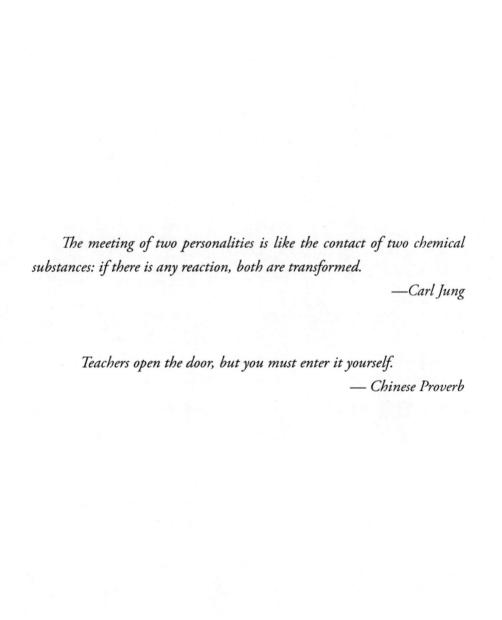

The meeting of two personalities is like the contact of two chemical substances: if there is any reaction, both are transformed.

—*Carl Jung*

Teachers open the door, but you must enter it yourself.

— *Chinese Proverb*

The Extraordinary Ordinary
A Tantric Fairytale

Andrena Woodhams

authorHOUSE®

AuthorHouse™
1663 Liberty Drive, Suite 200
Bloomington, IN 47403
www.authorhouse.com
Phone: 1-800-839-8640

First published by AuthorHouse 2/11/2009

ISBN: 978-1-4389-3310-8 (sc)
ISBN: 978-1-4389-3311-5 (hc)

Printed in the United States of America
Bloomington, Indiana

This book is printed on acid-free paper.

About the Author

In 2000, while living and working in Vienna with her Austrian husband, journalist Andrena Woodhams' existence turned upside down when she experienced a life-changing reaction to Lasik eye surgery. She later learned that she had a metaphysical reaction to the eye operation - it not only affected her physical sight, but how she perceived the world. Within a year, she divorced, gave up her career as reporter and presenter at BBC World Television and eventually sold all of her possessions in order to research and understand what had happened to her. She spent the next seven years in retreat, working with teachers of different spiritual traditions, learning yoga, breath work, somatic and energy bodywork, psychology, Tantra, shamanism and other healing modalities. Catapulted into the exploration of consciousness, using her own body and understanding as a guide, she underwent a radical personal transformation that now serves as the basis for her teaching. This is her first book.

Preface

If there is one thing I've learned, it is that the universe doesn't reveal her secrets lightly. It takes courage, discipline, perseverance, and above all, a willingness to let go. Because the extraordinary ordinary isn't something to achieve, but what lies in the depths of your being once everything else has been stripped away.

Becoming a woman for me was an epic. Like many females of my generation, I was taught that if I were good, eventually I would marry and live happily ever after. Stuff of myths and legends. I loved reading these classics because I always knew eventually things would work out in the end. But *living* a heroic journey is different. I didn't know what would happen, only that a sea of events was taking me further and further away from everything I had ever known, believed in, or understood.

This story is a journey into madness and back. It takes place in cities I know well, London and Vienna, however the events and characters in this book are fictitious. Vienna *is* the cradle of psychoanalysis, so certain real locations and public figures are mentioned, but all other characters and events described in the book are totally imaginary.

I wouldn't wish my experiences upon anyone, and yet if I were given the choice to do it over, I would say yes, because it has made me what I am today.

A woman. Gracefully, divinely, majestically, a woman.

October
Vienna, Austria

Fairytales aren't supposed to end this way, I repeat as my feet crunch along the leafy pathway toward the Vienna Woods, high in the hillsides cradling the city of Vienna. The branches of chestnut trees groan in the icy air, the wind howls in my ears. I am oblivious to everything around me. I have become numb over the past few months, since I learned that Vandana had cancer. She was *his* wife, my rival in love. I wanted her gone. And now she is.

What did Eugen tell me? Be careful with my thoughts, because they can become reality? *What have I done?* As I crest the top of the hill, the wind swirls the brown leaves in pirouettes before my eyes. I push a fluttering strand of hair away and gaze upon the city that is now my home. On my left, the Danube, a dismal streak of grey water in the brown landscape, pushes toward the flatlands of Slovakia. On my right, Vienna nestles in the crook of the Danube Canal, steeples and spires emerging from the autumnal backdrop of ochre and auburn. If I had binoculars, I could find the church with its onion-domed steeple where Vandana's funeral is being held. Eugen is there right now, standing dutifully at her casket, head bowed, mourning a woman he never loved. Or so he said. *I'm not sure of anything anymore.*

3

I bury my nose in my scarf, glaring at the city as if my misery is its fault. Six months ago I left London to come here to marry the man I loved. Instead, I find myself enmeshed in a sticky spider web of tangled family relationships — and death. I place my head in my hands, wishing I could find the peace of mind I crave. I wish I were somewhere, anywhere, but *here.*

A low, deep knell rings out from the city far below, followed by another bell, then another, and soon the cacophony of metallic sounds makes me lift my head. Wearily, I brush a few leaves from my trousers and start down the path toward the city. I hate myself for coming to Vienna, for leaving my career and everything for which I had worked so hard behind. All because of this restlessness inside of me that whispers that there is more to life. This feeling has been insistent all my life, pushing me to achieve, pushing me to succeed. The best marks at school, the top university, it launched me into television, moved me to London, and now here to pursue a relationship I should have known couldn't work.

I've been running. Always running. Until now.

2

By the time I arrive home, it is dark over the city. The narrow cobblestone streets are filled with bicycles and buses and clattering trams. The smell of firewood is in the air; sidewalk vendors sell roasted chestnuts and *Kartoffelpuffer*, soft rounds of hash browns grilled over a coal fire. Bland comfort food for a bland, comfortable life in a bland, comfortable city in middle Europe. It is autumn, Eugen explained to me, and this means it is time to eat pumpkin goulash and wild mushrooms and drink the season's new wines. Soon, it will be winter with more rituals just like they always have done for centuries. Everything in Vienna is predictable, and that is how the Viennese like it. And why I don't. I complained to Eugen that Vienna feels like a straight jacket. Try being an aristocrat, he answered, it's worse. That is why he married an exotic Indian when he was young. *Vandana.* Just the thought of her makes my stomach tighten.

I cross a cobblestone square, cut through a passageway that makes me feel as if I am walking through a mini cathedral, bypass a crowd of tourists ogling through the arched windows of the Café Central and I'm home. Using my shoulder, I shove open a heavy green door and walk under a massive entrance flanked by two stone Atlas figures shouldering ornate masonry. The four hundred year old building, with its faded ochre façade and rows of windows, overlooks the courtyard in stately boredom. A vast marbled room, the entire ground floor of the palace, envelops me like an inconsequential ant as I walk through the door. On either side of the grand staircase, somber family busts and massive oil paintings line the walls. The door behind me closes with a thud. I take the steps two at a time, my feet clattering on the cold stone floor, and unlock the door to our apartment.

Compared with the heaviness outside, the contemporary interior exudes openness and luxury. Soaring white walls, polished parquet floors, massive rooms with high ceilings and arched windows greet me as I walk inside. The combination of old world with a tasteful modern conversion is breathtaking. At the end of the foyer, a fire burns in the fireplace; a glass vase bursting branches of bright red berries rests on the white marble mantelpiece. As I drop my keys on the mahogany table in the entrance hall, I hear the delicate click of claws on the floor. Within seconds, a white cat with blue eyes and cream-colored fur pads into view.

"Minou!" I pull off my shoes and sit down to scratch my cat's chin, smiling as I feel her raspy sandpaper tongue on my hand. Jobs and countries have come and gone, but my cat has been an anchor for sixteen years. Minou tells me about her day in sporadic purrs, gives her ruff a few determined licks, then marches down the steps toward the kitchen where I know an empty food bowl waits. Knowing I won't get any rest until she is fed, I follow her into the drawing room.

And stop. On every surface is chaos. On the floor, on tops of tables, in open cupboards, in drawers left ajar, lie piles of books, stacks of papers, brochures, videos and boxes full of folders. In the corner, Eugen's priceless Empire secretary overflows with paper, business cards, receipts, tickets and flyaway scraps of goodness knows what. A half-open suitcase lies on the floor, spewing clothes like a clothing line— a rainbow of Izod shirts, a pair of jogging shoes stuffed with white tennis socks, a bundle of colorful silk ties snaking like miniature Chinese dragons in every direction. Shoes tumble along the corridor leading to our bedroom.

But it's the paintings that upset me the most. Stacks of large, unframed canvases lean like dominos against the wall. Eugen must have pulled them out before he attended the funeral. Vandana's paintings. I try to shield my eyes from looking at them. It's no good; the rich textured layers of swirling red and black and gold beckon, willing me to stare into the pictures. The writhing figures are too provocative, too dark, too — *sensual* to make me feel comfortable. They remind me of Gustav Klimt's blatantly sexual canvases that I saw at the Belvedere Palace when I first arrived in Vienna. His most famous, *The Kiss*, I could bear, but his others — society femme fatales in billowing silk gowns, naked mermaids with creamy breasts, mythological and Byzantine figures in flowing mosaic robes and long trellised hair — were so erotic that I had to leave the room.

Sexuality. Shadow. Death. The Viennese are obsessed with these three things. I give a little shudder as I turn the canvases against the wall with a determined flourish, then nudge the shoes out of the way and wander into the kitchen. At least this is one place where Eugen's mess hasn't dared to encroach. Placing Minou's food on the floor, I try to forget my irritation by stroking her while she eats.

"You weren't at the funeral."

At the sound of Eugen's voice, a cacophony of emotions explodes in my chest. I look up and see his large frame leaning against the doorway. I get up faster than I should have, and feel the room tilting toward me. Eugen reaches out to steady me, but instead of taking his hand, I place mine against the wall and look down, waiting for the dizziness to pass.

I try to make my voice normal. "I couldn't go. I just couldn't."

7

Eugen crosses his arms and leans against the doorway. His tone is icy. "As my future wife, you should have been there. What will my family think?"

I look away, not wanting to catch his eyes. "I couldn't attend the funeral of your ex-wife. I can't pretend to cry."

"You never cry anyway."

I get up and walk to the refrigerator, brushing the cat fur from my legs with short, irritated strokes. I cried enough to fill the Danube Canal over the past few months, but he doesn't know that. London, Geneva, Brussels, Milan, he's been away on business since our troubles began. Meanwhile I'm living in a city where I know no one, ostracized by Eugen's family, ignored by his friends. I grind my teeth together, trying to keep the words from spilling out, but it doesn't work.

"Can *you* cry?" I take a bottle of wine from the fridge. "You didn't love her, either. I saw it. You weren't around to watch her die."

I bang the refrigerator door shut to emphasize my point. *Not even five minutes and we're at it again.* As a peace-making gesture I offer him wine, but he dismisses it with a shake of his head. Pouring myself a large glass, I glance at him out of the corner of my eye. Why are we hurting each other like this? He's everything I have always wanted in a man. I'm just as taken by him as when we first met a year ago. It was his eyes that captivated me. Sparkling blue behind small round wire frames. I love his eyes; I'm always removing his glasses so that I can have a better look at them. They comfort me, smile at me, crinkle when he laughs, which is most of the time. Aquiline features set off by a shock of black hair and a neatly trimmed salt and pepper beard. Caring, funny and as sharp as a whip. Not yet fifty, Eugen made a name for himself in the financial world by tracking money laundering in Austrian banks, one of the drawbacks Austria has to contend with as the closest Western European country to the East.

Mafia pressure led Eugen to hold his interviews incognito, so it was a scoop to get him to talk on my television program. When I gave him the mandatory handshake in the television studio, it was all I could do to keep my knees from knocking. I don't remember what he said during my interview. I sat in my chair, transfixed, feeling this curious warmth in my body, as if someone had poured warm honey into my heart. After all these years of searching, I knew I had found my equal. It was worth the wait. *It's him,* was all I could think. *This is the man I've been looking for all my life.*

The memory makes me take a step toward him. "I didn't mean —"

Eugen fiddles with a cufflink. "It's called duty," he answers. "You'll have to get used to it. You Americans never understand protocol. There are certain things you have to do when you belong to an old Austrian family."

I bang my glass on the countertop louder than I intend. "Your family *hated* Vandana! They only accepted her once they knew she was going to die. No wonder Catholics love martyrs. The dead are safe. And they don't sell secrets." I frown, glaring at him.

After a moment of shocked silence, Eugen's mouth starts to twitch as if he is trying to hold something back, but then he gives up and bursts into laughter.

"Not bad! You managed to insult my family, my country's religion, generalize and judge all in one sentence. That's good. Very good." He picks up the wine bottle and pours himself a glass, smiling to himself.

My frown wavers. "I take it I was being spiritually incorrect again?"

He throws me one of those naughty smiles of his. "Not my Annabel. Never."

I smile in spite of myself. The tightness eases from my shoulders as I hold out my glass for Eugen to fill. How lucky I am. Whereas I frighten most men, Eugen thinks I'm funny. He takes my glass and places it on the countertop before gently pulling me toward him. I stiffen, then relax against his chest, enjoying a brief respite from the torturous feelings that have been haunting me.

"We didn't do anything wrong."

"I *knew* better!" I answer quietly. "I encouraged you to leave her."

Eugen's chest tightens for a second, then his ribcage loosens as if he is unwinding inside. "How many times do I have to say this? I would have left Vandana anyway. It was only a matter of time."

"I pushed you to do it." My eyes catch his, begging him to understand. "I can't lie to myself anymore. I used every one of my feminine wiles to get that woman out of your life." I want to cover my face in shame. "I don't need anyone to tell me what I did was wrong. I *know* I did."

"Let me go over this one last time," he says slowly. "When we met in London a year ago, my marriage was already over. Vandana was living here until she found another place to stay. We fell in love, and in a *coup de foudre* I invited you to live with me, which meant you had to quit your job, and Vandana had to leave. It was messy, but what else could we do?"

"We put her in a mental institution," I whisper.

He closes his eyes as if to block my words. "Vandana's admittance to Steinhof was going to be temporary. How could I know that she had cancer — no one did until it was too late." For a few minutes, we are quiet, rocking gently back and forth. It feels safe, a refuge where I can forget the big, bad world in which we live. I hear his voice murmuring in my ear. "Why do you insist on taking the blame for this?" When

I don't answer, he exhales. "We will get through this." He places his hands on my shoulders and begins to gently massage them.

In the silence of the moment, I feel an inner whoosh, as if a damn breaks inside me and the tension I've been carrying begins to drain toward my feet.

Eugen gently maneuvers my shoulders. "I don't understand why you don't learn to do something to relax your muscles, like yoga."

"I jog."

"Not the same thing. Yoga is a way of doing inner work, not just exercise."

"You always talk about *inner work*," I say. "I never know what it means. Sounds New Age."

But this only makes Eugen laugh. "It's been around longer than that." He points to the bookcase in the hall. "Socrates, for a start. *The unexamined life is not worth living*. Or what about the inscription on the Temple of Delphi? *Know Thyself.*"

I harrumph.

"Okay, what about this: *Understand this if nothing else: spiritual freedom and oneness with the Tao are not randomly bestowed gifts, but the rewards of conscious self-transformation and self-evolution.* The Hua Hu Ching."

"But why is that important?"

"Well," he says, softly thumping my shoulders a few times, which brings small tingles of electricity racing up and down my arms. "Let's see. It leads to happiness. Diminishes fear. Reduces stress. Increases tolerance and compassion. Makes you a more loving person. Improves your health. Makes you sleep better. Need any more reasons?"

"Mmmmm," is all I say. His massage has done wonders. I circle my head slowly, then move my shoulders, enjoying the open feeling at the back of my heart. "I was taught we are what we do."

Eugene smiles. "You might find that's not exactly true. You're much more than that. It's not what you do, but how you do it. If you don't believe me, visit the newspaper vendor on the Graben."

A smile spreads across my face. "Herr Dietmayer? I love his shop!"

Eugen looks suitably impressed. "I'm glad you've discovered him. Herr Dietmayer is a walking dictionary of spiritual wisdom."

I give him a dubious look, but underneath I feel a tug inside me, wondering if he isn't right. Eugen knows about things I never have dared to look into. Meditation. Yoga. Spirituality. Things far away from the fast-paced stressful life of a television presenter. The moment beckons, asking me to start to trust again, to trust the process, to trust life, to trust love, but then I remember Vandana. She trusted Eugen — she even married him — and look what happened to her. I remember her death, I remember my guilt, and with that, my mind jumps to attention.

"I've got to get my life in order." My brain grinds through my to-do list for next week. Suddenly a red light flashes in my mind's eye, and a reminder flag starts frantically waving. "I forgot — Max and I are doing a package tomorrow."

Eugen straightens up. "Again?"

"It's just a news story." In spite of myself, excitement creeps into my voice. "It's a pleasure working with him."

"It should be. He's one of Vienna's rising stars." Eugen walks over to pour himself another glass of wine. "You see a lot of him."

My mind ignores his last statement, and soon erases it from my memory. Of course I saw Max when Eugen was gone. He was my lifeline. I open the cutlery drawer as a hint for Eugen to set the table for dinner.

"Tomorrow is *Allerheiligen*," Eugen muses, ignoring the open drawer. "All Saints Day. I wonder what Max's up to." He glances in my direction. "Careful, love."

"But you introduced him to me!"

"Because you were looking for work, and I admire his." He wipes his hands on a dishtowel. "But there is something about that man I don't trust."

After dinner, we get ready for bed. Trying to remove my contact lenses with my toothbrush in my mouth, I scribble *contact lens solution* on my growing list of things not to forget. In bed, I curl up next to Eugen, spooning my body against his. My brain, however, is elsewhere. It repeatedly checks things off my list, trying not to forget hairspray and face powder and camera for tomorrow's shoot. Eugen reaches over to turn off the light. As I close my eyes, willing my mind to stop spinning, the tips of Eugen's fingers begin to caress my shoulder.

My mind screeches to a halt, leaving a strange inner vacuum echoing in my brain. *Vandana's funeral was today.* Against my will, the muscles in my lower back tighten as his fingers slowly work their way around my arm and toward my breast.

My arm slides over my chest in one quick movement. "Not tonight."

For a moment Eugen does nothing, then I hear the bed creak as he turns onto his side and props his head in his hand. The light from the moon shines on his profile. I see hurt and concern on his face.

"Is everything OK?" he asks softly.

"I don't know," I answer hesitantly. "Ever since Vandana's death…" Talking about sex is never an easy topic for me. I open my mouth once or twice but my jaw feels stuck, as if someone has wrapped tape around it. "It's just — sometimes —" I pause. "I — think sex is stupid."

Eugen throws his head back and laughs. "Sex isn't stupid! *You* may be stupid, but *sex* isn't stupid."

He caresses my cheek with a finger when he sees the hurt look on my face. "Those weren't my words. I was quoting Osho."

I frown, still smarting from his words. "Who's Osho?"

"Otherwise known as Rajneesh. He was a rebel Indian guru who landed in California in the seventies." He sees my eyes starting to glaze, so he changes tack. "He tackled a lot of issues that most spiritual people try to avoid, like sexuality and anger. He taught that nothing is negative. Anger and sex are just what they are. Anger and sexuality. It's our relationship to these things that is the problem." Eugen slides onto his side and opens his arms, inviting me toward him.

Relieved to have been let off the hook, I snuggle against him. "I guess I'll have to add him to the list of spiritual masters I need to study."

He brushes my hair away from my face and kisses my forehead. "Don't bother. He might be a bit of a challenge. But I can tell you why *I* used to think sex was stupid."

I look up, relieved. "*You* think sex is stupid, too?"

He smiles. "I *used* to. It's not easy for us for men. Just think. We derive pleasure from the same organ through which we pee." He waits for me to laugh, and when I do, he adds his punchline, his eyes crinkling as he gives me that adorable smile of his. "Remember. God has a *great* sense of humor."

I don't know how Eugen has done it. What could have been an embarrassing moment has become a tender one. It's moments like these when I remember why I fell in love with him. I lean over and give him a kiss. Then, wrapped in each other's arms, we fall asleep.

3

Allerheiligen
All Saints Day

The next morning, I am infused with an excitement I haven't felt in a long time. I kiss Eugen, shower and change, gulp down a cup of tea, grab my fleece hat and gloves and reporter bag, and tear out the door, my boots squeaking on the marble as I skip down the stairs. Pushing open the heavy front door, I hear a melodic clip clop and quickly step back as a shiny black carriage drawn by a pair of chestnut horses whips by. The owner, dressed in a natty black cape and bowler, tips his cap as the carriage passes by. Vienna is in love with its past, and has made big business of it. Thousands of tourists come here to wade in nostalgia. Carriage rides, cafes, long lunches, slowly meandering trams, long evenings drinking local wine in the vineyards surrounding the city, the concept of time takes on a new element here. Vienna is not a place for those looking toward the future, but for those who want to wallow in the past. No matter what happens in the world, it will happen later here. Hitching my bag over my shoulder, I stride toward the Graben, the broad pedestrian street that curves toward St. Stephen's cathedral.

The roofs of Vienna are drenched with a golden glow; birdsong merges with the sound of clattering hooves. Blinking in the sunlight, I wonder why there is no one on the streets before remembering it is a national holiday. Turning up the wide graceful arc of the pedestrian Graben Street — Graben means grave — I peer into the newspaper shop that Eugen mentioned last night. Like the hundreds of little shops in Vienna, the *Trafik* is a hole in a wall, only a door's breadth wide, and barely long enough for two or three people to stand inside. A bell tingles merrily as I open the door and a muted aria from Tosca wafts toward me. I flatten against the wall as a customer walks out, whistling with the music as if it were a top 40s hit. Music is always on everyone's minds here — even storekeepers and taxi drivers discuss the latest opera as if it were a television series. Although the shop is crammed with newspapers and magazines, the atmosphere is congenial and warm. Other *Trafiks* smell of stale tobacco, but everything in this one seems different, more alive. I breathe in the rich smell of orange and bergamot, appreciating the tea candle burner I see the owner has placed in the corner. No wonder this shop was written up as the most popular *Trafik* in Vienna.

Herr Dietmayer beams when he sees me. "*Guten Morgen!*" He pulls a copy of my favorite newspaper down from the wall. "Have you slept with a hanger in your mouth? I haven't seen you smile like that since you came to Vienna —" He scratches his head. "Four months ago?"

"Six," I answer, blowing on my hands to warm them.

The *Trafikant* — Herr Dietmayer told me that is what his job is called — nods. "What has caused this sudden happiness?"

"I'm working today. Like you."

He raises his eyebrows. His bald head glistens in the soft lighting. "Most people would never dream of working on a holiday. They think work is punishment."

I drop my bag on the floor. "I love working. It makes me feel important. Worthwhile. As if I am helping make the world to be a better place. Silly, huh?"

He shakes his head. "When you stop thinking you make a difference, a part of you begins to die. And then you become like the many walking dead that I see on the streets." He folds the newspaper and gives it to me.

"Walking dead?"

He shrugs his shoulders. "Most people, unfortunately. Somewhere along the line, they compromise, blame others for their failures, and eventually convince themselves life is to be endured, rather than lived. And their souls wither. They might live long, but they died young."

"I know what you mean," I murmur as I dig in my wallet for money.

The *Trafikant*'s gaze is so intense I can feel it through my coat. "You're at that point, I can see."

I look up sharply, but it is as if he never said a word. He smiles innocently.

I take a closer look around me. In between the magazines and newspapers, I discover crystals, small bottles of natural oils, even a row of colorful Tibetan prayer flags hanging from the ceiling. Eugen's right. Herr Dietmayer's little shop *does* feel like a miniature temple.

"And *you* make a difference?"

The owner smiles, his forehead wrinkling where his hair once grew. Behind me, the door opens and an elderly man in a dark loden coat shuffles in, dragging a fat little dachshund behind him.

"I *know* I do."

The shopkeeper pats my arm. "Working makes you feel great, to others it is a burden. So it isn't *what* you do, but *how* you do it, that matters."

I try to ignore the loud intentional huffing and puffing behind me. "Then why do anything at all?"

Before I say anything further, Herr Dietmayer winks at me as if to say *watch!* He beams at his customer. "*Guten Morgen*! How is little Hansi?"

The man grunts an answer, but soon, prompted by the shop owner's questions, he begins to recount his dog's latest visit to the vet. I watch in amazement as the *Trafikant* nods his head as if the dog's digestive problems were the most interesting news he has heard in ages. By the time the old man turns to leave, he is smiling. He even excuses himself as he squeezes by.

"Did you see that?" Herr Dietmayer says as the door closes. "Every person who comes in my shop receives my smile. This is what I choose to give my customers. Newspapers are my income, but I consider my real job is handing out smiles. And, if I'm lucky, some people will pass my smiles onto others. I reckon one smile can reach at least a hundred people a day."

I hand him a five-euro note. And something else. Respect. "You should work for the Vienna tourist board. You might be able to change the image of the grumpy Viennese."

The *Trafikant* gives me a mysterious grin. "Maybe I'm doing just that. In my own way." He gives me my change. "Leave room for magic in your life, Frau Jones. And it will appear." Before I can respond, a little bell on the door jingles, and the next customer squeezes me out onto the street.

4

By the time I reach our meeting place, the cold winter sun is well in the sky. There, by the subway entrance, I spot a figure bounding toward me, a red scarf fluttering behind him. I would recognize that scarf anywhere. It's Max Krankovich. His black hair, thick and wavy, is drawn back into a neat ponytail, a red ski cap pulled down just above his brown eyes. His sharp, sleek features remind me of a Doberman pincher, loyal and protective.

"Do you know how difficult it is to force a camera crew to work on a national holiday?" he says in his heavily accented English. He thrusts his cell phone in the pocket of his black leather jacket before shaking my hand. "And to think I used to be a communist. Unions are different once you have to negotiate *against* them." He points to a car parked on the street. "We must hurry, the camera crew is waiting."

I grab his sleeve as he starts to turn. "Just a minute. What is All Saints?"

Max taps his forehead. "I forgot Americans don't celebrate their dead."

"Celebrate our dead?" I ask incredulously. "We have a hard enough time accepting old age."

Max turns his mouth down at the corners. "Thank your cosmetic and pharmaceutical industries for that. They must be held accountable for what they have done to generations of innocent people."

I raise my hand. "New rules. You are not allowed to criticize my country before twelve noon." I look at my watch. "Two hours to go."

Max doffs an imaginary hat and grins. "*Jawohl.*" He smiles as he wraps his scarf around his neck and pulls his ponytail clear. "I haven't seen you in awhile. Eugen must be in town."

I sigh. "Vandana's funeral was yesterday."

Max fumbles with his keys. "It does not surprise me Vandana died of cancer. He was a coward to leave town while his ex-wife was dying. But to leave you alone, when you knew no one here, is unforgivable."

Not wanting to say something negative about Eugen, I stand silently at the car door. *I've already told him too much as it is.* During the traumatic last months of Vandana's illness, Max was my only contact with the outside world. Eugen first introduced him so that I could find work in television. But as the months wore on and Eugen was constantly away, I retreated further into myself, unable to do anything Vienna was famous for; too angry to sit in a café to watch the world go by, too tormented to attend its famous opera or concerts, too unhappy to visit its museums. Max coaxed me out of the apartment, enticing me with concert tickets and tours. Eugen was never around to help me negotiate the endless bureaucracy that moving to a foreign city involved. But Max was always there. Solid, dependable Max. I've worked with journalists like him all my life. I could trust him with my life.

Max slides into his car and reaches across to open the door for me. "Let me tell you something about aristocratic families. Living in a palace is like living in a golden cage. Everything's for show." He slams the door and starts the engine, smiling as he hears the powerful BMW roar into life. "I bet he wanted you to go to her funeral."

I glance sharply at him. "And?"

Max jams the car into gear. "And what?" He glances at me. "That's what's important to aristos. It's all image."

I slouch into the seat, staring in front of me.

Max taps me on the knee. "His ex died in a mental institution. Do you know what that means?" He purses his lips waiting for an answer that won't come. "It means his family *wanted* her to die. With all their connections, she was never moved to a hospital until it was too late." He zigzags along the narrow streets and soon zooms onto a two-lane highway heading west. He brakes hard and honks before swerving into the passing lane, blasting the horn as if any car in his way was a personal insult to his masculinity. "You told me he didn't even answer his cell phone while he was gone! Doesn't that make you suspicious?"

I place my hands on the edge of the seat to keep my balance. "Enough."

Max's eyes widen when I sees my face. Instantly he puts his foot on the brakes and the car slows down. When Max next speaks, his voice is softer, more present.

"I'm sorry. Really. But there are a lot of shysters in the world, and I want to protect you from them. Be careful with Eugen. He isn't all that he makes himself out to be." He cocks his head at me, observing my silence, then rubs his hand along the small of his back and groans. "My back is killing me. Those homeopathic pills you gave me didn't work."

I give him a suspicious look. "Did you *take* them?"

He flashes a guilty grin. "Give me an extra strength painkiller any day."

That's Max in a nutshell. Modern, results-oriented and impatient. He might be rough around the edges, but I appreciate his honesty. Slowly, as Max begins to tell me about our work, my worries with Eugen disappear and I start to focus on the story at hand. Along the way, Max points out people carrying bags filled with flowers and candles.

"We are doing a quick two-minuter for general syndication. The hook is All Souls Day in Vienna. You find the angle."

I flip through a folder he gave me, looking up every once in a while to ogle at the crowds. "Everyone's enjoying themselves."

"We Viennese *like* our melancholy." He smiles wistfully. "All Souls was my favorite holiday when I was young. It gave me a sense of belonging. Onki always spent the day with me."

"Onki?"

"My uncle. I'll introduce you to him one day."

We drive along an enormous red wall that surrounds what looks like an ancient walled town. Every mile or so, I see large gated entrances surrounded by clusters of little wooden stands selling food and flowers. Throngs of chatting crowds pour in and out of the gates, and still more stream from the red trams that rattle toward and away from the town.

"This is the Central Cemetery," Max explains as he circles around the parking lot until he finds a silver van parked at the edge. "It is as large as Vienna's downtown, and is one of its most popular tourist attractions."

"A cemetery is a tourist attraction? What is it with you Viennese?"

Max parks the car and pulls the handbrake hard. "We love the past. On All Saints, Onki and I would scrub the family graves before taking pictures to send to relatives in Croatia."

"You took *photos* of your family's graves to send to relatives?"

Max nods his head eagerly. "Many people do, especially those whose families live far away. That way they know their family is being taken care of."

I shake my head. "You Viennese are too morbid for words. You worship your dead."

"We are obsessed by them. Some call Vienna the city of the dead."

Feeling the flicker of an idea rattling in my brain, I pull out my reporter's pad and begin to scribble. "I've found our angle. Now go."

Max leaps out of the car and thumps at the window of a van where two burly men lie asleep. While he talks to the crew, I use the rear view mirror to powder my nose and chin and dab on a bright lipstick. Although I rarely wear make up, cameras are harsh and will make me look washed out if I don't apply it with a heavy hand. For the same reason, I adjust a colored scarf around my neck before easing myself out of the car.

At the cemetery gate, he pauses and looks at me. "Would you mind filming this on your own? I want to rush to my family." He smiles shyly and produces a bag of red candles and a large bunch of dahlias.

"If you edit it," I say with a smile. "Come back in an hour. I should have it in the can by then."

"Deal." Max gives me a kiss on the cheek. "You know I'd do anything for you." He holds my shoulder for a moment, then bounds through the gate and is gone.

It's a pleasure being with someone whom I can trust I think as I watch him disappear. Then, with the crew trailing beyond me, I wander through the gates. Inside is another world. Vienna's Central Cemetery feels like a park, with trees and shrubs and park benches and gravel walkways, except that, as far as I can see, are only graves. Row after row of them, all washed and scrubbed and lined with flowers and flickering red candles. Between the rows, entire families wander, chatting and calling to children as they stroll along the paths, admiring the graves as if it were the latest fashion. Vienna does love its dead. Unlike where I was born in the American Midwest, here death is a part of life, not something to be avoided. In fact, if I were to guess, it is probably something the Viennese look forward to all of their lives. I wander along the graveyard with the crew, pointing out the shots I know Max will need. Establishing shots, medium shots, and the essential cut-aways, used as visual transitions to link the story together. A few interviews, and lastly I film my piece-to-camera — talking to the lens while ignoring the crowds behind us. In an hour, the footage is in the can. By evening, the hour long video will be edited into two minutes and downloaded to networks around the world.

In what seems to be no time at all, Max is by my side, glancing through the camera viewfinder. "Great work. Now to the car."

"I thought we were done!" I cry. "I was congratulating myself that that was the fastest story I've produced in awhile."

Max gives me a mysterious smile. "Now comes the surprise. I sold a second story to the networks. Might as well. I've paid a camera crew for a day's work."

"Where to?"

"Mauthausen."

When I don't react, Max furrows his brow. "You *do* know it was a concentration camp."

I roll my eyes. "Of course," I lie.

"Good. And the anniversary of *Kristallnacht* is in a week."

I groan. "Not *another* World War II story. I must know more World War II stories and locations in Vienna than most tourists."

"I want you to know the real story of what happened."

I curl into the car seat. "If you're not talking about death, then you are obsessed with the pain of World War II."

He smiles. "It's my job. I do it well."

"And this new television series of yours is on World War II?"

Max gives me a smug smile. "You know me. Would I do anything else?"

5

The crew follows us as we drive along the highway. As soon as the car picks up speed, Max begins a running monologue with one hand on the steering wheel while the other gesticulates wildly.

"The SS built Mauthausen concentration camp in August 1938. Over 200,000 prisoners were imprisoned there because of their religious beliefs, race, criminal record, or because they were homosexual or prisoners of war. Half of all prisoners were murdered."

I glance out of the window at the well-kept farms and tidy villages rolling by. The gentle scene feels far away from the horrors of World War II.

Max's voice drones on. "*Kristallnacht* happened three months after Mauthausen opened. The name comes from the sound of the glass windows of Jewish storefronts breaking on November 9th 1938. Over a hundred Jews in Vienna were killed. Thousands were taken away to places like Mauthausen."

I tear my eyes away from the window and force myself to focus on the story at hand. "*Kristallnacht.* The night of shattered glass. Who did it? The Gestapo?"

Max throws me a triumphant grin. "*That* was the beauty of the Nazi campaign. It wasn't Nazis, but ordinary Viennese. The police stood by and watched the rampage. The Nazi government fuelled a

26

fear that already existed. A few communication tricks, and they had support for their war programs."

He pulls off the highway and we bump down a narrow road, the camera crew following us. Twenty minutes later, we pull up at a parking lot in the middle of nowhere. The warm autumnal weather is gone, replaced by a cold wind that slams into us as we walk toward a plain iron gate, our equipment dragging behind us. At first, it looks unprepossessing; a simple prisoner of war camp, just like I have seen in hundreds of photos of World War II. But in real life it seems less dramatic, smaller, somehow. Tiny huts — if they were any smaller I'd call them sheds — assembled from roughly hewn wood line either side of a broad walkway. On my right and left, I see signs and placards attached to the walls. It looks so — dare I say it — banal. As I glance down, a few sparrows land at my feet, searching for food on the dirty concrete floor.

The infirmary, I whisper to myself, reading a sign on the wall as I walk in. Inside, apart from a desk and a few tables, the room is bare. My boots thump on the wooden floor as I scan the room, looking for an ideal place to film. I hear Max coming up behind me so I turn toward him. "Prisoners must have come here when they were ill."

"Do not be naïve," Max snaps. "This is where prisoners were tortured."

"Here?" I look around. "It looks so — so *ordinary*."

Max nods when he sees the shock on my face. "The doctors called murder *Frühsport*, or morning exercise. Over there — " he points to a photograph of a rusty bathtub, " — prisoners were doused with ice-cold water until they froze to death."

In the corner I see a photograph of a person, no more than skin and bones, slumped in a bathtub filled with water. Is it a man or a woman? I can't tell. The body is no more than a limp bag of skin and bones. An icicle hanging from the tub makes me realize that the photo was taken in winter. Instinctively I pull my coat around me as the wind slams against the shed. A sickening feeling begins to rise in my stomach. *Don't get emotionally involved,* I tell myself. *There is nothing here you haven't read about in history books.*

Max pulls a list from his folder and thrusts it into my hand. "Have a look. Doctors working here called these techniques *Sonderbehandlungen,* special treatment."

I glance at the list. The prescriptions read as follows: *To be left standing in sub zero temperatures until frozen. To be gassed. To be shot. To be given injections.*

Doctors wrote these prescriptions. Not the SS. Not Nazis. Just doctors. People who thought they were doing their part to improve the human race. People who felt so threatened that the only way to feel safe was to exterminate anyone who was not of their race, ideology or creed. All in the name of self-defense. I shiver, feeling the numbness that has engulfed me the past few months begin to melt. Feelings start to emerge, black, sticky feelings that make my legs feel heavy and thick, as if I'm walking through tar. I try to stop them, but my mind slides *there.* Being a victim. Imagining what it would be like to be a prisoner, to wear those horrible black and white pajamas, to know that the moment I walked through the gate, I was dead. Fifty years later, the place still breathes the stale breath of death.

I had thought that crimes of humanity were big things, large things, horrific, horrible catastrophic events with neon lights that blink and warn *Here it is! How evil!* But crimes lie in the small things in life and are done by people thinking that they are *helping* humanity. *The road to hell is paved with good intentions.* Abusers and victims, victims and abusers lived and worked here, shoulder to shoulder, day after day. People died here. Abusers killing victims because they thought the victims were the abusers. My mind grinds to a halt. And that is when I get it. Abuser and victim are two sides of a coin. Germans were angry, they were frustrated, they were desperate, and they found someone to blame for their misery. Germans were the abusers, Jews, the victims. Germans felt *they* were victims, and that gave them the self-righteous anger to eliminate their perceived abusers. Victims and abusers. What a vicious circle — and one that continues today.

"I'm going to the gas chamber," I whisper. "Go get some establishing shots and meet me in ten minutes."

The cameraman heaves the camera on his right shoulder and grabs a box of lights. I thread the cord of the microphone up my back, loop it around my neck and attach it under my scarf, being extra careful to make sure nothing touches the microphone head. A light wind or the slightest touch of material can sound like a raging tornado on a sound track, rendering the shot useless. I then place the small recorder box at the other end of the microphone in my coat pocket and tuck the wires out of sight, then run my finger along the edge and turn the microphone on. Now fully miked up and ready to film, I slip into the next room. Here, according to the plaque on the wall, thousands of bodies were burned with mind-numbing regularity. I gaze numbly at the furnace. It's no larger than a pizza oven.

Max's voice whispers in my ear. "Apparently the stink of burning carcasses carried for miles. People living here claimed they never knew." He gives me a smug smile. "No one wants to know their country is the abuser. Why do you think your country doesn't want to show body bags on television when it fights its endless wars?"

"Max," I say, biting my lip with concentration. "Stuff it. Everyone is an abuser. Even you."

I ignore the shock on his face, concentrating on powdering my forehead while pulling a brush through my hair. Ten minutes later, the assistant holds a piece of red foil over an upturned light, which throws a soft pink glow onto my face.

Max's voice penetrates the heavy silence. "Rolling!"

I stare at the camera. "Walt Kelly, the author of Pogo, once wrote *We have met the enemy, and he is us.* Once we blame anyone who does not agree with our perception of the world — we become victims. The other becomes the enemy. He can be killed without a bad conscience. That's what happened here. People killed innocent humans because they *thought* they were helping the human race. A terrorist to one culture is a freedom fighter to another. The only difference is perception."

While the soundman helps me remove the microphone, Max barks, "It's a wrap!" Then turns to me. "You've got what it takes."

I notice a different sheen in his brown eyes when he says this, and realize this was more than a simple news story. Max has something else in mind. And whatever it is, I've just passed the test.

6

On the way back to Vienna, I huddle in my coat, wanting to sit with my emotions for the remainder of the journey. I look out the window, gazing dumbly at the hundreds of red candles flickering in the gloom in every cemetery we pass.

Max pulls in front of the palace and stops, reaching behind his seat. Then, with a shy smile, he hands a small package to me. When I look inside, I see it is full of small cat toys.

"For Minou. I forgot to give it to you the last time I saw you."

His soft spot for animals endears him to me. "Minou will love it," I say, smiling. "Why don't you give it to her yourself?"

Max looks at his watch, but I know he always has time for my cat. He parks on a side road and we get out, our breaths blowing little puffs into the evening light. The street is deserted, the cobblestones grey and damp in the early dusk.

"You live in one of the most enviable locations in Vienna," Max says, helping me heave open the heavy wooden door. I smile knowingly. Eugen told me this was the most beautiful of his family's palaces in the Austro-Hungarian Empire. After the gloom of Mauthausen, the openness in the spacious, airy interior feels bright and welcoming.

"Eugen isn't here," I say, noticing Max throwing a suspicious glance around the apartment. My voice echoes toward the ceiling.

Max removes his leather jacket and red scarf and holds them to his chest like a security blanket. But when he sees Minou strolling around the corner, tail held high, he instantly forgets his discomfort and drops on all fours, dangling the new cat toy before her. Minou, sitting upright like a bowling pin, accepts the compliment like a queen. Regally she dismisses the toy, and within minutes, she crawls into her meditative cat position on Max's lap, tucking her front paws under her and closing her eyes.

"Minou and I see eye to eye when it comes to our needs," Max calls behind me as I walk into the kitchen to make tea. "We hiss when we are angry, purr when we are happy, and walk away if we don't like the situation."

I watch Max swinging a toy mouse by the tail in front of Minou, his eyes shining as he gazes at my cat. For a moment I observe the two of them playing with each other. Beneath Max's antagonistic behavior, his gentleness with animals warms my heart.

As soon as the tea's ready, Max puts Minou on the floor, then stands up to follow me into the drawing room. At the room's threshold, the chaos glares at me. I hear a hoot of laughter behind me.

"This is incredible! How long has he been back?"

"Almost a week," I say under my breath.

"It looks like a bomb went off in a homeless shelter!" Max saunters toward a coffee table that has all but vanished under a mountain of papers and picks up a pale lavender notebook. "What's this?"

"Come on, Max." I put our mugs down on a side table and take the book from him. It is beautiful: the cover is textured with a batik motif, the inner pages are handmade rice paper. "Don't be nosy."

Max grabs it back and flips it open. "I'm a journalist. I'm *supposed* to be nosy." He stops as something catches his eye. A dark flush seeps up his neck like a water stain on blotting paper, leaving bright red patches on his cheeks. Within seconds, his neck starts to bulge as if he were holding his breath.

I reach out for the book. But instead of giving it to me, Max turns it so I can see inside, so I lean over to look at the page that Max is proffering to me. In a second, the room feels incredibly hot, so hot that I want to go and open the windows and let in some air. At first glance it looks like a journal with photos and drawings crammed in between the pages. There are diagrams of naked bodies with details of both a man and a woman's genitals. A tiny, spiderlike scrawl points to small arrows along the shaft of the penis. I know that handwriting. I would recognize it anywhere. It's Vandana's.

The door bangs. Max drops the lavender book on the coffee table as if it were a hot iron. It slips sideways, bringing a cascade of papers onto the floor. Max moves toward the door but I pull him back with a look that says, *too late!* In a panic, he drops onto the ground, trying to scoop up the papers. Not knowing what to do, I grab his cup of tea. At that moment, with Max on the floor surrounded by papers and me passing him a cup of tea, Eugen walks into the room.

Eugen glances sharply at me. I know I look as guilty as I feel.

Without looking at either of us, Eugen strides into the drawing room and, without a word, removes the papers from Max's hands and places them on the coffee table. He then takes the lavender book, walks over to his desk in the corner of the room, slides open the middle drawer and places it inside, turns the key to lock it, and pockets the key in his wallet. All of this is done without a word. When he is finished, Eugen walks toward us, leans against the wall, crosses his arms, and stares at me. Not at Max, but at *me*.

No welcome, no *Grüsse Gott*, no clicking of heels or shaking of hands. Not a word. In the silence that follows, Max gets up from the floor and dusts off his trousers. Eugen's eyes follow his every movement.

"So what scandal are you preparing to unearth?" I can hear Eugen is exercising enormous control to keep his voice level.

Max's shoulders hunch forward in an attempt to appear nonchalant. "A series called Victims and Abusers. The largest project I've ever done."

"Who is financing it?"

Max pulls his mouth down. "You're not interested in the content, just how much it will make."

Eugen tilts his head as if to say *touché*. They remind me of gladiators circling each other before a fight.

"Dr. Brandemberg. It's our first joint production."

"*Rudi* Brandemberg? We went to school together." Eugen speaks to me for the first time. "His wife's Emma. She's American and rich; he has the title and the castle."

"He's part of the old boys network," Max grumbles as he picks up his leather jacket and prepares to go. He turns to Eugen with exaggerated politeness. "I read in the paper that your wife was buried yesterday."

A look of pain crosses Eugen's face. "Ex-wife. We had already started the divorce proceedings before she died."

Max turns around. "Sorry. My sincerest regrets. So were the tabloids correct? Did she really go crazy?"

"Max!" I say, horrified. "Have some respect for the dead."

He shrugs his shoulders. "I figured that since she was an ex, it didn't matter."

"Just because you separate doesn't mean you don't have feelings," Eugen says quietly. "You also should learn to leave other people's things alone." He looks at me. "That means you, too. I'm very disappointed that you have stooped to such levels." He takes his glasses off and begins to polish them. "I need to lie down. It's been a long day."

Sensing that he has gone too far, Max sleeks his hair back into his ponytail. "Annabel did a fantastic job today. She needs to be back in television."

Eugen turns his head in my direction. "I'm not stopping her."

I step forward. "That's not true. You thought it wouldn't be a good idea once we are married. You said — "

His voice becomes strangely monotone. "I said I would never *stop* you. Whether I want you to work is another question."

Max grins. "I want her to present the series."

I swivel my head in his direction. "*What* did you say?"

His grin becomes wider when he sees my face. "You heard me. Consider today your screen test. You need to kick start your career again."

For a moment I forget Eugen, forget his anger, forget everything but look into Max's face. "You're offering me a contract?"

"The best there is. It's EU money. There's enough to go around."

Eugen rubs his neck. "I assume this series will be drudging up Austria's murky World War II past again?"

Max's eyes smolder as he looks at Eugen. "Austria did a great public relations job, convincing everyone Hitler was German and Beethoven was Austrian. It's time it pays for its past mistakes."

Eugen looks at me before giving Max a strained smile. "Why stir up old pain?"

Max leans toward Eugen, passion surging out of every pore of his body. "At least I have the courage to face old pain. And I help people while they're still alive."

And with that, he grabs his jacket and walks out the door.

7

Autumn fades into winter, and I feel the changing of the season in my soul. I serve dinner in silence. The wind howls outside the windows, making the walls of the palace reverberate with each gust. Dried leaves spiral in the air, hitting the windows like small bullets before twirling off into their unknown destiny. Even the large oak tree in the courtyard sways in a macabre dance with the wind. Clearing the table after dinner, my footsteps echo in the rooms while I walk from the kitchen to the dining room and back. I stop at the window to watch the clouds, low and black in the evening sky, stroke their wispy undersides against the gentle sloping hills of the Vienna Woods. When I arrived in Vienna, I spent hours pacing the rooms, watching the sunlight streaming through the large half circular window onto the wooden floor. I thought that I had fallen into a dream come true. But I'm not too sure about that anymore. I saw something in Eugen that I had never seen before — something that unsettles me. Perhaps Max was speaking the truth after all.

After dinner, Eugen and I relax by the open fire, nursing thimbles of grappa. Finally Eugen breaks the awkward silence. "You can't take that job."

"Why not?"

"I told you I don't trust Herr Krankovich. And I certainly don't trust Rudi Brandemberg."

"After the last few months, can I trust you?"

He ignores me. "If you produce a program that will increase people's fears, what reaction will it create? Will it make people angry, or will it make people reflect upon the situation more deeply?"

Stubbornly I look into my glass. "I have to make a living. If I were to bring my moral attitude into everything I reported on, I wouldn't have a job."

"I'm talking about it from a longer view."

I give Eugen a sidelong glance. "You mean a *spiritual* view."

He nods. "I wish I saw more spirituality in television."

"You never watch television!"

He gives me a cynical smile. "And you do?"

My shoulders drop. I shake my head, ceding the point. "Look. I know there is a lot more to life than my career. But I have to earn money. Besides, I don't see you living so spiritually. Whenever it comes to emotions, you go off into spiritual flights of fancy. When it gets close to the bone, you leave."

Eugen goes rigid. "Spirituality — "

"I've had enough of spirituality for the moment," I snap. "Spirituality is only a word for getting what you want."

Eugen takes his glasses off and puts them on the mantelpiece, then places his hand on my arm. "Why are we *always* fighting?"

Something snaps. My mouth opens and a tide begins to rise from within me, an ocean of words coming up from my stomach where I've squashed them for months and months but now there isn't anything holding them back so up they come, bursting out of my esophagus with the ferocity of a riptide at sea during a squall.

"I want us to get real! Vandana's dead, and we are partly to blame. You put her into a mental asylum and told me that it was for the best. You helped me visualize bringing love into our lives. I even did that funny ceremony you told me you learned in India. But what you really wanted was for Vandana to be gone."

Eugen's cheeks flush. "Vandana made herself ill. We are not to blame for what happened. Her presence was poisoning our relationship."

His hand isn't gentle and loving, it feels as sharp and aggressive as a claw. I remember Vandana's hand felt the same way, bony and grasping. I didn't want to see her, Eugen prohibited me from doing it but I had to, *someone* had to visit her, for God's sake. She was locked up and dying in an insane asylum — a dog would have been treated better than that.

I'll never forget standing face to face with a woman dying for a man who no longer loved her. All she could do was ramble about some nonsense she called the extraordinary ordinary. How changed she was from the glorious, bright-eyed Indian woman in their wedding photo. She seemed so frail that the wind could blow her away, her dark skin sallow, her long black hair lifeless. She was dying, she knew it and I knew it, but she didn't look sad. To me, she held a look of triumph on her face. I knew what it meant. I might have won the battle, but she had won the war.

"Vandana's gone," I whisper to Eugen. "But the damage has been done. We don't need her to poison our relationship, we've done it all by ourselves."

"No!" Eugen flings his glass in the fire.

It shatters on the hearth, causing the embers to crackle and spit with anger. As I stare at this uncharacteristic burst of emotion, Eugen slips his fingers underneath my hair and pulls my head back to gaze into my eyes. I see golden flecks flashing in the blueness, so deep, so powerful that I physically feel his eyes drink from mine. I fall into his arms, soaking up the protection they give me, and close my eyes to concentrate on my feelings. Behind my closed eyelashes, I imagine what love looks like, what it *feels* like. It feels, no it smells, like a rose garden. An exquisite fragrance coming from a bed of red roses, their petals moist with dew, early in the morning when their perfume is the strongest. I breathe deeply, enjoying the heavy scent. The deeper I breathe, the more fragrant it is.

I stop and open my eyes. I *do* smell a delicate scent, but there aren't any flowers in the room. I nuzzle into Eugen's chest, but the aroma doesn't come from him. In fact, it doesn't come from any point in the room. I look at Eugen to see his eyes closed.

"Do you smell that?"

"Yes, it's roses," he murmurs behind closed eyelids. A smile is on his face. "Is that perfume you are wearing?"

My brain continues to spin, searching for an explanation that won't appear. I look about the room, inhaling. How can I smell something that isn't there? I sit up, touching my fingers to my face and my nose as if they can tell me what is happening.

Eugen is intoxicated by the smell. He takes another breath as if to inhale it into his system. "God that's wonderful."

"I'm not wearing perfume."

His eyes flutter open. He, too, realizes something unusual is going on.

Disorientated, I wander the room. The smell of roses is as powerful as before. The scent becomes stronger when I get close to Eugen, and it weakens when I walk further away from him. My essence begins to dance, lilting on musical notes that aren't there, twirling in colors and smells and the softness of the air. Until now, I had thought that each sense could do one thing: my nose smells, I taste with my tongue, feel with my skin, look with my eyes. But that isn't true. Each sense has the ability to do everything; it is only now that I have become aware of it. I can hear with my eyes, see with my nose, smell with my tongue, even taste with my skin. We live in the realm of the senses. I read that in one of Eugen's books. Suddenly I am lighter, freer than I have ever been in my life. The feeling is exquisite and weightless, as if I am floating on air. This is love. Romantic love. I close my eyes and spin myself around the room, feeling a shy smile of gratitude on my lips. My heart opens and words burst out of my mouth before I can stop them.

"The extraordinary ordinary!"

Eugen goes rigid. "*What* did you say?"

As soon as he speaks, the scent disappears. It is as the electrical current that brought it to us has broken — snap! — just like that. Within seconds, I hit the earth with a thud. The smile slides off my face and lands in a soggy lump on the floor, my shoulders sag under a cloak of shame. How could I let this happen? My mind busies itself inside my brain, smoothing out those wild emotions, sorting out and dismissing anything that it couldn't compute. In a few moments, it is as if nothing happened. Discombobulated and hurt, I hug myself tightly and gaze into the fire.

"What *was* that?"

Eugen takes a breath and exhales sharply. "Forget it."

I turn toward him. "But it was real, wasn't it?"

"I said I want you to forget it."

The words sound growly and low, as if they are being forced through his teeth. This isn't the smooth, peaceful Eugen that I know. My mouth drops open. "But *why*?"

Eugen takes out his handkerchief to mop his brow. He looks into the fire, as if the flames are talking to him, whispering things that I cannot hear. Something is wrong. Whatever happened has affected him far more than he wants to admit.

I think of the one spiritual word I know. "Is this what you call enlightenment?"

"No!" he answers forcefully. "I call it bells and whistles. Vandana called it the extraordinary ordinary. Funny you should use the same expression."

I keep silent. I have a feeling that one false word and he will explode.

Eugen gazes at me. When he does speak, his jaw is tight. "Listen. Vandana was able to do similar things. But she wanted more. Always more. She began to dabble in worlds I had never heard of. Occultism. Past lives. Tantra. Shamanism. It was like a drug. I got cold feet — I couldn't go where she was heading. She called me a coward. It ruined our relationship, and finally it ruined her life." He grabs my hand, holding it so tightly that it hurts. "You can go these places. But don't. Please don't. Not until you do your inner work."

I don't know why, but I don't like being in this room with Eugen. He frightens me. He looks twisted, tight, aggressive. The walls close in on me, making me squirm as I rest my gaze on his face. It takes every bit of energy to make my voice sound normal.

"Come now," I try to say, taking his hand in mine and squeezing it.

To my amazement, he shoves me away from him. "Wake up, you fool. It can kill you. Just like it killed her."

And he storms out, leaving me standing in the room. Alone.

8

The fury of the wind wakes me. Sleepily I pull the duvet under my chin, careful not to disturb Minou from the end of the bed, and roll over against Eugen. But the other side of the bed is empty. Instantly I'm awake, putting on my glasses as I pull on my dressing gown and stumble out of bed.

I find him sitting at his desk, fully dressed in a suit and tie, his back toward me, staring out the window. I tiptoe in the room and catch sight of his thin but muscular frame, his torso erect, his dark hair trimmed neatly in the back. In front of him lies a pale lavender notebook.

He starts when I call his name, and, with an audible sigh, he swivels around in his chair. I bend forward, thinking I can see tears in his eyes, but it could be the light on his wire-framed glasses. Something in his body language makes me pull back and give him space. Without saying a word, he takes a neatly folded handkerchief from his pocket and begins to polish the lenses. Once that task is completed, he picks up the lavender notebook and puts it into the top drawer and locks it.

"I'm off to London. A client wants me to trace some money."

I've heard that before. I step toward him. "You're running away again."

He gets up from the chair and glances at his watch. "The taxi's waiting."

"How long will you be gone?" I reach to touch his hand.

He pulls it away. "Questions. Always these pathetic questions."

I draw my robe tighter around me and pinch my eyes shut, trying to hold back the tears. My truth comes out in a whisper. "I can't live this way anymore."

In that moment, Eugen looks at me, really looks at me, and his eyes drop. He clears his throat. "Annabel." He stops. "Last night you — you activated a dimension outside our current understanding of reality. You can do it. I saw it in your eyes. I saw it in Vandana's eyes, too."

Hugging myself tightly, I keep my eyes pinched as if to keep his words out. My senses are on overload, my skin twitching as flashes of heat overwhelm my system. What he says is true. I know it. I can go these places; I did it when I was young, before I learned to shut my mouth. I remember lying in bed at night, begging God to make me normal like everyone else. I pushed it away and forgot about it until now.

Eugen's voice brings me back to the present. "You were right. I talk about spirituality — but in reality I've been fooling myself."

My heart feels so tight I can hardly breathe. I'm losing touch with the floor; I'm floating above the room, high above, watching our conversation. I remember doing this while listening to my parents bickering when I was young. If I couldn't remove myself physically, at least I could check out and leave. It made the pain lessen somehow, but it also made me numb. I clamp my mouth shut so tight my jaw aches.

"You don't know me," he whispers. "And you don't want to."

Desperation creeps into my voice. "Eugen, don't leave. I need you."

"Find out who you are. That's more important than marrying me."

The words tumble out before I can stop them. "I know myself!"

Eugen's head droops. "I said the same thing once. Little did I know." His voice trails into the air, his words as heavy as winter blankets. Silence hangs heavily between us. When I open my eyes, he is gone.

9

I run to the window and look down as Eugen's slim figure disappears through the courtyard and into the street. The door slams shut, and then there is nothing but the sound of the wind. For a few seconds, I stare through the window, not wanting to believe that he has left. *Again.* My footsteps echo in the large, cavernous rooms as I pace within my golden cage, absorbing the fury of the storm into my psyche.

Minou wanders toward me. I pick her up and hug her to my chest, my heart aching. With tears streaming down my face, I scratch her under the chin, taking solace in the raspy sandpaper feeling of her tongue as she licks the tears from my cheeks. But it's not enough. There is something burning in my soul, and I have to find out what it is. I put Minou down and march to Eugen's desk and tug at the drawer where he placed the lavender book. It doesn't budge. In frustration I start to rummage for the key. A few papers float onto the floor. Then a stack of pamphlets slides off the desk and tumbles onto the parquet with a bang, causing Minou to scramble under the sofa.

Something snaps within me and I sweep Eugen's desk clear. Pens and papers scatter like confetti. Surprised by my own wildness, I attack the dining table, overturning boxes of magazines. Still no key. My pent up anger from the past few months explodes. I run around the apartment like a wild animal and wrench open the drawer with a knife, ignoring the crack of polished wood as I yank it open. There, as if to taunt me, lies the lavender book. I throw myself onto the chair and flip through the pages, hoping to find something that explains what happened last night. Something to confirm that I am safe, that I'm not like her, that —

— *I, too, won't die like her* my mind whispers.

Photographs fall from my shaking fingers onto the floor. I bend down to pick them up. One is a group of people naked in a large room with a vaulted roof. Another is a strange ceremony with people dressed is provocative, flowing Indian scarves, a third looks like a ritual, but for all I know, it could be an orgy. My eyes veer back to the book. Vandana's handwriting, small and squiggly like a snake, stares at me, taunting me with its words.

Eugen's sexual problems are a nightmare. A tantric healing might help him. I try to explain that at the turn of the century French osteopaths developed a procedure to heal the pain we hold in our genitals, but he won't listen. 'You're not going to stick your finger up my ass!' is all he can shout.

The book drops from my hands and bounces on the floor before coming to rest next to the scattered papers. This isn't a spiritual text; it's nothing more than a sex manual, written by two sex freaks. Eugen's words float back to me. *You don't know me, and don't want to.* I kick the scattered papers. I have to go, move, do something. I can't go back to London; I no longer have a home there. Where can I go where Eugen and his family won't find me? I pull out my suitcases and throw my clothes into them, not caring about anything except finding my way back to reality again. Reality. *My* reality. I look one last time at my golden cage, then pull Minou from her hiding place and stuff her squirming furry body into her carryall.

I call a taxi and give him an address in the first district. By late morning, I am standing outside Max's door. If he looks surprised to see a disheveled me in his doorway, he doesn't show it.

"*Komm,*" he says quietly, taking my suitcases while I put the carryall on the ground and let Minou out. Max puts his hands on my shoulders, and then gently wipes away a tear on my cheek. "I have been waiting months for this," he says, and kisses me.

November
Allerseelen
All Soul's Day

"Breakfast surprise!"

I open my eyes, disorientated by the strangeness of my surroundings, and fumble for my glasses as a long series of insistent meows approaches. Blinking behind the thick lenses, the fuzzy haze disappears and Max swims into view, followed by a bundle of complaining white fur.

"I did not expect guests for breakfast." He sits on the duvet with a cup of coffee in one hand and a tray with a selection of everything he could find in the refrigerator in the other. With his innocent expression and his thick hair curling every which way in the dry winter air, he reminds me of a fallen angel. Max bends down to stroke my cat. "I will give Minou food, she is hungry."

As Minou trots after him, I note Max's sleek, well-toned body looks as good without clothes as it does with them. I lean back into the soft pillows, holding onto my head. I had far too much to drink last night. Max was my rock and anchor for the past six months, far more than Eugen, but *still*. I hadn't planned on being in his bed. I close my eyes, trying to will away the confusion. *I don't do this. I don't go from one man to another.*

Max returns, pulling a wrapped parcel from underneath a napkin with an air of mystery.

I unwrap it, peering tentatively within. A ménage of cuddly stuffed animals innocently stare back at me. Their fluffy smiles reflect my own.

Max pours coffee, scoops the animals up in his arms and formally presents them to me. "*Ahem.* They are officials of the little known but well respected *Animalgemeinde der Fremdenfreundschaft Wien.* I will translate. It is the Organization of Friends of Lonely Foreigners in Vienna. They bid you welcome on *Allerseelen,* or All Soul's Day."

"I thought that was yesterday."

"That was All *Saints* Day. Today is All *Souls* Day. *Very* different."

I shake my head at the intricacies of Austrian logic. Then, looking at the stuffed animals, I smile, pulling the sheets around my shoulders while shaking furry paws and felty claws in mock seriousness. They are adorable. And so is he.

Max crawls under the covers and places the animals around him as if they, too, are to be served breakfast. He flexes his muscles and collapses onto the pillows with a sigh of satisfaction. "I will make you so happy."

His words make my stomach lurch. "Don't say that! Eugen—"

Max puts his hand up. "You are lucky to be out of that womanizer's life."

My jaw tightens. "I can't believe he could be that unfaithful."

Max purses his lips. "Rudi should know, they were at school together. Apparently he was known as Vienna's Casanova. You know, a woman in every port. And you wonder why he traveled for business so often?"

When I don't say anything, Max sits up in bed and shakes me. "Annabel, wake up! That man nearly ruined your career, and he was about to ruin your life." His eyes bore into mine. "I am not like him. I am not part of that weird esoteric spirituality. My feet are on the ground. I adore you. I will support your career. And I will do everything to make Minou and you feel at home."

Unfaithful? It can't be. I feel something inside of me withering in this moment. Over the years as a hardened journalist, I had disciplined myself to focus only on things that were concrete: my career, competitive sports, a large home, new languages, new cultures, foreign countries to explore. I believed in big things. Important things. Things that I could write about, report on, talk about. But not love.

And then I had met Eugen. For a few precious months, I allowed myself to feel something that I had hoped and dreamed of since I was a child. I had begun to believe that romantic love exists. I discovered that love is full of small things. The feel of Eugen's arms. The warmth of his breath. The look in his eyes. My memories of Eugen make my heart slip sideways, and I feel it slithering into a softness that feels dangerously unstable and insecure. Even when Eugen and I fought, there was something inexplicable that made me go the extra mile — and then I stop myself. I won't go there. True love doesn't exist. He didn't love me, he was playing with me. What a fool I was. How could I have got wrapped up with a man who meditates? Escapism from reality, that is all it is.

I feel Max's eyes on me and turn to smile at him. He feels so certain, so protective. Maybe if I try hard enough, I can make this work. Maybe Max can help me drop the shackles of guilt that I have been carrying since I arrived in Vienna. He can help me reject, once and for all, this horrible past year. Forget the guilt. Turn the page. Start anew again. Max is loyal, ambitious, adores my cat and I know he adores me, we work together well, have similar interests and — and

I can learn to love him. I know I can. My eyes settle on his long curly hair, still uncombed. It looks like a mop.

"Have you ever cut your hair short?"

"My hair is my persona," he answers. "A ponytail speaks paragraphs."

"I know. That's why I asked." I don't say anything more, but I see that he has absorbed my words.

Max leans over and kisses me. Before I know it, we are making love. *Fake it until you make it*, I tell myself as I check out, imagining that I am on the ceiling, watching impartially as my body is contorted into all sorts of uncomfortable positions to satisfy Max's mounting excitement. First he begins on top of me, then we move onto our sides, no that doesn't work at all, he slips out, and so, panting, he sits on his knees like a rearing stallion, flips me onto my back, holds me by my thighs and raises my torso toward him. With a shout of satisfaction, he tosses my ankles onto his shoulders and tells me to hold on. I look at my feet dangling on either side of his ears, feel my lower back aching and my neck beginning to crick and hope he tires quickly. *I don't know why people go on about sex.* How well I understand the famous British Victorian mothers' advice to their daughters: *Lie back, close your eyes and think of England.* As far as I'm concerned, sex is overrated and under performed. It doesn't cross my mind to satisfy myself. I don't know how. I close my eyes and sigh loudly, hoping Max will think it is an orgasm.

Ouch! My eyes fly open. I struggle to sit up, my hand on my chin.

"What's wrong?" Max pants as he rolls off me.

"I think I've pulled a muscle," I say, rubbing my jaw.

Max shakes his head like a bear and looks around, dazed, before his eyes come to focus on me. "Do not worry. We have time."

He glances at his watch and swears under his breath, then jumps out of bed, grabbing my hand. I barely have time to wrap myself in a sheet before he pulls me through the apartment. It is nearly as large as Eugen's. The large dusty space, with tall ceilings and parquet floors, are linked by a series of double French doors, giving it a cavernous but airy feel. Its barren simplicity appeals to me. I'm not sure whether Max is intentionally minimalist, or he doesn't care, but the apartment has a Zen quality to it. Two thousand square feet contain a bed, a large Bukhara carpet, an Art Nouveau dining table and chairs, a black sofa and a desk. No paintings, no clutter, no pictures or knick-knacks or mirrors, just books. Hundreds upon hundreds of them, placed like sacred objects in shelves that line the walls from floor to ceiling. The shelves are painted in soft pastels of blue and yellow and are backlit so that the books stand out from the walls like textured, multi-layered wallpaper.

Max swings open the creaky French doors leading to an additional suite of rooms. "One will be our office. I will install faxes and phones." He turns and smiles. "The other room is for Minou and her toys." He flicks a switch, and suddenly two television monitors click on and I hear the harsh guttural tones of a newscast blasting forth. "I'll have cable installed this week," he yells over the noise. "Then we can see which networks have syndicated our news broadcast on *Kristallnacht*."

The sound of the television feels like an abrasive insult to my senses. That's one of the things I most liked about Eugen. He didn't like television. Called it chewing gum for the masses. I find the remote and punch the mute button. Instantly a loud silence engulfs us.

Max looks at me, dumbstruck. "What? You are a journalist and don't watch television? My God, you really did spend too much time with that crazy aristocrat." He lifts my chin up so that I can look him in the eye. "I'm going to drag you back into television, Annabel. And

I'm going to make a star out of you." He picks up a folder and hands it to me. "I'm late for a meeting. Here's your homework for our production meeting in London next week. I will be home tonight to talk it over." He blows me a kiss, throws his clothes on and runs out the door.

2

Leopolditag

St. Leopold's Feast Day

Within days, the apartment is filled with flowers, the floor is littered with cat toys, and I find little gifts under my pillow every night before I go to sleep. I can hardly believe that my life could change so quickly. With Max by my side, Vienna shows a gentler, friendlier face. For the first time I can relax into the essence of the city, which, Max quickly points out, is music. Never mind that Haydn, Schubert, Brahms, Beethoven, Bruckner, Strauss, Schoenberg, and Mozart lived here, Max explains, music vibrates in the Viennese soul. It is everywhere. Sometimes, Max tells me, it is as subtle as the many people carrying black music cases of various shapes and sizes through the city, other times it is blaringly obvious, such as a public toilet under the opera house that plays waltzes to us while we pee. Everywhere are recitals, quartets, symphonies, operas, operettas, concerts in cathedrals — which is how Max describes sung mass — and dozens of tourist concerts touted downtown by young students dressed like Mozart look-a-likes in eighteenth century costume. Nice, orderly Vienna suddenly appeals to me. That sense of sliding into the abyss is gone.

In the morning, I tackle the production office, rearranging it to suit my working needs. Putting things into order always makes me happy. I stop to stroke Minou, remembering the nerve it took to move to London as CNN's financial correspondent. I loved being *the* Annabel Jones of CNN. I was always on the run, always reporting the latest crisis, breathing work as if my life depended upon it. If I'm lucky, I'll soon be back on the career track again. This television series is a godsend. The shrill ring of my cell phone makes Minou jump and jars me back into the present. As I grab the phone, my eyes swerve towards the clock. Only one person would dare call me so early.

"She's *dead?*" Chloe's voice barks when I tell her the news.

I wrap my dressing gown around my waist. "It's been a few weeks."

"*That's* why I haven't heard from you," my best friend muses. "Let me close my office door, I don't want anyone to overhear us."

Despite being born with so much money, Chloe More-Hamilton works harder than anyone else I know. She has a full time job as literary agent, and has more men in her life than I can keep track of. In her spare time, she sorts out the increasingly spectacular and chaotic messes into which her family seems to get stuck. In the middle of the chaos, Chloe executes the role of The Great Protectress, wisely helping family and friends when they are down. I hear Chloe's footsteps and the sound of a door closing. "How *dreadful!* Imagine, you wanted her gone, and now you got what you wanted."

I flinch as I sweep Minou onto my lap. "You wouldn't believe Eugen's behavior. He wasn't even there when she died."

"Sounds like you are less enamored with lover boy."

I hope she doesn't remind me of all the soggy words of love that I poured out in her kitchen in London. "That's the understatement of the year. Three days after she died, he was off again." I give an irritated tug at Minou's ruff. "Probably to see another woman."

"How do you know that?"

"Take my word for it," I say firmly. "So I moved out."

"Hang on, ducky," Chloe says. "Let me see if I have got this straight. You move to Vienna to be with your prince charming, who leaves his wife, who conveniently dies *anyway*, and then, instead of resting on your hard earned laurels, in the magnificent palace and in the arms of your rich, aristocratic soul mate, you *move out?*"

I hear the click of her lighter and long inhale. Every time Chloe lights a cigarette, she usually asks about my sex life. Quickly I change the subject. "Speaking of men, how's Robert?"

"Gone back to his wife."

"Robert is *married?*"

"It was my idea to give Robert the boot," she says nonchalantly. "I am simplifying my life. I'm getting rid of anything that weighs me down. Clothing, jewelry, even men and bothersome family members."

"That *is* new," I say. "What happened to the agony aunt in you?"

"She is asking herself what lies behind the protective armor of wanting to help others."

"And that is?"

"Behind every great mother figure is a control freak. When you help others, you are in control. You tell yourself you are doing it for others, but probably you do it to feel better about yourself."

I can't believe what I am hearing. "Where did this insight come from?"

"A Tantra course Robert dragged me to in Paris before we broke up. I'm doing another next week. A particular Frenchman whom I know will be there."

"Isn't that to do with wild sex?" I ask, trying to keep the suspicion from my voice. In the recesses of my mind, misty figures of copulating couples begin to dance like poisonous snakes, their bodies undulating in the reddish haze. The silence on the phone beckons. I clear my throat. "Sorry, what did you say?"

"I said, why aren't you back in London?"

I hesitate. "Because I am in another relationship," I answer quietly.

I hear a loud guffaw down the line. "*Two* men at once? Well done! I *knew* you had it in you. Who is he, not another aristocrat I hope?"

"He's one of Austria's television stars. He's got substance. And a ponytail."

"He sounds divine. How's the sex?"

"Come on, Chloe!" I say, exasperated.

"Don't tell me you *still* aren't keen on sex," she chides gently.

"It is about as good as it is going to get," I say, sighing.

"Don't say that. Sex *is* important. Sex will take you to places words will never reach."

"Max seems to enjoy himself well enough. We are good friends."

"That's a cop out. Don't fall for that good friend routine most couples eventually fall into."

"Compromise is part of life." Time to change the subject. "We'll be coming to London soon on business."

"Marvelous!" she whoops. "Come stay. I may be into frog legs by then."

3

Kristallnacht
The Night of Shattered Glass

The days get shorter and the nights longer. Vienna prepares herself for the long winter months ahead. Workmen crawl over fountains, boarding up bronze statues and stone cherubs and basins with large faded green planks that remind me of bomb shelters. The outdoor tables lining the sidewalks outside the cafes disappear, leaving the broad pedestrian areas looking open and forlorn. The drabness of winter has set in. On a grey and overcast winter day, Max and I thread along the narrow streets glistening with the late morning's frost to meet Rudi Brandemberg, the executive producer of our series, and the source of our joint income. Silently we walk through another courtyard that opens into a large open space, as large as two football fields, framed by massive stone buildings. In the center, on either side of a broad street slicing through the field, two large equestrian statues rear silently at each other in an open display of majestic radiance. Clusters of people, dwarfed by the size of the surrounding buildings, huddle in groups as they watch children and dogs run amongst the statues.

Max pulls on my sleeve, making me stop. He sweeps his arm in front of him as if he were a tourist guide. "Heroes Square. It exudes power, doesn't it?"

On my left and right, massive, imposing buildings project their heavy facades, columns and statues in bristling and imposing defense. "It looks too grand for such a small city."

"Austria is small now, but before World War I, it was the heart of the Austro-Hungarian Empire." He pulls his knit cap off, his hair falling over his face. "It's hard to have all this grandeur and no empire to go with it." His mouth pulls down at its corners. "Imagine. Over seventy years ago today, *Kristallnacht* happened. People ran along these streets, vandalizing stores and beating up people while the police stood by and watched. Ordinary people destroying shops, burning synagogues, forcing Jews on their knees to scrub the streets with toothbrushes while onlookers laughed. All because of what happened here."

I look at him questioningly.

Max points to a massive neoclassical pile of stone lined from end to end with pillars. In the center I see a massive balcony. "That's the National Library," Max says. "Hitler announced that Austria would join the German republic from that balcony. Seven months later, *Kristallnacht*. The rest is history."

Everywhere I look, people tramp along with pinched and preoccupied faces, hunched over as if the heaviness of the atmosphere is too much to carry. Even though the architecture is beautiful, my eyes only see a pervading melancholy. I seem to remember seeing that balcony framed in a sepia photograph. Hitler was waving at a sea of cheering crowds.

"I thought Austria was annexed."

Max snorts at my ignorance. "That's what Austrians want the world to believe. This square was so crowded with frenetically cheering people that you couldn't walk. People came from all over Austria to welcome Hitler's arrival." He points to a large four-lane road at the end of the square. "The Ringstrasse — that is the road built where the city walls once were — was lined with flags and people screaming *Heil!* as he drove by. Hitler was greeted in Vienna like a God."

I look around me, imagining crowds screaming frenetically, flags with swastikas flying in the breeze, the grinding sound of tanks making their way along the Ring road. I feel a pang in my stomach as my eyes skim the buildings and the passers-by. Suddenly everything looks very, very ugly.

"I forgot Hitler was Austrian until I arrived in Vienna," I say sheepishly.

Max stands in front of me, mesmerized by an image that only he can see. "My father was here. He welcomed Hitler."

"Is your father still alive?"

His eyes glitter with anger. "I asked my father what happened during the war, only to receive the evasive answer, *I don't remember.* In Germany, people *had* to look at why it happened. But in Austria, people said, *It's Germany's fault* and turned another page in history."

I stare at this man I am now in relationship with, and I realize just how little I know him. "Why do you always get so riled when speaking about your country?" I ask quietly. "Everyone makes mistakes."

Max gives himself a shake. "Other countries learn from their mistakes. Mine wallows in them." With that, he turns on his heels and walks away.

4

"It'll only take two seconds," I say as I open the glass door. "I want to pick up a newspaper." I really want Max to meet the *Trafikant*, but I don't tell him this.

A pleasant chime sounds. Herr Dietmayer beams as if the leaden and overcast day was filled with diamonds. "*Guten Morgen!*" He pulls a newspaper down from the wall, raising an amused eyebrow as Max crinkles his nose at the smell wafting from the tea candle.

"Verbena and lavender for inner stillness," Herr Dietmayer explains as he hands me my paper. "I thought it appropriate for the *Kristallnacht* anniversary."

Before I can reach into my pocket, Max throws a five-euro note on the counter. "Glad to hear you haven't forgotten."

I shake Herr Dietmayer's hand. "This is my producer, Max Krankovich."

Judging by Max's stiff reaction, I sense I have made a social faux pas by introducing a television personality to a lowly shopkeeper. But if Herr Dietmayer notices Max's offhand manner, he doesn't show it. He hands Max the change. "I know your TV programs. Some are excellent."

I peer over Max's shoulder to a small bookshelf behind Herr Dietmayer. Psychological books, self help books, tarot cards, Bibles,

61

books on the Vedas, Kabala, Tao and the Bhagavad Gita; tomes on healing, diets and alternative medicine, astrology, past lives, witchcraft, even Tantra. The library is a veritable A-Z of spiritual literature of all sorts, from the esoteric to the banal.

Max eyes dart suspiciously around him. "Do *you* watch television?"

"I choose not to." The shopkeeper hoists a bundle of newspapers onto the counter with a grunt. "All that information made me feel depressed, so I stopped. But I read a lot. It's one of the perks of this job."

"Max is the person responsible for showing me much of Vienna," I explain, putting a gloved hand on Max's sleeve. "But it always feels so heavy here."

Max turns to me. "That is part of the Viennese character. Either people are moaning about the future or they are complaining about the past."

The *Trafikant* nods his head. "Yes, the energy here *is* heavy. That's one of the reasons the Viennese are cranky. And why we have so many angels."

"Angels?" Max furrows his brow.

Herr Dietmayer points outside his shop. "Keep your eyes on the tops of buildings. You will find there are statues of angels looking down upon you from the most amazing vantage points."

Max puts a protective arm around my shoulders. "Vienna needs all the angels she can get. Deep down, all Austrians hate each other."

Herr Dietmayer looks surprised. "You think that?"

Max nods his head. "Trust me. I know my country."

The shopkeeper takes out a pocketknife and with a neat upward movement, slices through the cord holding the papers. "That *thought* must weigh terribly on you."

Max scratches his forehead. "It's not a thought. It's the truth."

"Is it now?" the shopkeeper asks, smiling peculiarly. "Are you sure it's the truth, or is it a *thought* that you have decided to believe?"

Max stops mid-scratch. "What *are* you talking about?"

Herr Dietmayer shifts his weight as he swings the rest of the newspapers behind him. "When you think the thought, 'All Austrians hate each other' how do you feel?"

"Angry." Max puts his hands on the small of his back and begins to rub it.

The *Trafikant* nods his head. "So the thought 'All Austrians hate each other' makes you angry." He turns to me. "Do *you* think that?"

I shake my head. "I don't know whether all Austrians hate each other."

He turns back to Max. "So she doesn't think that, but you do. It is only a *thought*. It's your perception of reality. And it makes you angry."

"What else is there to do?" I ask, curiously.

"You could *drop the thought!*" he says, grinning at Max. "I'm not saying *do so*. But — how would you feel if you weren't carrying around that thought?"

Max looks around the shop as if it had suddenly become too small for him. "If I weren't thinking that all Austrian hate each other?" For a second he blinks, disoriented. Then he shakes his head, pulling hard on his ponytail as he glares at the shopkeeper. "I like my anger! It gives me the energy to fight this *scheisse* city."

The *Trafikant* steps back, amused. "You *like* feeling angry!"

I glance at Max and nod my head. The *Trafikant* is right. Max *does* like feeling angry.

Max thrusts his nose in Herr Dietmayer's face. "And it's happening again."

I look at Max. "*What* is happening again?"

"A*nger*," Max says. "Can't you feel it? Anger is a rising tide that sweeps everyone up without noticing it. Take World War II, for example. In the 1920's and 30's, Germans were a normal, hardworking people who felt frustrated, downtrodden, and frightened of their future. Then Hitler came along and tapped into people's feelings of victimization. He funneled anger into righteous patriotism." He jabs a finger into the air. "Anger has power; anger makes people feel important. Anger gives meaning to peoples' lives."

The shopkeeper continues to smile. "So anger gives meaning to *your* life. Oh dear. I can see why your back hurts."

Max swivels round. "How do you know I have back problems?"

Just then, the chimes ring and the next customer squeezes in. Not wanting to get further into the conversation, I give the shopkeeper a little wave and drag Max through the door. Outside, I take a deep breath, thinking the atmosphere has a lighter feel than when I walked into the shop. That's always what happens when I see Herr Dietmayer. For a few minutes, we walk in silence. I glance at Max, noting his frown.

He stops, flicks his scarf around his neck and puts both hands on my shoulders. "Why do you let spiritual charlatans get to you like that?"

"At least he's pleasant." I say, hating that I have to defend myself. "That's more than I can say about most people I meet here."

Max shrugs. "So he's a good businessman. He'll do anything to sell more cigarettes and newspapers."

I'm about to open my mouth to respond, but then choose not to. No matter what I say, Max won't believe it. That's just the way he is.

5

The restaurant is tucked up a side alley covered with climbing vine sprinkled with orange and red leaves. The stark modern glass exterior on the ground floor is a pleasant contrast to the crumbling fifteenth century walls that frame it. Through the window I see a handsome lanky man with short grey hair sitting at the corner table sipping a glass of red wine. Rudi Brandemberg unfolds himself and stands up, his blue eyes resting on mine before he raises my hand to his lips in the old fashioned greeting I saw Eugen often use. Max had explained that the name Brandemberg was a door opener to the tightly knit circle of *in* families of Vienna. What he didn't mention, but I know, is that he is dying to be on more intimate terms with this man.

Max shakes Rudi's hand. "Greetings, Meister Brandemberg!"

"Allow me." Rudi holds a chair out for me as a waiter, dressed in a long white apron, hurries toward us with two menus. "Herr Krankovich is flattering me. I am only in my position at the Opera House because of my wife's money." His British public school English is as perfect as his manners. Polite, distant and reserved.

"Allow me," Max repeats as I open my menu.

It's pumpkin season. Pumpkin goulash, roasted pumpkin with garlic and cinnamon, pumpkin ravioli, pumpkin soup with pumpkin seed oil, pumpkin with dumplings, pumpkin stew, and even in the deserts I see pumpkin pie, pumpkin strudel and pumpkin ice cream. I like that the Austrians eat with the seasons. It makes me aware of the passage of time and the abundance of nature.

Max grins. "Be careful with the meat. There are many tasty dishes in Austria, but sometimes it is best not to look too closely at the ingredients."

"I'll order myself," I insist, smiling as I watch Max imitate Rudi's manners. "This is the only way I can learn German."

"*Jawohl,* my linguist!" Max grins, leaning back in his chair. He looks on tolerantly as I order in halting German.

Hoping I have understood what I have ordered, I close the menu with a satisfied snap and hand it to the waiter.

Max points in my direction. "It is nice to see an Anglo Saxon make an effort."

Rudi barely glances in my direction. "I wish my wife did."

"She's American, right?"

Rudi's eyes swivel toward mine. "How do you know?"

"Eugen, uh, Vasoy told me. Apparently you went to school together."

My first name basis with Eugen has the appropriate effect on Rudi.

"What a small world," he drawls, pouring *Sturm* — the season's slightly fermented unfiltered grape juice — in our glasses.

"This is only available for a short time," Max interjects, handing me a glass. "It reminds me of autumn."

As I take my glass, I notice Rudi's smile isn't as smug as before. "How do you know Eugen?"

"We —" I still have a hard time speaking about Eugen in the past. "It was because of Eugen that I came to Vienna."

Rudi studies me intensely. "Then I have also heard of you."

I sit awkwardly under his gaze, staring uncomfortably at my glass. Max comes to my rescue and puts a protective arm around my shoulders. "I wasn't going to let him do to Annabel what he did to other women."

"Max has taken me in," I say as I self-consciously take a sip from my glass. It tastes like cider, only sweeter. "It's delicious."

Rudi swirls the liquid in the glass. "Wise decision. Eugen is known for his, say, less than gentlemanlike behavior with women. Poor Vandana. I would have been sorry if you were to experience the same."

"The same *what?*" I ask curiously.

Rudi deftly changes the conversation by raising his glass. "Shall we drop the formal *Sie* and go by *du?*"

We clink glasses formally. Max looks pleased. "Thanks — Rudolph."

Rudi gives a gracious bow of the head. "Rudi. I saw the report on the anniversary of *Kristallnacht* that you sent to CNN, Max. It has been running since this morning." He throws me an appreciative look. "You're good, Ms. Jones. You will be a fine addition to the series."

"Annabel," I say. I feel my smile becoming firmer. I always feel comfortable talking business. It's just emotions and relationships that seem to catch me out.

He nods his head. "Annabel. Lovely name. It rolls off the tongue so beautifully." As the waiter clears our plates, he pulls out a document and flips to a page where I see a number of signatures. "You are also expensive."

"You get what you pay for." I turn to Max. "When are you going to sign the contract? I need to arrange my schedule."

Rudi's smile is like butter. "Don't worry about that."

"But that's not professional," I start to say. "You are hiring me."

"And we are living together," Max says, glancing in Rudi's direction as he speaks. "You will be paid through my company. So you don't sign."

Rudi sees me frowning. "Don't worry, this is how we do things here. Your salary is guaranteed. And I expect your input in the project."

I don't like this, but I'll have to let it go.

Rudi looks at his watch as he gathers his things. "I'm sorry, I have a meeting near the Hofburg."

"I'll get the bill," Max says, waving Rudi on.

He acknowledges with a slight nod of the head. Standing, he raises my hand just short of his lips and clicks his heels together. "I'll give your number to Emma. I'm sure she'd love to meet another ex-pat." As he scribbles his private number on the back of his card, he smiles at me. "We have a place in Carinthia. You—" he puts a cap on his fountain pen and places it in his jacket pocket before correcting himself. "Both of you must stay with us sometime."

6

Martinstag

St Martins Day

Max makes the ultimate sacrifice the day before we leave for London. With a solemnity accorded to a funeral, the controversial ponytail is ceremoniously lopped off by one of Vienna's more prominent hairdressers. He emerges from the hairdressers looking forlorn, clutching a carryall bag to his chest.

"I said I would do anything for you," he says, peering in the bag. "But that was difficult. I couldn't let them throw my ponytail away. I will bury it in the *Zentralfriedhof* cemetery next time I am there."

He looks so downtrodden that I ruffle his hair. "Do you go often?"

"I meet Onki there. Tell him about important things in life. Like you."

"The Viennese are obsessed with death."

"Vienna is called the *city* of death," Max explains as he takes my hand. "Death is part of life. Life, death, transition. That's why we like to celebrate the passing of time. Each day has a meaning; each season has its traditions. Like today. *Martinigansl* day."

"Martini what?"

"*Gansl*, goose," Max repeats as if I were deaf. "It's roasted and served with purple cabbage and dumplings and this season's wines."

So that was what all the restaurants were advertising! "Because?"

"Why do we eat goose today?" He reaches to pull on a ponytail that is no longer there. "Something about a saint in the fourth century who gave his cloak to a beggar. It's the anniversary of his birthday I think."

My eyes nearly pop out of my sockets. "You eat goose because it's the birthday of some man who lived over fifteen hundred years ago?"

He smiles. "You see? Vienna is revealing her treasures to you."

That evening while packing for London, I watch as Minou, wild-eyed and skittish, sprays paper across the floor as she stalks an invisible prey. I bend down, telling her that Max and I will be gone for a week.

"Frau Darinka will spoil you," I explain, picking her up.

But Minou won't have it. With a wriggle, she drops onto the floor, tail in the air. I look at her with a pinch of guilt. I hate leaving her. Only when I crawl into bed does she snuggle in my arms to tell me that she will miss me, that she understands that I need to be away, and that she will be good.

"No overeating," I whisper. "And no peeing on the carpet in protest, either." But she only purrs.

7
London

After sleepy Vienna, London pulses with life. Endless streams of people weave amongst the lines of red double deckers and shiny black cabs squealing cheerfully along the roads. As the taxi squeals to a stop outside Chloe's large white Victorian house in Notting Hill, a wave of nostalgia overcomes me. I lived in London for nearly a decade. My friends are here, I transitioned from young woman to adult here, I made my career here. No wonder London feels as comfortable as an old shoe.

Chloe opens the door with a bottle of champagne under one arm, a hammer and Christmas wreath under the other. "We'll handle the champagne and bags, you the wreath," she says to Max, handing him the hammer and wreath. "Bang it on the door but for God's sake don't bring the house down."

We drag the bags into the hallway while Max, with a look of self-importance, tackles the chore given him. I look around the kitchen and smile at the familiar chaos in front of me. Because of my friend's job at London's most revered literary agency, piles of newspaper clippings make a permanent home on, and under, her kitchen table.

Chloe removes a hair clip with one hand to allow her long tawny hair to tumble around her shoulders, then opens the champagne and pours it into three glasses.

I look Chloe in the eye. "You look good. *Something* has happened."

"*Mais oui*," she says, giving me a seductive smile.

I pause, trying to remember the latest Chloe man. "The Frenchman!"

"An ophthalmologist," she answers with a toss of her hair. "He performs that laser surgery on people with shortsightedness."

"Lasik, I think it's called," I say. "I'm interested in it. You know I have appalling eyesight."

"How could I forget the first time I saw you in your dreadful spectacles? You looked like Adam Ant."

"That's why I got contact lenses," I say, grinning.

"Jean Luc's doing *my* eyes next week," Chloe says, pulling a cigarette out from the pack. "He has a private clinic in Paris, but comes to London a few days a month to do surgery in Harley Street."

"Are you afraid?"

"He's good," she begins, then adds with a smile, "I mean, as a surgeon of course." She throws me a come hither smile. "Just think. Perfect eyesight. No contact lenses, no glasses, nothing between me and life."

I twirl the champagne glass between my fingers. "I *like* this man. He obviously is great in bed; he makes my best friend happy, and makes people see. Does he walk on water as well?"

"You'll see for yourself," she says as she puts a cigarette between her lips and reaches for her lighter. "Jean Luc is coming for dinner tonight."

"Sounds like you like him."

"More than what's good for me," Chloe answers, her eyes watching the cloud of smoke drift into the air.

Max walks into the kitchen and drops the hammer on the table before wiping his hands on his jeans. Chloe holds out a glass of champagne. "Do we kiss or shake hands? And where is your ponytail?"

Max instinctively draws his hand through his hair, but there is no ponytail. His hand drops to his side, as if disappointed. "It's my new image," he answers. "It is supposed to fit my new bourgeois lifestyle."

Chloe looks sharply at me. "You're not trying to remake him, are you? We like ponytails in my literary circles!"

I respond to Chloe's glare with a guilty shrug.

"Obviously your literary circle is profitable," Max says, shaking his head at the champagne. "A beer will do. How much is this house worth?"

"Max!" I cry.

"I *inherited* it," Chloe laughs as she walks into the hallway. "Let me show you to your room, then I'll get a beer for a partisan without a ponytail."

"Think of the people who work all their lives and never will be able to live like this," Max continues, gaping at the portraits as we mount the stairs.

Chloe, clearly amused, answers sharply. "Don't be so quick to pick up the mantle of the disadvantaged. We all come into the world with something. Whether it is money or wit, we all choose to do whatever we like with them."

She opens the door to my favorite room, the yellow one, facing the back garden. Pale winter sunlight streams through the large windows, lighting up the bedspread and thick curtains in large, old English rose patterns.

"Here's your room. An entire Turkish family, with all their dependents, squats in the guest bathroom when I don't have guests. I've thrown them onto the streets while you're here. But please, don't feel guilty."

Max throws back his head and howls. "I like it!" he cries, grabbing me by the waist and kissing me. "Mistress Chloe, we will get along fine. Now, is it true what Annabel has told me? That you love men? How many boyfriends do you have?"

Chloe gives her long hair a shake. "Hundreds," she says with a naughty smile. "And there is always room for more." She stops and thinks. "Well, until now."

8

Chloe is lighting the candles on the mahogany dining table when Jean Luc arrives. The oval dining room, with its high ceilings and Georgian proportions, is shaded in a soft glow, and is decorated in an abundance of red and orange, with bowls of lilies and berries in crystal and silver. The color scheme overflows onto the side table and into the entrance hall, where dozens of red tulips are placed in strategic positions under the soft lighting.

Jean Luc drops a dozen red roses onto the table in order to use both arms to sweep Chloe into his arms. *"Mon amour."* To my amazement, Chloe blushes like a schoolgirl. I like him instantly. He is of medium height, with curly gray hair brushed back to show a high forehead, a lovely smile, an open countenance and strong features. He looks like a man who knows himself.

"Val is behind me," Jean Luc whispers as he slips off a long black cashmere coat and hangs it in the closet in the hall. "It looks like she's on her own."

Chloe removes her apron. "Not again? She runs through more men than—"

"You do?" I interject with a grin.

"Jean Luc and Valentine are old friends from his Tantra days," Chloe whispers before turning to greet a petite woman walking through the door. Swathed in layers of shawls in tones of brown and orange, her black straight hair framing a round, heart shaped face, Val reminds me of mother earth on a warm day.

"Val darling," Chloe coos, indicating for Jean Luc to remove a place setting from the table. "Meet Annabel, another ex-pat." As they air kiss, I feel a slight tension in the air.

Chloe fidgets with a package of cigarettes as she glares at Val's back. To my amazement, Jean Luc sweeps Val into a full two-armed hug as he did Chloe, except that they don't kiss. It seems so private, so intimate, that if I hadn't known he was Chloe's man, I would have thought he was Val's.

"Tantric hug," Chloe huffs. She throws the cigarettes on the table and stomps into the kitchen.

Soon the dinner party is in full swing. The guests are talking animatedly with each other; the atmosphere is warm and inviting. It makes me realize how much I miss the sociability of London. If London is a river, then Vienna is a pond. Eight months in Vienna and I know precisely four people. One died, one I don't see, one is a shopkeeper and I live with the last one. No wonder I'm so dependent upon Max. My cheeks glowing from the wine, I sit back and watch him enthusiastically making a point with his empty wine glass as he talks with Val across the table. With his ponytail gone, his raw forcefulness has become more tamed, more acceptable. He is handsome, intelligent, amusing. *And he loves me.* A warm feeling rises from within as Max's voice breaks through my reverie.

"You look *wunderschön* tonight."

Acknowledging his gaze, I raise my wine glass.

"*Prost!*" Max downs the contents and slips his arm around my shoulders before turning to Val. "Say that again. You do yoga and Reiki — that Japanese healing thing?"

Valentine gives a throaty laugh. "I'm a *Reichian*. Like Wilhelm Reich. You, know, that Austrian somatic thing?"

Max's eyes nearly pop out of his head. "*Mein Gott,* don't tell me people still study his work!"

I turn to him. "Who is Wilhelm Reich?"

Max removes his arm from the back of my chair and helps himself to another glass of wine from the bottle resting at Jean Luc's elbow. "Just a discredited Viennese psychiatrist."

As Chloe returns with cake on a silver tray, she glances at Max's wine glass, and nods imperceptibly for Jean Luc to refill it.

"We Austrians are very suspicious of people who don't drink." I notice Max's voice is slightly slurred when he speaks.

"It is a crime *en France*," Jean Luc says. "What did Pablo Picasso say? *Love is the greatest refreshment in life.* So I'll stick with that."

"You *must* drink," Max insists. "Let me fill your glass."

"*Merci*, no," Jean Luc says politely but firmly.

"Oh!" Max exclaims loudly. "You are on a *diet!*"

I'm right; Max has had too much to drink. "Max!"

Jean Luc gives a diplomatic smile. "Alcohol lowers my energy and dims my awareness."

Max gives Jean Luc a bleary look. "But it relaxes you."

"If I am with friends, a glass of champagne tastes *magnifique*, but otherwise, I can do the effect myself." Jean Luc grins mysteriously and changes the subject. "I take it Reich is not highly considered in Austria?"

"What do you expect?" Max shrugs his shoulders. "He went insane."

Val takes a sharp breath in, as if the words hurt her. "Reich died in a federal penitentiary," she says emphatically, "But that doesn't *mean* he went insane."

Jean Luc picks up a fork and takes a bite of cake that Chloe has placed in front of him. "Marvelous, *ma belle*." He pulls the cake toward him for a second helping. "Last week, I operated on a Viennese who knew a lot about Reich. He explained that between the first and second world wars Vienna was *the* hot spot of psychiatry."

I take a plate from Chloe and help myself to some cream. "I can't imagine Vienna being the hot spot of anything."

Jean Luc smiles at me. "It was strange. I realized that I had taken a Tantra course with him in California years ago."

Max splutters. "Tantra! What is that, a sect?"

"Sex, darling," Chloe answers, "not sect."

Everyone laughs except Max.

Jean Luc turns to Val. "You were on that course, you might remember him, tall and thin with a beard. His wife was Indian. He's called de Vasoy. Nice man."

Now it is my turn to choke. "Eugen got his eyes done?"

As the color drains from my face, Chloe puts an arm around Jean Luc. "Uh, darling. I think you just operated on Annabel's ex."

Jean Luc's eyes open wide, and I see him give me the same look as Rudi did, as if, suddenly, he knows who I am. I can just hear what's going on in his mind. So that's the little snipe who stole him away from his wife. I feel a rush of feelings fighting each other, on one side I want to defend myself, to blurt out the entire damn story in its entirety, to use this dinner like a confessional, to say it wasn't my fault, I didn't know she had cancer. But before I can, I feel Max's protective arm around me.

"You don't know how Annabel suffered under that womanizer, Jean Luc. Don't believe all he tells you." And with that, the conversation is over. Smiling to himself, Max reaches across the table for the bottle of wine. Halfway there, he winces, his hand shooting toward the small of his back.

Realizing that neither of us wants to talk about Eugen, Jean Luc throws a look of concern at Max. "Your back hurts?"

Max rubs his back. "I forgot my pain killers. Can you give me some?"

Jean Luc looks at Val. "Perhaps Val's work would be more helpful. After a two hour session, you'll feel like a different person."

Val watches Max rubbing his lower back. "You must have a lot of stress in your job. Do you often get angry?"

Max snorts. "Don't tell me that Reichian stuff is true."

Val smiles at Max. "You can also go to a chiropractor. Cracking your back will help relieve any unexpressed emotions you might be holding."

Max glares at his wine glass. "Now I've heard everything."

"Everything?" I interrupt.

"Emotions tied within the body," Val explains to me. "Pain is one way your body speaks to you."

Max looks defiantly around the table. "That's stupid. I've got a bad back. So did my father, and my grandfather before him. And you tell me this pain is because I have a particular attitude in life?"

"Patterns run in families," Val interjects. "Have you ever caught yourself reacting to things the same way your father did?"

I jump as Max bangs his wine glass on the table. His face is crimson, his hand is clenched, his eyes narrow into slits. No one speaks.

Max answers in a low voice. "I have nothing to do with my father." He pauses before continuing. "He was a bitter, angry man."

It seems even the flickering candles are waiting for what will happen next. The silence dances between us. Then — boom! — it is broken. A bustle of activity, a clink of glass, the chink of tableware, a hushed word massages the awkwardness back to normal.

Chloe stands up. "Coffee anyone?"

My jaw starts to throb as I look off into the distance. I'm furious at Max for getting drunk in front of my friends. That Jean Luc knows Eugen. And that I can only stand here, tongue-tied, unable to say anything.

Val gives me a look of sympathy. "Does your jaw hurt?"

I rub it slightly. "Strange, it's seemed to flair up in the past few months."

We all get up from the dinner table and start to bring the dishes into the kitchen. She gives me a knowing smile. "Are there a lot of things you haven't dare to say in the past few months?"

I glance sharply at her. "How do you know that?"

"I'm a Reichian therapist," she says, smiling mysteriously. "That's my job."

"So Reich was Austrian? Like Freud?"

She nods her head. "What your friend said was true. Vienna was the cradle of psychoanalysis. Some of the best psychoanalysts came from there." She hands me her card. "If you want to know any more, just give me a call."

9
Andreasgebet
St Andrews Day

The next day the production meeting goes smoothly. Apart from his growly voice, Max doesn't show any adverse signs of his alcoholic binge. All we have to do is survive tonight's feast — I have a St Andrews dinner tonight — and we're home free. St. Andrew's in Scotland involves whisky, bagpipes and haggis I explain to Max. In Austria, he answers, it's much less exciting, only a prayer to St. Andreas in the evening.

"I'm glad we're in the UK and not in Austria," I say as we collapse in a taxi after our meeting. As we bounce our way through Hyde Park on our way to Chloe's house, Max turns and puts an arm around my shoulders.

"The conversation yesterday got me thinking. Do you know Wilhelm Reich wrote a book that predicted the coming of World War II?"

I'm surprised he's brought up the subject again. "So he's more than *just* a discredited Viennese psychologist."

Max ignores my dig. "He wrote *The Mass Psychology of Fascism* in 1933. In it, Reich said every man has a fascist inside of him begging to be set free."

"How did he know that? By interviewing people?"

"No, by watching their bodies."

"He could see that by observing body language?"

Max laughs. "He also said that Fascists were sexually repressed neurotics. Shortly afterward, he emigrated to the USA."

I tap my fingers on the seat. "I'm not surprised! Vienna, the city of death. The city of sex therapy. Interesting."

"Aren't you living in the right place," Max says, tussling my hair.

Not wanting to show my hurt, I dig in my purse until I find Val's card. "That does it. I'm booking a session with Val. Production expense."

Max laughs. "And how will I classify that one?"

"Research," I say. "If Wilhelm Reich is as interesting as I think he is, then he might be the link I was looking to put in the program. Vienna's gift to the world."

10

But when, a day later, Valentine motions me to sits down, I'm suddenly not sure anymore. She is a very different person than the boisterous American I met at Chloe's. Her voice is deeper, her manners slower. I look around me. Her office is bare except for two chairs facing each other and a large massage table. Soft music plays in the background.

She gives me an open smile. "So why are you here?"

I respond with an uneasy look. All of a sudden, the room seems too small. It smells of incense, stuff from the seventies, stuff I never liked. I adjust the cushion underneath me. I have to restrain myself from fidgeting. "I want to know more about unconventional Austrian therapy."

She nods. "Let's talk about you. That will give you what you need."

I nod more openly than I feel. I don't like talking about me. That's why I'm a journalist. I interview others. I'm the one in control. And right now, I feel very out of control.

"Max is your partner, right? Handsome man. Do you find him attractive?"

My eyes flick from one side of the room to the other. I nod my head.

"Sexually?"

"You're as bad as Chloe." I look away, but her eyes keep pulling me back to her, gently probing inside to all those places I hide from the world. I want to bolt from the room.

"So you're not sexually attracted to him." She pauses. "Have you told him this?"

My eyes pop open. "Of course not! That would hurt his feelings!"

"And you wonder why your jaw hurts? There are a lot of unexpressed feelings in there."

I can't sit in the chair anymore, it irritates me. As she motions for me to take my clothes off, my heart begins to race so fast I think it will explode. "It's more than that." I peel off my clothes as casually as I can, considering what I am about to say. My tongue seems stuck to the roof of my mouth, but the words keep coming. "It's not Max. Every time I'm with a man, I start to lose sexual interest in him. For a while, I can fake it, but then I start to feel repulsion." Feeling as if I have climbed Mount Everest, I lie on the massage table and close my eyes, feeling my stomach fluttering nervously. Instead of relaxing, every cell in my body is on edge. It reminds me of the time I visited a hypnotist. She couldn't put me into a trance. I had felt proud, as if I were stronger than she. No one is going to take me where I don't want to go.

Instead of responding to my heroic admittance that I lack sex drive, Val simply nods and holds two fingers to my neck. "Now breathe. Give me an audible sigh when you exhale."

I take a few shallow breaths. A yawn overwhelms me, then another, and within seconds I slip into blissful slumber.

"Breathe!" I wake up with a start, wondering where I am. Val sighs loudly, urging me to imitate her. Sleep, that's all I want to do, what's wrong with sleeping, leave me alone. I start to slip into no-man's land when I feel her shaking me.

"Breathe!" I hear again, coming from what seems far away. "In and out."

Every fiber of my body rejects this simple word. *Why can't she leave me alone?* I feel her forcing my hands into a fist. Her hands feel warm to the touch.

"Clench your hands. Pound them on the table. Breathe. Loudly. Sleep is your body's way of resisting."

Resistance? This isn't resistance. I'm just tired. I clench my fist and breathe, making a small self-conscious sigh on the out breath. Val holds two fingers to my temple and presses the indentation at the back of my neck.

"Ow!" I scream.

Val's pinch brings me sharply back to the moment, and, against my will, I inhale deeply. With that breath, *something happens.* Something beyond my control, something that starts deep within my solar plexus, something that gets stronger and stronger and then —

My body jumps as if it has been plugged into an electric socket. I freeze. *What is going on?* I hear Val's voice and sense her moving around my body, pushing here, pulling there. For the first time in my life, my body is obeying another master than me. This out of control feeling brings upon a complete, overwhelming panic that causes me to clench my lips and tighten every muscle in my body. My body, the one thing that is so part of me that I have never even questioned it, is coming alive. *And it has nothing to do with me!*

A strong prickling sensation like champagne bubbles begins to run up and down my arms. What's happening to my fingers? Although I try not to, I can feel them starting to curl like the gnarled hands of an old woman. If that isn't bad enough, my face muscles begin to tighten, and

I can feel my lip drawing itself down over my teeth making my mouth forms an "o". Deep in my throat, a deep Oooohhhhhhhhh starts to make its way from inside my belly up into my throat. I summon all my strength to clamp my mouth shut just in time. If I hadn't been careful I would have screamed. *I don't like this one bit!* As Val moves along my body, pulling my arms over my head, running her fingers along my jaw, pressing points on my neck, my command center is verging on breakdown. My head rocks from side to side. A wave of heat ripples up my torso. My right foot jerks back and forth uncontrollably. With every passing second, something else is pinging with tension, snapping, like electrical wiring gone mad.

You are faking this! I hear myself shrieking internally. *Tell her to stop!*

And then, just as it is unbearable to continue one second longer without breaking down into a jumble of quavering limbs, I ask myself a question. *Who is the me telling me that I am faking this?*

Everything in that moment stops, and in that extraordinary realization I become aware of two things. I am not this voice. And I contain it. *There are two me's!* I had always thought that I was this prattling voice. I know it well. This is the me that endlessly makes lists, doesn't let me sleep, hums songs nonsensically, tells me that I am stupid, repeats conversations over and over again with *I should have said...* Now I am aware there is another me, a much larger me. The second me encompasses the first. It is so large that I can watch my body jerk and hum as if it were a scene in a movie. There is no judging or condemning, no sadness or fear. It is curiously detached but at the same time, connected. In this moment, I feel a little give within me, and it is as if a wide belt that had been hitched tightly around my chest loosens a few notches. I take a deep breath, a really deep breath, realizing that what I had been doing before was taking in oxygen but not breathing! Savoring the coolness of the air swirling in my lungs, I breathe deeply, then again and again. It almost feels as if my breath is breathing me. My body's external twitches become less irregular, and this releases streams of delicious champagne bubbles up and down my body. Warmth radiates from my heart. Everything around me seems to flow with the silkily smooth in and out movement of my breath. I feel delicious and blissfully free of stress and fear. It is a sensation unlike anything I have felt before.

"Open your eyes, and sit up slowly," I hear.

As I do, I put a hand to my forehead. It feels foreign to my touch. *You are in London*, the first 'me' reminds me. It is no longer at war with the second 'me'. This feeling of peace is delicious, almost intoxicating. I'm at peace with the world. Slowly I sit up.

Val is sitting on the chair in front of me, smiling. She looks remarkably beautiful. In fact, everything in the room does. "How's your jaw?"

"I forgot that I had a jaw." My joints feel as if they have been lubricated with honey. I clear my throat a few times before I find my voice. "I had the most extraordinary realization. There are two me's!"

Val laughs. "It's quite something to realize you aren't that neurotic voice inside your head, isn't it?"

I nod my head in wonder. "The second 'me' is serene. Peaceful."

"The second you is your *soul*."

My heart flutters. *My soul!* "You mean it really exists!"

"Of course it does. All those spiritual texts weren't written for nothing."

"And what about the other 'me'? The one prattling on that I was faking it?"

87

"That 'me' is your *mind.* You are not your mind, although it would love you to think that." She laughs. "There is an expression that says *The mind is an excellent servant, but a terrible master.*"

"It's true. It is so critical." I stare in the distance. Time seems as rich and thick as pudding. I could wallow in it for hours. "But why is my mind so frightened of my soul?"

"Because your mind will die with your body. Your mind, like your body, is temporary. But your soul will live on. It cannot die. Your soul is so large that your mind cannot understand it."

I flex my joints. They all feel as if they have been lubricated. In fact, my body feels as supple and strong as a panther. "Is that why I feel so large?"

"Yes. You have expanded so that you can feel your soul *and* your mind. So, in effect, you have become much larger. How does it feel?"

Hmmmm. I blink, trying to focus on her face as I get up to put my clothes on. I have to stare intently at my shoes in order to place my feet in them. I feel as if I have on a different body than when I walked in. "Is this what happens when people meditate?"

She smiles. "Meditation takes you *out* of yourself. I've helped you come *inside* yourself. So now you know what it feels like to skim the depths of who you *really* are." She stands up and smiles. She knows she doesn't have to say anything more as she helps me to the door.

11

"It was — " I search for the right word. "Extraordinary."

Yawning, I drop onto Chloe's large overstuffed chair as she arrives with a pot of tea and a plate piled high with pieces of homemade shortbread. After an initial high, I was so tired I sent Max to our congratulatory drink with our production partners so that I could spend the afternoon resting in bed. I smile sleepily at Jean Luc, who takes his coat off and relaxes on the sofa across from me.

"Why did my mouth and fingers curl up?" I blink a couple times to get my contact lenses to settle in my eyes.

"*Tetni*," Jean Luc explains, taking a cup of tea from Chloe. "It's a standard reaction when your body resists energy."

When I shake my head in confusion, he puts his cup down and speaks slowly.

"Most doctors know *tetni*, but don't understand what causes it. That is because the concept of energy is not included in western medicine."

"Most people only feel energy when they work out — or sex," Chloe answers, placing the porcelain teapot on the table and sitting down on the sofa next to Jean Luc. "Of course I prefer the latter."

Jean Luc smiles as he lifts Chloe's hand to his lips. "When you are first aware of energy, it feels out of control. Your mind goes ballistic,

and your body clamps down for what it thinks will be World War III."
As he talks, he holds his hand out and tightens his muscles. I see that
naturally his fingers curl forward slightly. "It's a bodily reflex. When
that happens, keep breathing and open up to the energy, and *tetni* will
pass."

Chloe slips her shoes off and curls up next to Jean Luc. "Delicious.
Just like a really good orgasm."

"Don't you think of anything else?" I say with a faint smile.

"Why?" We laugh.

Jean Luc places his hand on Chloe's knee. "*Mon amour*, let me see
if I can explain it a different way. Reich discovered something Tantric
scriptures have written about for thousands of years. That *everything*
is energy. This energy emanates from Source, God, Love, Universe,
whatever you want to call it. Quantum physics says the same thing.
This is what Albert Einstein wrote about when he wrote $E=mc^2$."
He smiles and squeezes Chloe's hand. "I love Einstein. He also said
Gravitation is not responsible for people falling in love."

Chloe looks at him. "All you can talk about is love."

He gives a look of feigned surprise. "Why? It's the best energy
there is!"

We all laugh.

"And why is energy important?"

"It takes Einstein's equation off the page and puts it into real
life. It helps you experience union with the source of all that is.
Consciousness."

I look beyond them through the window. A faint yellow glow
from the lamppost seeps through the pane, lighting up the quiet tree
lined street. "Unity. That is what I felt. As if my mind and my soul
had met. That is why I felt so peaceful. So — large."

Jean Luc gives me a gentle smile. "You were larger, because you realized you weren't just your mind."

"And why did my body jerk like that?"

"It wasn't used to all that energy. The jerks were blockages — like traffic jams — in your system. As more energy enters you, it moves your body out of the way to accommodate the flow." He takes a sip of tea. "How does it feel to receive more of yourself?"

For a moment I pause, thinking about the extraordinary series of events that have led me to this moment. "Knowing myself. Until today, if someone had asked me if I knew myself, I would have categorically answered yes. Now I'm not sure."

Both Chloe and Jean Luc laugh. "Welcome to the club."

I hesitate before asking the next question. "How is Eugen? I wanted to ask the other night, but didn't dare."

"Deep into his own process of self inquiry."

I want to ask more, but don't know how to phrase my question. I don't even know if I have any questions. It just feels nice to hear his name. "Is that another word for inner work?" I ask hesitantly.

Jean Luc takes a sip of tea. "It begins by looking at your greatest fear."

I lean back onto the sofa. "Well thank goodness I don't have one," I say lightly.

Chloe stubs her cigarette out. "Annabel Jones, don't lie."

"Sounds as if Tantra is your path." Jean Luc says with a tender smile.

"Tantra!" I feel a flutter in my solar plexus. "That's for stupid esoteric fools like Vandana."

"Careful about dismissing something you don't understand as stupid," Jean Luc answers. "Everyone's fears are different, so everyone uses different tools to get there." He turns to Chloe. "Tantra is a pleasure for you, because your greatest fear doesn't lie in sex, but commitment."

She tosses her head. "Like you."

He smiles at her. "Like me. As I said, everyone's fears are different."

"And Tantra is…" I look at the both of them.

"Tantra is for people who have challenges with sexuality. And that means everyone," he continues firmly. "In today's world, anyone who says they don't have a problem with sex is in denial. And I happen to know a great Tantra teacher in Vienna."

December

Krampus

Day of Krampus

By the time Max and I return to Vienna, it, too, is transformed. A week ago we left a dusty masterpiece of pompous architecture. Now it feels like a cozy town dressed in wreathes and ribbons and candles. Shrouded with powdery snow and bedecked for Christmas, it is filled with villages of wooden stands selling hot wine and chestnuts, bustling crowds and magical shimmering decorations that light the cold dark streets with a warm glow.

Even Max's apartment has been transformed. Our concierge, with the help of Minou, has prepared for our arrival. Little baskets of miniature Christmas cookies wait in the foyer, a sweet smelling Christmas wreath hangs on our door, and a large *Adventkranz*, a pine branch decoration with swirls of ribbons and four red candles, graces the dining room table.

The following day Max meets me for another Viennese tradition, sipping hot mulled wine at a Christmas market. I'm not sure if it is because of my Reichian session, but I feel more at ease with myself, with my situation and, well, with everything, really. The city looks brighter, more intense, more magical. I never imagined Vienna could be so wonderful. It has the surreal feel of a wonderland, as enticing as a new lover, full of unexpected surprises at every turn. I roll my neck in a circle, marveling at the freedom I feel in the joints. And that's when I see it. There, high up, on the tops of the buildings. Angels. Round fat cherubs, willowy Madonnas in flowing robes, dynamic Athenas.

"Look!" I cry. "The *Trafikant* is right. There *are* angels everywhere!"

"What angels?" Max asks, frowning. The *Gasse*, the Austrian word for street, is so narrow that our footsteps echo against the stone walls. On either side, lampposts are covered with posters offering an array of Christmas concerts in churches and concert halls throughout the city.

"Statues, silly," I say, pointing to the rooftops. "Vienna *is* a city of angels. They are secretly keeping an eye on everyone walking below."

Max rolls his eyes. "Great. Now I feel as if I am being watched."

"I feel protected by them."

Max's brow furrows. "Journalists *don't* believe in angels. They know it's only a way the Catholic Church makes people lose touch with reality."

I give Max a playful shove. "Why *not* believe in angels? I didn't believe in energy, either, and now I know it exists."

Max gives me a suspicious look. "Don't go esoteric on me."

I laugh. "I'm pragmatic. It's to my advantage to give them the benefit of the doubt."

Max slings an arm around my shoulder. "There is only one angel I believe in. And that is you."

Arm in arm, we walk into a large open square that has been transformed into a little village of snow-dusted stalls lined with sweet smelling pine boughs. Each booth brims with brightly colored candles, soaps, children's toys and hundreds of hand painted Christmas ornaments. Stalls offer roasted sausages and Hungarian *Langos*, large deep fried crispy pancakes slathered with butter and garlic that are a throwback from the Austro-Hungarian Empire. Snow squeaking underfoot, we follow the scent of orange and nutmeg and cinnamon to a stand selling hot mulled wine and dozens of varieties of Christmas cookies. Children race through the crowd with switches and twigs in their hands, giggling as they hit each other on the legs.

"That's typical for *Krampus*," Max explains as he gives me a cup of hot mulled wine. "*Krampus* is Devil's Day."

As I sip my drink I watch the children scamper, screaming and laughing, through the crowds. The warm liquid slowly descends into my belly. "You have a day for those who are *bad*?"

"The original *Krampus* was a pagan god with horns and a black curly beard who lived in the dark forest. Christianity turned *Krampus* into the devil, a symbol for the dark side of human nature. In Vienna, *Krampus* is a children's excuse to be naughty. But in the countryside, *Krampus* is a day to get back at people who have done you wrong." He selects a gingerbread cookie from a plate offered to us by the stand owner and waves it under my nose. "So be careful how you treat me."

I take the cookie and pop it into my mouth, enjoying the spicy cinnamon and nutmeg flavor. "Had I known it would be so nice at Christmas, I wouldn't have agreed to go to Chloe's. But you can go, you know."

He puts his arm around me to guide me in the direction of a stall selling *Bratwurst*. "I couldn't leave Onki alone. But Minou has allowed you to go."

We huddle over our plate, poking toothpicks into bite size pieces of steaming sausage. A happy glow surrounds us. I hook my arm around Max. "Do you know that Austria has amazing countrymen?"

Max beams. "Well, yes, I do. Me, in fact."

I kick some snow in his direction. "Seriously. I want to include them in our series. Like Wilhelm Reich and his therapy."

Max gives me an odd look. "Everyone says Reich's a fraud."

I can hear Jean Luc's words echoing in my brain. Was it only last week that I was willing to dismiss everything that I couldn't understand?

"Now I understand why Reichian therapy isn't popular. Because people dismiss things their minds can't understand."

"I need scientific proof," Max answers, distractedly poking a piece of sausage into the mound of mustard.

How can I put what I feel into words? Before the session, I would have dismissed such things as energy and souls and body armor and coincidences. I would have dismissed my soul, because that is what it was, a concept. But after the session, I can't do that because it is more than a concept, it is an experience. And if I close my eyes and ignore my surroundings, like I do every night now before I go to sleep, I can still tap into that feeling of my soul. It feels all warm and fuzzy — with about a million watt voltage attached. I take a moment to find the right words.

"Your series is about war, isn't it? Well, what I experienced in the session was like an inner war. On one side, I had my mind telling me what I *should* feel and *should* do. But then another part of me began to emerge. A dark part." I search for the right words. My eyes light up. "My *Krampus*. It was wild and uncontrollable."

Max eats the last piece of sausage. "You paid someone to do this to you?"

I frown, trying to hide my irritation. "As long as my mind didn't want to accept this dark side of me, the war inside me increased. But when I surrendered, a most wonderful feeling came over me. I won the battle. I think — I think I even met my soul."

I feel the doors to Max's mind slamming one after the other. He finishes his *Punsch* and takes my cup. "Now I've heard everything. Let's go."

It's amazing how much it hurts to hear him dismissing something that is so important to me. "Look, Rudi wants my participation in the series, so here it is. Austria didn't just provide the world with Hitler, one of the greatest bad guys in history, it provided the world with a way to avoid such a tragedy happening again."

Max turns to me. "What *are* you saying?"

"*I met the enemy, and he is us*, remember? During my Reichian session, I met my enemy within. By confronting this side of myself, I found peace. It was temporary, but for the first time in my life, I experienced what total inner peace feels like." I hesitate, then decide why not, he'll think me crazy anyway. "If we all found this feeling, and could keep it, World War III needn't happen."

"How can a journalist be so naïve?" But when he sees my hurt expression, he relents. "Look, Reich is only one person. If you want to bring this theme into our series, you will have to find more than that."

I feel as if I have been given a reprieve. One by one, the bells begin to ring, their sonorous tones washing over the city, announcing one o'clock. I eat in silence, listening to the gongs echoing across town. "Who do you know who understands psychology?"

Max pauses before answering. His voice sounds like a rusty door giving away reluctantly. "You might ask Rudi's wife. I've never met her, but he says she is the queen of therapy."

Rudi's wife! Emma is American too. I can hardly contain my curiosity.

"Give me a week." Excitedly, I give him a kiss and I run off, eager to give Emma a call.

2

St Nicholas Tag
Day of St. Nicholas

The next morning, I wake to find the television blaring from the kitchen and Minou curled up at the end of the bed, a bright red ribbon around her neck. I scratch behind Minou's ears, listening to her rumbling purr as she recounts her adventures while we were gone. Within minutes, Max marches in with a tray holding two steaming cups of hot chocolate and a plate filled with flaky squares of warm strudel filled with cream cheese.

"*Topfen Golatsche.* To celebrate St. Nicholas. Minou said this was your favorite breakfast." He sets the tray on the bed and breaks off a bit of *Golatsche* to feed her. He dusts the flaky pastry from her fur. "St. Nicholas rewards those who are good all year."

I nibble on the pastry. "Wasn't yesterday *Krampus?*"

Max sits down next to me. "Yesterday was for those who are bad; today is for those who are good. Like you." He picks up a small blue velvet pouch from the tray and places it into my hands. "I wanted to give it to you in London, but now is the time."

"Max, no!" I cry, pushing the pouch away. "Take it back."

"I will throw it away rather than do that," he says, crossing his arms.

I stare at the pouch, not daring to open it. Memories come surging from my subconscious, images of when I first met Eugen. I remember looking into his eyes and knowing, without a trace of doubt, that he was the man with whom I wanted to spend the rest of my life. It might have been a dream, but my goodness it's hard to let it go. I press my folded hands to my lips and watch as Max carefully opens the leather drawstrings and pulls out a beautiful diamond and sapphire bracelet. Snapping it around my wrist, he holds my chin between his thumb and index finger and looks me deeply in the eyes.

"Stay in Vienna, *Annabelchen*. Together, we will make it work."

3

The Café Central's buzzing atmosphere reminds me of the Oyster Bar in New York's Grand Central Station. Its stone columns, arches and chandeliers make me feel instantly as if I am in the center of things. Sitting at a small round marble table in the corner of the room, I watch a continuing throng of waiters and tourists coming and going as Rudi's wife Emma breezes up, her Yorkshire terrier trotting at her heels.

"Rudi has raved about you since he met you," she says kissing the air on either side of my cheek.

More petite and round than she sounded on the phone, Emma is in her late forties, with well-cut mousy brown hair, a perfect eggshell complexion and large eyes hidden behind a stunning pair of glasses. She waves an imperious hand at a passing waiter.

"Café Central used to be Vienna's literary café. Now it's a tourist trap, but I still like the atmosphere." She drags me toward a display case to choose from the dozens of pastries and cakes and orders a piece of apple strudel for her and one for her dog. By the time we return to our table, two large cups of cocoa are waiting for us, and — under the table — a small water bowl for the dog. Emma lowers her plate onto the floor for the terrier to lap at the whipped cream. "So. Are you depressed yet?"

"Depressed?" I pick up a fork and start to cut into the strudel. The crust is warm, the apple filling melts in my mouth. It is the most delicious pastry I have ever tasted.

She rolls her eyes. "*Everyone* who moves here gets depressed. It's part of the Viennese experience. I nearly died when Rudi dragged me here twenty years ago. Every foreigner I know has had to go into therapy at one time or another to survive living here."

"That's why I wanted to talk to you," I say, wiping the crumbs from my lips. "What do you know about Wilhelm Reich?"

"Very controversial. Why do you ask?"

I take another bite. "I am looking for something positive to put into the series."

Emma flashes a naughty grin. "Positive? Now wouldn't that be a change! Every time I watch one of Max's programs I end up wanting to murder a few hundred people." She nibbles at the strudel before looking up at me. "Why someone as controversial as Reich?"

"I had a Reichian session in London."

Her eyes grow even larger behind her glasses. "Is it true? Can it make you crazy?"

I put my fork down. I might as well tell her the truth. "No, the opposite. I now know what it feels like to be sane. I — I even met my soul."

A piece of strudel falls from Emma's fork, but she is so engrossed in the conversation she doesn't notice. "Good God! Reichian therapy isn't so far from Freud!"

I look confused. "What are you talking about? Freud wasn't interested in the *soul*. He analyzed the *mind*."

She looks curiously at her fork when she sees nothing is there. Her eyes drop to her lap, then she calmly picks up the piece of fallen pastry with her fingers and pops it in her mouth.

"How's this for a well kept secret? Do you know that there was a *fundamental flaw* in the translation of Freud? His psychoanalytical writings have been translated into the study of the *Mind*. But Freud wrote *Seele*, which means *Soul*."

My mouth drops open. "*Seele* was translated as *mind*?"

She nods her head, her eyes shining. "Isn't that wild? In German, *Geistig* is the correct terminology for mind. But Freud used the word *Seele*. And *Seele* correctly translates as a man's essence, or *Soul*."

"But that changes the entire interpretation of Freudian work." I pull out my small reporter's pad to scribble a few notes on it. "How could something so important be mis-translated?"

Her words tumble out of her mouth as fast as water running down hill. "Remember it was the early part of the 20ᵗʰ century," she starts and catches her breath before continuing. "Science was in, and God was out. It has been said that the American psychoanalytic movement wanted to present psychoanalysis as a serious medical study. If this is the case, it is easy to understand why they chose *diseases of the mind*. It fit their scientific interpretation of the world far better than *diseases of the soul*."

"So Reich and Freud were searching for the same thing, to bring peace to man."

She nods her head. "A generation apart. Freud was an old man by the time Reich came around. Like many top specialists, he got his students to do his research. That's why he sent Reich to the Steinhof insane asylum."

"Steinhof!" I gasp. *That's where we sent Vandana.* The color drains from my face.

"Vienna loves its mental institutions," Emma continues, unaware of the effect her words have on me. "There's a marvelous art nouveau church on the grounds. There's also a memorial to the Nazi's clandestine euthanasia program. Steinhof is where the Nazis systematically killed the mentally ill." She puts her cup of cocoa down with a decisive thump. "It's about time someone shows the positive side of Vienna's insalubrious past."

"Max isn't exactly thrilled about my idea."

"I'll drop a few hints to Rudi," she says. "When it comes to finance, I carry some weight." She leans back and studies me. "So what are you doing for New Year?" When I shake my head, she claps her hands with pleasure. "So it's settled. Come stay in Carinthia. It'll just be Rudi and the kids." She waves her hand for the waiter to get the bill before turning to me with a shy smile. "I think I've just made a friend."

4

Zweite Adventssonntag
Second Advent Sunday

With a candle set in a red jar tucked under his arm, Max turns off the blaring television and puts on his coat. I already know the ritual. He must be preparing to take the 71 tram to Vienna's Central Cemetery.

"What will you do for Christmas?" I ask, dangling the end of Max's red scarf on the ground for Minou to play with.

Max puts both arms around me. "Do not worry. Minou and I are preparing an intimate Christmas dinner, just the two of us."

"You *can* come to London, you know that."

"No, go and enjoy yourself. I wouldn't feel right leaving Onki. I'll pick you up and we'll drive to Rudi and Emma's for New Year. I can't wait to see their *Schloss*." He heads toward the door as Minou swans around his feet. Suddenly, mid-swan, she flops over on her side and stares into space. Instantly we both drop on our knees to examine her. Minou doesn't seem to be in any pain. Within a few minutes, she gets up, only to fall over again.

"Oh poor thing," I say, bending down to stroke her. "I was afraid of this. She's nearly seventeen." I bite my lower lip.

Max looks up at me, his eyes moist with tears. "I love this cat more than anything else in the world. You had better prepare yourself. We Viennese know death when it calls."

After Max leaves, I spend the rest of the morning on the phone with Minou on my lap. I don't like to think of death. I don't like darkness, either. I know we die, but I just don't see why life had to be created this way. It's wrong. Searching to avoid these gloomy thoughts, I bury myself in my work. Surprisingly, it doesn't take long to organize an interview at the Steinhof mental institution. Apparently a Dr. Berger knows a lot about Wilhelm Reich, and would be happy to talk to me. Carefully placing Minou by her bowl brimming with an extra dose of cat food, I pack my notepad in my case and scoot out the door. At the end of the street I hesitate, look at my watch, and turn in the direction of my favorite *Trafik*, telling myself I have to pick up a newspaper to read on the tram on the way out. I believe my own lie. Hardly a day can go by without a visit to his temple shop.

I have to admit it. Christmas in Vienna is beautiful. Not overdone, not commercial, but just right. Since the *Kristkind* — the Austrian fairy that brings presents — only shows up at Christmas Eve, the first Christmas trees are appearing on the streets just now. To my amazement, in one day, the Graben has been instantly transformed into miniature pine forest. Storefronts glimmer with shimmering strings of white lights hanging from the stone balustrades like long, slender icicles. Stamping my feet outside the *Trafik*, I notice that even the wrought iron lamps on either side of his door have magically become fanciful candy canes. As I open the door, I am enveloped in a rich smell of orange and cloves. The *Trafik* is crammed with people holding steaming mugs in their hands. I count at least six, plus Hansi the dachshund in a miniature red sweater with tassels. It feels more like a country pub than a newsstand. Although everyone barely has room to bring their mulled wine to their lips without bumping each other, no one seems to mind.

"*Grüß Gott!*" Herr Dietmayer beams over his customers' heads. "Come have a mug of *Punsch* and some home made Christmas cookies!"

"There's plenty of room!" a woman in a long green loden coat pipes up. Everyone laughs good-naturedly. I bend down to stroke the dog before working my way forward.

The *Trafikant* hands me a steaming mug of mulled wine. "Where are you off to now?"

I plunk my case on the counter and take a sip. "Steinhof."

A man puts an arm around the woman next to him. "We got married there."

"You got *married* in a mental institution?"

"*Nein!*" he chuckles. "Otto Wagner designed the church on the grounds. One of the most important Art Nouveau buildings in Vienna. Exquisite."

I laugh. "Only in Vienna can a mental institution be a cultural experience."

The woman gives me a tender smile. "It's beautiful, really. If you go now, watch for the crows. The hills and trees above Steinhof are the sleeping places of Vienna's birds in the winter." She gives her mug to Herr Dietmayer. "*Danke* and Merry Christmas. Or should I say Happy Hanukkah?"

Herr Dietmayer laughs as he takes the cup. "I celebrate all religious holidays."

"That's a good way to get more vacation," the woman in the loden coat answers. We all laugh as they are decanted out the door.

I shake my head in wonder as Herr Dietmayer reaches up and pulls a newspaper down from the shelf and folds it.

"Are you always in such good humor?"

He smiles. "Most of the time." For a moment the little shop is quiet.

The question blurts out of my mouth before I can stop it. "How do you do it?"

He looks pleased that I asked him a personal question. "I choose to say things that support people. Other thoughts I keep to myself." He gives the change to a customer, pats him on the back and smiles.

"You don't seem as if you have a lot of other thoughts."

He laughs. "Not as many as I used to. But let's get real. We *all* have dark thoughts. It is what we *do* with them that counts."

I frown. "I want to get rid of mine."

The *Trafikant* taps his forehead. "*Oi-vey!* You can't get *rid* of thoughts. If you try to resist, it will drive you crazy!" His bald brow wrinkles with concern. "That isn't why you are going to Steinhof?"

I shake my head. "I'm doing some research on Wilhelm Reich."

His eyes open wide. "Interesting man. Why him of all people?"

"I had a Reichian session. That's why I'm aware of my thoughts."

"It's humbling to realize how much inner pollution we carry within us. No wonder we have so much pollution in the world."

I furrow my brow. Where does his wisdom come from? Max explained that *Trafiks* began after World War II as a way for disabled war veterans to earn a living. But Herr Dietmayer isn't disabled. If anything, he looks healthier than most merchants I run into.

"What does the state of the world have to do with my sewer of a mind?"

"More than you think. Everyone is walking around filled with judgments, criticisms and complaints, mostly aimed at ourselves. Our *outside world* is a reflection of our *inner world*. So the best way to clean up outer pollution is to start by cleaning up inner pollution."

"Inner pollution equals outer pollution," I say. "Interesting way to think of things. Does that apply to everything?"

"Of course! Take war, for example, as it seems your country likes it. Outer war happens only when a people are fighting an inner war. Reich touched upon this when he observed people's bodies in Germany and Austria before World War II. By observing how they held their bodies, he could see their internal wars, especially anger, that they were carrying around. He knew that sooner or later, it would translate as outer war. And he was right. Along came Hitler, and the rest you know."

"Aren't you discounting a lot of other factors?"

We stop talking as the door opens and a customer walks in. Herr Dietmayer beams and hands the young man a mug of hot mulled wine.

"I'm not discounting anything. All I am doing is pointing out that people who hold an inordinate amount of anger and fear — whether it comes from their economic situation or the food they eat — will sooner or later feel the need to control the world as they see fit. They will find an outlet, and it normally is *out there*, rather than *in here*, in themselves."

The door chimes and several people squeeze in. He leans forward. "I want to share something with you. There are no good guys. There are no bad guys. People just *are*. Period. In order to have day, we must have night. Good, bad. Shadow, light. Krampus and St. Nicholas." He points to his heart. "Heaven and hell are right here, Frau Jones. The entire earth is contained right here, in our bodies. This is what the bible meant when it referred to free will. It is what we do with it that matters."

5

High on the hills of *Baumgarten Höhe* I see them. Crows. Hundreds of them, spiraling in the cold winter sky like swirling black leaves in a windstorm. As I get out of the tram and walk up the hill, pale green iron gates come into view, then an enclave of imposing brick buildings. I wander past the grim porters lodge, then along a path running between the buildings to a large stone church with an enormous golden dome flanked by two towers. The church, *Kirche am Steinhof*, is without a doubt beautiful, but who in their right mind would want to get married in such a dismal setting? My last visit to Steinhof Psychiatry Hospital was so painful that I had hoped never to come here again, and yet here I am, only a few months later, doing the same thing.

The complex is empty and soul-less, reminding me of one of those model towns under glass cases that you see in architectural offices or in museums. Wide gravel paths run in methodical, orderly patterns through manicured lawns that connect bulky neoclassical beige buildings with large windows called pavilions. It's quiet here, a sleepy stillness, but it's not peaceful. It is anything but peaceful. It was here, Max told me, that the Nazi regime performed some of their most unspeakable crimes against a civilian populace. It was here that sterilizations, mass murder of the mentally ill and handicapped children were an everyday occurrence. Drugs, injections, withdrawal of food, and a particularly brutal method of electric shock killed 3,500 people — all performed under doctors' orders. Many of the medical practitioners, Max told me, continued careers in high positions in the Austrian government after the war. Every building, every shrubbery, every person I see seems as if they are shouldering the weight of the past. *What a place to die.* An overwhelming feeling of sadness envelops me. I heave a deep sigh, then turn and look for a sign directing me to Pavilion 21.

As I push open the heavy glass door and walk into the building, I am thrown back into the modern world again. Voices, machines, telephones echo in the dreary institutional hallway, men and women in white lab coats bustle by, patients shuffle in and out of doorways. I stand in the middle of the hall, looking for someone to point me in the right direction.

A young man in a pale blue tracksuit and curly black hair walks up to me with a bright smile. "Who do you want to see?"

I'm just about to respond when a short man in a white coat and slippers turns the corner. His hair, long and greasy, is smeared over his bald head; his coat is rumpled and stained. He blinks myopically at me through large thick glasses. "Who do you want to see?"

I'm not sure who to answer. It is as if both men were in their own bubbles, neither acknowledging nor seeing the other. I look at one, then the other, then throw my hands in the air and toss my question between them like a bone between two dogs.

"Dr. Berger. I'm the reporter who called this morning."

The young man's voice drops to a whisper. "Finally! I knew you would come. I've tried for weeks to get word of the conspiracy out."

The man in the white coat interrupts him. "Follow me." He turns and shuffles down the hallway.

Confused, I gaze back at the young man, expecting him to be angry, but he's not. As docile as a puppy, he wanders off, talking to himself.

The encounter leaves me disorientated. *The white coat works here, the other is an inmate.* I follow the man in the white coat, my heart pounding in my chest. I feel as if I'm walking into *One Flew over the Cuckoo's Nest.* The halls look like any hospital corridor, bland colors, vinyl floors, clean, airless and dead. *This place has no soul.* And neither do the patients. A loud wail pierces the air, causing me to peer self-consciously into a large dormitory room. Behind the netting that covers one of the rollaway beds, a woman gazes at me with the flat eyes of a fish. Another wanders the room talking to herself as she shakes a fist in the air. I pull my head back like a snail, unsure why I feel so embarrassed. It is as if I am witnessing these people's *Krampus,* but they can no longer hold it inside of them. The man in the white coat points down a corridor and strolls away, his slippers flapping noisily.

I'm admitted immediately. Dr. Berger, a woman with short-cropped hair and tired eyes, waves me into her spacious but poorly furnished office. It looks like any governmental office; functional, cluttered and insipid.

When I mention Reich's name, she shifts in her chair, explaining in a hurried tone that her interest in Wilhelm Reich does not reflect Steinhof, then listens while I assure her that I want *her* opinion, not her institution. After a long pause, she leans back in her chair and points to a portrait of Sigmund Freud hanging on the wall behind me.

"Dr. Freud was the most famous of the Viennese School. In the 1920's, he was already considered a God in this newly formed arena called psychoanalysis. Freud sent young Reich — still a student — here to interview patients to see whether the newly discovered Freudian theories were correct." Despite her initial hesitancy, Dr. Berger's eyes sparkle with enthusiasm. "But Reich soon discovered that his professor wanted him to do the impossible." She tilts her head toward the door leading to the outside corridor. "As you can see, many patients aren't *capable* of talking about their relationships with their mother or sister."

A loud scream interrupts us. She stops talking and tilts her head to the side like a nanny waiting for a child to calm down. When we hear nothing more, she continues. "Since Reich couldn't analyze what the inmates *said*, he began to observe their *bodies*. He came to the conclusion that every syndrome or complex Freud had written about wasn't just a *thought* held in a person's mind. It showed up in how the person *held* his or her body. This is how Reich developed his theory of *body armor*."

"Body armor?"

Another scream from behind the closed door. My heart races, but this time Dr. Berger doesn't even stop talking. "The outside world can hurt us, so from a very early age, we develop mechanisms to protect ourselves. We tighten our jaws to hold back things we want to say but don't dare." Speaking through clenched teeth she continues, "Soon it becomes normal to talk this way."

I think of Chloe. "The British stiff upper lip."

She laughs. "Exactly. Not just people, but entire cultures adopt patterns of body armor. Just as you absorb your parents' way of looking at life, you will absorb their breathing patterns and how they hold their bodies."

Another scream pierces the walls, this time followed by various thumps. Dr. Berger sighs, looks at her watch and stands up. "It's too noisy here. Let's take a walk on the grounds, shall we?"

Outside, the cold wind blows along the lawn. Dr. Berger wraps a scarf around her neck as she points to an old man, stooped with age, shuffling toward us. "Look at his back. Doesn't it look as if he is carrying the burden of the world on his shoulders?"

The old man leans heavily on his cane, mumbling to himself. As he passes us, he raises his eyes, his gaze vacant.

"If you were to talk to him, you would find out that he believes he *must* shoulder the world's problems. He cannot fathom what it is like to live another way. That is, according to Reich, because his view of the world has been imprinted into his body structure." She watches him hobble on his way. "His body armor is an extreme case. But he is an example of how rigidly a person's perception can distort their body."

I watch the man limping away. "You're right. When we get older, we say that we are *set in our ways.*"

"Of course this is only one of many factors that cause illness and pain. But that is principally what Reich calls body armor."

"Is it possible to release body armor?"

"That's what Reichian work claims to do."

I look again at the old man. "So if he were to have a session, his body could start to change shape?"

She nods her head as we turn and walk along the gravel path toward the entrance of the compound. "That's what Reichian work *claims* to do. Apparently, when body armor is released, the person's *body* is not only more open, but so is his *mind.* Body and mind are linked. When one becomes flexible, so does the other."

"And what would that give him?"

"The next time a difficult situation comes along, he might not react like he used to. A certain amount of flexibility can give him the chance to act a different way, perhaps a better way. In other words, he can handle life's curveballs easier than someone who needs to control their surroundings to feel safe. This can bring a sense of well-being and ease."

"But that's fantastic! Why doesn't your institution use his work?"

She glances at me, her eyes troubled. "Have you *had* a Reichian session?"

When I don't answer, she thrusts her hands in her pocket before speaking. "When I was a student, his work interested me so much I had a few sessions. What happened so confused me I never had the courage to do it again. But I never forgot it, either."

"What happened?"

"I had spasms. I couldn't control my limbs. I ran hot and cold. My fingers started to curl up like this, and my mouth down."

"That's just your body's reaction when it resists energy."

"Resistance to *energy*? That is interesting."

We walk for a few moments. Only the sound of the gravel crunching under our feet breaks the silence. Finally she speaks.

"I wish western medicine would be more inclusive of other ways of thinking that are outside of our current understanding of life. Like energy. I don't understand it, and yet it is a building block of so many things we do. One of the things I have noticed is the *energy* some inmates have. Sometimes it seems as if they are about explode. The amount of sedatives we have to use is phenomenal." She shrugs her shoulders. "If you want my opinion, modern medicine doesn't understand what happens when someone loses their mind. All we can do is sedate our patients, care for them, and hope that they will return to normal."

"That is already a tremendous amount," I say softly. "It can't be easy to work here." At the door, I turn once more to her. "Would you say Reich's work hasn't been incorporated in psychiatric treatment because it hasn't been understood?"

She nods. "Reich was too advanced for his time."

"And Freud. Was he looking at diseases of the *Soul* or the *Mind*?"

My question makes her raises her eyebrows. "I'm glad you know about that. Freud was creating a new profession that was hard to define because it was neither a medical discipline nor a religious one. As you know, common knowledge still believes Freudian work is in the mind." She gives me a tired smile. "Personally, I think healing can only occur in the soul."

I thank her and walk along the path, reflecting upon what I have just learned. My mind is spinning with excitement. Suddenly the idea of working in the series has become more enticing to me. I pull my scarf tighter around my neck and bury my nose in its warmth. It is almost midwinter. In the short hour I was here, darkness has nearly fallen.

In the distance, a car stops and a tall figure gets out and slams the door. Curious who would arrive in a mental asylum at this hour, I watch the figure walking toward me. There is something that looks familiar. The impeccable cut of the coat, the dark green hat on his head. I stop, leaning forward, squinting as I try to see through the increasing gloom. Those long strides, head held erect, gaze in front of him, always on the horizon, to keep his vision as wide as possible. *It can't be.* My stomach lurches, my heart pounds so loudly that it roars in my ears. It's Eugen.

He, too, stops when he sees me. After a moment of shock, he reaches for my hand, but when he sees me pull back, he stops.

"I thought you had gone back to London."

I falter under the weight of this sentence. He thought I had left for London? Is that why he hadn't looked for me? But no, that couldn't be true; all he had to do was call my old address. A jumble of thoughts bounces around my head while I gaze at him as if he were a portrait that has come out of storage, a face I know intimately, but now realize I hardly know at all. He looks thinner, tired, unsure of himself. His hair, thick and wavy, curls at awkward angles as if it, too, isn't sure of how it should behave. Even his well-trimmed beard looks greyer. But it is his eyes that I notice. Unlike the rest of his face, which seems to be undergoing an enormous strain, his eyes, without the constraint of his glasses, have come alive. They focus on me with an intensity I have never seen. As I try to make sense of my rambling thoughts, I hear a rustle behind us. It's the old man whom Dr. Berger and I had seen earlier. He obviously wants to speak to us, but his mouth can't form words. Glancing quickly behind him I see his cane on the ground.

Instantly Eugen leaps forward to pick the cane up, talking to the old man as he leans on me. Silently we lead him toward Pavilion 21. It is a relief to do something rather than talk to each other. Dozens of unspoken accusations float in the air between us.

"What are you doing here?" I finally ask when a nurse runs out to help the old man into the ward. I can hardly speak, my tongue seems stuck to the top of my throat.

"Picking up Vandana's things. She was in Pavilion 10, over there." He looks around at the somber buildings. "What a place to die."

"It wasn't our fault, remember?"

He winces and thrusts his hands in his pockets as he looks into the distance. "Why didn't I help her earlier? By the time she came here, it was too late. She was screaming and chanting and babbling to herself. No one could understand what was happening to her —"

"How do you know?"

His eyebrows knit together. "How do *you* know?"

I struggle to find the words. "I came to see her, when you and your family left her to die."

Eugen reacts as if my words were a dagger. "I *told* you not to do that. I distinctively told you not to, and you disobeyed me. How *could* you?"

My jaw drops, and words — black and sticky like tar — pour out of me. "How could *you* bring me to Vienna under false pretenses? You and your weird sexual rituals."

As soon as the words leave my mouth, I wish the earth would open up and swallow me alive.

He drops his arms and with that, his resistance.

"So that's why you left." In the evening light, his eyes flash as dark as sapphires. "I want to be honest. You're right, I didn't contact you. I wasn't ready. I wanted to look at my relationship with myself before returning to a relationship with a woman I loved. And that is you."

He stops as if he has said too much. He closes his eyes and takes a deep breath. "I've relived our last night together over and over in my mind. I wish I had acted differently, but I didn't." He looks in my eyes. His words are slow, articulate, measured. "Let's forget what happened. Please."

An inner war rages within me. My mind scrambles through its memory banks, scooping up all the reasons why I could never accept a man who abandons me, who has strange sexual urges, who

— *who loves you,* interrupts my soul. *And you love him.*

Wrong! Time out! Cut! screams my mind. My jaw sets. Not that it matters anymore. Everything is already ruined. I pull at my scarf. It suddenly seems so hot, the atmosphere so oppressive, that I want to run, far way from Eugene and a part of my life I'm desperately trying to forget.

"I can't," I say. "I'm working."

Eugen's eyes start when he hears my words. At first, it is as if he has misunderstood and has to recall my entire sentence. Then he breathes in sharply. "With *whom* are you working?"

I take a step back. If only I could have rephrased it in a different way.

"Rudi Brandemberg."

It takes a few seconds before Eugen's face registers the full implications of my statement.

"Max. That bastard! I knew I could never trust him."

I take a step toward him. "Eugen — let me explain."

He shakes his head, stepping back. "No. Don't waste your energy. I don't want to know." And he turns and walks away.

6

Dritte Adventssonntag
Third Sunday of Advent

My mind and heart contain a jumble of feelings and emotions swirling inside me. They follow me as I listen to the latest production of Wagner at the Opera House, sitting next to Max, huddled on the red velvet chair in the theater box, glancing into the protective cloak of darkness. They are in the harmonious voices of the Christmas choirs floating into the cathedral ceilings of the baroque City Hall, they are in the bells that ring to announce the third advent Sunday, they are each voice that soars into the heavens and begs me to remember what happened during those fateful months before Vandana died. I push the memories away, but my mind has other ideas. As soon as I relax and let the music seep into my soul, my mind scurries through its memory banks and triumphantly parades Eugen's last words to me. *You don't know who you are.*

My reply echoes in response. *I know myself!*

— *God, you were self- righteous!*

I squeeze my eyes shut. Has my mind always been such a tyrant? How it prattles on, with nonsensical melodies, phrases and taunts. *Soul,* I beg, Why *can't I hear you?*

— *Face your fears,* my soul whispers.

— *And he had an eye operation!* my mind butts in. *Ooh, how he's changed. But you left! You really blew it.*

My thoughts follow me as Max and I celebrate our two-month anniversary with dinner at the Hotel Bristol. The evening washes over me, the words, the lovely silver and crystal and mahogany paneling, the flattering maitre d' who compliments Max on his latest works. But it all feels hollow, empty, as if I am doing something terribly, terribly wrong.

At home my thoughts follow me as I soak in the bath, hoping the feeling of dirtiness will wash away. They follow me to the bedroom, where Max awaits with passion in his eyes. I know better than to hope to feel a faint spark of sexual attraction. *What is wrong with me?* I watch him pump himself into iron-jawed ecstasy and give an internal sigh of relief as he explodes like a roaring bull and collapses over my body, panting furiously. Silently I count to one hundred before moving away from his arms and slipping out of bed.

"What are you doing?" Max says from behind closed eyes.

"Getting a drink of water," I answer. "Making love makes me so thirsty."

I can feel Max watching me as I go into the bathroom and drink a glass of water, then come back to bed. Then, rolling away from him, I close my eyes and return to my inner world.

Max fumbles to turn on the lamp. As the light clicks on I twist around to see Max gazing at me, his black hair falling over his eyes like a forelock. He props himself up on one elbow. "You have a problem with sex, don't you?"

The words pierce me like an arrow. I pull the duvet around me. The pale golden glow of the room feels as harsh and invasive as his words.

"Why don't you talk to Emma?" he asks quietly. "She might know a psychiatrist or a sex therapist."

I let the words waft over me, biting my lip to prevent myself from crying. I can't tell him that he hurts me when we make love, that I feel a vague sense of repulsion when he touches me. Max reaches out to touch my shoulder. But instead of welcoming his hand, my body flinches as if recoiling from his touch. Max lets out an audible sigh and rolls away in disgust.

I lost Eugen to my fears about sex. I'm not going to do the same with Max. My jaw sets. I sit up in bed, squashing my feelings of repulsion inside me, and grab hold of Max's arm. "You're right. I have a problem. And I want you to know I'll do everything to make this work. Just give me time."

Max glances at me. "I'll ask Emma about a sex therapist I heard her talking about."

"I — I know a Tantra teacher in Vienna."

My voice trails as I see Max's eyes roll toward the ceiling. His head falls back against the pillow with a tired thump. "You need a professional."

"Jean Luc and Chloe know her."

Max shrugs his shoulders and pulls the sheets over his shoulders. "I don't like you getting involved with esoteric nonsense. I'll call Emma."

"No, don't," I say a little too quickly, but Max pulls the sheet around his shoulders and closes his eyes as if my presence is too painful to bear. I turn away, feeling vulnerable in my emotional nakedness, and fumble to turn out the light. Then, in the safety of the dark, I let my tears flow.

In order to pacify Max's fears of the esoteric — as well as my own — I decide to classify Tantra as sexual therapy. *It's not that I don't like sexuality, my body doesn't,* I think as I pick my way along a cobblestone street toward my first appointment. I feel the urge to run in the opposite direction. This isn't psychotherapy, this is *Tantra.* It is dark, esoteric, sexual, and *verboten.* When it comes to my fears, it gets full marks. An internal battle rages as I walk along the street. Half of me, the half that made the appointment, drags the other half, which is in the process of throwing an internal tantrum. And I'm in the middle, watching my legs and arms moving as I walk along the street, wondering if there is a sane cell left in my body. I check the piece of paper where I scribbled the address, push open the large double door of an imposing Baroque building and walk up the polished stone steps. An attractive woman a few years older than I with long blond hair and pale blue eyes shakes my hand and introduces herself as Lisa. She is comfortably dressed in a cotton sweater and leggings.

"Good to see you are wearing exercise clothes. Take your shoes off," she says, using the German informal *du* and smiling briefly. "And close the door behind you."

This is what a Tantra teacher looks like. My mind goes wild with judgment. I pull off my boots and walk into the office. The room, with its high ceilings and paneled wood floors, is bare except for a few candles flickering in one corner.

Lisa sits down at the desk and indicates for me to take a seat. "*So. You don't find your partner sexually attractive,*" she says, taking a sip of tea.

"Max," I say lamely.

She smiles. "Okay. You don't find Max sexually attractive."

Instantly I regret revealing this condemning piece of information. But I had to — I could hardly keep from crying when I made the appointment.

Lisa noncommittally nods her head. "How about when you pleasure yourself?"

I cock my head to the side. Perhaps I didn't understand.

"That is what we call masturbation," she says. "Self-pleasuring is a much nicer word, don't you think?"

I'm not used to talking about intimate things with a complete stranger. I stare at her in silence, knowing I look as stupid as a cow chewing her cud.

"All right," Lisa finally says. "How *often* do you self pleasure yourself?"

My eyes run from one side of the room to the other. My forehead perspires slightly and I feel a claustrophobic twinge in my gut. I try to search for an adequate answer, but get none.

"I — I've never masturbated," I whisper.

She laughs a deep-throated laugh. "Now that's something. How old are you?"

"I'm nearly forty," I say as I feel my cheeks flush. *Get me out of here!*

Lisa writes a few sentences down on the piece of paper. "How long have you not found Max sexually attractive?"

"I'm not actually sure I ever *did* find him attractive," I say slowly.

Her eyebrows flicker momentarily. "So why are you with him?"

I stare at her as if I am in a deep, impenetrable fog. Once again I say nothing. The silence drags between us.

"Right," she finally says. "So you don't know why you are with him. And why didn't he come to the appointment with you?"

"It's my problem, not his."

"Do you want to save your relationship?" She takes a sip of tea. Her eyes feel as if they are piercing into me.

"Of course," I say indignantly. For a split second I look at her angrily. *How dare she!*

She continues to stare at me, her hand poised over the sheet of the paper.

My shoulders fall with my bravado. "I'm not sure of anything anymore."

Her gaze softens. "Good. That feels honest. Tantra is nothing more than being honest. With yourself, with Max, with the world. Truly honest about your feelings. Not what you *should* feel, or *could* feel, but what you *do* feel. Sometimes those feelings are frightening to accept. The hardest thing is to be honest with yourself." She puts her pen down. "If you want to save your relationship, tell him how you feel. If you are concerned it will hurt him, tell him that as well." She smiles. "So it's up to you. Do you want to work with me?"

No! screams my mind. I imagine it dancing a few steps like a boxer before a match. *Look at her, with incense and candles and Indian knickknacks. You can't take someone like this seriously.* But I know that voice. It's the part of me I dragged kicking and screaming to this appointment.

"Yes," I say, more firmly than I feel. "So why *do* I lose interest in sex?"

She smiles and sips her tea. "When sexual interest goes out of a relationship, it is an indication that things aren't well *within* the relationship. Perhaps there are hidden tensions or aggressiveness that neither of you dares to admit. If so, it will come out during sex."

I rest my chin in my hand. "I don't think women like sex as much as men."

Lisa puts her teacup on the table. "Don't fall for that. That's what we were brought up to believe. It is what our culture and society and religion teaches. *But there is no physical reason for it to be true.* In Tantra, for example, women are the initiators. A woman is a Tantrica, but a man is someone who follows Tantra."

"So why do women lose their libido?"

"Because women are taught to forgive and forget. But our bodies say *I'm still angry*." When she notices me giving her a suspicious look, she drops the pencil on the desktop. "Let me share something with you. Your body remains in integrity with what you *feel*. Words can lie, but not your body. Bodies *never* lie."

As she is talking, she gathers a few mats under her arm. She then places them in the center of the room and asks me to lie down on the floor facing upward. When I do this, she lies down next to me.

"In Tantra we have specific names for our sexual parts because penis and vagina don't describe the sacred aspect of sexuality. Therefore we call the penis by the Tibetan word *vajra*, and the vagina by the Indian word *yoni*."

Still in awe that she can speak so openly about things that I have always considered taboo, I watch as she lies down and places one hand, palm down, below her belly button, and the other she holds over her *yoni*.

"This is the pelvic curl," she explains. She takes a deep breath inwards, rocking her pelvis forward. Then she slowly exhales while rocking her pelvis backward.

"But that is the movement you do when you make love!"

She grins. "Precisely."

I think of the Tantric hug that Jean Luc gave Val when I first met him. It, too, seems so intimate that it was almost embarrassing. "Is Tantra always like this? Such things are normally reserved for intimacy!"

She shrugs her shoulders. "And in the dark, right? As if something is wrong with love."

That is the end of that conversation. Lisa rocks her pelvis back and forth, back and forth, while she talks to me. "This is called a pelvic tilt. Try it."

I'm so shocked I can hardly understand her words.

She ignores me. "Keep rocking your pelvis back and forth. This way, you are consciously using the three keys — body movement, breath and tone — while making love."

"Three keys?" I repeat.

She nods her head. "Movement. Breath. Tone. First rock your pelvis. Once you are sure of the movement, then add the breathing. The last thing to add is sound."

I place one hand on my belly, the other on the crotch of my pants. How I hate that word. What did she call it? My *yoni*. Awkwardly I begin to rock my pelvis. But my body won't work. The mat is too soft, the air too warm, her voice too mesmerizing.

I hear her voice, but it sounds far off, as if through a fog. "Breathe in while your pelvis is forward, breathe out when you arch your pelvis back. If you feel sleepy, breathe deeper."

A wave of drowsiness overwhelms me. I try to fight the feeling, but it is just as powerful as when I was in the Reichian session. The room begins to rock like a baby cradle, softly, cajoling me to close my eyes, just a little, no one will notice. My eyelids flutter closed, I try to open them but they have become so heavy. Before I know it, I am asleep.

A voice pierces my sleepy bubble like a needle. "Wake up."

My eyes flicker open. Lisa is on her knees looking at me. To my surprise, instead of compassion, her eyes are cold.

"Don't waste my time."

We glare at each other in silence. I dislike her tremendously in this moment. I can't believe I am paying someone to get mad at me. A flush of warmth rises in my cheeks, and I realize that I, too, am angry.

"I *will* continue," I say firmly. I start to rock my pelvis and breathe in rhythm. When I get tired, I pound my fist into the mat to wake up. Time and time again I want to sleep, and time and time again I pound my fist into the mat to force myself awake. After a few minutes, Lisa stops me.

"That will do for now."

I get up from the mat, feeling as if I have barely skimmed by an examination.

"The next time you make love, keep that movement in mind," she says. "If you feel drowsy, remember to add one of the three keys, and that will help you break through your resistance."

"Do other people feel so sleepy when they do these exercises?"

"Why are you so concerned about what happens to other people? Concentrate on what happens to *you*. It is *your* experience."

"I'm curious."

"Curiosity? Or perhaps you like to have everything under control?" She smiles. "If you think you have life under control, you are deluding yourself. Can you control the weather? Political outcomes? You can't even control what people think. The only thing in life you may control is *you*. At the end of the day, you can't even do that."

"I don't understand why getting angry at me was helping me," I mumble as I stand up.

She grins. "Really now? Didn't you notice that when you got angry, your tiredness disappeared?" As I mull over her words she smiles like a Cheshire cat and leads me to the door.

8
London

Christmas comes just in time. I breathe a sigh of relief when Max drops me at the airport so I can catch the early morning flight to London. I need to escape to familiar territory, and there is nowhere more familiar and welcoming than Chloe's kitchen.

As usual, it is the fulcrum of her literary works in progress. I drop my bag in the hall and wade through old newspaper clippings and Christmas invitations. Chloe, still in her dressing gown, her hair curling every which way, opens a bottle of champagne and pours it into two champagne flutes. She moves the piles of newspaper aside and squeezes in behind the table.

"Champagne and mince pies for breakfast, our favorite ritual." Chloe grins sleepily. "So, how's the sex life coming?"

"I ran into Eugen at a mental institution."

Chloe examines the fruity filling before taking a bite of her pie. "I ask you about your sex life and you answer that you saw Eugen. Freud would have a lot to say about that." She pops the rest of her pie in her mouth and washes it down with champagne. "Do you miss him?"

"No. Yes. I mean, of course I want to make it work with Max. " My mouth shuts on its own accord and stays that way, not daring to let out another word.

Chloe gives me a surprised look. "Max doesn't know you saw Eugen?"

"Of course not. It would hurt him."

"Oh? Or are you afraid he will think less of you if you told the truth?"

"I hate when you do that!" I reach for my glass of champagne.

She grins. "Honesty is always better, even if it hurts."

"That sounds like something my Tantra teacher would say."

Chloe taps my glass with hers. "Cheers for beginning something that must be petrifying to you." She digs through the piles of papers until she finds what she is looking for, a large black book, then points a long red lacquered nail at the front cover. "Read."

I lean forward and brush a few pastry crumbs off the page.

The basis of Tantric philosophy is energy. This universal energy manifests itself in polarities, such as male and female; night and day; good and evil. The aim of Tantra is to balance these opposite polarities within a person's body. This harmonious union of reacting opposites brings about a sense of well being that comes from being real, with oneself, with one's partner, and with others.

Chloe sits back and gives her hair a toss. "You see, unlike religions, Tantra prefers the individual to experience reality, not just believe something because someone thousands of years ago wrote it. Tantra understands that everything is energy. Polar opposites that form a union. And from this union — that's what making love is — life is born. Time and time again. Every second, life begins over again." She laughs. "Now that deserves another mince pie. I *love* a philosophy that uses making love as the basis for everything!"

As we simultaneously reach to pick up another pie, a loud, very un-Chloe-like hiccup overcomes her. Her eyes pop open and her hand flies to cover her mouth.

"Chloe, you're drunk!" I exclaim, collapsing in a fit of laughter.

"And you, Lady Ashtor, are *ugly*. But tomorrow I shall be *shober*, and *you* will remain ugly." She wipes a tear from her cheek. "Winston Churchill's greatest dinner party quip. You don't have anything to do in London, anyway, except to eat mince pies and talk to your dear old friend Chloe. Where was I? Oh yes. My *tresoir*, the deliciously hunkable bonkable Jean Luc. Now I'm going to attempt to be serious." She flicks a few crumbs on the floor. "When I do Tantric exercises with Jean Luc, I feel connected with him, to myself, to the world. As if we are all one. Pretty pathetic, huh?"

"It's not pathetic at all," I say. "It's something I've been waiting for all my life."

She smiles one of her irresistible mother hen smiles and looks at her watch. "Darling, I *must* fly. I have to give an appearance at work before the holidays begin. Now don't forget. Tomorrow at 9:00. You can perform a throwing-out-the-contact-lenses ceremony tonight before going to bed, you'll never need them again."

I get up from the table, my legs a little wobbly. "Only you would give me a Lasik eye operation for a Christmas present."

"You'll see. Perfect eyesight will change your life. Whoops," she says, grabbing hold of the table to balance her. "Three glasses and I'm giddy. Bad form, this abstaining from drinking." She stretches her foot out to find the slipper and her toes give a triumphant wiggle as they slip inside.

I give her a bear hug. "I miss you," I say. "It's hard living in different cities."

"Now don't get too touchy-feely on me," she says. "Remember I'm British."

"Yeah, Yeah." We both smile. I look around. "Where are your cigarettes?"

Chloe looks sheepish. "Jean Luc doesn't like smoke," she says, shrugging her shoulders. "Don't say a word. I was going to stop anyway."

9

The next morning, the taxi zigzags through streets jammed with double-deckers and black cabs and Father Christmases — cousins to Santa Claus — in bright red costumes and beards. Throngs of Christmas shoppers surge along the sidewalks, ebbing in and out of stores like a river flowing downstream. I swim with the tide, past post cards of the Royal family hanging from news agents — as my *Trafikant* would be called had he lived in London — on my way to Jean Luc's office in Harley Street. There, in the waiting room, I sit, myopically blinking at the world. Without my contact lenses, the world is a mirage. Lost and insecure in my blindness, I float in a world of blurry lights and movement. As the nurse leads me toward the operating room, Jean Luc greets me with a nod, his surgeon's gloves and mask in place. Gone is the talkative romantic, replaced by an efficient professional doing his job.

"This is Chloe's friend Annabel," he says to his team as he points me to what looks like a dental chair. "Now. Lie down and we will anesthetize your eyes."

The nurses surround me, some calling out numbers, others adding anesthetic eye drops to my eyes. Once they are numb, a contraption is fitted on my eye to hold the lids open.

A voice floats from behind me. "Now stare at the red light."

As I do, I feel a slight pressure against my eyeball. Jean Luc recounts each step of the procedure. My ears listen to his soothing voice as a rhythmic click click click occurs in the background. My nose records a slight acrid smell, as if something is burning. Five minutes pass, then the same procedure on the other eye. Ten minutes later, I sit up in the chair, a little dazed. A nurse dabs a few tears away from my cheek.

"What time is it?" Jean Luc asks.

I look in front of me. There, on the wall, is a clock. I didn't even know that it was there. Even though my vision is watery, I can see the white face, the black hands clearly marking the time.

"11:30 am," I say, blinking in watery disbelief. "Oh my God, I can see." And I burst into tears.

10

Heiliger Abend
Christmas Eve

The pealing bells of the St. Peters church announce the beginning of morning service. I'm already awake, surfing behind my closed eyes in the space between sleep and awareness, taking in the sensations that drift toward me. Pale morning sunlight streams through the French windows onto the garden below. A cold breeze brushes my cheek with a cool featheriness. I pull the duvet close to my chin and look out the window. The world is so immediate it takes my breath away. The frost on the window, the tiniest of twigs on the branches of the trees feel so close I could touch them. It is as if I am wearing binoculars. But it's more than that. I feel as if I am waking up from a deep slumber. There is a sense of wonder, a deep inner tranquility, a feeling of peace. I can *see*. *Really* see. In these few precious moments, it seems as if I remember *who I am.*

Annabel Jones, who is she? Then, as I start to remember, questions begin to fill my brain. *Why am I living in a country I don't like?* A thud of apprehension hits me. I turn my head to the left, bringing a mahogany chest of drawers into focus as another thought arises. *Why am I working in television when I never watch it?* This thought makes

135

me blink. I raise myself on my elbows and let my gaze fall on the picture of Max next to my bed. *Who is this man?* I fall back on the pillows and let my breath flow out of me, gazing at the ceiling as if it can answer the questions swirling in my brain.

— *Now you've done it*, it whispers. *You've gone crazy.*

And that's when I begin to sneeze.

11

Stephanitag
Boxing Day

Chloe comes in with a cup of tea and a description of Boxing Day lunch.

"We have leg of lamb and Yorkshire pudding and parsnips and mashed potatoes and gravy." When I don't react, she puts a hand on my forehead. It's hot to the touch. "God you look terrible! I do hope you'll live to see the New Year."

I blow my nose for the millionth time. Since the operation, the days have melted into endless sleeping and sweating and shivering. I've had a complete meltdown of my body, and a meltdown of my mind. It has left me so confused that I can't think straight. "This is the worst flu of my life. I don't even know what day it is."

"Boxing Day," she says. "Remember? The day we British exchange presents? Jean Luc is here. It's lunchtime."

Three days have gone by. I try to sit up, but my dizziness is so great I nearly fall over. Promising Chloe I'll be down, I manage to dress into a halfway presentable person before slowly shuffling down the stairs to Chloe's dining room. I have to stop and hold my head three times to prevent myself from fainting. At the table, I barely have the energy to eat. Although I am aware of Chloe's and Jean Luc's eyes on me, I can hardly look at them. After lunch we retire to the drawing room with tea and mince pies. As I wrap a blanket around my shoulders and huddle close to the fire, Jean Luc sits in front of me, takes both of my hands in his, and looks deeply into my eyes.

"You were fine when I checked your eyes after the operation. Are they OK?"

"Perfect," I say. "That's the problem. Something else has changed."

I hesitate; it isn't easy to find the words. I look down to his hands. They feel warm and comforting. "Something radical has shifted. I can see. Really see." I wait to see if he will say something, but all I receive is an encouraging look. "My life. If you can call it that. But I'm only layers. Just layers." I stop, not wanting to continue.

Jean Luc leans back to look at me as if he were examining a rare specimen. "Ah. You had a *metaphysical* reaction to the operation. How interesting."

I try to keep the irritation out of my voice. "I don't know what that means."

He tilts his head to the side, as if searching for the right words. "Your perception of yourself and your world has shifted. Is that right?"

Everything around me is so familiar, but I can't seem to put meaning to anything. I bring my hands to my face, running a finger along the outline of my cheek as if to reassure me that everything is as it was. "If I don't do something, I will die."

Chloe's brow knits together. "That's a bit melodramatic, isn't it?"

Jean Luc shakes his head. "No, my love. I know exactly how she feels."

I think of the *Trafikant's* words. "Perhaps not physically. I might live for years, but something in me will die. Or I will become ill."

Jean Luc puts a hand on my shoulder. It feels so calming I have to stop myself from leaning forward to kiss it. "Some people get cancer. Or a near death experience. You, dear Annabel, have had a rather dramatic wake up call."

Chloe tosses her hair. "Why didn't this happen to me?"

He rubs Chloe's neck. "It doesn't happen to everyone. There are no scientific studies of this phenomenon. But I have noticed many people making radical changes after the operation." He looks pointedly at me. "Like your friend Eugen."

A wracking cough overwhelms me. As Chloe runs to get a glass of water, Jean Luc pats my back. "Don't worry too much about that now. You need rest."

"What do I do?" I whisper. "I hardly have the energy to walk up the stairs."

"That's because you have been using your energy to keep yourself together all of these years," he says quietly. "Going places, doing things, always on the run. And now you've stopped."

"It's the end of the road. What a pathetic human being I am. If I were a war reporter and had a breakdown, it would be different…"

"Stop," he answers. "Then you would have thought that your breakdown occurred because of the stresses of war. No, this type of breakdown is as hard as they come, because there is no reason for it. You are incredibly strong to have allowed this to happen to you. From now on, you are ready to do your work."

"Inner work?"

"It's also called *self-inquiry.* Can you do anything else?"

I collapse back on the sofa. "Not anymore."

"Rest assured things are happening as they should," he says gently. "Continue Tantra. Relax and sleep. Reflect. Start analyzing everything in your life. You might find there are a lot of things you thought were true are only a perception." He smiles. "And drink lots of water. Doctors orders."

January
Sylvester
New Year's Eve

The tunnel that leads me from the plane into the airport feels like a birth canal, long and dark, patiently nudging me into the unknown. The moment I enter the Vienna International Airport, my senses are dulled by a sense of oppression. But now, I don't know whether it is Vienna, or just me. I have been walking in a fog all my life, and only now am I aware of it. As the doors to the baggage claim swoosh open, I emerge, blinking nervously through the skiers and holidaymakers milling at the exit for something, anything that looks familiar. There, a red scarf winking in the crowd. It's Max with a bouquet of red roses in his arms. I blink again. His mane of curly hair is gone, replaced by a crew cut.

He grins and ruffles the top of his head with a hand. "It's called a hedgehog."

I find myself missing his ponytail. When I frown, he grins. "Minou told me to do it. We have been cleaning in preparation for your arrival. She is complaining she has dishwater paws." He takes my suitcase from me.

"How is she?" We weave amongst the crowds toward the car park and walk outside. The cold wind blasts into my face, making me grab hold of Max's coat in order to keep my balance.

He tosses my suitcase in the back of the car. "Missing you. You look terrible. *Schnell*, it's a two hour drive to the Brandembergs and I don't want to be late."

After I collapse in the car, Max revs the engine, then takes off towards Vienna to pick up a present for Emma before we head south to Carinthia. We circle the Ring, the street that hugs Vienna's most prominent buildings, then wind our way into the heart of downtown and park along a narrow alley. As we get out of the car, I notice the city has transformed itself once again. Its cloak of Christmas paraphernalia has been replaced by massive stages with strobe lights and special effects. Statues of cherubs and angels and winged Madonnas look impassively from the rooftops at the crowds of revelers surging amongst the stages and onto the streets.

Max glances around him and beams. "You see, Vienna isn't always traditional. Tonight will be one wild outdoor party. The entire downtown will be so crowded you won't be able to walk."

Puffing, I follow him as he marches by stands selling everything from *Bratwurst* to beer. As we turn the corner, I stop to look at the strange sight in front of me. Dozens of stands, once filled with Christmas ornaments and gingerbread hearts, are now selling — pigs. Pink pigs. Fluffy pink stuffed pigs. Cookies in the shape of pigs. Marzipan pigs. Plastic pigs. Pig key chains, pig magnets, pig paper, pig decorations, pig trinkets. *Chachkies*. It's a Yiddish word spoken by Jews in Vienna, and, glancing at the army of collectibles around me, now I understand its meaning. Dust collectors. Any second, I expect the usual tirade from Max about the useless waste of capitalism. Instead, I receive an innocent smile. Grabbing my hand, he walks toward a stand and begins to sift through the pigs with the eye of a connoisseur, eventually handing a marzipan pink pig with a four-leaf clover in its mouth to the stand owner.

"Please don't tell me I have to eat that," I say, watching the owner wrap the pig.

"It's for luck," he answers. "If you eat it, it will bring bad luck to you."

Viennese logic goes over my head. As Max continues to browse with enthusiasm, I peer into a box filled with small leaden figures. When I look closer, I see pigs, lanterns, horseshoes, even treasure chests.

"What are these, miniature toys?"

"Those are *Bleigiessen*," Max explains. "We use them to tell fortunes." He scoops a few figures out and calls to the stand owner to add them to the package. "I'll show you how tonight."

Back in the car, my head is so heavy it drops forward once, twice, and soon I am fast asleep. Hours later I wake up as the car bumps upward along a dirt track through a mature forest of beech and pine trees. Suddenly, like a stage set, lights flash on and the castle appears, its jagged profile glowing in the starry night. As we get out of the car, a bell sounds and the heavy wooden door creaks open. Rudi's face peers out. He shakes Max's hand before turning to me.

"Leave the bags, Hans will get them shortly."

"*Danke*," I say, dragging myself through the door.

Rudi takes my arm as he shows us to our room. As he leads us up a further flight of stairs, Max's eyes bulge like ping pong balls in the dim lighting as he gazes around him. Darkened portraits of ancestors sitting pompously in their gilded frames line the walls on either side of us, glaring upon us as if we were intruding in their musty silence. The wooden boards under the long Persian floor runner that lines the passageway creak underfoot. Rudi opens a heavy door to reveal a large room with a massive fireplace and a four-poster bed. I see a few streaks of brown coming down the ceiling in the corner and recognize the telltale marks of a leaky roof.

Rudi follows my eyes and smiles patiently. "The upkeep here is horrendous."

I glance at him. "You don't know whether this castle owns you, or you own it."

He gives me a perplexed look. "That's what my father used to say." Shaking his head, he closes the door.

I flop on the bed and put my head in my hands. That sentence was written all over Rudi. He is walking in his father's footsteps. *I had better watch my mouth!*

Max bends down to look at me. "What's wrong?"

"I shouldn't be here," I say. "I'm too ill."

"Maybe you should get a flu shot."

"That's not it," I say quietly, then pause, unsure how to continue. "Remember I had Lasik surgery before Christmas…" My voice trails as I glance at the rich embroidered golden cloth on the bed. The threads are so sharp and clear that I can see each and every one individually. Without my contact lenses, the world seems so much more immediate, closer somehow. I look up sharply. "Have you ever awakened and seen the world differently?" When he gives me a quizzical look, I add, "More than physically. As if you lived in a three dimensional world, and suddenly you are aware that there is a lot more depth that you never knew about?"

He squints at me. "Perhaps you had an allergic reaction to the operation."

I rub my eyes. The damp sweat on my brow tells me I am running a fever. "It's more than that. It is as if I can *see*."

"Of course you can *see*. That's why you had the surgery." He puts a hand on my arm. "Annabel, you worry me. You seem changed somehow."

Not wanting to answer, I lean against Max's chest. I can't put my feelings into words. I feel disorientated and confused. Things I have always taken for granted, such as sceneries, relationships, conversations, even something as simple as a person's eyes, look new, different, deeper. I have a sense that I have been lightly skimming on the surface of life, and suddenly the plug has been pulled, drawing me deeper into an abyss that I didn't know was inside me. I sigh and bury my nose into his chest, appreciating the warmth radiating from his skin. Surprised by my frailty, Max gently strokes my hair for a few seconds. Then, without saying a word, I get up to splash some water on my face and go to my bag to give Max an orchid that I had bought at the airport.

"For Emma. Give it to her with your pig. She'll love it."

We wander down the long creaky stairwell, following the muffled sound of laughing through rooms and corridors and land in a corner turret where the kitchen now is. The thick stone walls with their miniature windows look incongruous with the French Provencal country kitchen interior. As we walk in, I spot Emma in the corner on her knees, adjusting her son's collar. She is dressed in tan suede *Lederhosen* and a fine green open-necked sweater with silver buttons. In the distance, Rudi helps a man in a dark green loden jacket prepare the drinks. Max marches up to Emma with the marzipan pig and the lead figures in one hand and an orchid in the other. Emma's gaze takes Max in from his hair to his figure, calculating and adding plus and minus points as she internally packages him in her own social agenda. I can see she is surprised by his off hand, cool figure, and the flower touch tips the balance in his favor, and that he meets with her approval.

Emma peers into the package before giving it to the man in the loden coat.

"What a darling."

As Max wanders over to Rudi, Emma presents her two children who curtsy and click their heels as they are introduced to me. While the men pass the drinks, we lean against the kitchen table, skirting important issues while making small talk about the children and the holidays. Although we are moving our mouths and making sounds, we aren't really communicating. How much of my life has been wasted passing time like this? I watch Emma smother the children with kisses before they scamper off to play. Her eyes follow the children out of the door. "The years go by so quickly."

"You love your children, don't you?"

She gives me a sad smile. "They are the light of my life. Don't you want any?"

I think of the hours spent discussing that subject with Eugen. He wanted children; I was afraid they would limit my career. But now — now I feel differently. Suddenly I would do anything to have a child. To settle down, to grow a family, to root. To love. With a start, I realize that I have used the word all my life, and I don't really know what it means. As Emma describes the planned renovations in the castle, her voice fades into the background as my eyes settle on Rudi and Max. Huddled together in the distance, they probably are talking about Austria's economic problems and the latest political scandal and how difficult it is to make a living these days; everything but how they are feeling and who they really are. I hear my voice breaking into Emma's soft prattle. "How is your relationship with Rudi?"

She frowns, taken aback by the directness of my question. "It's based upon compromise. Especially on my part."

I take a glass of soda water from the butler. "What do you mean?"

"I gave up my career to follow Rudi to Vienna when he inherited the castle." She wipes her forehead with the back of her hand as her eyes flicker to the dining room where Rudi is standing. "I never wanted to live here."

"Did you ever talk to him about this?"

"Heavens, no," she says with a shrug. "That would open up a can of worms and make my life miserable. He is becoming as authoritarian as his father, and doesn't even realize it. Besides, I couldn't leave the children." She smiles in their direction and tugs her sweater down to disguise the extra kilos around her hips. "So I choose not to say anything and to eat my frustrations away." She signals the end of the conversation by clapping her hands. "Hans, dinner."

We follow the butler into the gloomy dining room and stand around the table watching him place the wine on the sideboard. Rudi, his mouth terse in concentration, walks around the long oval dining table, eyeing the line of chairs. With military precision, he moves a chair to the right, then studies the table again and nods to himself.

"His father had brass tacks nailed into the floor to mark where the chairs are supposed to be lined up," Emma whispers to me as she indicates where we should sit. "Rudi used to think it was funny, and now he's doing what his father did. God forbid if he continues in this direction."

The children chatter boisterously throughout the meal, lightening the otherwise heavy atmosphere. While the butler pours copious amounts of wine in the glasses, Emma passes around plates of turkey and grilled vegetables and a salad of wild mushrooms on a bed of lamb's lettuce with dark pumpkin seed oil dribbled on top. Impatiently, I wait for Emma to pick up her silverware, and then attack the salad.

Ever since the operation, I have eaten like a bear. Something is burning like a furnace inside me, razing layer after layer of — what? Ego? Personality? I can't find the word, but all I know is that whatever is smoldering inside me, these people around me think is *life*.

"You must not have eaten in weeks," Emma says, eyeing me as I try not to wolf my food.

Max lifts his glass for the butler, who circles the table with a bottle of wine. "Annabel is on a strange diet. She has lost five kilos in two weeks."

"Emma eats like there is no tomorrow," Rudi says, unfolding himself from the table to wave the butler in his direction to refill his glass. "But she gains weight."

"Here I am," Emma says as she leans over to dust the crumbs away from her youngest child. "You can talk *to* me, not about me, in my presence."

Rudi indicates for the butler to open another bottle of wine and leave it on the table. "Why can't I speak about you in front of you, Emma darling?"

"Don't you remember how your parents always talked in front of us as if we did not exist, except as an extension to their egos? So kindly speak *to* me in my presence."

Rudi smiles at Max. "Emma's latest discovery with her therapist. She's been going for fifteen years and I can't see it has made any difference."

I raise an eyebrow in Rudi's direction. "Didn't you hear what Emma said?" The moment I ask this, I want to put a hand over my mouth, but it is too late, and I feel a heat growing in my chest as everyone's attention focuses on me. "Your wife asked if you could not speak *about* her, but *to* her, and yet you continue to do the same thing." I turn to Emma. "It *is* as if you didn't exist. No wonder you're in therapy."

Max's jaw nearly drops in his plate. If he could put a paper bag over my head at that moment, he would. "Annabel doesn't understand our culture."

I swivel toward Max. "Maybe not, but I know what I feel. And it feels so much nicer when you speak *to* me."

Although my words are soft, they are as strong as steel. In that moment, two things happen; I feel Emma's appreciation and know that from now on, I have been moved from acquaintance to friend. At the same time, I see Rudi's eyes opening, and sense a flash of recognition, as if he, too, is taking me in.

Rudi gives his head a slight bow as if to cede the point. "I'll do my best darling."

Emma's eyes nearly pop out of their sockets. Breathless, she leans forward and touches his arm. "Thanks, honey."

I take a long sip of water to cover up my smile. Max, on the other hand, leans over to nudge Rudi.

"Be careful my friend. You won't like what Annabel wants for the series."

Rudi leans onto the table to gaze in my direction. "Tell me. I'd love to know."

A flicker of excitement creeps into my voice. "I think it will make the series more internationally appealing. A ten-minute insert, all filmed in Vienna, with two, maximum four interviews. The increased cost to the budget will be minimal."

I can see Rudi appreciates my budgetary considerations. "And the content?"

"The first episode aims to show how Austrians defined themselves as victims during World War II. It is well known that they were collaborators, welcoming Hitler into Vienna and embracing Nazi ideology with fervor." My enthusiasm for the subject gives me a boost of energy. "The role of victim is dangerous, because once a people defines themselves as one, they will find an abuser. This time, the Jews were blamed. They were made to be non-human. Demonized. Incredibly enough, although Germany and Austria were *aggressors*, they thought of themselves as *victims*. They felt they needed to protect themselves from Jews. Never once did they consider themselves to be wrong. Victims become abusers, who become victims, and so forth. It is one of the most vicious cycles that exist. It is what starts wars."

Rudi pours wine into both his and Max's glass and leans back with an appreciative smile. "An excellent overview. I can see you've done your research."

My eyes flash with excitement. "But what if all outer wars are results of wars we have within us? If we are able to resolve our inner wars, then we have found a way to end the vicious cycle of victim and abuser."

Rudi looks confused. "But what does this have to do with Austria?"

I lean forward. "More than you think. We tend to forget how wildly popular Hitler was, *and* that he was democratically elected."

"Never mind that he was a vegetarian non-smoker who loved children," Emma interjects.

"People in Germany and Austria followed Hitler's policies blindly, demonizing anyone who did not agree with their way of thinking."

Rudi reaches out to pour me more wine. "And you want to add —?"

I put my hand over my glass and shake my head. Ever since my Reichian session, the thought of wine makes my stomach turn. "Austria gave the world Hitler. But Austria also gave people a way to understand the inner war that each of us has inside. To get to know ourselves. Psychiatry. Psychology. Somatic therapy. Vienna, or the Viennese way of thinking, has brought this gift to the world. Therapies that are so revolutionary they are barely understood, even fifty years later."

Max rolls his eyes. "She means Wilhelm Reich."

Rudi push his chair back from the table. "Wilhelm Reich?" He shakes his head. "Didn't he go insane?"

"But Sigmund Freud wasn't crazy," Emma pipes up. "Nor was Viktor Frankl. Or Josef Breuer. Or Alfred Adler. Annabel's onto something."

Rudi looks Emma in the eye. "All those people were Jews."

Emma bristles. "So what? Vienna *was* a Jewish city before World War II."

"Jews," Rudi drawls. "The biggest victim-culture of all." In the shocked silence that follows, he serenely pours himself another glass of wine. "And I'm not going to finance another program showing Jews as victims of the Holocaust. The Nazis exterminated communists, gypsies, gays, and other minorities, but all you ever hear about it is Jews."

Emma looks as if she has been frozen on ice. Mechanically, she turns to the children and nods, indicating that they can leave the table. The two children stand up and bow to us politely, then dart toward the sitting room, where the butler has lit a fire in a massive stone hearth.

She throws Rudi an icy smile. "I think we've had enough wine." Once the words are out of her mouth, she dismisses them, and with that, her husband. She turns to me with a determined air. "How was London?"

Rudi gets up from the table and returns with another bottle of wine. He glares in Emma's direction, but she resolutely looks away.

"Wonderful," I answer, the atmosphere making me shift uncomfortably in my chair. "At least until I had the surgery. I think it's the reason I got sick."

Max gives me a strange look. "You've been talking in non sequiturs since you got back from London. What does one thing have to do with another?"

I retreat into myself when I hear this. Max is right; until now I would have thought that they have nothing in common. But now I know that everything is connected. Nothing occurs by happenstance. The realization makes my head dizzy.

Emma senses my confusion. "I've heard colds purge your system of toxins."

"The surgeon told me I could have had a metaphysical reaction to the operation."

Rudi gives me an acerbic smile. "Metaphysical? Isn't that a big word."

Max laughs loudly. "She also believes in angels."

I flash an exasperated smile. "I'm not the only person. So does the *Trafikant*. And Eugen."

Emma looks at me curiously. "Eugen who?"

I feel Rudi and Max's eyes on me. "Von Vasoy."

Emma's eyes open wide. "We haven't seen him for years."

Max is too busy draining his glass of wine to notice my questioning look. I turn to look Rudi in the eye. "I thought you and Eugen were best friends?"

Rudi clears his throat. "We see each other now and again." He adjusts his cufflink before looking up. "It's nearly midnight. Shall we go next door?"

Max leaps to his feet to help me out of my chair. "Good idea."

I follow everyone into the library. Outside under the floodlights, the children scour the landscape for fireworks, their laughter and excited squeals floating in through the windows. The fire pops and crackles in the small but cozy room. In a few minutes, Emma returns from the kitchen with a silver tray in her hands. On it is a blue and white porcelain bowl containing the curious figures we bought at the market. Next to them I see a large candle, two spoons and a bowl of ice water.

Rudi's eyes light up when he sees the figures. "*Bleigeissen!*"

Emma sits next to Rudi and gazes at her children playing outside. To my relief, the antagonistic tone from the dinner table has dissipated. We huddle around the tray, watching Max place a figure in the palm of our hands. The air in the room becomes warm, intimate, mysterious. I place my figure — a little treasure chest — in a spoon and hold it over the candle, as if I am performing a sacred ritual that has been done for thousands of years. Emma and Rudi are as engrossed in the procedure as I am.

Max holds his hand over mine to steady it. "Careful, don't spill, or you will bring bad luck on your family."

I'm about to laugh when I see that he means it. Max drops his voice, whispering that when the figure is melted, I should pour it into the cold water. Then he will read my fortune from the shape it takes.

"It's like reading Chinese tea leaves," Emma murmurs as she places her figure in the spoon and holds it over the candle. "Rudi says you do this well, Max."

He looks up earnestly. "My uncle showed me how. He taught me a lot about old superstitions and rituals that bring good and back luck."

I look up. "You can't tell me you are superstitious."

"Careful!" He steadies my hand again. "Why do you think we have so many angel statues in Vienna? We have a reverence for the magical, and we need all the help we can get to protect ourselves from bad luck."

"But you don't really believe in that, do you?"

"There, it's done," Rudi says, pointing to mine. "Into the water!"

Quickly I pour the melted lead into the water. Steam hisses up as we watch the liquid wiggle like a silvery worm before freezing into place. Emma does the same, then Max pulls the twisted shapes from the bowl and wipes off the dripping water.

"What does it say?" Emma asks, her eyes as round as saucers.

He turns it backward and forward, his eyes absorbing the shape. He sits back on his heels and sighs, looking at Emma. "Strange. You will walk away from a person who could help you."

Emma looks confused. "I don't need any help. I wonder what that means."

"Five minutes before midnight," Rudi interrupts, turning on the radio and nodding to the butler to open the champagne and fill our glasses.

Although it could be pond water as far as my taste buds are concerned, I take a sip of champagne as my eye falls on the second piece of lead. Max scoops it up and drops it in his pocket as we sit, listening to the announcer counting down on the radio as the old year fades away. At midnight, the deep, resounding gongs of the St. Stephens church begin to toll, announcing the end of the year. As the bells fade away, the soft sounds of violins begin to play the familiar strains of *The Blue Danube*.

"At least that sounds a lot nicer than *Old Lang Syne*," I murmur.

Max furrows his brow. "You mean everyone doesn't play *The Blue Danube* at the beginning of the year?"

"The fireworks have begun," Emma says, pointing at the window into the inky blackness beyond. The children squeal as puffs of red and blue and white dot the horizon in every direction. She turns to me and clinks my glass. "What will you do when the series is over? Where will you live?"

Max pulls out the second piece of twisted lead and drops it in my glass. "With me." He turns to the others with a grin. "That's what the shape says. We are getting married."

Everyone explodes with excitement, me included, although I'm not sure exactly why. As the music swells, Rudi and Max sweep Emma and me into their arms for a waltz. Gaily we twirl around the room, laughing as the lilting melody on the radio lulls us into more champagne and cheers and dancing. Everything seems so gay, so easy. If there is meaning in life, then this, too, is meant to be. Max's arms feel strong and secure. Surely in them, I will be happy. His eyes catch mine and we smile. In that moment, I know I want this relationship to work. And I can sense that Max, too, can feel my determination.

"I love you," he whispers as we twirl around the room.

2

The four-poster beds squeaks as we collapse onto it and lean back into the pillows. I close my eyes to stop my head from spinning as I feel Max pulling off my shoes and tugging at my skirt. The crisp cold air makes me come alive. What did Lisa tell me? Three keys. Breath, movement and tone. My inhibition loosened because of the champagne, I wiggle my hips to help Max slip off my skirt and stockings, then breathe again and sigh verbally as I exhale. Sitting up, the rush of champagne makes my nasal passages clear. I breathe deeply, feeling the fresh air pumping through my body, making me feel as supple as a panther. Coyly I push Max onto the bed and begin to caress his shoulders, my fingers flicking under his shirt onto his naked torso with feathery touches. My touch begins to excite Max, who lunges for me but I shake my head and pull back, forcing us to go at a slower pace. A wave of numbness overwhelms me, tempting me to go to sleep, but, remembering the Tantric exercise, instead of succumbing to this feeling, I breathe again, deeply. To my amazement, the tiredness fades and I start to feel each pore of my skin reaching out to touch his. My body shivers and a long dormant inkling of sexual excitement begins to ripple through me. Slowly I begin to remove Max's clothing.

Max pulls me toward him but this time, rather than surrendering passively, I match his energy with my own, rocking my pelvis and breathing deeply as our bodies intertwine. *It's working*, I think, closing my eyes to concentrate on the feelings within my body, opening to the enjoyment of his caress, guiding with increasing confidence and excitement his hands to where I need to feel touched.

But something isn't right. Instead of working with me, I feel him struggling against me. Confused, I open my eyes, reaching gently to bring him closer. But the opposite occurs. His eyes narrow, his muscles tightening under my fingers. Then, unexpectedly, he pushes me aside and sits up.

"Stop dominating me!"

I shake my head to try to clear it from the alcoholic fuzz. "But I only wanted to show you what I liked."

He rubs his hands through his hair as if searching for a ponytail that is no longer there. "You never did that before."

I give him a confused look. "I'm applying what I learned in Tantra."

"Why don't you go to normal therapy?"

"I'll go to any therapy that works," I say. "And it was working. I was enjoying making love to you."

"I *hate* when a woman tells me what to do," he growls. "Sex should be a place where I can do what I want." He sits up and slides his feet to the floor, hunched in his boxer position.

I pull the sheet up to cover my body, trying to make sense of it all. I look at him, really look at him. Before I can stop myself, I blurt out, "You are *angry*! Why?"

"As if *you* don't know." He gets up to turn the lights out, and then I hear a loud squeak as he climbs into bed and turns away from me. Only when the protective blanket of darkness covers him does he speak. "You were acting like a prostitute."

The words sear into my breast, but I am too stunned to say anything more. I place my hand on his shoulder, but he brushes it away. Confused and unsure what to do, I roll onto my side and squeeze my eyes shut. My life is starting to unravel before my eyes. I need to talk to Lisa, and soon.

3

Heiliger Drei Könige
Epiphany

The drive home is accompanied in silence.   The streets of Vienna, empty and forlorn, seem cheerless compared to the liveliness of Christmas. With the window decorations and pine wreathes and candles and lights put away, the city takes on a lonely, deserted air. As soon as I walk into the apartment, I scoop Minou into my arms and crash into bed. Minou, sensing my lack of energy, decides to do away with the traditional *Why did you leave me* punishment and takes up her post on the bed as watch-cat. Alternating between sleeping curled in my arms, or placed in her meat loaf position, paws neatly tucked beneath her, she quietly conveys a sense of peaceful surrender.

Listen to me, she purrs. *Sleep until you are no longer tired; eat when you are hungry; hiss when you are angry; spend hours meditating on life; purr when you want love; accept whatever comes as perfect. The time will come again when you will want to play.*

Finally, I have no choice but to accept her wise advice.

The last days of post-Christmas lassitude drag by in sleepy predictable monotony. Every evening a lone, hollow clang rings, followed by another and another, the deep tones echoing through the apartment, heralding that another day is over. I lift my head from the pillow to listen to the multitude of peeling and clanging bells as they reverberate from the different points in Vienna. Like clockwork, I hear the click click click of Minou's paws walking across the parquet floor toward me, and soon Max will be back from the sport club. Then he will switch on the new flat-screen television that sits like a crown jewel in the sitting room. The television is so loud so that I can hear it throughout the entire apartment. I hate how he turns it on when he comes in, but it keeps him occupied, and allows me to sleep. It is the only thing I have the energy to do.

Days float by. During this time, I wander around the apartment in a daze. Everything is the same, but at the same time it is different. I am in chaos. I have run into a dead end. There is nowhere to go. The world continues as before. Trams come and go; I cook for Max in the evening, he sits on the sofa and watches television, I cuddle Minou, take a bath and go to bed. I dare not mention my fragile state of mind for fear that Max will think I am mad. I feel raw, like an onion that is being peeled, layer by layer. But an onion is only layers, so this analogy doesn't help me. Because all that is left is the abyss. That black abyss of not knowing who I am. I can't tell anyone, because they'll say something stupid like "Oh you are finding yourself." And I'll punch them. Because anyone who uses this sentence is so firmly entrenched in themselves — or who they think they are — that they have no idea how ignorant they sound.

My random thoughts follow me as I open the door when I hear the doorbell ring. Three children, dressed in colorful long robes and turbans, wearing crowns on their heads, wish me *Prosit Neuejahr* as they sing. Their soft voices caress my soul, and I lean against the door, a smile on my face as I listen to the lilting innocence of their young voices. After I put money in their clinking collection tin, one child wearing a black beard, her face painted black with coal, takes out a piece of chalk and writes at the top of the door:

$$20 - C+M+B - 05.$$

"Today is January 6th," she explains. "The day of the Three Kings. This chalk message will grace your door all year, telling everyone who comes to visit that Caspar, Melchior and Balthazar have stopped by this dwelling to leave their blessings." She smiles at me. It is time for the New Year to begin.

4

By now Lisa's office feels as if it is the one place where I can get some sane answers. She takes a sip of tea as I recount what happened.

"He called you a prostitute?"

I nod my head, the memory making my cheeks burn. "And doesn't want to talk about it. As if my new changes are threatening to him."

The sweet smell of incense floating from the joss stick burning in the corner of the room makes me rub my nose irritably. I don't need to mention my state of mind after the operation to her. She already knows that I've started to unravel.

Lisa shakes her head. "You are beginning to transform, and he isn't. If he doesn't come to a session or two, he will be left behind."

"Why should Max come?"

She sits back in her chair and looks me in the eyes. "Because he is with a woman who has a problem with her sexuality."

I look at her in confusion. "But it's *my* problem, not his."

She puts her cup down and straightens the papers on her desk with an air of impatience. "This is one of the oldest deceptions in history. Whenever one person in a relationship has a problem, the reality is often the opposite. It is the *other* person in the relationship who has the problem, but cannot accept it. It is dumped onto the partner, who conveniently accepts it as their own."

I never thought of that! "So Max *also* has a problem with sexuality?"

"Sounds like it. It doesn't let you off the hook, but it might allow you to feel some compassion toward yourself." She stands up. "So let's see how you got into such a relationship. Let's dance for a few minutes. I want you to mimic me." After putting on some music, she begins to stomp her feet flat-footed on the ground in rhythm with the drumbeats. Weaving around the room, she engages me with her eyes, beckoning for me to come closer, to look at her, to admire her. I feel as if she is weaving a spell around me, taunting me. Her look is too deep, too intense, too *sensual.* Nervously I flick my eyes toward the corner of the room, the floor, anywhere but in her eyes.

Lisa stops dancing. She looks at me a long time before speaking. "Why can't you look in my eyes?"

I feel like a rabbit caught in the glare of headlights. I've lost the ability to blink. My mouth opens and closes, but nothing comes out.

Lisa's gaze softens. "Are you afraid that I will make a pass at you if you stare at me?"

Do I dare to say what I feel? I look at my feet. "I am afraid that if you make a move toward me, I have no choice but to accept it."

"And where are *you* in all this?"

I don't understand. "What do you mean, where am *I*?"

She puts her hands on her hips. "What I mean is, what does Annabel want? If I want to come on to you, you *do* realize that you can say no, don't you?"

I look at her, stupefied. In fact, I hadn't realized that at all.

She shakes her head in frustration. "*So* many women have this problem. They don't realize that *they can say no.* They give their power away to the men they are with. It is just like your relationship with Max. You don't have to do what he wants. If you do, you feel resentment, and then you get back at him by blaming him."

She chews her lower lip for a moment, as if to consider what to do next. I sense a change of tactics, and, when I see her walk over, turn the music off and drag two large cushions into the middle of the floor, I know I'm right.

"Sit on one," she says, patting it. "Cross-legged. Facing the other pillow."

Reluctantly I do what I'm told.

"Now imagine that Max is the other pillow."

I look at her curiously. I won't like this exercise, I know it. "What does this have to do with my sexual problem?"

Lisa ignores me. "Now. You are going to tell Max why you are angry."

"But I'm not angry." I cross my arms.

She raises an eyebrow. "You're not? We'll see about that. Hit the pillow."

I feel heat surge in my face as I stare at the pillow. A tear spills onto my cheek.

Lisa hands me a box of tissues. "Do you know women cry when they can't express their anger? And men become logical."

"I'm *not* angry," I sniff. "I just don't want to do this."

"So what are you feeling, right now?"

I stare at her. "I — I don't know."

"You don't *know* what you are feeling? What is it? Anger? Sadness? Joy? Fear?" She continues to look me in the eyes.

More tears roll down my cheeks. My head is in a fog. "I don't know," I say. "I just don't know."

Lisa backs off and I immediately feel a sense of relief. She cocks her head and stares at me for a few seconds. "Were you told all your life what to feel?"

My eyes open wide. Of course I was.

"Emotions are simply energy," she explains, handing me another tissue. "You don't have to be frightened of them. Remember, *you are not your emotions.* You are much more. Think of a child. One minute they scream, the next they laugh."

"I am supposed to imitate a child?" I ask. "Children are cruel."

"Children can be cruel, but they let their emotions flow, although *unconsciously.* When we grow up, we learn to stifle or distort our emotions. But emotions are meant to flow through you. The difference is that you can be conscious."

I am not my emotions. That is a liberating thought.

"Can you express anger?"

I physically recoil. "I've never lost my temper in my life."

"Uh-huh." Lisa nods her head. "I thought so. So you have a problem *knowing* when you are angry. Were you allowed to express anger when you were young?"

I reflect on my formative years. My childhood felt like a war zone. I lived on tenterhooks, never knowing when I would be in the way of an emotional grenade. In order to protect my sensitive feelings, I became the family pacifier, attempting to defuse conflicts or confrontations before they happened. "I was too well brought up to lose my temper. Only the men in the family could express their rage."

"In our society, women are not allowed to express anger. But anger is just anger. It isn't directed at anyone."

"I was taught anger must be controlled."

"That is what we have been *brought up* to believe. But it is the opposite. We need to learn to express anger *responsibly*. Where in your body do you feel anger?"

I look at her blankly. "I — I don't know. Even speaking about anger makes me feel hot and uncomfortable."

"It might help you if I tell you where *I* feel it. I feel my anger in my solar plexus. And what does it feel like?"

She closes her eyes, and her face begins to change. Although her features relax, her face begins to turn red. The atmosphere of her office seems to become warm. Instantly I feel guilty. *What have I done to make her angry?*

Behind her closed eyes, she says, "I've found my anger. It feels *hot*. It feels *powerful*." She nods her head for a moment, and clenches her fist. A second later, she opens her eyes and smiles. The anger is gone. She continues talking as before. "The energy of anger is very similar to sexual energy."

My mouth drops open. "You can change your emotions just like *that*?"

She shrugs and smiles. "Just in case you are wondering what anger has to do with your sexual problem, many people who have problems with sexuality also have problems expressing anger." She grins as me. "Beat the pillow."

I contemplate the pillow for a few seconds. My jaw begins to ache.

"Come on. *Hit* the pillow. Tell Max what you feel."

I tap the pillow, self-consciously listing a few of my complaints in a low voice. Then I turn to her. "It isn't his fault, you know."

"Don't talk, hit," Lisa orders.

A trickle of sweat runs down my back. Silence descends as I stare at the pillow.

"He called you a *prostitute*. A whore. You want to make love, and instead verbal abuse is thrown at you, intending to make you feel guilty for what you feel."

Don't lose control! my mind shrieks. Then something in the bottom of my spine like a red-hot wind flushes through me and I explode. My voice jumps and I scream, beating the pillow furiously with my fist.

"I hate you!" I scream into the pillow. "You lied to me! You did everything you could to make me leave Eugen! You made me leave the one thing in this world I love most!"

My truth fuels my rage even more. I scream and swear until my voice becomes a slurred unintelligent wail that crescendos into one long solid shriek, and then slowly subsides as I lean forward onto the pillow in front of me, sobbing uncontrollably. I brush the tears away, but it does no good. They keep welling up and spilling onto my cheeks, dripping onto my shirt, my notebook and the floor. I wipe my eyes, but they still overflow in an unending flood of water.

Lisa hands me a tissue, but other than that, she says nothing. For minutes, the only sound is my sobbing.

"You might find you will be a bit unstable," she says as she leads me to the door. "Be easy on yourself until we next see each other."

5

What do I have inside me, I think as I walk slowly home and drag myself into the apartment. When I open the door, I am relieved to find myself alone. The rest of the day I feel the effects of this experience. It is like a floodgate inside me has opened, and a very deep sadness wells out of my pores, flowing with the tears that cascade down my cheeks. I wonder how long I have been walking around with this anger and sadness. Probably for years. Red-eyed and exhausted, I sit in an armchair for hours, feeling wave after wave of sadness pour out of me. Minou, sensing my sorrow, sits on my lap and sets up the loudest purr she can muster, but I can barely stroke her.

In the evening Max comes home and sees me sitting in the chair staring blankly into space. He drops his jacket and keys on the table, kicks his boots in the corner and goes to the refrigerator. In a few minutes he returns with a beer in one hand and waves the other in front of my face. "What's wrong?"

"I had my second Tantra session," I say with a gravelly voice.

Max looks at me oddly. "You sound hoarse."

"I've been screaming."

He looks closer at me. "You pay for someone to make you scream? What a waste of money."

When I don't answer, he flops onto the sofa, flicking on the television, changing channels with a speed only a man can achieve.

"Why don't you go for a session?" I croak. "Then you can decide how beneficial it is, or isn't."

He points the remote control at the television. "Do you know why America muddles in the affairs of other countries? Because Americans don't know they are alive. Secluded in their little work cells and their armored vehicles, I mean SUVs, stuffed with a diet of sugar and fat filled junk food, being served in convenience stores where they never know anyone, it is no wonder Americans feel alienated. They need war to feel that they are alive."

I hold my head in my hands. "Can't we talk about something else?"

Max tosses the remote on the table. "*Na, ja*. So then what do Americans do? Ahh, then they discover *spirituality*. Hype to make them feel alive. Look at you, wallowing in self-pity when you have a roof over your head. You don't know what sadness is. Go speak to a homeless person, then you'll know what life is all about."

"Stop it!" I bring my hand to my jaw. It's begun to ache again. "You don't know what I feel." *Be truthful,* Lisa's voice comes to me. "And you —*You* are part of the problem." Saying this makes my voice tremble.

Max's lip curls. "So now *I'm* part of the problem?"

We glare at each other as the silence drags between us. I lick my lips, dried and chapped from the screaming, then clear my throat. When the words come, they roll out of my mouth slowly, as if every syllable needs to be annunciated clearly.

"Let me try again. My Tantra teacher encouraged me to be honest with you. Being honest is the hardest thing I have ever done. I don't think I've been honest with any man in my life. I don't think I've been honest with myself." I look down at my lap and take a deep breath. "I know this will hurt you, and that upsets me. But I have to say it anyway. I wonder if I left Eugen too soon. I didn't give it enough time."

Max starts when I say these words. I'm afraid if I stop I won't be able to continue, so I speak quickly, the words tumbling out of my mouth in a quiet staccato.

"That's not all. I'm — I'm not sexually attracted to you. I'm not sure whether I ever was." My fear of confrontation is so great my body begins to tremble. After I finish I stare into my lap to try to gather myself together.

Max's right hand twitches against the sofa. Flick. Flick. Flick. I look into his eyes and see something that I have never seen before. *For goodness sake, I am frightened of his anger!*

In the silence that sits heavily between us, my eyes silently plead for him to understand.

"Is that all?" he finally says, coldly. "So much for sexual therapy."

"There is another thing," I say. "I'm not sure if I can marry you if things don't change. I want you to go to Tantra with me."

"You call Tantra therapy?" he hisses. "Why don't you go to a psychologist?"

"I'm going to a person who is helping me."

Max bangs his beer on the table. "This woman, she doesn't even have a doctoral degree."

"Why don't you meet her? Then you can decide."

Max juts his jaw out. "You and your pseudo-spiritualism full of angels. It is only a game for rich Americans. Besides, *you* have the problem."

And he storms out of the room.

6

The ring of the telephone wakes me up. It's night. Minou lies curled up in a ball next to me, one paw over her eyes. I blink in the dark. I must have fallen asleep on the sofa. I croak into the phone a hoarse hello.

"What's wrong with your voice?"

It's Chloe. I try to clear my throat. "Thank God it's you. I don't think I could have spoken to anyone else at the moment."

"Are you ill, ducky? You sound like a foghorn."

"I've been screaming."

A surprised pause greets me. "You're not the angry type."

"I didn't think I was either."

I can almost hear the light bulb going on in Chloe's mind. "Of course, it's Tantra, isn't it?"

"And my relationship with Max. It's going from bad to worse."

I imagine her giving her hair a good shake. "What did you expect?"

"Expect!" I croak. "I had hoped things would get better!"

"Look, Tantra is like a microwave. Whatever is in the relationship will get more pronounced. Unspoken things will come up to be cleared. Whatever love you share will also become stronger."

I cough once more. "How are things?"

She giggles. "I've got a surprise for you. My literary agency is invited to the Opera Ball in Vienna. We have a box. That means I can invite friends. It will be a great weekend away for Jean Luc and me. Besides, I want to know how well Max dances."

"What a useless friend I am. I should be inviting you and Jean Luc."

"There are friends and there are acquaintances. Use the word *should* with an acquaintance, but not with a friend. With a friend, you just are. And *you* are invited."

"So you'll be coming to Vienna?"

"Middle of February, darling. So hold out until then." And she's gone.

7

I gaze abstractedly at our production schedule, but after my Tantra session, my mind has a hard time clicking into gear. Glancing at my watch, I drop my pen and gather my coat and scarf and head out to meet Emma. I haven't seen her since New Year, and her voice sounded urgent. I trudge by the *Trafik*, flattening myself against the wall of a building as a horse and carriage clops by, then walk along the cobblestones until I reach the large double doors of Café Central. Stamping my feet as I unwrap layer after layer of winter clothing, I glance at the stone arches and columns as if it is the first time I had ever seen them. *How beautiful it is here.*

Emma, sitting at a small table to the left of the entrance, looks up from a magazine and gives me a wave. Her Yorkshire terrier is by her feet.

"I've already scouted out the desserts. You need one, you're too thin."

She gives a waiter an imperious wave, ordering two coffees and an *Esterhazy torte*. In a few minutes, he appears with a silver tray carrying two cups of coffee, two glasses of water with small spoons resting across the top, a triangular slice of creamy beige and pink-layered cake and a bowl of water for the dog.

"I wish they wouldn't fill the order so quickly. I feel guilty watching all the tourists wanting to sit down as we chat over empty cups."

"We can stay as long as we want," she explains as she digs into the torte. "In a good *Kaffeehaus*, when we finish our water, the waiter will bring another glass. And another. He should continue to do so until we are finished."

She finishes the torte and places the plate on the floor for the dog, then licks the cream from her fingers. "Is everything all right with you and Max? You hardly said a word to each other when you left."

I rub my jaw before lying. "Just a little squabble, that's all."

She gives me a blasé look. "It'll pass, just say you're sorry and cry a little. It works every time." She raises her hand to order another pastry — this time a *Topfen Strudel*, before turning to me with an enormous smile on her face. "I *had* to meet you. I've been thinking about what you want to do with the series. It's fantastic."

I wrinkle my nose. "I got the distinct feeling Rudi doesn't want to go forward. Not with Reich, anyway. He's too controversial."

"But I do." She digs in her bag and pulls out a small notebook. "I've been doing some research. Reich died in prison, but he *wasn't* crazy. You are on to something."

The waiter arrives with a piece of golden strudel filled with soft white curd cheese. I feel the plate. It's warm. Taking a bite, I relish the sensation of feathery pastry filled with soft sweet cheese, not too sweet, not too heavy. I take another bite. My God, when it comes to desserts, the Viennese take the cake. It's nice to sit in a beautiful café, eating exquisite food and drinking some of the best coffee that I have ever had, talking to a friendly face. This is what Vienna is all about. Life here runs at a slower pace than the rest of the world. It slows my mind down, puts my disordered world into some sort of perspective. "Sigmund Freud," I say almost in a daze. "Wilhelm Reich. I need one more viewpoint. In order to make a sequence on film, I need three angles. Three people."

Emma gives me a triumphant smile. "That's easy. Viktor Frankl."

I take another bite. "Viktor Frankl?"

She nods. With a deft flick, she pulls out a pair of reading glasses and balances them on her nose as she looks through her notes. "Frankl, like Freud and Reich, was also a Jewish psychiatrist. But unlike Freud or Reich, he was thrown into a concentration camp."

Memories of Mauthausen flood my mind. I put my fork down. "So what happened to him?"

"He endured unspeakable horrors at both Auschwitz and Dachau. But instead of the camps breaking his soul, it strengthened it. He decided that he was taking part of one of the most extraordinary experiments that man could do — an attempt to de-humanize a sector of the human race. He decided that he would survive, and use his experiences in the camp to form his theories. And, miraculously, he did survive, and came up with his theory now known as the Third School of Viennese Psychiatry."

"Which is?" I look up to study her face. Her eyes are shining with excitement, her fingers flipping through her notes.

"That man's primary motivational force in life is his search for meaning."

A lightning bolt hits my solar plexus. "Another word for spirituality." Automatically my hand digs in my bag for my reporter's pad.

She nods her head. "He called it Logotherapy. It's a talk therapy based upon the understanding that every man is searching for meaning. This, he believed, is the motivating force behind every person's search for happiness."

"The marriage of mind and soul." I push away my plate and begin to write. "And Frankl, too, left Vienna?"

"After he was let out of a concentration camp," she says, taking the last piece of strudel between her fingers and popping it in her mouth. "His book *Man's Search for Meaning* is one of the most inspirational reading materials I know. Finding meaning in a concentration camp was something, I can tell you. These experiences formed the basis for an entire field of psychological work called *transpersonal therapy*."

"Transpersonal what?"

"Therapy. I looked it up." She opens her notebook for me to see. "There, you see? The word comes from Latin. *Trans* means beyond and through, and *Persona* means mask, or personality. It's going beyond trying to understand the personality. It views the individual identity through the soul."

I stop writing. There it is again, the word *soul*. I look up to catch Emma's eye. "Are you saying that the beginning of the Mind-Body-Spirit movement began in *Vienna*?"

Emma's eyes smile back at me. "Yes. Psychoanalysis began here. But Freud and his psychiatric work was only the beginning of a revolutionary trend to understand the self."

"This confirms what I thought," I say, scribbling so fast that my hand can barely keep up with the words. "Vienna has given the world an extraordinary gift. So extraordinary that it still isn't accepted. Even here." I waive my hand for the bill. "This is all I needed."

She gives me a shy smile. "*Something* has to come out of the fact that I have spent the last fifteen years in therapy."

I pause. "Freud, Reich, Frankl. Curious that they are all Jewish."

Her eyes begin to shine. "Remember that Vienna was *full* of avant-garde thinkers around the turn of the century. You wouldn't believe how many of the artists, musicians and scientists were Jewish."

She pulls the terrier's leash, causing the little dog to jump up. "Do you realize that before World War II, Vienna had a population of 1.9 million people? That's 700,000 more than today. Of that, nearly 200,000 were Jews."

"How do you know this?"

"Research," she says with a smile.

My eyes widen when the realization hits. "You're Jewish, aren't you!"

Emma gives her head a curt nod. She grabs the bill from the waiter's hand and waves off my attempts to pay. "My family was. We were part of a powerful Jewish family that had to flee Vienna in the 1930's. The same time as Reich, Frankl and Freud." She juts her chin forward as she throws down a few bills. "And I am not allowed to bring my children up to know their Jewish heritage. Only the aristocratic side." She leans forward again and lowers her voice. "That's why I want you to include this in the series."

I put my pad back in my bag as I listen to her words. "Curious. Rudi seemed so anti-Semitic."

"He wasn't," she pouts. "Not when he was young, anyway. His father was an officer in the *Wehrmacht*, the Austrian army, but he told me he learned from his father's mistakes." Her mouth pulls tight. "Now he taunts me by saying our children don't want to be known as Stein the shopkeeper, only Brandemberg."

I gather my coat and jacket and take a last sip of water before standing up. "Max is convinced this won't fit into the series. Like it or not, I'm a hired hand, not a producer. I have to do what he says."

Emma gives me a terse smile. "But *I* hold the purse strings. And I don't care what Max and Rudi say. It is time to set the record straight. For me. For my children. And for my people." She stands up, pulling on her coat with defiance. "*That's* why I want you to put this in the series."

8

With Minou on my lap, I flip through Reich's *The Mass Psychology of Fascism*. The more I look through the pages, the more amazed I am. It was written in 1933, when Nazism was still considered no more than a political party. It answered a question I could never understand, how millions of cultivated, hardworking individuals could let themselves be seduced by Hitler.

Every man has a fascist inside of him begging to be set free. All it takes is a demagogue who can ignite our paternalistic and authoritarian impulses to turn murder into a mass movement.

I read this over and over again. He's right. Max would say that Bush has achieved the same thing, convincing Americans to support a war to find weapons of mass destruction. Even though the weapons were never found, Americans still supported the war as justified. Then, when things go sour, they become disenchanted, forgetting that they voted for him in the first place. Victims again. Soon it will be someone else's fault. Or some other country's. Anyone's fault but our own.

Before I can read any further, the door bangs in the distance. Minou, startled, struggles in my lap. As I put her on the floor, Max storms in, throwing his sports bag against the wall with disgust. He throws his coat on the sofa, kicks his shoes onto the middle of the floor, turns the television on, and flops on the sofa.

"I can't exercise anymore. I'll have to make an appointment with the doctor. My back is killing me. If this keeps up, I won't be able to go to the Opera Ball."

Beyond him, the television flickers images of orange and yellow and red flashes. Another war somewhere or another.

"Why don't you turn off the television? I'm sure that doesn't help your stress."

"How can you say this? You're a reporter, *mein Gott*!"

That's exactly what I've been thinking. I don't like television, so why am I working in it? But I can't verbalize this yet; it will rock my life even further. We both turn as we hear a soft thump behind us. It's Minou on the floor. She looks dazed and is struggling to get up. In this moment, everything is forgotten —television, Wilhelm Reich, our difficulties. Time slows down. The only thing that matters is my cat. Max looks up as I rush over to pick her up. Minou wriggles, not wanting to relax into my arms, so I carefully set her down. With our hearts in our mouths, we watch her wobble away, paws splaying right and left as if she is skating on the slipperiest ice rink. Although it is only a few feet, the journey seems to take forever. Finally, she collapses in her basket and stares, gazing into space.

The rest of the evening passes in contemplative silence. I wait for Max to get to bed. Then, in the silence of darkness, I creep toward the corner of the room were Minou is lying in her basket, her eyes glittering in the inky blackness. I drop next to her, putting my arms around her and put my head on her fur to take solace in her rumbling purr. My sadness is so great I am unable to sleep. And so, quietly, I begin to tell Minou her story. How I found her, so many years ago, on the streets of Brazil when I was a young reporter. How she dutifully followed me from country to country, learning Portuguese, then American, then English and finally German. How important she is to me. Her purr sporadically rumbles in reply, telling me how much she loves me, that she doesn't want to go, but she knows that it is time. She carefully washes my hand, making me hers. *Our time together was our gift to each other,* her eyes say. She stares at me, and I her, as if we want to drink the vision of each other into the depth of ourselves.

In the morning Max finds me asleep on the floor with Minou in my arms. When I awake, moving my stiff limbs, she struggles to get up, but her legs are too weak. Three times she gets up, only to fall down, panting heavily.

"It's her time," Max says, bending down to stroke her gently.

Minou licks his hand, but stops, her breath rasping erratically.

I know he is right. "I'll get the vet," I say in a quiet voice. "I need some air."

9

I cut down the main pedestrian street, weaving between delivery vehicles and bicycles as workers shout to each other under the watchful eyes of the traffic police. My breath blows rings in the cold morning air as I trudge down a small side street to ring the office bell of our local veterinary to tell him the sad news. I extract his promise to come by noon, then turn back, marching as quickly as I can to get back to Minou. Then, before my mind can protest, I open the door of the *Trafik* and walk in.

"Don't bother with the newspaper," I say, shaking his hand with a tired smile. "I just wanted to say hello. It's a coincidence I was walking by." As my eyes focus on Herr Dietmayer, I see a pale, shimmering white light around him. With his bald head, it almost looks like a halo. I blink but the light doesn't go away.

He puts both hands on the countertop. "You know there are no coincidences. I can see you know that, even if you might not want to admit it." Herr Dietmayer's forehead creases in worry. "What's wrong?"

My lower jaw starts to tremble. "My cat." I stop, afraid I am going to burst into tears in front of him. Looking at my feet, I murmur, "She's dying. I know she's just a cat, but…" A tear slips down my cheek.

He reaches out to hold my hand. His skin, although wrinkled, is as warm and soft as a baby's. "She's not *just* a cat. It doesn't matter *who* you love, whether it is a mouse or a cat or a person. But *how* you love." He pauses, letting my hand go.

I take both hands and thrust them into my pockets as I bite my lip. "I love her more than anything," I whisper. "She's just a cat, but she's all I have."

"You need to get back to her." His tone is brusque. "What time is the vet coming?"

I give him a strange look. *I didn't tell him the vet was coming!* "Noon."

"Listen carefully. We all have more of a choice when we want to die than we think. And the more conscious that is, the more beautiful the death can be."

"Death can be beautiful?"

"Of course," he says. "Just as beautiful as birth. Because that is all life is. Birth. Death. Transition. All the gifts of life. And as you know, that is what Vienna holds. Death. It has a wonderful understanding of this phenomena."

"But my cat is just an animal."

"Humans have individual souls, but animals have group souls. That is the difference between us. And yet nowadays, humans are so out of touch with their souls that they can't feel the rhythms of life and death. Animals are much more in tune with the cycles of life than we are."

"You see things so differently. But it makes sense to me. It all makes sense."

"Life makes sense, once our perception shifts." He moves his weight from one leg to the other, as if he is suddenly tired. "You begin to flow with life, rather than against it. You begin to accept that nothing is under your control."

"I am learning that I am the maker of my own destiny," I start to say.

"Can you stop your cat dying? Can you stop grieving for her?"

Tears start to fill my eyes. "No."

His voice softens. "Sorry, it is just that death makes me cut to the chase. Nothing is more sacred in life than death. In a larger sense, you are in charge of your destiny, but that is a very large sense indeed. But I can tell you, once you release your hands from the tiller of your little boat that you call your body, and start flowing down the river of life where you are supposed to go, life begins to feel so much easier. And so, if your cat has chosen now as the time to die, then you must let her go free. Love is not sticky and wants to hold onto things. It is true abundance, because there is always enough love. So feel. Feel her love, and feel the loss fully. Feel all the depth of love that death brings. And it will give you a gift you will never forget."

And, before I can say anything, he drops his eyes to the counter, and I see that he, too, is in tears. "Go now, and God bless," he says as I turn and walk out the door.

10

Max is sitting by Minou's basket when I return. I drop on my knees, and, as the *Trafikant* told me, begin to tell Minou how I love her. How I will be with her until the end. How I will not abandon her at the end of her life. The hours pass, and soon I hear the doorbell. My feet feel like lead as I answer the door.

By the time we return to Minou's basket, she is having difficulty breathing. There is no need to examine her; we all know the moment has come. Time seems to slow down, so much that I can feel not only its linear quality, but that it, too, also has depth. It is so deliberate, so deep, that it is as rich and thick as pudding. With Minou in my arms, I walk onto the terrace where she loved to sun herself. The day is bright and sunny, the blue sky and sunshine feel as crisp and clear as life itself. In the distance I see the Vienna Woods, where months ago I walked to avoid Vandana's funeral. Now, I understand why Eugen had to attend his ex-wife's ceremony. Not for other's eyes, but for his own. Death needs to be acknowledged as part of the flow of life, as flowing as the olive waters of the Danube Canal that slowly float by.

Minou stares into space as Max leans over and kisses her, then he stands back as the small grey haired Hungarian in a white coat and kind eyes pulls out his medical bag. Tears pour down my cheeks as I kiss my cat hurriedly goodbye, realizing that she is in pain and needs to go, then, holding her in my lap so that she is comfortable, I watch as the vet injects her with the relaxant. Instantly I feel her little body unwind. She stretches out her paws one last time, crossing one daintily over the other, and falls asleep, her head resting gently on her paws.

The vet then stands over her and looks at me, his eyes full of compassion. He tilts his head in Minou's direction as if not wanting to wake her.

"May I?"

Tears streaming down my cheeks, I nod, then watch as he injects her a second time to put her to sleep. All of us, even the vet, are crying by this time.

We wait a minute. I look out onto the Vienna Woods and infinity beyond, not able to bear what is happening in my arms. The vet rests his hand on her body.

"*Bizarre*, her heart won't stop beating," he says. "I gave her enough."

Then I remember what the *Trafikant* told me. I need to release my physical connection with my cat. I close my eyes and imagine the cord that links our hearts together. It is there, as clear as day. A white, wispy string, as light as a ribbon floating in the breeze, stemming from my heart into my cat's body. In my mind's eye, I untie it from my heart, but every time I want to release it, the cord snakes its way back to my heart. Three times I do this, but every time it returns. I open my eyes and see the veterinary taking out more serum for a second injection. I then look down to see Minou's mouth opening and closing. She can't breathe.

The vet moves toward me but I shake my head silently, my eyes glued to my precious cat.

It's all right, Minou, you can go, I tell her from deep inside of me. *I'll be OK.* In that moment, her heart stops. Something whooshes past me and flashes toward the hills in the distance. I feel her soul as clearly as I feel the wind on my cheek. In that moment of separation, I realize the true depth of our love. It is endlessly giving, forgiving, a love that lives on, even though her body is now dead. And that is how I receive her last, and greatest gift to me. My heart cracks open as I understand, at last, the gift of unconditional love.

11

The red 71 tram swings its unhurried way toward the Central Cemetery on the outskirts of Vienna. Max and I stand, holding the bag between us as we gaze at the red brick wall of the cemetery. It's been running beside us for miles as we stop at each gate to let people on and off. Finally the tram rumbles and squeaks as it slows in front of Gate 4. We are the only ones to get out. The doors close noisily before the tram rattles on its way. We watch it go, feeling the silence descend upon us. It is late afternoon. In an hour, the cemetery will be closed. A large cloud casts a dark shadow over us as we walk through the stone gate and into the cemetery. The only sound is the wind blowing through the trees and a raven cawing in the distance.

"Hold the trowel under your coat." We tread as surreptitiously as we can through the gravestones, each holding a red candle under our arm. It was Max's idea to bury Minou at his family grave, even though it is illegal in Austria. But anything was better than putting Minou's body in the vet's sterile bag to be cremated.

"This is the Jewish section," Max whispers. "I prefer to approach our family grave this way to avoid being seen."

The deeper we go, the more abandoned I feel. Alone. Acres and acres of statues, crypts and tombs, old and forgotten, tilted at awkward angles, covered with ivy and infested with weeds, beckon with forgotten serenity. I slow down to gawk at the multitude of monuments in front of me.

"How many people are buried here?"

"Over three million," Max says. The somber tone of voice sounds as if he were describing the latest architectural wonder. "This is one of the largest cemeteries in Europe. We have over 330,000 monuments."

I stare at tomb after tomb of Jewish names. *Singer, Levy, Braun, Bauer, Engel, Weiss.* Hebraic script. Stars of David. We walk under the stern gaze of statues of warrior angels and tear-stained eyes of weeping women. The gravel path winds through a forgotten forest of tombs that whisper that time doesn't matter, nothing really matters because no matter what you do, you will end up here, your name in stone, falling into the earth again. My heart catches in my throat, making me cough nervously. *From earth you come, and to earth you shall return again.*

"How many Jewish people lived in Vienna before the last war?" I whisper to Max, trying to keep my mind off of the content of the bag in his hands. I look at the sea of graves spreading in front of me. It looks like a small village of stone monuments. *In loving memory of … never to be forgotten …* But the words inscribed on the tombs aren't true. These tombs haven't been cared for in years.

"Two hundred thousand or so," Max answers, turning right and left among the tombs, walking through the maze with a familiarity that amazes me.

"And how many Jewish people live here now?"

"About seven thousand."

The extent of the extermination of the Jewish people in Vienna hits me. Looking at the sea of graves in front of me, I realize that Emma is right. Vienna *was* a Jewish city. No wonder it feels as if it has lost its soul. Because, in many ways, it has. The ancient soul of Vienna lies here, amongst these graves. Amongst a part of its population that no longer exists. I drop my gaze to my feet as I feel another wave of tears coming on. We plod through the overgrown paths that cut through row after row of mossy, vine covered, crumbling gravestones.

Finally we turn into an area that seems tidier, the graves more modern. Max stops and gently places the bag in front of a small patch of brown grass surrounded by a low wrought iron grill. Inside are various stone plaques. Max looks right and left before stepping inside the plot of land and drops to his knees. Silently I pass him the trowel and watch, blowing air on my gloves to keep them warm. Max, biting his lip in concentration, scrapes a hole in the hard earth at the corner of the family plot.

"I wasn't around when my father died," he says as he digs. "Sometimes I dream of him wailing at his grave, crying for me to come to him, begging my forgiveness."

Suddenly I feel very tired. Tired of fighting for justice. Fighting with Max. Fighting to bring my stories of good news into a world that only wants to hear bad news. *Why am I working as a reporter when I don't watch television?* Fighting a life that isn't my own. This isn't why I was born. I was born to do something else. But what? The answer to this question lies just beyond my reach, somewhere in the ether of my dreams, tantalizing me in moments such as these, moments that I know are marking themselves upon my memory like stone. I shiver and look around. It is getting darker by the minute. I lay my gloved hand on Max's arm.

"Max. I know what to do. You can forgive your father. Now."

Max responds by throwing the trowel down with a bang. "Forget it. I will never forgive him. OK, pass her basket to me."

I'm not sure whether the heaviness in the air comes from Minou or my realization that Max will always hold his rage close to his heart.

My shoulders sag as I open up the bag and remove the basket. Minou's lifeless body feels strangely heavy. She is curled inside as if she were asleep. I try to memorize the last sight of my beloved cat as Max places the basket in the hole as gently as he would place a sleeping baby in a crib. Together we begin to shove dirt in the hole. It pains me to see it spraying indifferently over her white fur. This shouldn't be, she should react, jump up, meowing a complaint at this harsh treatment. But instead she lies still and silent. *Dead.* I close my eyes, unable to take the sight of her body being covered by earth.

We breathe a sigh of relief as the last shovel of dirt lands. Carefully, we plant a small rose in the earth, then Max places the two red candles on the mound and lights them. The candles flicker in the fading light.

Now that it is over, I let my tears flow. My heart feels tender and open. The emotions that flow through it are unbearable. I had no idea that love could feel this way. Like a rainbow, it contains all of the feelings that I know, anger and sadness and joy and frustration. *She's gone*, I keep telling myself. *She's gone.*

Minutes pass. The moment shimmers, stretches, and is over. Raw and exhausted, I get up. For a second I am disoriented and confused. Turning my head to the left, I see Max standing a few yards away, facing a small tomb at the end of the family plot.

Without looking at me, he asks, "Would you like to meet Onki?"

I look around, but we are alone. It is so dark I can barely see him. For a few moments, I listen to the wind rustling through the branches, waiting for someone to appear. But Max doesn't move, nor does he turn around. He stands with his back to me, talking under his breath, his words forming a soft continuous murmur. My mouth drops open when I realize what is happening.

"This is Onki?" I whisper, not wanting to believe what is in front of me. "But — but he's *dead!*"

Max turns and smiles, his brown eyes shining innocently in the flickering candlelight. "Of course. He's been dead for fifteen years. But I still talk to him, just like I used to, and he responds sometimes, just as he used to." He drops the trowel in the bag. "It is comforting to know what he will say." Then, with a smile on his lips, he turns to walk past the rows of silent tombs and into life again.

February

I wake up to whiteness. It must have snowed all night. I slowly sit up and rub my eyes. They feel raw and oversensitive to the touch. I turn to see Max sleeping peacefully next to me, and feel soothed by his presence. For days after Minou's death, we spent hours talking about her as if our words would keep her alive. If it hadn't been for Max's willingness to grieve so openly, I would have put on a stiff upper lip, telling myself to get over it, Minou was just an animal. But Max taught me that grieving is a very essential part of life. If you don't feel death, he told me, you can't feel life. I had no idea that underneath this tough journalist exterior lay such a sensitive person. In order to experience the majesty of the mountains, you need to descend into the darkest of valleys. In his words, *feel the abyss.* I thought it was an extraordinary choice of words, as that is exactly what my eye operation gave me: the realization that I have an abyss within me, we all do. And if we can't hold the abyss of death, we can't hold the joy of life. Vienna holds death well, Max explained. It's joy that the Viennese have a hard time with. That's why they love music. Holding all that death without joy, they need all the music they can get.

Max looks as innocent as a child in his sleep. His mouth, slightly open, is soft, his closed eyes calm and serene. Minou's death has opened my heart in ways that I never could imagine existed, and as a result, it has brought us closer. With newly found tenderness, I lean over to kiss him, then slip out of bed and hurry to get ready for breakfast with Emma. She insisted she had to see me, and it's the only time I can squeeze her into my busy schedule.

I walk outside to find the city resting placidly under a blanket of white that billows gently with the wind. Snow drifts against cars and buildings, creating miniature art forms that rest softly against the window ledges and make peaked caps on the parked cars. Everything has a muffled, dampened feel, is softer, more forgiving, somehow. As light and puffy as meringues, it rests on the shoulders and heads of statues, piles high on the edges of fountains, cloaks the stone winged Madonnas and graceful caryatids adorning the doorways with fluffy white capes, draping a feathery white duvet over cars and bicycles. Absentmindedly I look at my watch, then, seeing that I have a few minutes to spare, I run my glove over a small white bonnet on the little stone cherub before opening the door of the *Trafik* and slipping inside.

The bell chimes pleasantly and a waft of orange and cinnamon blends with the soothing sounds of a morning violin concerto.

Herr Dietmayer's eyes pinch in concern when he sees me. "I haven't seen you for a few days. Is your cat —?"

"She died a few hours after I left you." I look away, embarrassed to feel another wave of tears coming on. Trying to keep the tears back, I blink again, irritated to see a faint whitish haze appear around the *Trafikant's* head. If I look directly at him it disappears, but if I relax, it comes into focus again. Confused, I bend down to dig in my bag for money. With a few murmurs of condolences, Herr Dietmayer discreetly looks away, placing the newspaper on the countertop in front of him with a gentle smile.

I hesitate for a moment, wiping my tears away with a tissue that he passes to me. "Do you remember that conversation we had a few months ago? About allowing magic into my life?" I clear my throat. "Well, it's happened. In a big way."

His eyes seem to deepen somehow, become more intense. Without saying a word, Herr Dietmayer reaches under the countertop and pulls out a dog-eared sign.

GESCHLOSSEN
CLOSED

"Hang it on the door and give the doorknob a twist. We don't want to be disturbed."

A little warily, I pull off my gloves and hang the sign on the doorknob and lock the door. I feel as if I'm playing truant. I like being here, but I know Max doesn't approve of my deepening acquaintance with Herr Dietmayer. He's just a shopkeeper, Max keeps telling me. I thought Max was more egalitarian than that, but something tells me that this man is the only person in Vienna who can understand what is happening to me right now. I take a deep breath, searching for a way to begin.

"Before Christmas I had an eye operation," I say quietly. "After having been nearly blind without my glasses, I got perfect eye sight. But something else happened. I can see. Really see. As if a veil has dropped from my eyes."

Herr Dietmayer's eyebrows raise, and his bald head crinkles. "A *metaphysical* reaction to an eye operation?" He chuckles softly to himself. "What a sense of humor the universe has."

I frown. "I thought the expression was that God has a sense of humor?"

"God, universe, source, love, it's all the same thing. The important thing is that you were given a wake up call. And an extraordinary one at that."

I place my gloves on the counter. "A wake up call? That's what the eye surgeon called it." I notice the shopkeeper's surprised expression. "He's a friend who understands these things."

Herr Dietmayer blinks. "Spiritual literature calls it a wake up call, but you can use whatever term you like. It's something that impels you to make radical changes in your life." He smiles. "You are lucky to be surrounded by people who can explain it to you. I wish I had had that when it happened to me."

My mouth drops. "You had a metaphysical reaction to an eye operation, too?"

He chuckles to himself. "No, no, a wake up call. A traumatizing one, too. It took me years to realize it was the best thing that ever happened to me."

I want to ask him more, but he changes the subject. "So what looks different?"

I think for a moment. It's hard to find words to explain how I feel. "My life, and I don't like it. When I look at a person, it is as if I can feel what it is like for them to be alive. It's like intuition, but stronger. And sometimes — sometimes a person seems to glow." I glance at the shopkeeper while I speak, noting the pale whitish haze around his head. "Like you." I pause again. "It looks like a *halo*."

He smiles. "You're able to see my aura, that's all."

My eyes open wide. "You mean it's true? Auras and halos really exist?"

"Of course they do! What did you think; medieval painters had good imaginations? *Everyone* has them."

I purse my lips. "Why can I see yours so clearly?"

195

"Because I had to do a lot of cleaning up, so to speak, after my wake up call. More of me, more of my soul, radiates outward. No big deal."

I am dumbfounded. "*Saints* have halos. Not normal people like us."

He smiles. "Saints *are* normal people who have done a good spring cleaning during their lifetimes. How clearly you radiate depends upon how deep in yourself you are able to go."

I look around the shop. Everything seems so calm. No, it is Herr Dietmayer. He's not only standing still, he feels, well, still on the inside. "What is it about you that is different?"

Herr Dietmayer gives me a knowing smile. Not smug, just assured. "I think what you feel is my presence."

"That's your personality."

"No, it's my presence. I am more fully in my body than most people."

"But what *is* it?" I ask, not really understanding his last sentence.

He smiles. "You're feeling my energy."

I frown. "Energy? What's energy?"

"Everything is energy! Your *thoughts* are energy. Your *soul* is energy. Your *body* is energy. *Everything* in our solar system is energy." He knocks on the countertop. "Even this Formica countertop!"

I tap the countertop dubiously. "It seems pretty solid to me."

"It's just vibrating at a lower level than you are. If you don't believe me, try Albert Einstein. *All matter within the universe is comprised of energy.* That's what he meant when he wrote $E=mc^2$. But don't get caught up on all this metaphysical stuff. It's interesting to see that people radiate a little like the aurora borealis, but in the end of the day, it's unimportant." He leans forward. "Really. If you get caught here, you'll start to think you are special, and that will lead to disaster."

196

I think of Eugen's words. "Do you mean bells and whistles?"

"Precisely! Once you are aware that everything is energy, you'll never see the world again the same way. You will be able to see more of people's lives than they can see, and will be able to understand more how the universe works. Before you know it, your ego starts to crow like a rooster and you'll want to show off what you know."

I turn around to look out of the store, wistfully observing the crowd hurrying by. Each person is in his or her own world, talking on a cell phone, walking a dog, buttoning a coat, hurrying toward a fixed destination in a fixed world. Busy. So busy.

"I used to be like that," I say quietly. "I knew who I was, what I was doing and where I was going. Life was easier that way." I turn back to Herr Dietmayer. "I was fooling myself. I was only on the surface of life. I can see that now. Now everything is starting to unravel, and there is nothing I can do to stop it." My words choke in my throat.

He nods his head. "So you are starting to realize that there is nothing you control. Nothing. That's the paradox. In everyone else's eyes, you will look as if you are falling apart. All that is happening is that you starting to sink into a deeper truth. Very few people will understand what is happening to you. But things have to fall apart before they come back together. That's one of the rules."

"So what can I do?"

"Keep digging inside yourself. Keep searching for the truth. *The truth will set you free.* I think that comes from the Book of John."

My eyes open wide. "*Jesus* did this?"

He smiles when he sees my expression. "It doesn't matter who did it, only that they did. Anyone whose soul wants to wake up *has* to go through this. You'll find a lot of people talking about it, but very few are lucky enough to go through it."

I shake my head. "Jesus?" I can't believe what I have heard.

"Jesus, Buddha, saints, and many others. Don't get caught up with names, young lady." His voice takes on a harsher tone. He pauses, shifting the weight to his other leg. "This is a tricky place for the ego. A word of warning. All of these things will be so amazing you'll want to talk about them." He pauses. "But people don't like having their version of reality tampered with. They won't understand, even if they say they do. It will be a lot less painful for you if you keep these things to yourself."

Eugen's words come to my mind. "This search. Is this inner work?"

He nods his head. "Inside you. That's where you'll find all the answers you are looking for. Your truth. And that will set you free."

The abyss yawns. My truth? What is he talking about? As if I am Jesus? This is the talk of a madman. Besides, I am about to start a huge television production next week. Earning a living. Plotting my career. That's my reality. My mind shuts shop with a bang.

"I'm not sure if I'll have the time," I say, glancing at my watch. "I'm starting a very important project next week."

He looks a bit surprised when he hears this.

"Work? You won't be able to work—" but he checks himself. He shuffles on his legs and for a second I think I see him wince with pain, but when I look again, he is back to the soft gentle smile. He looks up as someone knocks on the door and nods to me to open the door. As I turn around, he hands me my newspaper with a silent wink and I slip out the door.

2

Mariä Lichtmess
Candlemas

The sun appears as I walk into the street. It's February 2nd, or Groundhog Day in the USA. So if today is sunny, the groundhog will hide from its shadow and that means winter isn't over yet. England doesn't have groundhogs, Chloe explained, but they do have badgers. Chloe made a point to tell me this holiday existed in England long before my country was born. It lies right between winter solstice and spring equinox so Pagans celebrated it big time before Christianity took it over and decided to rename it Candlemas so they can light candles for the Virgin Mary. I remember Chloe teaching me the rhyme her nanny sung to her when she was young.

> *If Candlemas day be fair and bright,*
> *Winter will have another flight.*
> *If Candlemas day be shower and rain,*
> *Winter is gone and will not come again.*

By the time I arrive at the Café Central, the sun is high enough in the sky to make the cobblestones sparkle with a dusting of fresh snow. The pale winter light shines against the ochre and pale green and terracotta baroque palaces and the stately grey of the museums, trying to warm the atmosphere with its pale winter rays. Looking at the tops of the buildings, I see my statues of cherubs and winged Madonnas perched upon the roofs, surveying with concern the last of the Christmas trees piled on the street corners, abandoned and forgotten like broken toys. Some still have remnants of tinsel fluttering in the breeze.

Candlemas means party time, Emma explains as I settle into the soft blue velvet booth near her. The Viennese barely have had time to go on a post Christmas crash diet, recuperate from New Year's alcoholic excesses and get a few days skiing in before *Fasching* begins. It's like carnival, but the Viennese celebrate it by dressing up in gorgeous clothes and dancing at balls.

"There is the Coffeehouse Ball, the Bon Bon Ball, the International Atomic Energy Agency Ball, the Philharmonic Orchestra Ball, the Opera Ball, even a ball for chimney sweeps." She looks up from counting on her fingers.

When I tell her we will be at the Opera Ball, she laughs and presses her hands together like a little girl about to receive a toy. "We'll see you there." Her terrier scurries under her chair as she waves a waiter over with a flick of her hand. "I'm on a diet, but I want you to try a *Krapfen*. It's like a jelly doughnut. Everyone eats them during *Fasching*." She gives our order, then places her hand over her mouth. "I should have sent you a condolence card for your cat."

The mention of Minou makes my eyes go moist. I bring my hand quickly to brush a tear from my cheek. "Sorry, ever since Tantra I can't hold in my emotions anymore ... "

"Tantric sex?" she exclaims, dismissing my sadness with an arch of her eyebrows. She opens her bag to pull out a small saccharin dispenser and clicks it several times in her coffee. "My my my."

The sun flashes through the windows in bursts, highlighting the multitude of arches and columns around me. I look up at the ceiling, knowing that my words are falling upon deaf ears.

"Tantra isn't just sex. It's about being honest. With myself and with others. It's hard work."

Emma leans forward and pats my hand. "We all go through stages like that. It took me fifteen years of therapy to know myself." She eyes the large, puffy pastry the waiter brought me. "You wouldn't mind if I had a bite, would you?"

I push the plate toward her.

She consumes the entire Krapfen in a few mouthfuls. "Sweets and sex, two things women never get enough of. Do you know Reich recognized that sexual repression had to do with many of the psychological problems of the world?"

"Wilhelm Reich was also interested in sex?"

"Darling, that's what got him into trouble! After he emigrated to the USA, he recommended that sex education be taught in public schools." She pauses for effect. "That was in 1948."

"Wasn't that the McCarthy period?"

She attacks the second *Krapfen,* delicately dusting off the powder sugar from her chin. "He was a communist, too. No wonder he was thrown in jail, right? He died of a heart attack two years later."

I put my coffee cup down. "So why do people say he went crazy?"

"Because many people wanted to discredit his work."

I think about what happened to me during my session. The spasms, the rush of emotions, the prickly feeling of energy racing up and down my body. "I can understand why people would be frightened of his therapy, because what happens is beyond the current understanding of reality. But in the end, it gave me the most wonderful feeling of peace.

It is transformational. I think if it could be explained, more people might try it."

Her eyes open wide, the expression of her face almost theatrical. "That's what I wanted to tell you. I've put Rudi on ultimatum. Either he supports what you want to add to the series, or I'll pull out my capital."

I fiddle with my cup. "Isn't that a little extreme?"

"Don't worry, I have my own agenda." For a moment, she tilts her face to the side, as if studying me. "So what about Max? Is he going to these — Tantra — sessions?"

"He refuses to go. He says it is *my* problem."

"Typical man," she says. She pulls out a pack of cigarettes and lights one. "To be honest, I can't say all those years of therapy have made me any happier, they've only made me more aware of my neuroses." She wipes the plate and pops her index finger in her mouth. "I'll tell you what, I'll put you in touch with my psychiatrist. He is *such* an interesting man."

I look away. What is happening to me is much more than sitting on a sofa discussing my mind's prattle or examining my childhood. That is talk, but mine is a physical process, wild and uncontrollable and transformational. I think of Herr Dietmayer's caution. But then again, Emma may understand. I lean forward. "The morning after Minou died, I lay in bed, trying to feel the inner peace that I felt during my Reichian session. I knew I needed something; I couldn't bear the sadness anymore. Suddenly, I felt a hot flash in my chest, as if someone had placed a hot water bottle on my heart."

Emma's eyes look like saucers behind her glasses. She is so engrossed with what I am saying that she misses the ashtray entirely, scattering ash all over our table.

"This warmth spreads through my body, radiating outward from my heart. I start to shimmer from head to toe. Then my fingers start curling up like an old woman —"

"What!" Emma drops her cigarette in the ashtray. "I thought you met your soul!"

"Oh, that was later," I say, "First came the battle. But my fingers curling up is no big deal, it's just *tetni*," I say, feeling like a pro. "*Tetni* is what happens when my body is resisting energy. So I breathe deeply, again and again like I was taught, and my fingers relax. Wave after wave of warmth spreads through my body. My body tingles all over. I felt as if I had dropped physically deeper into myself again, into my space of inner peace."

Emma starts to scratch her neck. "And this happened spontaneously?"

"All by myself." I keep my eyes glued on her face, watching her reaction.

The waiter appears and places another cup of coffee in front of Emma. She closes her eyes, then, when she opens them, it's gone. The connection between us has shut.

"Well. I'd rather watch pornographic videos while staying at a hotel. At first I was embarrassed when paying the bill. Now I just stare the receptionist in the eye."

"Does Rudi know?"

By way of answering, she looks away and flutters her hand for the bill. Surprised that she doesn't want to talk about it, I glance at my watch and start. I'm going to be late for my Tantra appointment. Pretending that the last part of our conversation didn't take place, she air kisses me and waves me toward the door.

3

As I leave the cafe, a tremendous wave of drowsiness washes over me. I can hardly drag one foot in front of the other. By the time I arrive at Lisa's, I am so sleepy I can hardly keep on my feet. I stifle a yawn as I collapse onto the chair.

Lisa, dressed in her habitual leggings and sweater, takes a sip of tea as she observes me. "Resistance."

I shake my head to try to clear my foggy head. "How do you know? I may be just tired."

Lisa gives me an amused smile. "*Everyone* has a reaction when they are being pushed beyond their boundaries. Your resistance makes you drowsy. That's very common. Certain people show resistance by getting angry. I even had one person who itched." She laughs. "He had a terrible time, scratching himself all over before a session. You hate your anger, don't you?"

I sit up straight. "But I *never* get angry."

"Oh no?" She gives me an amused smile.

I frown. "Why do I want to get angry? There was too much anger in my family. Nasty things were said. It was ugly. It hurt."

"Responsible anger is one thing. Trying to hurt someone is something else."

I nod my head, but Lisa can see I don't understand.

"You can be angry at someone you love," Lisa says softly.

I look at her with big eyes. "I — I can?"

"Of course you can. It's natural to feel anger. But we quickly tell ourselves that we *shouldn't* feel angry. We say *I shouldn't want to wring my partner's neck* or *I shouldn't want to kill my child*. Instead of *accepting* our feelings, we *reject* them." She pauses to see if I am following her. "These unexpressed feelings are stuffed into a pot, and left to stew. Over time, they turn into unclear emotions such as resentment and hatred. One day, anger hits the bottom of the pot and the lid blows. But what comes out of the pot isn't *anger*; it is your repressed feelings."

"So it's not anger that makes me want to say nasty things?"

She shakes her head. "Anger might get you to say your truth, and that might not be what your partner wants to hear. But anger is just energy — a cleansing energy that is powerful enough to clean all those emotions out. Because if all those unwanted emotions get stuck in your body, they could cause pain and even illness over time."

"But people in my family lost their tempers all the time. Anger hurts others."

"There are two types of tendencies. For people whose tendency is to lose their temper, the mastery lies in being able to *choose* when it is appropriate to be angry. Often people who have the second tendency — which is yours — are attracted to this type."

I lean forward in my chair. "And what type am I?"

"You are the type whose feelings are so deep inside that you don't even *know* when you are angry. So first I'm going to help you *find* your anger." She stops to let me digest her words. "Anger isn't negative. It keeps you in integrity. Think of it. When you are angry, you say what you feel, don't you?"

"It's true," I say slowly.

"There are exercises that will help you clear your anger. Alone. Then, once you have done that, you can be clear-headed to communicate your dissatisfaction with whomever you have been having difficulties."

"That sounds better than the endless snapping and arguments with Max."

Lisa smiles. "And you say you don't have anger? Anger can be very subtle. Nagging, bickering, pestering, whining or telling people what to do are all forms of expressing anger. You feel a victim of Max, but in fact you are a victim of your own anger. No one can make you angry if you don't want to."

"No one can make me angry if I don't want to." I pause. What a liberating thought. "And if I express my anger, how does it not turn into a shouting match?"

"There are some basic rules. Don't say anything to hurt someone else. Don't say anything you will regret later. And stick with saying how *you* feel. Not what the other person *should* be feeling, or what you *want* them to feel." Lisa starts to prepare the room. "Unexpressed anger is a problem in modern society. People aren't allowed to express anger except in war or sports. Why do you think there is such a proliferation of violent films on the market?" She tosses two large pillows on the floor and indicates for me to sit on one of them. I groan inwardly as I settle on the pillow.

"I want you to show your feelings. Women love to be the innocent victim. They feel someone else is doing something *to* them, making them angry, resentful, sad, depressed. So the first step is to recognize that you *can* get angry."

I throw a doubtful look at the bamboo cane in her hand. "I don't know why you want to make me emotionally unstable."

She hands me the cane and gives me a stern look. "For forty years you don't express your feelings, and you expect that in one session everything will be perfect. Healing doesn't work that way. Most people don't want to do shadow work, which is what this is called, because it is so painful. The worst part is that it will get more painful before it gets better." She adjusts the pillow in front of me. "Let's work on your relationship with your family." She taps the pillows. "Here are your parents."

My mouth becomes dry. She wants me to hit a pillow representing one of my parents? "*Why* do I have to hit someone who loves me?"

"It's just a pillow," Lisa answers. She gives the pillow a few whacks. "What's the big deal? Go ahead and hit it."

I raise the bamboo stick above my head. But instead of thumping the pillow, the stick hovers in mid-air. Waves of guilt wash over me. How can I do such a thing? Imagine if my parents could see me now. How horrified they would be! I lower the stick with an irritated look. "I don't want to do this. It's stupid."

She raises her eyebrow. "Don't *want* to, or *can't?*"

"Of course I can—" I start to say.

"Then do it." She throws her fist into the pillow. A large thump echoes in my ear. Her amused attitude irritates me beyond belief. I raise the stick in the air, but when I want to bring it down, my arm becomes paralyzed. It's as rigid of steel. It won't bend, it won't move, it just sits there, straight in midair like a mast of a ship, my fingers gripped tightly around the cane. Heat surges into my cheeks as I try to move it, but it won't budge. Finally, I drop my head in shame. My arm falls on my lap, the stick clatters on the floor. She's right. I can't do it.

Lisa lets me sit for a few minutes while I register what has happened. "If you can't hit a pillow, do you think you are afraid of expressing anger at those you love?"

I nod my head dumbly.

Lisa looks closely at me. "Did you always have to do something to be loved? The what's behind the over-achiever. True love is unconditional," she says quietly.

A wave of anguish rips through my heart when I hear these words. "I don't think I know what love is," I whisper.

Lisa's eyes are full of compassion. "I think you have another pot of emotions that you need to separate. Love and achievement aren't bonded. Love is just love. It doesn't *need* anything."

My body shivers as I hear these words. Yet another layer of protection drops away. "But this is only know this type of love I know."

Her eyes soften. "If you've never received unconditional love, how can you expect to give what you don't know? Then you beat yourself up for not being able to give it to others. Can you see it's not your fault? Until now, you were unconscious in this spot. But now you will be able to separate love from achievement. And that's a big step toward learning what true love is."

I put my head in my hands and burst into tears, my shoulders heaving. Lisa keeps unpeeling me, layer by layer, until I sit beneath her, raw and aching.

"That's good," she says. "Let the sadness out. It is natural to mourn love that you never received." She hands me a box of tissues. "You don't have to be so hard on yourself anymore. And that means you won't be so hard on others." She arranges the notes on her desk, a signal that our session is over. "You are really doing your work. I can see it. But if you want your relationship to last, it would be a good idea if Max would come to a session or two."

I feel so weak I can barely put my coat on. "I'll see what I can do."

4

Fasching

Mardi Gras

The week leading up to production is frantic with activity. I throw myself into my job and let life propel me forward, working around the clock and then collapsing into bed, my mind whirring with the increasing list of responsibilities. I know I'm being well paid, and want to do a good job. Scheduling the film crews, arranging the interviews, scripting what I want to say has me running around Vienna from morning to night, researching locations and drinking gallons of coffee to sustain me. Max and I hardly say two words to each other, finding it easier to communicate by email, even when we are in the same office. To say that I am relieved when Chloe arrives for the Opera Ball is the understatement of the year.

On the eve of the ball, my taxi skims along the Ring and glides through the imposing gates that guard the Hotel Schwarzenberg, the palatial hotel where Chloe and Jean Luc are staying. Once inside the gates, Vienna has been left behind; the spaciousness of the gardens feels like an old English manor house in the country, worn but elegant. As the taxi coasts toward the discreet entrance tucked into one wing of the palace, I adjust the shimmering orange satin of my gown, pleased I will have a little time with Chloe before the ball. Since I began Tantra, my weight has curiously dropped. Tugging at my now too large ball gown and unused to wearing high heels, I totter along the polished marble floor and down the steps into a room with barrel-vaulted ceilings and a warm fire burning in an ornate marble fireplace. A mahogany clock ticks contentedly on the wall, its pendulum swinging at the pace of luxury. Chloe drops her newspaper on the table next to her when she sees me. She is dressed in a long black silk dress dipping dangerously into a low v-line in the back.

"You look gorgeous," she says as we air kiss, then spins me around to admire my dress. "Don't be another Wallis Simpson."

"*A woman can never be too rich or too thin,* right? Well, I'm working on the rich part."

"But you're getting too thin."

I look down at myself. "I can't understand it. I'm eating like a wolf."

"When you find out your secret, tell me," she says, reaching down to wipe any dust off the seats before we settle into the leather armchairs in front of the roaring fire. A dapperly uniformed waiter takes our orders, then I slip off my shoes and fluff my gown as I tuck my feet underneath me. Our voices drop to a low murmur so that we still can hear the crackling of the fire.

The moment I have been waiting for has arrived. My relief flows out of me like a stream running down hill.

"Minou's death was hard enough, but Tantra has been a killer. Life was so much easier when I was under the illusion that I had everything together. I *thought* I was such a nice person, and I discover I have a sewer for a mind. I *thought* I was making strides in my sexuality, and Max calls me a prostitute." I glance at her. "If I weren't so pathetic, I would think it's funny."

Chloe accepts my string of complaints with a stoic nod of her head and pats my arm. "Chin up." She smiles, her eyes twinkling in the firelight as she leans forward with a conspiratorial air. "Listen. I've been dying to tell you. You wouldn't *believe* whom we ran into on the plane over here." She pauses theatrically. "Eugen."

The room tilts underneath me. "Did you speak to him?"

We hear Jean Luc's voice down the hall, talking to Max. Chloe looks at her diamond watch in dismay. "Damn, the boys are early." She lowers her voice. "We couldn't ignore him. Planes aren't that big, you know. But he is coming tonight."

Before I can answer, Max and Jean Luc arrive, looking gallant in their evening clothes, followed by a waiter with four glasses of *prosecco* on a silver tray. I look longingly in Chloe's direction, a million questions swirling in my brain. I take a glass of *prosecco* from the waiter with a distracted air.

As we clink our glasses, Jean Luc gives me a wink. "To Tantra."

Max reaches over to adjust the shawl around my shoulders before throwing a suspicious glance in Jean Luc's direction. "So it's your fault." Behind his smile, there is a slight edge to his voice. "Every time she comes back from a session, she looks worse."

Chloe turns to Max, her eyes sparkling. "Darling, don't you know how to seduce a woman? Tell Annabel she looks ravishing! She'll be eating out of your hand in no time at all."

But Max can only frown. "I wish Annabel would focus on what is important."

I wave my hand in front of Max. "I'm here, remember? Talk to me."

Jean Luc gives Max a bemused look. "Important things? Such as?"

Max downs his glass. "Other people's needs. Making the world a safer place, fighting poverty, defending human rights, you know, that sort of thing."

"I have all the battles I can handle," I say quietly. "Inside of me."

"You'd better get real fast," he answers, waving his empty glass to the waiter to get the bill. "We start filming on Monday, remember?"

Before I can reply, Jean Luc slips an arm through mine, gently dragging me along the corridor. "Breathe," he whispers. "It'll do you wonders."

While Max helps Chloe with her coat, she tugs at his sleeve. "Let me tell you, Max darling, Tantra takes courage. Most people study Tantra because they are obsessed with sex and are looking for an outlet." She tosses her hair and grins. "Like me." She slips her arm in Max's, and, with a sultry voice and slow smile, she squeezes his arm as we walk toward our taxi. "So, how's your love life? Details, please!"

5

The taxi pulls in front of the Opera House. As Max pays, Jean Luc helps me out of the back seat, then lightly pulls Chloe out of the taxi and into his arms. Together, we join the throng pushing through a sea of flashing cameras toward the entrance. I glance at the massive building towering above us. Flanked by winged horses under a bronze dome, it looks to me as if the architect couldn't decide on one style, so he chose them all; turrets and terraces and loggias, rose windows carved from stone, long rectangular and small square windows lined in wood, a gaggle of gargoyles. A line of bronze composers standing pompously on pillars, even a chimney or two sprouting between carved reliefs of flowers, columns and cherubs. It reminds me of a church, a museum and a national library built into one. Max told me that the Viennese critics loathed it when it was inaugurated in 1869, which prompted the architect to commit suicide. It confirms my suspicions that Vienna's energy was always hard on a person's mental health. It must not have been easy to live in the city of psychotherapy before it was invented.

Inside, the somber atmosphere is brightened by clusters of women in dazzling ball gowns moving like a sea of color up the staircase. The women may be the rainbows, but it is the men who are the peacocks of the evening. Rows and rows of commemorative medals sparkle on their breasts, striped silk sashes gather into a glittery order, proudly heralding

213

each man's values to the world. Everything around us sparkles, the flower decorations are magnificent, the feeling of expectation high. Nervously I peer around the bronze lamps and up the stairs to see if I can spot Eugen's tall figure in the crowd, but all I can see is a solid stream of color.

"The Austrian president will be here," Max explains as we climb the magnificent stone steps toward our loggia box on the second floor. "As well as heaps of international useless partygoers with more money than sense."

"Like us." Chloe giggles as we enter our box. Standing in the miniscule entryway lined in red silk, Jean Luc helps Chloe with her coat, then removes his silk scarf from his neck.

Chloe rubs her hand over Max's short hair. "You'll be mistaken for a banker."

Max fingers his silk red scarf with a grin. "I've just gone incognito. I'm still a communist at heart."

"Chloe More-Hamilton!" I hear, and a flurry of introductions with the other members in the box begins. The atmosphere reminds me of an intimate party within a party. I can see by Max's reaction that these are people who matter. For all his sneering, he laps up the atmosphere. Soon his discussion with a portly man with a shaved head and a pear shaped body is so intense he forgets me.

Jean Luc and Chloe stand next to each other, peering over the balustrade onto the floor below. The circular rounded walls are tiered with plush red boxes stacked on top of each other. It makes me feel as if I am in a large, bejeweled music box. The ceiling, with its massive crystal chandelier, reminds me of the lid. Below, a wooden platform has been built over the orchestra pit, creating a large, round dance floor. This is the bottom of the jewelry box. All along the walls, people chat and wave at each other while scanning the other boxes through binoculars.

As Chloe begins to talk animatedly to a neighbor about her latest book deal, Jean Luc smiles at me. "How are your eyes?"

"My *eyes* are fine. But my Tantra teacher is giving me a work out." I pull the bodice of my dress out to show him how loose it is. "I'm exhausted most of the time. And although I'm eating, I'm losing weight. Maybe I'm ill." My eyes scrunch in worry. "I hope I don't have cancer."

Jean Luc adjusts his cufflink. "*Ma petite.* If you want, I can prescribe a complete physical in London." He gives me a gentle smile. "But — let's just wait a few months. Fatigue, sleeping for hours, unexpected pains, trembling, emotional outbursts and even losing weight are typical reactions of a person undergoing deep shadow work."

The relief must be written all over my face. "Is that what this is called?"

He nods his head. "It goes against everything that I learned as a doctor, but I've come around to understanding that everything is connected. Mind. Body. Spirit."

I rub the tips of my fingers along the soft red plush of the seat as I ponder his words. "But my weight? How can it affect my weight?"

He pulls out a pair of opera glasses lined with mother of pearl and puts them to his eyes as he speaks. "You've heard of metabolism, right? The speed of your metabolism influences how much food you need to live. If your metabolism is high, you eat more because your body processes food quicker. If your are sluggish, your metabolism is slow."

"So you are saying my metabolism is increasing?"

"It looks like it, doesn't it?" He lowers his binoculars with a faint smile. "*Mon Dieu*, I haven't seen hairstyles like these since I used to attend all those balls for Paris' fashion week."

When I look confused, he slows down. "Your body is like an envelope that contains your energy. Your weight has less to do with what you eat, but how much you are clearing out old patterns that are blocking you from receiving more of your own energy."

He is about to raise his binoculars to his eyes but I rest my hand on his arm. What he is saying is too important to let go into social banter. "Explain this to me."

Immediately his eyes become deeper somehow, as if he is looking at me, not just my clothes and hair, but deeper than that, as if he is holding all of me in his gaze. "Of course." His voice, too, has become deeper. "Let me explain how energy works. Have you ever watched water run downhill? That's the best analogy I know to describe how energy works. It's always there, always flowing. Whenever we give it a chance, the water will trickle in, unless, of course, our defenses are so tight that we create a dam. So water, with infinite patience, waits outside, waiting for the dam to start to crack. And you know what, the water always wins." He chuckles to himself.

I give him a confused smile. "Someone once told me that everything is energy."

Jean Luc answers with a very matter of fact look. "That's true. So, if energy is all there is, and it is always flowing, always available, then it is us who are blocking it." When he sees I don't understand, he tries a different tack. "You know when you lack energy, you feel small, as if life is wearing you down. That is because you aren't able to hold much of your energy. *You are how much energy you can hold*. That is why, when you are bursting with energy, you feel big, as if the world is your clam."

"Oyster," I say, trying not to smile. "The world is your oyster."

"Oyster," Jean Luc repeats to himself. "The world is your *oyster*. I'll never understand the English language." He smiles to himself and clears his throat. For a moment, we turn and silently gaze at the sea of color around us. I look at his hand resting on the plush red balustrade. It is inordinately small for someone of his build. It could be the hand of a musician or an artist. I find myself wondering why Jean Luc decided to become a surgeon. How strange life can be! Imagine if he hadn't become a surgeon, or if Chloe hadn't gone to the Tantra class and met him, I would never have had the operation, and my life would be so different. Absentmindedly I watch the signet ring on his left hand glittering in the bright lights. He turns back to me and I smile, embarrassed to have been caught studying him so intensely.

"What about your Reichian session? Weren't you amazed?"

"But I experienced *tetni*," I say sadly. "My body resisted energy."

He laughs when he sees my expression. "It is *wonderful* that you experienced tetni! That means that you were willing to open to a new level of energy. Many people are so tight that they experience nothing, and so they think there is nothing there, and stop. They are in denial, and don't even know that they are in denial."

A newcomer in our box makes everyone jostle again. I feel as if I have been packed into a very ornate sardine can. My eyes skim the box, wondering when Chloe will join us. "But why did energy want to run through me?"

If Jean Luc finds my questions too deep for our social surroundings, he doesn't show it. Opening up his coat with one hand, he carefully deposits the binoculars into the inner pocket. "Energy is *always* there, always waiting to come in. Have you heard of the expression *Everything you need to know is right in front of you, if you only choose to see it*? Well, it's true. It is always *we* who are refusing life's energy and opportunities, not the other way around." He stops for a minute, as if trying to find the right words to express what he wants to say. "We are much bigger than we think. Our energy is much more than what we let in. In a sense, we are all walking around in prisons of our own making. The smaller the prison, the tighter we feel. The tension we hold in our body is phenomenal, and it is all because we are using our energy to try to hold on to what we know — which keeps us small — instead of opening to a greater energy that we don't. The blocks in our bodies are resistance against a larger energy that is nothing more than parts of ourselves we haven't yet owned."

I take the time to digest his words. "But if you were to ask anyone here if they wanted more energy, they would say yes. So why do we block it?"

He grins when he hears my question. "That's the paradox. Everyone wants more energy, but on *their* terms. And life doesn't work like that. We block emotions that we don't want to feel, like anger, or sadness."

There he is, talking in non-sequiturs again. "But what do *emotions* have to do with *energy?*"

He gives a small wave to Chloe, who begins to weave through the guests like a panther stalking through the tall grasses of the savannah. "*Mon Dieu.* I'm so glad you ask these questions, because they force me to explain something that now seems so obvious to me. You'll see for yourself. Once your perception shifts, it gets very lonely, because what is obvious to you will be right over most people's heads." Reaching out to grab Chloe's hand, he pulls her toward him and drapes an arm around her shoulder. "Emotions are waves of energy. E-motions. Energy in motion."

"E-motions. Energies in motion," I repeat, smiling at the logic of it all.

He nods his head. "Any emotions you can't feel get stuck in your body and dam the flow of energy into you. By opening to your energy, like you did in the Reichian session, or like you've learned in Tantra, or in yoga or in a number of body based therapies, you help release the blocks that prevent this energy from coming in. You allow more of yourself to come into your body, and therefore get bigger."

Chloe tosses her hair and grins. "Making love is my favorite way of tapping my energy."

Jean Luc leans over to kiss the back of her neck, then turns to me with a lackadaisical smile. "I agree. But what do you expect? I *am* French." He pulls the binoculars out of his pocket and hands them to me as if to close the subject for a while.

Chloe points to a box across the way, whispering in Jean Luc's ear something that makes him laugh, then nudges me and lowers her voice. "Speaking of which, do you *want* to see Eugen?"

"No," I say too quickly, and then reply, "Yes." I bring the binoculars up to my eyes to scan the crowd for his familiar profile.

Jean Luc puts his arm on mine. "You will see, it will all work out. Just keep your emotions flowing. That will keep you in the here and now."

"The here and now?" We turn around, not realizing Max was standing behind us, a look of irritation on his face. He waves his empty champagne glass in the air. "We are standing in one of the most expensive boxes at the biggest social event of the year and you are talking about esoteric trivialities?"

Jean Luc flashes his best doctor smile. "I know what you mean. I used to think that way." He turns and looks Max in the eye. "The here and now is all we have. Yesterday is gone, tomorrow is not yet here." His arm arcs in the direction of the dancers. "And I think the here and now is *magnifique*."

219

Chloe rests her hand on his lower back. "I second that. I *love* you. But there are times I don't *like* you." They both giggle.

Max puts his arm firmly around my shoulders and pulls me to him brusquely.

"I just want to love Annabel."

At first I freeze, wanting to pull away, but then I give way and let Max kiss me, trying to ignore the heavy fumes of alcohol on his breath.

Jean Luc quietly turns to whisper into Max's ear. "Listen to a woman's body language, my friend, and respect it. Then she will be yours. *Real love begins where nothing is expected in return*, I believe Antoine de Saint-Exupéry once wrote."

Max brays with laughter. "All women love to be told what to do. It's part of their character." Before Jean Luc and Chloe can respond, he turns to see who is walking into the box. "*Mein Gott* that's the head of our television station!" Handing me his empty glass, he saunters away, calling his name.

Just as Max leaves, the music announces that the opening ceremony is about to begin. This is what the Viennese do to introduce debutants who are no more than seventeen or eighteen years old to society, I was told. The crowd becomes quiet, the lights dim. Below, a long line of figures in flowing white gowns and three quarter white gloves pause, as graceful as fairies. Next to each young woman stands a young man, dressed immaculately in white gloves, black tails and white tie. The young men hold their partners as if they were dainty flowers that could be swept away with the slightest puff of wind. As the first lilting notes of the polonaise begin, the line of dancers move like one block of toy figurines, each couple twirling in perfectly synchronized tempo. As they swirl in unison, the white dresses billow outward like spinning tops as the dancers form geometric patterns of black and white; first lines, then circles, then squares. It is exquisite. Before I know it, the opening ceremony is over, and I hear the master of ceremonies call, "*Alles Walzer!*" The orchestra picks up the first waltz of the evening, and within minutes couples stream onto the floor, Chloe and Jean Luc following in their wake.

Chloe whispers something to Max on their way out of the door. He nods his head, but instead of returning to me, he continues to charm another member of the box, his glass waving enthusiastically above the crowd. I examine the fellow guests with a bored expression on my face. A few high flyers in the media world; heads of newspapers, one or two publishers, a trophy wife or two. I am painfully aware that my ability to perform small talk has disappeared with my bad eyesight. With a long sigh, I rake my eyes over the heaving crowd. It's going to be a long night.

6

A hand on my shoulder makes me turn. "So we found you at last."

Relief floods my face when I see Rudi's smiling face. He lifts my hand to his lips as Emma finishes air kissing a couple. The olive creaminess of her skin is stunning, the perfect backdrop for the jewelry dripping along her neckline. However unlike Rudi, who looks as if he were born for white tie, Emma looks lost in the swaths of beautiful material that make up her dress. When I kiss her I notice her shoulders tight and her eyes strained.

She flicks her nose in the direction the dance floor. "Did you see the flowers this year? How *could* they do something in such poor taste? The florist should be hung."

I was right, she is upset. "Are you all right?"

"Absolutely *fine*," she says with too much confidence to be believable. "Just one of those *compromise* moments. Sometimes I wonder if I'm not going to compromise myself to death." Nervously she fingers her diamond necklace.

Rudi ignores her comment. "I have business to discuss with Annabel," he says, extending his arm toward me. "And there is no better place than the dance floor."

As Max is nowhere to be seen, I look toward Emma, not wanting to leave her alone. But she waves me on, turning her back and whipping out a pair of binoculars. I take Rudi's arm and follow him out of the box. As we reach the floor, Rudi takes my right hand in his and puts his other hand on my waist.

"You look exquisite." His fingers twiddle the small pearl buttons that descend the back of my strapless satin dress.

The closer we get to the dance floor, the more people press at us from all sides. Finally we edge into the swirling crowd, where a huge mobile mass seems to be bumping happily in more or less the same direction around the room.

"Hold tight," Rudi whispers, and he launches us into the throng.

We are swept into the sea of dancers like a wave retreating from a beachhead. Dancing in the home of the waltz is an experience totally unlike what I had expected. I had imagined a Viennese ball to be a quiet affair of polite couples dancing genteelly with each other, but it is anything but that. The ball season is a time of frolicking, a time to let go of inhibitions and to be free. The crowd of bustling, talking dancers twirls and glides in concentric circles like a whirlwind of bodies. Tighter and tighter we turn, the dancers around me laughing as they gyrate into a swirling mass of skin and satin and starched collared sexuality. As we spin, I try to keep my head from whirling by focusing on one spot, but the colors whizz around me, overwhelming my senses.

"Emma has threatened to pull out her financial backing if I don't accept your input," he says as he rests his cheek next to mine. We bounce off another couple and I nearly lose my balance. "But I'm not one to easily cave into my wife's whims."

He pulls me toward him. My waist bends forward to meld into his; his hips slide slightly so that my hipbone rests gently against his middle, enabling his leg to press into the billowing satin emptiness between my legs. My body becomes an extension of his, my breasts press into his chest so close I can feel the outline of his shirt studs next to mine, we spin in tight circles, one-two-three one-two-three one-two-three, circling backwards, smoothly maneuvering through the crowd as he guides me with skillful pressure on the small of my back.

"You dance beautifully," he murmurs, pressing his cheek to mine.

I feel as if I were spinning on air. I enjoy the lightheaded feeling, glancing up to the ceiling to see the crystal chandelier sparkling all the colors of the rainbow. Rudi presses me closer to him, then twirls to the left, then once again, and we glide past a congested area of the dance floor and into an open space of evenly circling couples. I close my eyes and enjoy the sense of being part of something greater than myself, as if all of us are one great dance machine. The violins soar in the distinctive three-point waltz rhythm and I have a distinct feeling that we are encouraging the music to rise and fall with each twirl. Rudi bends to say something in my ear. I smell a mixture of eau de cologne and the rich but not unpleasant aroma of perspiration mixing with the starchiness from his collar, and a distinctive masculine scent emanating from his skin. I enjoy the synchronistic movement of our bodies, spinning round and round but our torsos are one, and I feel the heat between our bodies as if I am on fire.

A couple bumps into us, causing me to slip and lose my balance, but Rudi deftly catches me and pulls me tightly to him. "Relax! Balls used to be sedate affairs before the Viennese waltz was invented. Only married women were allowed to dance in such a loose and immoral style." He laughs. "Rather like modern dancing is considered today. I consider a Viennese ball is a time to explore the darker side of yourself. Last century, it was a time when prostitutes and ladies of society mingled." He throws his head back and laughs, his eyes sparkling. "This is more than a ball. It is a part of our *culture*. Johann Strauss wrote music for it, Gustav Klimt designed clothing for it, ballets and operas were written about it. Arthur Schnitzler wrote a story describing a masque ball held at a private house in the Vienna Woods where partners swapped with other invitees, so that they could act out their desires with total freedom. But the mask had to remain in place upon the pain of death, because members of the soiree met naked."

There is something in Rudi's behavior that makes me uncomfortable, but at the same time I feel the inexorable pull and excitement of the forbidden. My mind flutters on the notes of the music as I imagine the dance floor full of couples dancing naked. The racing of my heart is unbearable. I'm sure he feels my skin warming inside my clothes, the beating of my heart, the dizziness that entices me not to care about anything but this moment. His lashes, long and heavy, flutter against my cheek as he bends down to nuzzle my hair. He breathes deeply. "I have wanted to do that since we met."

"I thought we were talking business," I say, trying to clear my fuzzy head.

He ignores my comment. "Even buildings were created for our magical, mysterious balls. I must take you to the Hotel Orient." When I give him a questioning look, he adds, "My dear, it is known to all in Vienna, but never spoken of. It is said Emperor Franz Josef, Orson Wells, Nietzsche and many of Vienna's wild men frequented the hotel. Orsen Wells filmed a part of his classic film *The Third Man* there." His voice drops. "It's a unique part of Vienna's darker side. It was built at the turn of the century for intimate rendezvous of the upper classes. Rooms are rented by the hour. They are decorated with round beds and Jacuzzis and miles of red velvet."

Each time I spin, I become dizzier and dizzier, my senses intoxicated. The feel of his muscular body, the smell and the touch of his hands overwhelm my senses, causing me to close my eyes, but even there, behind my closed lids, erotic scenes in the Hotel Orient flash and beckon.

The music comes to an end. Rudi deftly twirls me in the opposite direction so that I can regain my balance, but my legs are still swaying with the music by the time we stop. I had never dreamed that such rigorous waltzing could be so erotic. In my head, the sound of the crowd twines and leaps with the lingering chords of the violins. I feel Rudi's breath on my cheek, warm and enticing and I see that he, too, is intoxicated with the moment.

"I've tried to keep myself away from you, but it's no good. I dream about you. Come to the Hotel Orient with me. We can even write it off as a business expense." He chuckles as if we both are sharing an inside joke.

Behind him I spot Chloe and Jean Luc standing on the dance floor, holding hands as they gaze into each other's eyes. I stand for a moment, blinking, unsure of my surroundings, trying to balance on firm ground. What is this feeling inside of me? Confusion. No, deeper than that. Boxed in, trapped. Anger! How dare he put me into an impossible situation. If I say no, I have to deal with a bruised male ego. If I say yes, I will betray Emma. No, I will betray Emma either way, because she'll blame me if she knows her husband made a pass at me. I close my eyes, feeling my heart flutter nervously in my chest. "And if I say no?"

"You wouldn't."

My smile becomes fixed. "Try me."

"I'll let you go."

My eyes shoot open. "I thought we were discussing whether or not I am going to include Wilhelm Reich!"

His eyes harden. "So did I, but Emma's silly attempt to blackmail me has raised the stakes."

As my mind races, trying to figure out how to extricate myself gracefully, I look at Rudi's face. I see a frustrated man behind his handsome facade. A man full of compromise, a man who has put lineage over his desires, marrying a woman for her money, doing the right thing, just as his father did. I see a very unhappy man. I think of Emma chatting about nothing with people she hardly knows, draped in the costliest of silk and satin and shod in jeweled evening shoes, spending fifteen years in therapy because she doesn't want to see reality, sacrificing her life to be with her children. The thought of Emma makes me close my eyes and pull my shoulders forward to protect my heart. My breasts strain against the bodice of my dress as a trickle of sweat runs down my back. And then, out of the blue, I think of Vandana and all my memories well up inside me, forcing me to *see*. I wasn't a victim, I just thought of myself as one. And I'm not a victim now. How do I get out of this? By staying in my integrity. Saying what I feel, even if Rudi doesn't like it. Taking a deep breath, I will myself to be calm and stare at the crowd of dancers, as if considering his proposal. Then, using every ounce of energy I can, I look toward the ground. "I can't, Rudi. I'm a friend of your wife. And I don't betray friends."

Rudi's eyes glaze. "Don't be a moral fool," he whispers, pulling me into his arms. His breath pants in my ear. "It won't hurt anyone."

His voice is too loud, it screams in my ear, echoing hollow promises and unfaithful lies. How did I get into this situation? Here I am, thinking I am going to discuss business and I'm having to defend myself. *Can't men think of anything else?* The lust in his eyes, combined with his desperate pawing, makes me cringe.

"Let's go back to Emma."

My voice falters as I am jostled into a corner. I take a breath, trying to clear my head as I reach down to adjust my dress, but before

I know it Rudi pulls me toward him. My shoes slip from underneath me and I fall into his arms.

"Who gives a damn about Emma," he whispers, leaning forward and flicking a tongue in my ear.

A look of disgust crosses my face as I feel the warm stickiness. I sense the ghost of Vandana looking at me, wondering what I will do, and all the memories from my former life with Eugen rise up from within. My spine sets, the sordidness of it all makes me sick. Rubbing my shoulder against my ear to clear the repulsive wetness away, I give a push, harder than I intended, which catches Rudi off balance.

"I do. And I'll tell her if you don't stop now."

Rudi tumbles backward, bracing his fall by grabbing onto my shoulders, his fingers pressing hard into my bare skin. Wincing with pain, I stand still, unsure what to do next. A long silence follows. When he looks up a few seconds later, my heart catches in my throat when I see his eyes.

"I'm pulling my backing out of this whole damn series. That will serve you bitches right for trying to blackmail me."

I peel his hands off my shoulders. My eyes flash. "You wouldn't."

He grins, mocking me. "Try me."

"You bastard. Max has been developing this series for years."

He coughs, trying to clear the emotion from his voice. "I'll lose money, but I can afford it. Unlike the both of you."

The atmosphere is stuffy; there isn't enough air to breathe.

"I'd rather quit," I say, closing my eyes as I try to calm my breathing.

"It's a deal. That gets Emma off my back." Rudi gives me a triumphant smile. "God you're gorgeous when you're angry. I'm sorry you are such a fool. The invitation stands. Call me if you change your mind." He pulls on his cufflink. "If I hear a word about any of this, I'll pull the plug. And I'll make a point of crushing any project Max wants to do in the future." The music changes. Rudi glances at his watch and gives me his arm, smiling coldly. "Let's wander over to the midnight quadrille, shall we?"

My hand acts as an umbilical cord between us as we skirt through the sea of jostling bodies pouring onto the dance floor. Everywhere around us, people are sorting themselves into parallel lines with men on one side, women facing them. We squeeze through a traffic jam of tailcoats and satin and waving arms and within moments, despite the crowd, we wiggle between Emma and Max. With a determined smile, Emma pulls Rudi toward her and gives me a hopeful smile. I look away, unable to bear the irony of this moment.

"Did you close the deal?" Max asks in a low voice. His hands feel clammy. Not wanting to answer, I close my eyes, preferring to focus on the notes of music swelling from the orchestra. I know this melody. It's the distinctive two-point rhythm of Strauss' *Fledermaus*. I put my hand onto my forehead; it is hot to the touch.

"What's wrong with you?"

"I'm sorry," I say faintly. I can barely stand. I'm still reeling from the consequences of our conversation. What will Max say when he discovers that I've quit? As a couple jostles into place across from us, I close my eyes halfway. Nothing feels real anymore. I'm in a surreal dreamlike state. My eyelashes form a soft halo around the room, making everyone undistinguishable, just flashes of colors, including the man who arrived with that tall woman on his arm. Of all the people in the room, what is it about his face when all the others blur together? The line of his jaw is delicate, more intelligent. His eyes have that blue clarity, they remind me of Eugen — I freeze, not wanting to believe my eyes.

It *is* Eugen. I blink and open my eyes to make sure I'm not imagining it. It takes me a few seconds to absorb the newness of his appearance without his beard and glasses. Our eyes meet. Eugen's eyes widen as he runs his finger under his starched collar. Max's hand tightens in mine, and I realize that he, too, has seen Eugen. In unison we look in the direction of the dance master, wondering if we have time to move to another spot. But it is too late. The midnight quadrille begins.

"Curtsy to Max," Rudi whispers, "then take his hand and walk in a circle with the opposite couple."

A feeling of déjà vu hits my consciousness as I curtsy to Max, then to Eugen, who twirls and deposits me back in Max's arms. My eyes veer to Max, then back to Eugen. Now that Max's hair is short, I muse, he looks different. My eyes wander along the line of his jaw. It's not so strong, and yet that, too, looks familiar. I take the scene in fully. Both men stand in front of me, dressed in identical jackets, shirts, ties. The same size, the same hair coloring, build and features. I gaze at one, then the other as we go through the mechanical movements of the dance. Although life has shaped them differently, giving one a more refined look, the other a rougher appearance, these two men have been made from the same universal cookie cutter. I gasp at the realization.

They could be twins.

Not knowing what to do, I keep staring at their faces. I register rage and betrayal on Max's face when I hold his hand. He hands me to Eugen, who glares with icy anger as he spins me on my way back to Max. Feeling like a fish caught in a school of sharks, I continue to dance, mechanically turning here, walking there, not knowing what to do with my eyes, avoid Rudi, curtsy again to Eugen, then back to Max's arms.

Max turns me the wrong direction, but Rudi guides the both of us back to our proper places in line. The music soars as the line moves three steps forward, three steps back, two steps right, two steps left, an English chain, taking the man's hand and swinging our partners, then the women's hands, round and round in a chain, we are women and men, dancing the dance of life. That is all life is, a dance. I can exchange partners but it is still the same dance. Different men, cultures, jobs, but to me, they are the same. I am dancing the same relationship as before. Relationship. With myself. With those whom I love. And with those I do not know. That's all life is. A dance.

My feet slide to a stop, and for a moment I watch the swirling colors and churning movement around me. When I was young, I used to love to put my eye to a kaleidoscope, turning it round and round as the crystals formed an endless mysterious array of shapes and sizes that entertained me for hours. Dancing in this glittering, oversized jewelry box, I feel as if I have been transported back to the kaleidoscope of my childhood. I gaze toward the ceiling, feeling the heat of the lights on my skin and watching the shimmering sparkles from the chandelier scattering across the crowd like miniature diamonds. It's beautiful, but something is missing. What's different about this? What has vanished from my childhood?

The answer swirls and twirls around me with each rustle of fabric, each touch of a hand upon mine, each whiff of perfume. It repeats like a soft drumbeat in synch with the rhythmic patter that our feet make upon the wooden floor.

Me. When I am present, everything changes. I am the observer, perceiving life through the lens of my kaleidoscope. When I bring myself into the equation, I'm like the eye of a hurricane, unaffected by the winds that whirl around me. As my eyes lower from the ceiling to the swirling movement around me, I drop deeper into my feet. I feel a little heavier, rooted and connected to the earth. This gives me a platform through which I can observe the chaos around me. Everything around me is moving, impermanent, shifting, but I remain the same. I am the one looking through my kaleidoscope, choosing my partner in the dance of life.

And I am dancing in the arms of the wrong man.

My cheeks flush, my heart stuttering in my chest as the dance ends. Breathless and dizzy, I close my eyes, feeling the rush of blood in my ears. There is nothing stopping me from leaving the room except that my feet are stuck to the floor. Eugen has seen me with Max. It's too late. He'll never want me back. Not after this. I feel him staring at me right now. I can't look at him, nor am I able to walk away. I might as well spend the rest of my life right here. I try to remember my anger when I left him, my outrage when I read those words in Vandana's diary, my fear of dying like her in a golden cage. It all seems so unimportant now. Everything seems inconsequential except for the warmth that I feel in my breast, radiating outward like a shimmering light that encompasses the entire opera house in its wake. And I know that it comes from his eyes.

7

Rudi gives Eugen a smile of strained grace as he shakes his hand.

"It's been a long time." With the smoothness of a snake, he pats Max on the shoulder as if he were a prizefighter. "Annabel and I don't see eye to eye on the series. You'll have to find someone else to present it."

All around us, I feel as if everyone has ended their conversations and raised their heads to look at us. As both Max and Emma look at me with dumbfounded amazement, I nod my head tersely before looking away. My body is trembling from head to toe. The utter hopelessness of my situation is more than I can bear. I try to focus on the music, the lights, the gay chatting, anything but the uncomfortable moment. But it doesn't help; time seems to drag on unbearably. To my relief, within seconds Rudi is gone, pulling his wife behind him like a wayward dog, swallowed in the crowd of colors, materials and movement, leaving me watching their retreating backs in disbelief. Max is so shocked that for once he has nothing to say.

Eugen's voice breaks the silence. "Vienna's self-appointed Don Juan. He's known to chase every attractive woman in town, whether married or not." He takes a neatly folded handkerchief from his pocket and pats his brow, then slips it smoothly into his pocket again. "I should know, he chased my ex-wife for years."

Although he is talking to the woman next to him, I know he is speaking to me. I stare dumbfounded at Eugen, opening my eyes wide as if that would help me understand the words I just heard him say. That's impossible, Eugen is Don Juan, I know it, he was always abandoning women. I know this, I repeat to myself, so it is true. As I think about it, my mind whirls back, searching my memory bank. I blink once, gazing in front of me but only seeing one face, Rudi's face, leering at me on the dance floor. A stone falls into my stomach with a sickening thud.

"Rudi chased Vandana?" I whisper. "I thought you were friends."

Eugen gives me a confused look. "We might have gone to school together, but that's a long way from being friends. No one in their right mind would trust a man like that. He's as ruthless as they come."

I've never heard his voice sound so bitter. I inhale sharply as I rake my eyes over the woman standing next to Eugen. She isn't even pretty, I tell myself, looking at a younger image of myself. How dare she be there, standing next to him? My mind taunts me with images of Eugen going home with her, smiling and joking with her as he once did, and then making love to her in his bed. Our bed. My face becomes so warm that I put my hand to my cheek. The rush of blood roars in my ears. Everything is too much for me, the room begins to spin and I close my eyes, reaching out to Max's shoulder, trying to keep from falling.

Suddenly, without saying a word, Max grabs hold of my arm and drags me along the carpeted steps. I hardly have time to struggle into my coat, and without saying goodbye to Chloe or Jean Luc I am pulled out the door.

8

My head is pounding by the time we get home. I collapse into bed, my ears still ringing with music and laughter and the rush and swirl of people. Under the duvet, I lie perfectly still, my eyes closed, my breathing slow and labored. Hopefully I can have some quiet. I need to make sense of all. One thing is clear; Rudi is one of the biggest bastards I have ever met. Why didn't I ask Eugen rather than taking his word that Eugen was a womanizer? I slide under the duvet, praying for sleep to come. I've lost my job, my source of income, Max's respect, and have only earned Eugen's hatred throughout the process. I have nothing. Through my closed eyes I feel Max looking at me. With each breath, cords of guilt wind themselves around my body.

The smell of alcohol wafts toward me and I feel Max shaking me. "Don't pretend to sleep, I know better."

I open my eyes and see Max sitting on the bed next to me. His muscular torso glimmers in the soft evening light. His glittering eyes make me want to cover my nakedness. I pull the duvet toward me, but he jerks it away, leering as my naked breasts are exposed. I draw the duvet up to my chin. "More happened tonight than you think. Let's leave it until tomorrow, can't we?"

He snatches it away from me, laughing as I scramble to cover myself. "I saw you with Rudi," he says, rolling on top of me. "He fired you, the bastard. Probably because you were trying to get him into bed."

I take the sheet to wipe the tears off as they spill down my face. "How can you think that? I don't flirt with husbands of friends of mine."

"You need to be taught a lesson, little girl." He pulls my hair back, pinning my head to the bed. Looking deep into my eyes, he bends down and kisses me hard, prying my lips open with his tongue. Before I know what is happening, I feel his knee wedge between my legs, forcing them apart, as his hand snakes its way down my belly. I wrench my head away from him, gagging as I try to catch my breath. I put my hands on his chest and push, but all Max does is laugh.

"This is fun," he says, taking both arms and pinning me to the bed. "I always did have a fantasy of raping a woman. Just enjoy it."

I feel crucified with my arms splayed on either side of the bed. I twist my body this way and that to wrench myself free. "I am going to scream if you don't get off me."

"Not if I kiss you," he says, fumbling between my legs. I feel something between my thighs and cry out, wishing with all my might that I could close my legs, but I can't. I feel open and exposed to the world.

Then Max thrusts inside me and something in me snaps, making me roar like a tiger. A blast of energy surges through me, as powerful as a cyclone, pumping my body with so much strength that I twist from his arms and leap out of bed in a matter of seconds. In a flash I fly into the bathroom and bolt the door.

Max pounds on the door, laughing. "Come now, it was a joke."

But I can't do anything, cannot respond to his calls, cannot talk, cannot see. My body feels as if it is on fire. I cry hot, angry tears, jamming a towel into my mouth to gnash its fibers, and then I scrub my body from head to toe, as if to cleanse myself of his touch. Soon Max gives up and goes to bed. I crawl into a small ball on the floor, remaining locked in the bathroom the entire night, silently sobbing. The next morning, the sound of the wind wakes me up. When I hear Max moving around the apartment, I unlock the bathroom door and cautiously look out. Everything looks normal, as if nothing happened. But something has. In me. Silently, I tiptoe out of the bathroom and throw on a sweater and jeans, then get my coat and scarf.

As I pull on my coat, Max emerges from the kitchen, staring at me with bloodshot eyes. I resolutely step back to keep the distance between us. The atmosphere is stifling me. The silence yawns between us like a crevice. Then, before he can say anything further, I slip out the door and am gone.

9

By the time I drag myself through the grounds of the Hotel Schwarzenberg the pounding in my head has lessened. The garden, with its rambling paths and stone statues, is covered with a heavy dusting of snow and laced with bird song. Stamping toward the hotel entrance I try to breathe but the tight belt around my chest is so tightly cinched I can only wheeze.

Chloe, her tawny hair curling every which way around her shoulders, pulls a white cotton bathrobe around her as she lets me in the room. The delicate strains of *Wiener Blut*, one of Vienna's most famous Johann Strauss waltzes, rises and falls in the background. Normally I'd be embarrassed to intrude on what is obviously a romantic weekend, but I am beyond caring. I need help, and now. I pull off my boots as Chloe pats the bed next to her. Jean Luc emerges from the bathroom, shaved and emanating clouds of eau de cologne. He gives me a kiss on the cheek and settles on the bed. Between sniffs, I tell everything, from leaving Eugen to quitting my job to Max's near rape. Finally it becomes too much for me and I burst into tears, my shoulders heaving. Everything I have worked so hard for is gone. My career dreams are shattered, and so are my hopes of living with someone I love. I feel like a raw pile of flesh, so pummeled by life that all I can do is sob in despair.

There is a discreet knock on the door and a smartly dressed waiter arrives with a tray piled high with croissants and canisters of hot coffee and milk. Jean Luc arranges the breakfast things with surgical precision, then picks up a croissant as if it were a delicate specimen.

"Do you realize that although the croissant is a French symbol, it was created by a Viennese baker to celebrate Vienna's successful rebuttal of the last Turkish siege in Europe in 1683?" He runs his finger lightly along the curve of the croissant. "The crescent is the symbol of Turkey."

What is he talking about? "*Kipferl*, the Austrians call it," I whisper as I crawl on the bed. "It means crescent in German." I lean into the pillows, holding my crumpled tissues tightly in each fist.

"Napoleon brought the *Kipferl* to France, where it was renamed the *croissant*, the French word for crescent." He raises a finger in the air. "But the French recognize the historical connection by calling *all* pastries, *Les Viennoiseries* — Viennese pastries. Lesson over." He smiles. "So how do you feel?"

I shake my head, appreciating Jean Luc's attempt to get my mind off of my situation. I wash a croissant down with a cup of café au lait. With each bite, the tight belt around my chest begins to loosen.

Chloe reaches out to hold my hand. "What do you need?"

"Time to think," I say quietly.

Chloe gets up to rummage in her suitcase, then pulls something out which she drops in my lap with a metallic clang. When I look down, I see it is her house keys.

"Get on a flight to London. Spend the weekend at my house."

"Have another Reichian session while you're there," Jean Luc suggests. "That might help you get a clear head."

I nod my head at the both of them. Within minutes I'm watching Chloe book the flight, putting it on her credit card with a wave of her hand to keep me quiet. Within fifteen minutes, everything is arranged. I stand up, feeling wobbly, but stronger than when I first arrived. I give both of them a hug.

"I need to go home and pack."

"We'll be back Sunday afternoon," Chloe says. "Be easy on yourself."

Jean Luc looks at me. "Let me give you one of the rules of life. When you think you've hit rock bottom, that is when magic happens. I don't know how it works, but it does. When you surrender, doors open to let something new in."

"Can you be more specific?" My voice sounds as weary as I feel.

"*Naturellement,*" he says. "Your spiritual path — "

"I'm not on a spiritual path," I snap.

He laughs. "We are all on a spiritual path, whether we want to admit it or not. But don't worry, the word spiritual doesn't exclude love." He looks at Chloe. "Loving a person can be the most wonderful path that there is." His eyes twinkle. "And I have news for you. After you left the ball I had a chance to talk with Eugen."

"He hates me," I say quickly.

Jean Luc gives me one of his best French smiles. "If you love him, let him go. If he returns, he was always yours. So focus on yourself. Trust that everything is working as it should."

"Do I have a choice?"

He shakes his head. "No, but it will be a lot easier if you surrender to what is, rather than what should be. Trust, Annabel. You'll see everything is working as it should."

March

The apartment is as silent as a tomb. There is no delicate click of Minou's claws to greet me, no blaring television or clang of pans in the kitchen. Just the sound of the furnace blasting heat through the large, empty rooms. With my heart beating furiously in my chest, I close the door and pull off my coat and boots as the midday sunlight filters in through the French windows. But even the feeble rays on my back feel cold and impersonal. I tiptoe into the corridor, hoping that Max is gone so I can pack and leave in peace. I stand with my ear cocked; waiting for a sound, any sound, but there is only silence. I breathe a sigh of relief and stride into the bedroom to throw a few clothes into my bag, then roll it into the sitting room to scribble a note to Max on my way out.

As I approach the sofa, I stop; startled to see an inert figure slumped on it. I inhale sharply, as still as a statue, as if remaining motionless will make me invisible. My shoes feel frozen to the floor. Hearing movement, Max looks up, dropping his hands over his knees like a lifeless doll. He must have been this way for hours. Our eyes meet. Cords of guilt tighten around my chest as I see his bloodshot eyes and his haggard look. The cords squeeze my chest tightly, making it difficult to breathe. I feel stiff and awkward, remembering when I begged Eugen not to go to London. I thought he was so cruel. Now

I've come full circle, knowing that it is just as painful to leave as it is to be left. Another chink in my resentment against Eugen falls away as I see Max's haunted look mirroring my own.

"Where are you going?" His voice is a gravelly croak.

I hunch my shoulders forward. "London. I need time to think."

"How can you do this to me? You abandon the series, and now you're abandoning me."

I wish he would be angry. It would be so much easier to leave if he were banging around the apartment, screaming like he normally does. Then I can be the victim, the violated woman, and turn and leave without a guilty conscience. To see Max this way makes my heart wrench in my chest. In his mind, I am the bad guy, I have abandoned him, both in work and now privately. I can feel his pain; it makes my mouth dry when I realize that I am the cause of it. My shoulders drop.

"My taxi's waiting."

His eyes take on a pleading look. When I make a move, Max lunges forward to catch my arm, his fingers tightening around my wrist.

"Don't leave. I — I don't know what got into me."

A bead of sweat makes its way down my back. I straighten up and take a breath. The words tumble out of my mouth like pebbles bouncing down hill.

"I want you to promise I will be paid for the work I've done. Please."

To my surprise, my request isn't thrown back into my face. If anything, it seems to deflate him more. He nods his head before letting it fall onto his chest, swinging forward as if his neck had been snapped.

"Anything. I'll do anything for you."

His acquiescence doesn't make me feel better. I look at him, heartsick to think that I have to leave like this. Then, before I change my mind, I turn and walk out of the door, dragging my suitcase with my leaden heart behind me.

2

London isn't the same without Chloe. The familiar squeal of the taxicabs, the cheerful banter of the taxi driver, the heaviness of the English coins in my hand, even the tourists snapping pictures of the live toy soldiers guarding Buckingham Palace no longer give me the pleasure they once did. I had been happy in this city. London, with its penchant for eccentrics and idiosyncrasies, trends and traditions, reminded me of an overgrown village. I used to love interviewing the latest financial scandal or gossiping with a girl friend over tea and scones at Brown's Hotel, enjoying the squeak of old stairs and tatty carpets, or strolling Green Park with its fleets of canvas lawn chairs politely waiting to be sat in.

But now, as I take out the keys to unlock Chloe's door, twisting the multitude of locks once, twice, three times and de-actifying the burglar alarm, smelling the emptiness in the hall and kicking aside the junk mail and flyers that have been pressed through her letter slot, I realize that something has changed. *Me.* Shivering in the cold, badly insulated house, I turn up the thermostat, then drop my bag in the hall and walk into the kitchen to put on the kettle for tea. Unable to accept all that I have lost, I feel ill at ease in London, uncomfortable to be alone in Chloe's house, and most of all, uneasy in my skin. Like a robot, I go through the motions of making a cup of tea, then collapse at the kitchen table, hunched over the steaming cup, blowing on the hot liquid. I am so miserable that I barely notice that the toppling piles of newspapers, manuscripts and articles have been swept away from the table. For the first time, the kitchen is clean and paper free. I had wanted her to do this for years, and now it no longer matters. Nothing matters to me anymore.

The rest of the day doesn't progress in a linear, normal fashion, but shapes itself against the emotions that rise in my breast, faster and faster until they spill out of my eyes and onto my lap. I flip through books, wander from window to window, write in my journal, take a nap on the sofa, but mostly I turn the scenario of the Opera House over in my mind, looking for ways in which I could have reacted differently, turned the situation around, altered the course of history for one minuscule moment. But all of the scenes end up like this one, with me crying on the floor in an empty house in London. Alone. Jobless. And nowhere to go. I considered myself successful, but everything that I have achieved has stemmed from fear. Fear of failure. Fear of abandonment. Fear of love. When I look within, I see nothing but fear. Fear. That's all I am. And I've spent most of my life running from it.

I wish there was someone to see, something to do, anything to take me from this hollowness. But there is no way out. I am at the end of the road, and there is one place to go. Inside. Making an appointment with Val was easy the first time, because I had convinced myself it was research. But now I know better. My arm feels like lead as I make the call, hoping against hope that Val is away, but she picks up and books me in. I hang up and collapse on the ground like a rag doll. The call saps all of my strength. Only when it is dark do I drag myself upstairs and fall into the dreamless sleep of the dead.

3

"Clothes off and on your back," Val says as I enter her office the next morning. I want to talk but she shakes her head and points to the massage table in the middle of the room. Obediently, I undress and lie on the table with an air of apprehension as she washes her hands and returns to the room.

Trying to make myself comfortable I take a breath, sighing as I exhale, but why has someone put a pile of bricks on my chest? My breath is short and shallow, my energy so low it is hard to breathe. A wave of irritation floats through me. Why am I doing this? I yawn for what seems forever. Resistance. I respond to the sleepiness engulfing me by taking a deeper breath, and another, and another. And — as quickly as it came, the drowsiness disappears. Suddenly my head begins to itch ferociously as if my scalp were covered with biting, irritating lice. More resistance. I reach up to scratch it with both hands, digging my nails deep into my scalp. As the itching fades, yet another feeling overwhelms me. Impatience. Edginess. Restlessness. It takes all my will to hold myself from getting up and walking away.

Instead, I breathe. Again and again, sighing loudly with each exhale. Val presses points on my spine, pulls my arms over my head, kneads here and there on my body. I breathe again and again, waiting for something to happen. Minutes pass. Then, so subtly that I have to check to see if I'm not making it up, I feel something. A tiny movement coming from inside. It stops, so I breathe into it. My body starts to jiggle as if it had been plugged into a light socket, light tremors working their way up and down my spine. I breathe again, and the tremors increase in volume, getting stronger with each breath.

Stop! my mind screams, hunkering down as if for a war. I freeze. My body is being taken over by something stronger than it, causing my feet to jiggle as a rippling begins to work its way up my torso. My muscles tighten in a frantic attempt to keep my body still.

Part of me is aware of my mind trying to make sense of it all. Recriminations bounce in my head like wildly clattering beads in a baby rattle. My parents. Max. Emma. Rudi. Eugen and Vandana. I'm being judged by the most cruel of inquisitors, *me*. I *knew* better than to fall in love with a man loved by another woman. My heartlessness in getting Vandana out of my life makes me sick. Just the thought of her brings waves of self-loathing and guilt. I feel the belt around my chest tightening, tightening, as if it wants to squeeze all the life out of me. I try to breathe, but my body contracts against myself. And this is when the awareness strikes. Satan, hell, sins aren't *out there*. Hell is right here, in my body. I am much bigger than the tight energetic suitcase that I am in. I am encased in a prison of fears. Fears disguised as judgments, self-righteousness and blame. And no one constructed this prison but me.

"Keep breathing!" Val's voice sounds as if it is coming from far away. I squeeze my fists together when another bolt of energy rips through me, causing my chest to lift off the table, and then slams down as my feet kick upward. Then my body begins to flap — yes, flap — like a fish out of water. I don't have time to be frightened, I can barely keep myself from exploding into all four corners of the room, and soon I have lost contact with Val. I am bathed in sweat; tears squeeze from my shut eyes, saliva dribbles out of my mouth, but I don't care, I can't care, I can barely keep up with this never ending hurricane of wild, powerful snaking energy that has turned my body into a piece of leather fluttering in the breeze.

You are faking this! my mind screams as it flings against my skull. By now, the cacophony of sensations ripples like a snake, up, up my neck — and wants to come out my mouth. I tighten my lips, but the energy is stronger than my muscles, parting them to let a voiceless scream burst from my throat. I snap my jaws shut in horror.

But Val has another reaction. "Scream!" she cries, hopping around the massage table, pressing and prodding my flailing limbs. "Go with it!"

I can scream? In that moment I drop all resistance, and with a last distraught shriek, my mind releases its clutches on me, and I tumble backward into my abyss. Like a horse leaping out of a starting gate, a scream bursts out of my mouth with such power that it makes my entire body quiver in aftershock. But once it is out it continues, one long steady note diving and twisting in the air, filling the four walls of the room with a sound so primitive, so powerful that it needs no words to express itself. I scream, really scream, like I have never done before, a scream of rage, a scream that makes the incessant roaring of a hurricane seem tame, a scream that blasts beyond the room, beyond the office, into all of London and into the heavens. I scream and scream until I no longer have any voice, it gurgles in my throat as I cough and gasp for air, spitting phlegm into a tissue held in front of me, and then I scream some more. I scream with pain, I scream with anger, I scream with frustration at being *here*. In this world of pain. Injustice. Poverty. Death. I am endless, but I live in a limited world. The pain of living is excruciating.

How long will this take? my mind bleats anxiously as it bounces wildly back and forth with each jerk of my head. *It will end when it ends,* responds a soft voice that comes from deep within me. That soft voice isn't bouncing but floating peacefully, observing my writhing body from within and from without, as if it were able to hold both at the same time. It is much larger, richer, more embracing than my mind. *Ahh, my soul.* It is where my sanity lies, because it is not dependent upon anything *out there,* not what anyone else says, not anything that happens, but radiates from within, like a candle flickering brightly inside my heart. My scream becomes clear, the pitch dropping to one solid bellowing sound, so deep that it seems to emerge from a place so old that I can feel roots and moss and swinging vines and can smell the rich black soil that is the source of everything that grows from the earth. I scream, twenty minutes, thirty minutes, an hour, I can no longer tell how much time has passed. Perhaps I will scream forever. It doesn't really matter. Nothing matters but feeling this scream, embracing it, owning it, becoming it. And when this happens, the note is long and clear, filling the room with my sound, reaching deep into the depths of my lungs for a power and volume that would make any opera singer blush with pride.

When the scream ends, echoing against the walls of the office, my body gives little shudders, twitching here and there, and then silence. And it is then that it happens. I surrender. Waves of forgiveness flow through my body, along my muscles, up to my chest, and with an internal sigh, the gentle energy of forgiveness eases the cinches on the invisible belt squeezing my chest as easily as a lubricated bolt sliding open. I gulp for air, amazed to feel my breast raising and lowering with ease. Gallons of air float effortlessly in and out of my lungs, and I can feel my chest rising and falling with each breath. It is as if my breath were breathing me. The mindless prattle is gone, replaced by clarity of thought, a feeling of the moment, embracing everything around me in a love that is so soft and so powerful that it brings tears to my eyes. Effervescent bubbles of love and gratitude wash over me as my body hums and purrs like a generator. I feel accepting of the world, accepting of myself. I am, at my source, unconditional love. Everything else — fear, sadness, even aggression — is a denial of *who I am*. This is the message at the bottom of the abyss. There is nothing else but love.

I hear Val's voice near my ear. "How are you?" The sound echoes in my skull, as rich as caramel. I didn't remember she had such a lovely voice.

I open my eyes and blink, trying to get my bearings. Above my eyes, the ceiling is swirling with bright colors that sparkle and flicker in every direction.

"The ceiling." The deep timber of my voice surprises me.

"That's energy," Val says quietly. "It's beautiful, isn't it?"

I could spend hours looking at it. I turn my head and see that she has bent down next to me. I can see all the details on her face as if they were under a magnifying glass. She radiates beauty. Her lips part into a smile.

"And how do *you* feel?"

Her question takes me aback. I can feel the edge of myself expanding beyond my body, far beyond the room, radiating like a crystal into the depths of the universe. Connected to everything that there is.

"Me? Oh yes, there *is* a me." I run my fingers along my leg just to make sure. It feels foreign to the touch, as if I have run a marathon, and have come home with another body, one that is so much more open and flexible. I turn toward the ceiling to lose myself in the colors as tears roll down my cheeks. Tears of gratitude. For life. For love. Because it is one and the same.

"Drink lots of water. You'll need it after a marathon session like that. You were running *a lot* of energy."

So that is what Jean Luc meant when he said running energy. "But all that jerking and screaming — is that *normal?*"

My question makes her laugh. "The energy running through you hit your blocks and armor. So your body needed to jerk and twist to accommodate it."

"And my throat?"

She smiles. "There were a lot of screams locked in there, weren't there?"

I twist my head around, noticing how flexible it is. "Is my armor gone?"

She laughs. "The armor around your chest opened when you surrendered. But your armor around your throat is so thick it will take time. Don't worry about it. As you saw, egos will fight to the death before they let go." She helps me sit up.

I look around, feeling as if I have slipped on a new body. Everything feels so fresh, so immediate. "Why can't you remove all of it?"

"I don't want to turn you into a mad woman."

I give her a questioning look. "You're exaggerating."

She shakes her head. "I'm afraid not. Your body is very wise, far more than your brain. And so if it has created a block, there is a good reason for it. Armor does two things. First, it individuates you. It makes you different from others. Secondly, it protects you. If you were brought up in an environment where your parents fought, or imposed their ideas of what is right or wrong onto you during a time when you should have been experimenting by making your own choices, you start to armor yourself. It shuts others out, and keeps you intact. You close down, only hearing or seeing what you have been taught is safe. Life becomes survival."

"So I created armor to protect myself."

She smiles. "Right! *You* did this to yourself. No one did it to you. You consciously limited yourself, but as you take responsibility for your life, you can open to other parts of yourself that have been cut off." She helps me on with my coat. "So screaming isn't important, but *what it releases in you* is."

"Is that why you didn't tell me to scream?"

"Everyone releases differently. The important thing isn't how far you go, but how much you can integrate it into your daily life."

"I had so many questions to ask you." My voice trails. I take a deep breath, relishing the air swirling in my lungs. "Can you come for tea tomorrow? Jean Luc and Chloe will be back."

She nods her head as she helps me off the table. Spontaneously, I give her a hug before making my way with a firm step toward the door.

4

By the time I return to Chloe's, it is midday. The session has made me incredibly thirsty. I drink about a gallon of water, and, suddenly aware of how tired and sweaty I am, I wander upstairs and run the water for a long, hot bath. Sinking into the steaming water, I close my eyes in mindlessness, absorbing the sound of the dripping faucet, the sharp tingling smell of pine bath salts, the silky fluidity of the water caressing my skin. Time and time again, I take a deep breath and exhale, listening to the masses of air releasing from my lungs. I marvel at the openness in the cavernous expansion in my chest. The extraordinary thing about this process, I realize, is that it runs backward. Only when my body armor *eased*, did I recognize that I *had* it. As if I were walking around with bricks on my shoulders. If someone had pointed out to me that I am carrying bricks on my shoulders, I would have responded that I like things this way, thank you very much. Only once the bricks were gone, could I feel the open space they left. I splash the water with my toes, trying to formulate how the process works. There is no way I could have forced the armor to release. It is a process of surrendering. Trust.

I finally give up trying to figure out what happened and lie mindlessly in the water. Slowly, without even becoming aware of it, an overwhelming sadness overcomes me. I splash a little, not liking what I'm feeling. It's sticky and black, like mud. *Why can't this water wash away the feeling of dirt?* Memories of the night of the Opera Ball invade my pores, forcing me to remember my feeling of helplessness as Max jammed his knees between my legs. My muscles contract as I close my legs together, my hands fluttering in the water as I try to push the thoughts away.

Lisa's voice floats in my memory. "Have you ever seen your *yoni?*"

I remember being horrified. "Why would a person want to do that?"

She had shaken her head, as if I were a wayward child. "So many women have never dreamed of looking at what is their greatest treasure. The *yoni* is the most exquisite part of your body. It is where you receive your greatest pleasure, from yourself and from your partner. It is where you give birth. Is there not anything more sacred than that?"

"It is dirty," I had answered.

"So many women think this way. She is a part of your body. How could anything God has created not be perfect?"

Her words had looped around my brain, searching for a pigeonhole so that they could be compartmentalized, analyzed and understood. Round and round they went, but what she was saying just didn't fit with how I was taught to see the world. My vagina? You don't show pictures of such a thing. That just wasn't done.

As if previewing my reaction, Lisa pulled out several manuals on subjects such as Sacred Sexuality and The Divine Feminine. "Do you realize that we are living in a very fundamental era?" Before I had time to answer, she continued, "We are still heavily influenced by patriarchal thinking. When you were young, women were still considered the inferior race. But that's not true. Our ancestors in the matriarchal societies — 20,000 to 30,000 years ago — revered women because only they could give life. Men respected women's innate wisdom. Women are connected to the Earth — Mother Earth — in ways that men can only envy."

She sat back and smiled at my reaction. "It's something to realize that we are far more prudish than many of our ancient cultures."

I felt as if she was taking a hammer to my most precious beliefs, blasting them away one by one. And yet, somewhere I already knew this. I remember Lisa opening a book and pointing to a page showing hundreds of diagrams of the *yoni*. I stared at her finger running along the pictures as if she were showing me her favorite flowers in a plant catalogue. She had explained that Japanese, Chinese, Indian, even Arabic cultures worshiped the *yoni*. It wasn't just a body part to be classified for fertility or disease.

"Look at how unique she is. As individual as a person's face."

I found myself leaning over the book to study the pictures. I couldn't help it. *Yonis* are different as the petals on a flower. Some were brownish, others pinkish, some large and fleshy, others narrow and thin. To my amazement, I learned that the Arabic culture has thirty-eight classifications for the *yoni* alone. Honored and worshipped, it was the source of life itself, and therefore studied in great detail. Her looks, her taste, and her pleasures.

"The *yoni* has been regarded not with shame, but with awe and reverence for thousands of years," Lisa had explained as she closed the book, indicating the end of another lesson. Then she gently looked at me, one woman to another. "It's quite a shock to realize how imprisoned you have been by your own society's beliefs, isn't it?" It was a very touching moment.

Not long afterward I remember sitting naked in front of a mirror, as Lisa had instructed, in order to look at her for the first time. I squeezed my eyes shut at first, and then slowly opened them. It was a wonderful moment. I felt as if I had thrown off a cloak of humiliation that I had been wearing and hadn't even known it. Shame is a human invention, not divine.

But now, as I lie in the warm water, I sink beyond that layer of disgrace, deeper into myself. The drip of water in the bathtub sounds like a clock. I feel as if I am falling into another world rather like Alice in Wonderland. I am still in my world, feeling warm water and smelling bath salts, but behind my closed eyes, I am in a place as real as my tiled bathroom in London.

In this Alice in Wonderland world, the three dimensional rules that have governed my life don't apply. Time isn't linear, but can be manipulated. I can speak to the characters, and they to me, as if by extra sensory perception. I see three figures standing in a neutral hazy background. I am all of these people. The first, a toddler at the age of three, with sparkling blue eyes and curly golden hair, is me when I was young. There I am again, aged thirteen, awkwardly thin with long blond hair and buckteeth and glasses. The last 'me', an immaculately dressed Barbie doll with long blond hair, is twenty-one. These three aspects of myself face me and smile expectantly. After an initial moment of surprise, the observer 'me' speaks to the three girls, not with words but with my mind. *Let's make friends.*

Instantly the hazy background disappears and a new location comes into focus. Surprised, I see that we are all in my childhood bedroom in the Midwest, with its pink carpets and cheerful wooden beds placed in front of the large window overlooking a perfect green lawn. I feel the smoothness of the starched pink tartan bedspread underneath me as we pile on the bed together. With the relaxed familiarity of a slumber party, we gossip and chat amongst ourselves about relationships and parents. The main topic of our conversation, however, is how difficult life was.

I feel a catch in my throat. Something happened back then, something that was terribly, terribly wrong. It is so frightening that it has been hidden from me all of these years. Uneasily, I bend down to the toddler and ask gently if it was she. She shakes her head and spreads her chubby arms wide, her smile bright and trusting. With infinite tenderness, I embrace her little body to my breast, discovering that in my Alice in Wonderland world, bodies aren't fixed like in ours. As I hug her, she melts into me like honey. Now her bright and smiling self is within me.

With trepidation, I turn to the second me, the awkward young teenager. But she isn't so easy to question. She turns away from me, holding her thin body as rigid as a board, curving her shoulders forward in shame.

"It's you, isn't it?"

The tenderness in my voice makes her look at me from behind her rigid self-defense, and she nods her head curtly yes. Her confusion and shame makes my stomach flutter. A trapdoor opens within me, and the feelings of the sexual abuse that occurred in my youth spill forth. I begin to cry as other memories begin to float to the surface, fleeting glimpses here and there. A friend of the family. I am alone. I want to cry out, but am forced to keep quiet, to accept whatever happens to me, even if it means allowing his fingers to wander where I don't want him to go. The part of myself that is observing the scene expresses no judgment or shame, only offers explanations to why I act in a certain way now. *No wonder I can't say no.* I had to do what I was told, that is how I was brought up, and he was a friend of the family, after all. And now, thirty years later, I look upon this poor, lonely, misunderstood girl, and am able to feel the pain and guilt she could not understand. I open my arms wide, so wide that she collapses sobbing into my arms. I pull her tighter toward me, but instead of the resistance that comes from two bodies touching, I feel a soft give and look down to see her disappear into my heart. She, too, has become incorporated into me, but with a bittersweet aftertaste. I will always be wounded. But it is now a wound that will begin to heal.

Looking around, I see the last me, the Barbie doll, stand up from the bed and stretch as if she doesn't have a care in the world. But I can now see behind her air of defiance. I scan her face with concern; but I can sense only a flickering shadow of myself. Already by that age, I was numb. It was what I had to do in order to survive. As I smile, holding my arms out with tenderness, her defiance fades and she falls into my arms, crying tears of shame. And she, too, disappears into me. Warmth spreads upward toward my face as I feel an explosion of heat in my beating heart. The air fills with a softness of rose petals; the water caresses me like a lover, washing the feeling of dirt away. There was never any dirt, only memories of a situation that was terribly, terribly painful.

As I open my eyes, I become aware that the bath water is lukewarm and my cheeks are wet with more than just steam. As I get out of the bath, I feel a deep sadness, but I feel whole. A newer, gentler sense of myself has been birthed.

5

The sun filters onto the long flat green, highlighting the mottled peeling bark of the large plane trees that line the wide alley that divides Hyde Park into two. There is nowhere more beautiful than England when the sun is shining, and suddenly its appearance is like an invitation for everyone to pour into the park to enjoy the fresh spring day. Twittering birds fill my ears, the happy shouts and laughter of children and dogs yapping as they race in circles on the lawn, the clop clop clop of a sleek bay hunter and rider returning to the stables in Buckingham Mews, sounds so loud and crisp, as if they were being projected by a microphone. My eyes drink in the trees and grass and blue skies that dance around me. I never knew there were so many shades of green; the dark green of the park benches, the pale soft green of the grass stretching in front of me, the intense flashes of green in the buds sprouting from the brown branches of the trees, the very essence of life springing from a long dark winter. I feel that if I look close enough, the scene around me would be nothing but millions of dabs of color in a pointillist painting.

Life has taken on an immediacy that is outstanding. Waves of gratitude swell with bittersweet sadness. I had been sexually abused when I was young. Over and over, the sentence repeats in my mind, but I can hardly believe it. Now I can understand my attempts to protect myself from men 'attacking' me. Not knowing that this wound lay deep within me, it only compounded the older I got, and then I began to punish myself for acting as I did. It makes sense that once my fear belt released, memories would surface. My only job is to accept and feel them fully.

Back at Chloe's later that day, I eat a huge take-away from the local Indian restaurant, then clean the kitchen and prepare for Chloe and Jean Luc's arrival. As I wash up the cups in the sink, another wave of tears washes over me. My situation hasn't changed — I'm still alone, jobless, and don't know what will come next — but it doesn't frighten me as much as it did. Although I still feel raw, there is a trust that things are unfolding as they should. I crawl into bed just as the sun is setting and for the first time since Vandana's death, I fall into a deep, untroubled sleep.

6

With Chloe and Jean Luc's return, the house comes alive again. The telephone begins to ring; footsteps clomp up and down the stairs, an aria from Puccini's *La Boheme* lilts from the library as Chloe and I prepare tea in the kitchen, complete with crumpets and cucumber sandwiches. My body doesn't feel quite the same twenty-four hours after my session. Although I slept for more than twelve hours, I feel as if I have been run over by a truck. My voice is gone; I ache everywhere, especially around my upper chest and neck. Trying to keep my mind off the pain, I focus on cutting crusts from the brown bread and place thinly sliced cucumbers on the buttered slices.

"Normally your kitchen looks as if a bomb has gone off in a paper factory," I say as I arrange the sandwiches on a platter and sprinkle watercress around the edges.

Chloe laughs as she swirls hot water in the teapot to heat it. She doesn't have to comment about my hoarse voice, she knows I had a session with Val.

"Jean Luc says he prefers to see the marble tabletop when he eats."

I give my friend a tired smile. "Jean Luc is still the only one?"

Chloe fluffs her hair playfully. "Nearly six months now. I think I've broken my own record. I wasn't even that faithful to my ex-husband."

She laughs and goes to the sink to pour the water out, then places two teabags, one for us, one for the pot, in the teapot and pours boiling water inside. "Ignore everything your soppy old friend Chloe told you in the past about using men before they use you. Because she was wrong. After all these years, she's learning what it is to love."

"I can't believe what comes out of your mouth these days."

Jean Luc pops his head into the kitchen, a suit bag hanging over his arm. "Val called. She'll be over in a minute." He stops as his cell phone rings. Picking it up, he shrugs and blows us a kiss, then his face disappears.

As my eyes follow him dragging his suitcase up the stairs, the penny drops. "He *lives* here, doesn't he?"

Chloe flicks her tawny hair away from her face as she gathers the tea things on the tray. "You could say that."

I never thought Chloe would risk settling down with one man, and that makes me happy. I gather the tea things and follow her into the hallway. By the time we enter the library, Jean Luc stands up from lighting the gas fire, which roars to life. Crackling merrily, it lends a soft warm glow to the late afternoon grayness.

As I butter the hot crumpets and pass them around on plates, Chloe settles next to Jean Luc and begins to pour the tea. "Something doesn't make sense. Why did you quit your job? You weren't fired were you?"

Like a bad dream, I run through the scenario at the opera ball as if to make sure that it really happened. The scene shoots into fast forward and I see Rudi pulling the plug on the project, destroying Max's career — I rip the film out of my inner projector and throw it away. I already have one disaster on my plate with Vandana; I don't need to ruin another person's life. "No, I wasn't fired," I say quietly. "I quit."

Chloe drums her fingers on the edge of the sofa and narrows her eyes as she looks at me through her long eyelashes. "Just like that."

I find the strength to nod my head. "Just like that."

"Annabel Jones, don't lie to me. You kiss goodbye to a year's salary and the chance to kick start your career? Can you manage financially?"

I look away. "I'll be OK."

Chloe hands me a cup of tea. "Will you stay with Max even if you aren't working with him?" Jean Luc puts his hand on Chloe's arm as if to say, *slow down!* but that's Chloe, she bores right to the point, and if you don't like it, then tough. That's one of the things that irritates me most, and at the same time, why I love her so.

"I don't know," I say quietly.

Chloe looks at Jean Luc, who looks down at his hands for a moment. The silence in the room is unbearable. Jean Luc looks into the fire.

Just then the doorbell rings, breaking the atmosphere with its ringing chimes. Jean Luc jumps up to get it. Blankly, I look toward the fire, and then I feel a hand on my shoulder. It's Chloe. She pulls me onto my feet, and then does a remarkable un-Chloe-like gesture, wrapping me in her arms as if I were the most dainty of flowers. It feels surprisingly intimate. Our bodies melt into each other. Any traces of self-defense disappear, leaving me blubbing uncontrollably in her arms.

It is only when I have blown my nose and had another cup of tea that Jean Luc and Val enter the room. As I throw the crumpled tissues in the fireplace, I realize that they discreetly had been talking in the kitchen to give Chloe and me time together.

"I've been showing Annabel the wonders of a Tantric hug," Chloe explains as they walk in.

Jean Luc grins and opens his arms to me. "Want another?"

"Uh, no thanks," I say, collapsing on the floor.

Val rests on the large overstuffed chair by the fire. "Don't be surprised if you feel fragile," she says softly. "After you open like that, your body will contract again. All sorts of things may happen, muscle pain, cramps, even uncomfortable memories or feelings might arise."

I close my eyes, staring into the blackness behind my eyelids. There it is, the face of the poor girl with the long blond hair and her slightly buck toothed grin, her long legs gangly like a colt, her shoulders hunched forward in shame. I can still feel the tightness in her heart, the shame she carried in her breast, as heavy and cold as a stone. It was her fault. It must have been her fault, or it wouldn't have happened. After all, he was a grown-up, and everyone knows that grown-ups know more than children. My hands start to shake and I knot them between my legs, right there where he touched me. I hear a voice coming from far away.

It's Chloe. "What's wrong?"

I open my eyes and blink at my best friend. I try to shake the image from my mind, but it won't work. It hangs like a neon sign in my brain, blinking red, waiting to be exposed. Can I tell her my secret? In front of Jean Luc and Val? What will they think of me? I open my mouth and watch as the words come tumbling out.

"I remembered," I say softly. "I — I was sexually abused." My words end in a whisper. I hope no one can hear the trembling in my voice.

Chloe's eyes go moist, and I can feel that she wishes to hug me all over again. "Oh poor darling. That explains a lot!"

"Now you know why it isn't healthy to remove all your blocks," Val says quietly. "You already have enough to deal with, don't you?"

Val crosses her legs and studies me for a moment before giving a sidelong glance to Jean Luc. It's hard to imagine this tiny woman had the power to manage my flailing body for three hours. "You know I was going to attend that Tantra seminar in Austria over Easter. I rented a lovely chalet near Salzburg. But I can't go. It's going to cost a bomb to cancel the entire thing." She turns and smiles. "Why don't you go in my place?"

Before I answer, Chloe flings her arms around Jean Luc. "I'll take it for the rest of the ski season." She turns to me. "That way, you can go anytime. Perhaps you'll let Jean Luc and me spend a romantic ski weekend or two."

Considering that Chloe likes skiing as much as she likes getting up early in the morning, I know she is doing this for me. Her gracious generosity overwhelms me. And so, for the umpteenth time, I burst into tears.

7

The heaviness of Vienna embraces me as the plane lands. Unlike London, where the first signs of spring are in the air, Vienna is still in the clutches of winter. It is grey, in-between weather. Bits of grimy snow lie dumped between the cars, a cold, angry wind whistles through the streets, causing people to hold their hats as they totter along the cobblestones. Winter is not yet over, spring is not yet here. It is a time of waiting.

There are no flowers or waiting arms at the airport, only an empty space where Max would have been. With no deadline to meet, no job to go to, I take the train into the town center, rolling my suitcase along the pedestrian Graben, not knowing where to go, not wanting to go back to Max's apartment. And that is how I end up standing in front of the *Trafik*, watching my arm open the door so that my eyes can feast on his colorful prayer flags and my nose can inhale the reassuring lavender and orange smell as if it were my last gulp of air. I peer in to see the *Trafikant* standing as usual behind the counter, his eyes closed, a faint smile on his face, his rounded hands resting, palms together, on the countertop in front of him as if he were praying. When he hears the little bell jingle, his eyes gently open as if he were emerging from a deep and peaceful sleep. His face crinkles into a warm smile when he recognizes me.

"*Guten Tag!* I haven't seen much of you. Been skiing?"

I have to clear my throat before I answer. "London."

He stretches his hands over his head, then looks up and carefully adjusts one of the Tibetan prayer flags that have come loose from the ceiling. A man in a leather jacket squeezes in, demanding a package of cigarettes. Herr Dietmayer theatrically wrings his hands.

"Just ran out. Try the news stand by the cathedral."

Grumbling under his breath, the man pushes out the door.

"I don't need a newspaper," I say sheepishly, "I wanted to say hello." Embarrassed, I glance at the shelf where packages of cigarettes ought to be.

Herr Dietmayer follows my gaze. "I'm supposed to supply cigarettes, but I can't sell something that I know will harm people's health. So I stick to smiles and newspapers." His eyes close halfway as he looks at me. "What *have* you been up to?"

His look makes me feel like a rabbit caught in front of the headlights of an oncoming car. I look behind me, but I am the only one in the shop. I turn back with an uneasy look on my face. "What are you looking at?"

"Your energy — it's wide open."

Although I can see his comment was meant as a compliment, my eyes begin to water. What is wrong with me? Before, I never cried, now I can't stop. How ridiculous it would be to cry right here, in front of a shopkeeper I hardly know.

"Cry, cry, my dear," he says as he takes a package of tissues and gives one to me to dab my eyes. "You are crying because you are open. That's it." He hands me another tissue as if I were the most fragile of porcelain.

I look to one side, pretending to glance at the postcards. "I lost my job, that's why I went to London. And while I was there, I had another Reichian session." I turn back to look at him. "Perhaps that is why my — my energy is different." I still use the word a bit too self-consciously.

Herr Dietmayer nods his head as a small smile spreads across his face.

"I thought you wouldn't be working for long. Once a person decides to do inner work, things sort of work out to give them the necessary time."

I can feel my chin dropping. "You *knew* that I would lose my job?"

He laughs. "Oh no, no, not that. But I know how powerful the energy of transformation can be. It's like Kali."

When I give him a blank stare, he digs around in the eclectic collection of postcards next to the cash register. While waiting, my eyes fall on a small poster advertising a Tantra course in the Austrian lake district a few hours west of Vienna. That is where Val was going. Tantra in Sound of Music country? The image of the von Trapp family hitting pillows in syncopated rhythm in Lisa's apartment bounces across my mind, making me smile involuntarily. I give Herr Dietmayer a sidelong glance as he pulls out a postcard of a black woman with a long, lolling red tongue and wild eyes.

"Haven't you heard of Kali, the Indian goddess?"

I shake my head as I stare at the postcard in front of me. The woman is remarkably ugly. She wears a long necklace of human skulls around her neck. Circling her waist is a skirt of human bones. She is dancing on headless figures that writhe under her feet.

"This is Kali," he explains, his eyes sparkling with pleasure as he gazes at the postcard. "She is a Hindu goddess who decapitates anyone who isn't strong enough to meet her integrity. Isn't she magnificent?"

I glance at the lolling tongue hanging from her mouth. "She's repulsive!"

"Because she incorporates the dark side of the feminine. Am I right in thinking that you have a difficult time holding the wild woman in you?"

I look again at the card. "Does she, um, scream?"

He chuckles when he hears my question. "Does she ever! She is no nonsense, clear integrity, absolute equality, and perfect compassion. Kali sees things as they really are. She is fiercely loyal. Western religion is frightened of the Kali aspect in women, and has tried to get rid of it, because once a woman has integrated her Kali, she can never be dominated again."

"A woman who has found her Kali can never be dominated again?"

"That's right. Kali leads to wholeness. Because a woman who hasn't incorporated her Kali isn't whole."

"So if I can connect with the Kali aspect of myself, it can give me courage?"

"The courage to do what?" he asks softly.

I feel tears brimming. "To leave a relationship I know isn't working for me. To leave a man who says all he wants to do is love me."

"Oh my, my," he says gently, handing me a tissue in preparation for the overflow. "That is hard." Herr Dietmayer continues to nod his head; his silence encouraging me to speak what my heart is saying and I don't want to hear.

Tears begin to flow down my cheeks. "I can't let guilt run my life anymore. I have to stick to my truth, even if it hurts him. There's room in my heart for one man, and that's not Max." My voice turns heavy as I think of Eugen. *And even he is gone.*

I am overwhelmed by the wave of shame that seems to well up inside me. I take a big gulp of air, feeling my breast rise up with the oxygen that flows into my lungs. "I used him," I say, more to myself than to anyone. The realization makes me start, and for a second I clamp my mouth shut, but it opens of its own accord and keeps forming words without any input from my brain. "I used him," my mouth says, without shame, but simply telling the truth. "I used Max as an escape from a situation I didn't know how to get out of. And I hate myself for that." Surprised by my freely flowing mouth, I look at Herr Dietmayer with wide-open eyes. It is only after a second that I remember to close my mouth.

"If you used him, then he used you," Herr Dietmayer says quietly. "Remember you are always with your equal in a relationship. So don't let guilt keep you in it." When I don't say anything, he whispers, "True compassion is hard." He smiles gently. "But most of all, you are learning to be compassionate with yourself. Once you see your dark sides, you have a lot more compassion for the dark sides of others. And then you can make a choice. Not from fear, but from awareness. Even choices that are painful."

I look down at the counter before glancing up to see his deep brown eyes looking at me. "It's hard to realize that I'm not the goodie-goodie I thought I was."

He nods his head. "I know very well what you are talking about." He looks beyond me, focusing his gaze in the distance, but I know that whatever he is looking at is much further away than the confines of his little temple shop. I take a moment to study him. He is wearing a soft beige sweater, worn and comfortable. On his left hand, I spot a small golden ring that looks Asian in appearance. And then I see them, tiny scars on his hands, like whip marks in his bronzed skin, as if he had been caught in a windstorm.

"Shrapnel," he says quietly.

I start, embarrassed to have been caught staring at him.

"I fought in Cambodia," he adds. My job was to *kill* bad guys."

My mouth drops open. Images of The Killing Fields spring to my mind. I look down at Herr Dietmayer's soft hands, and wonder how it is possible that those warm, grandfatherly hands could have once held a gun. "But you seem so peace loving — "

"I know," he says with a quiet and firm voice that clearly indicates he doesn't want me to ask anything further. A shadow flickers across his eyes, and I feel as if the energy in his little temple shop has become heavier. "But you've been honest with me, so it is only fair that I be honest with you. I can talk about shadow because I know it intimately. I was as tough as they came. It took a cosmic kick for me to see another way of thinking."

"A cosmic kick?"

"To realize that there are no good guys, there are no bad guys. Just people, doing the best they can. But the more our actions stem from love rather than from fear, the more aware we become. Shadows are nothing more than places in ourselves that we haven't looked at, parts of ourselves that might be too frightening for us to accept. The more of ourselves that we know, even those frightening or uncomfortable places, the more awareness we have, and therefore the larger we become. We become more compassionate and loving, even when making decisions that are painful."

A man comes in to buy a newspaper, and instantly the atmosphere becomes lighter, so much so that I almost wonder if I hadn't imagined our conversation a few moments earlier. I stand back to watch him exchange a few pleasantries as he sells a newspaper, then the customer, with a friendly wave, goes on his way. Herr Dietmayer's smile is back on his face as he turns to me. "So you have some time on your hands. What will you do with it?"

"I don't know." I look into the distance. It feels strange talking intimately with a man I know so little. No, it feels good. I don't know if I have the patience to wag my mouth and saying nothing, just to pass the time anymore.

"Have you considered taking a break to reflect on your situation?" Herr Dietmayer asks, handing me yet another tissue.

I take it with a quick thank you. "There's a Tantra course in Mondsee in a few weeks. I know I could go if I wanted to."

His eyes start to sparkle as he taps the poster on the side of the wall, the one I had been looking at earlier. "It's one of the best there is. I know the organizer well. Remember Jesus spent forty days in the desert? What about forty days in Mondsee?"

"I'm forty. I want to start a family. Even if it is a family of two, if you understand what I mean. But perhaps I've waited too late."

"You're right on time. Forty is when most women begin to deepen into themselves. Before that, they think they know everything." Herr Dietmayer pauses as if considering something, then flips open the countertop in front of him and walks toward me. I'm surprised to see that he is limping hard. "Just in case," he says as he pulls a card from his pocket. "Call me any time."

My eyes wander down his leg. Something looks wrong. Herr Dietmayer nods his head with a bittersweet smile.

"Amputated from the knee down. It took years for me to recognize it was the best thing that could have happened."

I am about to say something, but he smiles firmly, as if an iron gate has descended and I know not to press further. As he hands the card to me, he closes his hand over mine and gives it a squeeze before closing the door.

8

Max's apartment has turned into a squalid bachelor's dive in my absence. Now that the filming is underway, he is gone from early morning until late at night. I am asleep by the time Max comes home, and he is gone before I wake in the morning. The only words we speak turn immediately into accusations, Max calling me egotistical and I responding by calling him a rapist. I think both of us are relieved we aren't working together. It would be hell to try to keep up a professional front.

With mixed feelings, I learn that Max was able to pull in one of Austria's most well respected news reporters to fill in for me. I can feel my bruised ego wishing for revenge, hating that someone else is mouthing my script in front of cameras while I mope at home. I turn my cell phone off, preferring to use the silence to think about my life and what I want to do with it.

The few days pass quietly. I go for walks along the Danube Canal and wander the city, keeping an eye on the angel statues looking down upon me. But they, too, are silent, as if waiting for a decision to be made.

9

I haven't looked forward to a Tantra session as much as this one. As I slide into the seat next to Lisa's desk, I inhale the sandalwood incense, surprised how much I enjoy the smell.

She lets me finish my story as if I were telling her the weather. "I suspected sexual abuse. Remember I asked if you had a happy childhood?"

"You *knew* it?"

She speaks softly. "Many women suffer sexual abuse as children. What do you expect when we live in an era that labels sexuality as something dirty? Denial, denial, denial and the buck stops here. With frustrated men who take it out on little girls who don't know better."

I sit, absorbing this new information quietly. "I'm starting to heal a wound I never knew I had."

She takes a sip of tea. "Not only that. The cycle of victim and abuser is starting to unravel. It's about time."

"What about when I tried to make love to Max? He called me a prostitute."

"*Do* you feel a prostitute when a man finds you attractive?" Lisa asks softly.

I nod my head, not liking her question.

"So you feel a victim. And a victim chooses a man who abuses her."

The truth makes me very, very quiet. "And if I find my Kali?"

"You will *need* the energy of Kali, the energy of anger to transform. Clear anger is an affirmation of self. Think of it, you really mean what you say when you're angry. You are affirming who you are."

"I never thought of anger in this way before."

She scribbles a few words on a pad of paper in front of her. "If you are going to take a forty day retreat and go further into yourself, you're in for a rough ride. Many people won't like the direction you are heading, and will try to punish you for it. You are going into territory that hasn't been explored by many people, so your mere presence to them will be threatening. What is important is that you find *your* way."

"Max says I have become the most egotistical person he knows."

"He's right. You are egotistical." She grins. "And that's good. You have to be self-centered to find your integrity."

I give her a questioning look.

Lisa finishes writing and puts her pencil down. "Most people can't say no. So they do something they don't want to do, then they resent the time and energy they give. They are angry with the person who asked them the favor. But remember, *it isn't what you do; it is the intent behind your actions that counts.* So if you do something you don't want to do, you will radiate resentment. That is counter-productive."

"I have to be self-centered?"

"No! I'm saying be clear."

"But if I start to change my behavior, people won't like that."

"Right. People who are used to getting their way with you will find you irritating. They won't like that you now say no. They may even get angry."

275

"Why do I want them to get angry at me?"

"I see. So you would rather do something, then get angry with yourself for doing it. That can cause illness. Tell me. Is guilt a big thing in your family?"

"Guilt!" I cry. "I feel guilty because I used Max. I feel guilty because I plan on leaving him." There goes my mouth, telling the truth again.

Lisa shrugs her shoulders. "Let me walk you through guilt."

I keep quiet, knowing another lesson is coming up.

Lisa drops a pencil on the table. "Let's say I want to eat a cookie. I get up to go, but you ask me to stay with you. I have three choices. I can stay with you. Or, I can tell you I'm hungry, I want to get a cookie and I will be back. Or I can listen to you and say, I'm sorry, I didn't realize you wanted me to stay. I am hungry, but because I love you, I will stay with you." She looks at me. "All three cases are correct. There is no judgment in any of them. But you are being clear."

"That seems straight forward to me."

"But in reality, most people, especially women, tell their husbands that they will stay, but inside their minds they play a victim cassette, grumbling about all the times they can't do what they want because they have to please their husbands, their husbands are always so demanding, etcetera. Over time, that resentment comes out. How many women have you heard husband-bashing?"

I rest my head in my hand, amused. "A lot. Most, in fact."

"But it isn't the husband's *fault*. He has the right to ask the question. *She* needs to learn her boundaries, and have the courage to say no." She gets up from behind her desk. "If there is one cardinal rule I can give you, it is this: *Never do anything because you want to please someone. Do something because you want to, or not at all.*"

That turns everything I was ever taught on its head. If I didn't do a lot of things, what would people think of me? I like to be charming. I like to help people. That is a fundamental part of my personality. And now she says that I should become a sour-faced dour who doesn't help anyone? I'm still mulling over that sentence when she pushes the chair out from the desk.

"So tell me now how you feel about Max. Right now."

"I know he didn't mean it."

Lisa's eyes flash. She leans forward. "You can tell yourself these lies, but don't waste my time. Be honest. What do you feel about him?"

"I am being honest!"

Lisa brings her face right next to mine. "No, *honest*. It's a strange word to you, isn't it? You tell people exactly what you think they want to hear. Getting people to do what you want is called *manipulation*. A more polite word is *charm*."

My face turns bright red. *How dare she!* My mouth opens and closes as I try to hold back the thoughts raging in my head. They loop around like a broken record, becoming louder and louder in my brain. The room feels so hot I break out into a sweat. I rub the back of my neck, the perspiration making my hair moist, then wipe my hands on my trousers as if to remove the guilty sweat from my hands. But then I don't know what to do with them so I bring them in front of my mouth, as if to hold the words in, but it doesn't work any longer, my lips part and from deep within me, a river of words erupts like lava.

"He should be so lucky," I fume. "That I left Eugen for *him*, an angry upstart with a ponytail. He thinks he's such a great lover, but he's crap. All muscle and thrust." I clamp my hand over my mouth as if to stop anything further coming out.

She crosses her arms and smiles. "Good. There's your anger. And that's your truth." She gets up from her desk. "The session's over. You have some important decisions in front of you."

I close my mouth again, but my jaw is slack, there is nothing inside except for pure exhaustion. I'm horrified that someone has heard what is really going on inside of my brain, rather than the filtered version that I have always presented to the world. I have been humbled. Although it smarts, I know it is for the best.

10

Aschermittwoch
Ash Wednesday

The heavy wooden door beckons, pulling me toward it. There are hundreds of doors like this in Vienna, dark, mottled with age, offering peace and quiet to any passerby who needs time to ruminate, reflect, wonder how on earth life got to be such a mess. All streets in Vienna seem to have a church at one end or the other. Some are hidden, offering only a deceptively small door onto the street, so that when I walk in, I am taken aback by the cavernous interior. Others can't wait to bombast me with their towers and domes, eagerly ringing their bells so loudly that everything — the neighboring streets, buildings and even passerby — reverberate under foot. Some remind me of jolly round babushkas, their fat curved cupolas and squat onion domes dressed in cheerful pastel colors, others are as solemn and long faced as an old spinster, their heavy spiky steeples intent on piercing a hole in the sky. There are Evangelical churches, Catholic churches, Orthodox churches for the many people who wandered to Vienna from all parts of the Austro-Hungarian Empire. They reflect the many styles, peoples and traditions of this multi-cultural mélange of peoples. Perhaps this is why Austria is so heavily Catholic; it is on the border with the Balkans, it was filled with Jews and now overflowing with Turks, its religion constantly under threat from people who fiercely believe that their God is the only God that matters.

The door of the Jesuit church opens into a light and airy interior, as cozy a church as you can find in this city of baroque palaces, dressed in an orgasmic splash of colors. It's *Aschermittwoch*, Ash Wednesday. It's a time to kneel, to pray, to ask God's forgiveness. The sung mass has just begun, and I hear the sumptuous strains of Brahms's *Ein Deutsches Requiem* as I stand at the back of the church, hesitating whether to stay for the service. The pews are packed with people of all ages and sizes, attending the church service as if they would attend a museum. Inside it is as cold as outside, my breath smokes like a dragon into the still air. I bow my head to listen to the music, letting the sounds of voices lilt in harmony around my ears. I watch the priests in bright robes holding a golden chalice to the light, the sunlight flickering through the windows, putting on a show of beauty for everyone.

Seeing that there is no room in any of the pews, I head toward one of the elaborately carved confessionals. Here, no one will be able to see the tears streaming down my face. Tiptoeing carefully on the marble floor, I enter the enclosed space and collapse onto a bench, breathing in the musty smell of frankincense and candles. I feel as hollow as the space surrounding me. *Please show me the way,* I plead behind closed eyes. *I can't stand this pain any longer.* I wait, hoping the heavens will open up and God will come down to tell me what to do with clear numbered instructions. I try to make a pact with God, telling him that if things work out, I will be a good person, I promise. *Penitence.* I wait, hoping for a response, but I am met with cosmic indifference and a cold seat.

And then I get it. There is no one to bargain with. I'm not haggling with God, I'm making a deal with myself. I peer out of the confessional and look at everyone in the pews. That is what everyone here is doing — bargaining with God — as if he is a benevolent person who judges whether we are good or not. But God doesn't care one way or another what I do. God, I realize, is that energy that I felt during the Reichian session. It was so powerful that I know all I could take was a mere drop; only a sliver of its potential, and that was enough for an entire lifetime. It was so powerful, so strong, and yet so benevolent. If it had a voice, it would have said *So you want to open yourself to me? Then prepare yourself for my awesome power. Because I am everything, the dark and the light, the good and the bad, the day and the night.* It was so powerful that no one person can hold it all. That is God.

Forty days in the desert. Forty days. Leave everything behind, without knowing what will show up. No guarantees. No job. No man, no marriage, no commitment. Forty days. Learning to trust what will come as perfect.

When I leave the church, the angels and cupids from the rooftops gaze benevolently down upon me. I can feel their blessing every step I take.

When I get back to the apartment, Max is gone. It is empty and bare and depressing, the grey weather taunting from the closed windows, and everywhere I walk, I imagine I hear the click of Minou's claws on the wooden floor. The feeling of abandonment is everywhere. I stand at the window, staring unseeingly at the Danube Canal for a long, long time. Then I slowly get up, my body as heavy as lead, and start to pack. There is nothing to keep me here any longer. I know it is time to go.

April
Mondsee, near Salzburg

The lake glistens like a dark sapphire in the sunshine. The sky is blue and welcoming, white clouds with grey undersides float over still waters. I swivel my head right and left, easing the tension in my shoulders as my rental car bumps along the road that winds away from the lake. Glancing at the map next to me, I look up to see a chalet nestled in the hillside. It is just like Val described. The old farm building has wisps of hemp sprouting from between the rough-hewn wooden slats, a wooden fire bell on the slate roof that looks like a miniature birdhouse, and a balcony. On the top floor, a second terrace peers out from under the overhanging slate roof. Both are lined with window boxes overflowing with flowers.

I park, opening the window to breathe in the intensely fresh air. It must have rained earlier this morning; everything looks fresh and scrubbed for spring. A small cherry tree at the edge of the property flutters its blossoms in the air, cows moo in the field across the road, the smell of freshly cut grass drifts on the breeze from the farm down the road. Smells that tell me that winter is over and it is soon to be summer, of endless days spent doing nothing but lying on the grass and enjoying the warmth of the sun. I rest a moment, letting the quiet of the countryside ease the tension from the past few weeks.

Moving out under Max's reproachful gaze was one of the most difficult things I have ever done. His anger, cloaked under a blanket of unspoken accusations, hung in the air from the moment I woke up until I fell into bed at night. *How can you do this to me* whispered the silence between us, causing me to drop my eyes as I waded through the guilt-ridden atmosphere, trying to decide how to best go about the dirty deed of leaving. Guilt dripped behind me with every case I packed, oozed in my footsteps as I cleared out my office, squished underfoot as I trudged back and forth to my hotel room in town. My leaden gaze had to sweep over an area once, twice, three times before registering what was mine and what was his, but in the end, nothing mattered except leaving, and even that took all my strength. Everything I had once considered so dear — photo albums, books, presents, even Minou's carryall — was left behind. Through sheer exhaustion, I willed a new life to begin, one that would begin clean and clutter free.

And so it is. A wooden gate hangs precariously from its hinges, beckoning me to walk through it. I lug my suitcase along the path, pulling out the enormous key Val sent me, then open the door and walk inside. An eighteenth century wall clock, its pendulum ticking a slightly lopsided tick tock, bongs a greeting as I walk in. The coziness of the room is almost overpowering. Everything is wood, from the beamed ceiling to the benches that line the white plastered walls. Rag rugs in dappled green lie scattered across the rough wooden floor; a smattering of comfortable furniture rests beneath the contented gaze of pale green shutters. The low set, deep windows offer me a view of the lake from wherever I stand, and when I press my hand against the glazed tiles of the corner stove, I feel they are warm. Someone had been thoughtful enough to have turned on the boiler, and the idea of a bath seems too good to miss. And so, after pulling out my cell phone to text Val to say I've arrived, I retreat into a long, steamy bath in the stillness and quiet of the countryside. Then, with a twinge of apprehension, I turn off the light. My forty days have begun.

2

Over the next week, the days float into each other. I get up, go for a walk, make a cup of tea, sleep, and sit. Mostly sit. That was Herr Dietmayer's suggestion, together with writing in the leather-bound journal that he gave me before I left. Herr Dietmayer was overwhelmingly supportive of my decision to take a retreat, and encouraged me to sign up for the Tantra course. As we sat having coffee near my hotel, I told him how my guilt over Vandana's death had propelled me into Max's arms. He told me I should be grateful that Max helped me along my path. Soon, I'll learn how to be grateful for everything that happens to me.

"I don't care about a path," I replied. "I want to get my life in order."

He slowly rubbed one finger over the back of his hand, as if to smooth the fine white scars from his skin. "If your life is in order *inside* you, it will soon be in order on the outside. No matter what happens to you, everything is always perfect."

I impatiently pulled my earlobe. "Life is anything but perfect. One look at my life disproves that theory."

"It's not a theory," he answered, smiling gently. "It's a question of perspective. *The world is your mirror.* However you see yourself, you see the world. From my perspective, everything is as it should be." He laughed a deep throaty laugh. "Wouldn't you like to view the world that way? It makes life so much more enjoyable. And it creates a lot less tension in your body. Your back will feel better, too."

I rub my lower back. "How could you tell?"

"Don't worry, it's a common thing when you go through transition. Gurus often ask their students complaining about backache, *what are you holding back?* In other words, it is a part of you that doesn't want to let go of a situation, or an attitude. Your energy has stopped there, and is creating pain, which is your body's way of bringing your attention to something."

"But Max has back problems," I said, frowning. "I don't see him changing."

"The pain doesn't have to do with transition, but the emotion that is behind it," he explained. "With back problems, the emotion is often anger. So *are* you angry?"

I gave him a sheepish smile. "Until a few months ago, I would have said no."

He patted my arm. "Great! That's the first step, owning your anger. Recognizing it isn't a negative emotion. In transition, it's a friend. Then learning to let it go responsibly. Keep going, and you'll find the moon, and not get caught up with the finger that points to it."

When I gave him a confused look, he put his cup down so that he could use both hands to explain. "It's a parable. The moon is where everyone wants to go, but a lot of people get caught up with the finger, rather than focusing on *where* it is pointing."

I still didn't understand.

"Once again, it's not *what* you do, but *how* you do it. If you wanted to, you could go the religious route and become well versed in one or all of the world's religions, quoting the Bible or the Koran or the

Torah or the Vedas." He smiled. "Or you could go the New Age route, talking with angels and learning about energy vortexes and listening to channeled voices. You could learn to *live in the now* and *be, not do*, meditate, repeat mantras or sit with a shaman. Or the yoga route, mastering breath and body, or the healing route, learning medicine or acupuncture or any one of the healing modalities. Or the self help route, learning to visualize or be coached or undergoing psychological analysis." He paused to take a deep breath. "But it won't bring you to what you are seeking."

"I'm seeking?"

He gave me a quizzical look. "Of course you are. You're a seeker. People like you have been around for thousands of years. You want more than just to live a good life; you want to know why you are living here on earth. And you're just realizing that external things such as a man or a job or a family won't give you the inner peace you crave. So now you have begun to seek *inside* yourself. And that is a good thing, because that is where you will find it. But don't get caught up on the tools."

"Tools?"

"*Tools.* Don't think that following a spiritual path will help you anymore than self-help or psychology or Reichian work, religion, or even Tantra. These are all tools. To be used and then discarded when it is time to move on. It's not the tool that matters, but what it opens in you."

"Even religion?"

"*Especially* religion. Religions are just bowls that hold spirituality. The problem begins when you confuse the bowl with what it contains. Consciousness is far too *vast* to be contained by anything man made, like religion or language."

"That sounds sacrilegious."

287

"Not at all. Both language and religion define the limits of a culture's reality. And they fulfill that purpose magnificently, as long as they are allowed to grow, which unfortunately doesn't occur in religion as often as it should."

"You think *religion* should be discarded too?"

"I'm not saying anything should be discarded!" he answered. "But so many people get side tracked because they never look where they need to, and instead focus on the tools. All I am saying is that *you have to do the work*. Period. Because that is why you are here. To know *who you are*. But that is what most people avoid all of their lives." He stretched his legs in front of him and smiled at me.

"I've already done some inner work," I said, still not sure if I was using the word correctly. "Reichian work. And Tantra."

"That's why I'm giving you this pep talk. Now take these tools and use these forty days to drill deeper into yourself. Because you already have what you are looking for." When I gave him a doubtful look, he nodded. "It's all there, in you. What's in between you and whatever you are looking for is your inner garbage. It takes a lot of self-forgiveness to get through that. It's a path of fire."

"Come on, nothing can be that bad."

He gave his head a little nod. "I'm afraid it is. It will feel like," he stopped as if searching for the right words. "Like willingly sinking into the mire." He gave a little chuckle, as if recognizing how melodramatic it sounded. "The only way out is *down*. Just keep sinking, and ignore what your mind will be screaming. Keep sinking, down, down into yourself, accepting and feeling everything that comes up. Your mind will go wild, telling you that you will be stuck forever, but it isn't true. Trust that everything that is happening to you is part of the process, and eventually you will fall inside." He smiled. "It's worth it."

I shrugged my shoulders and looked at my watch. It was time to go. "I don't think I have much choice."

He chuckled. "No one goes into their inner garbage whistling and smiling. The only reason to go there is because you can't go anywhere else, right?"

I nodded my head. "That's exactly right. I have to do it."

"So go, and go deep. Because the faster you fall, the sooner you'll get through."

"And how will I know when I'm there?" I could hear the tentativeness in my voice, but I felt silly asking questions that I already should know the answers to.

"There isn't a *there*," he said, but when he saw my face, he smiled. "When you don't have to ask. You'll know."

I remember leaning forward toward him. I had to ask one more question. I dropped my voice. "Tell me," I said, dropping my voice to a whisper. "How do you do it? How can you be happy? How can you be —" Against my will, my eyes glanced at the space where his leg should be.

He shifted his weight. "Happy with a body like this?" He reached his warm, grandfatherly hand forward and patted my hand before ordering the bill. His voice sounded like a murmuring brook. "It comes from accepting myself. All of myself. The good parts as well as the bad. That's why I can accept the world as it is. I *know* that everything is perfect. Just as it is." He paused to pull out his wallet, waving away my offers to pay. "Some people use the expression *waking up* — but that has so many different connotations I prefer to use the word *presence*. Being present with what is."

"The extraordinary ordinary?" I said hesitantly.

"That's a lovely term," he answered. "Whatever you want to call it, for me it is *embracing*, rather than *discarding* life. As it is, in its entirety. That's when the ordinary *becomes* extraordinary."

That is when he gave me a small leather journal and a pile of books that he considered useful. Told me to take my watch off and to find my own rhythm in life. And be prepared. Because once I started looking within, I should be primed for my unconscious to heave a big sigh and let rip.

3

I gaze out from the balcony, warming my hands with a cup of hot steaming green tea. Wisps of fog loll on the lake, playing hide and seek with the sun as they stretch their fingers to tickle the lower edges of the hills. Far away on the opposite shore, the grim presence of the jagged granite mountain face rises in majestic silence. I am surrounded by primary colors. Bright red geraniums. Intensely green grass. Dazzling blue sky. Rolling green pastures tumble down into the lake, the color of which changes from grey to emerald to turquoise in minutes. Snug, tidy farmhouses dot the hillside; tractors industriously turn the first mowing. A deer cautiously makes its way across the field and bounds into the woods.

I wake when I want to, sleep when I want to, eat when I want to, read books Herr Dietmayer gave me. No, consume books. The floor by my bed is littered with my favorites, *The Power of Now* by Eckhart Tolle, *Awareness* by Anthony de Mello, *Loving What is* by Byron Katie, *Spiritual Enlightenment* by Jed McKenna. Modern philosophical books by Ken Wilber and Gary Zukov, books on sexuality by David Schnarch and David Deida and Margot Anand, books on healing and health by Barbara Brennan, Carolyn Myss, Christine Northrup, fictional books by Paolo Coelho and Aldous Huxley. They tell me, over and over again, exactly what Herr Dietmayer told me. With each book, my perception of the world shifts, opens, and my mind searches for more. These authors are all friends on the path, reassuring me that I am not alone in my quest. They give me a different understanding of the world that I live in. I ponder new ideas as I go for walks, sleep and sleep and sleep some more, feeling the years of stress unwinding in me.

But curiously, the more I unwind, the more irritated I become. The less routine I have, the more I implement rules. Ten times a day I look at my watch as my inner dictator orders me not to think, not to sleep too long, and to keep busy. I have to hold myself back from doing something, going somewhere, anywhere, but *here*. I find an urgent need to balance my checkbook, do my laundry, panic about my jobless state, plan my future, flick through television channels. If I busy myself, time flies, if I sit, my mind goes ballistic, making me look at my watch as if I were afraid I was missing something important. If only I could get out of here. Out of this house, no, out of Austria, no, out of Europe, no, out of the whole damn world — no, I realize with horror, *out of my skin*. Inside me, a million wires that have held my personality together for so long begin to unravel, leaving me in freefall.

From deep within my gut a low growl emerges. I jump up and start to pace the floor as a combination of hatred and anger and despair bursts within me like a boil. Hatred of myself, hatred of this country, hatred of its people, hatred of my friends, hatred of my family, hatred of the world. I never knew I possessed such self-hatred. A car drives by, and if I had had a machine gun, I would fire at its tires. A dog bark interrupts my silence. If he were near me I would strangle that mutt. *I'm a nice person*, I tell myself through gritted teeth. *I don't have these types of feelings.* But it doesn't work. Rage encompasses my entire being. I can understand Hitler, feel Attila the Hun's cruelty, embrace Stalin's policies in my soul. *I am a nice person I am a nice person* I repeat desperately, but by now, I no longer believe it. As I drop into the slime of the mire of myself, I want to kill, maim, and torture anyone in my sight. I want them to scream with pain and to fall on their knees and beg for redemption. I want to open my mouth and let a stream of obscenities out, so foul that the air will turn black. All the injustices of the world, all the killing and dying and starvation and heartbreak and despair, is within *me*. I feel disgust for everything. But my main object of disgust is *me*. Not knowing what to do with myself, I try to lie down, but the sheets feel like rough wool, I toss and turn and scratch, as if I could physically remove this leathery skin that has encased me. Herr Dietmayer's words float into my mind. *Keep sinking, down, down into yourself, accepting and feeling everything that comes up. Trust the process.* Oh oh oh I think as I circle the house like a caged animal, looking for something, some way, to get out of here. It is as if the process is gnashing and chewing me alive, burning through layer after layer of fermented rubbish in my mind.

Hour by hour I sit while my internal battle rages. I turn off my cell phone, I can't sleep, I can't walk, I can't eat, I can't read. All I can do is feel pain. Pain. Such pain. Why do I want to live in a world of pain? *This* is what Herr Dietmayer meant when he called it a path of fire. Vaguely I recall Vandana saying the same thing. I hiss internally as I march into the kitchen to grab an enormous bottle of mineral water, throwing the farmer outside the window a hostile look for good measure. Sitting down at the wooden table, I pour the water into a glass, watching as my shaking hand causes it to run over the cup and dribble onto the floor. For a moment, I watch the water spreading onto the table. Vandana also talked about a path of fire. *My cup runneth over with love.* My mind freezes. For a moment, the two images don't seem to match. Vandana and love. Love and Vandana. My mind clunks and whirrs like a lawn mower that has a stick caught in it, then stops violently, as if something has jammed the blade. I squint at the water.

Could Vandana have gone through this?   I remember her banging on our apartment door, begging Eugen for forgiveness. I had thought it was a woman's wiles to get him back, and pleaded with Eugen not to answer. But now, I'm not sure.

My eyes fixate on the glass in front of me. It seems so clear, so fluid, so purifying. Water. I down it in one go, feeling the liquid descending into my abyss. It feels good, so I drink another. And another. *Keep drinking, keep drinking* an inner voice says. What did Jean Luc say? *E-motions. Energies in motion.*

This is what is happening to me! This is an emotion. It was always within me, festering like a wound. By feeling this — all of this — I'm cleaning it from my system. In a flash of insight, I understand people who commit suicide, feel empathy for those who torture, maim and kill because of fear. This spot is so dark, so vile, that my body wouldn't let me go there until now. It would have been physically unbearable, because I would have identified with it, rather than let it flow through me.

I down two more glasses of water as if I've been thrown a lifeline. By now, my belly is bloated but I continue to drink, glass after glass, feeling that each drop of water is pulling me through the abyss. Over the next seven hours, three gallons of water go through my system. Time after time I go to the bathroom, knowing that the water has gone through me, purifying me. So this is what Herr Dietmayer meant when he said *there are no good guys and there are no bad guys. People just are.* Before the words didn't apply to me. I was a good guy. And people like Hitler were evil. But now I know that's not true. I have everything inside of me, the killer and the victim, the torturer, the rapist. I am all of that.

The mental battle ends in the afternoon, leaving me weak and exhausted. I get up and take a long shower, letting the water rinse the outside of my body like it has rinsed the inside. Too tired to flip through books, too tired to even sleep, I lie on the bed, my arms and legs splayed like da Vinci's Vitruvian Man, feeling energy purring up and down my torso. My body feels lighter, freer, more flexible and at the same time, stronger. Never again can I judge someone else for their actions, because I have been everything. No one is bad, no one is evil, they are only living life from that horrible place that I experienced a few hours ago.

I take a deep breath and find that I can breathe into my chest. Surprised, I try to delve into that sticky pain again, searching with my internal vacuum cleaner. Surely the black stickiness can't be gone. But it is. That rage is no longer part of me. So this is doing the work. No wonder people don't want to do it. But my God, when it is over, the feeling of lightness is so powerful, so free, that it makes everything worth it.

Over the next thirty days, I fight many mental battles. Some take longer to blow through than others. Every battle has its own strategy, and I use all the tools I have learned to get through them. Deep in the forest, where I hope no one can hear me, I scream like I did in my Reichian session. I pound pillows representing Max, Eugen, my parents, the world, and me. I babble endlessly in order to loosen the muscles in my mouth so that I can say things I always wanted to, but never dared. I write for hours on end. I dream a dozen dreams a night, dreams of feces and hollow, lifeless corpses. Sometimes the battles leave me so weary that I collapse on the bed in a daze that lasts for hours. Every time I emerge from a battle, I hope it is the last. But then another emotional wave rides up and I am off.

As each battle comes and goes, it becomes easier. The less I struggle against the process, but flow with it, the faster it goes through me. And with each battle, the lightness inside me increases. My vision becomes clearer, my sense of smell more acute, my taste buds come alive. I cry at the simplest things, a beautiful piece of music, a flower by the roadside, even the beauty of a bit of trash by the road. The world feels a softer place, a more forgiving place, and when I look inside, I know it is because I am finding that softness within myself. For the first time, I have an inkling of what Herr Dietmayer means. Perhaps he is right. Perhaps the world is perfect, in its own way.

4

A loud knock resounds through the house. The door squeaks open, and I hear a thump on the floor, as if someone has dropped a bag.

"*Grüß Gott* or whatever they say. God I hope this is the right house. Anyone home?"

I topple down the stairs to see a frazzled Chloe, sunglasses propped on her head. She looks like a ghost from a life I once knew, but everything seems so far away I have to blink before I can remember. Unaware of my confusion, Chloe gives her tousled mane a good shake as she struggles to remove her jacket, then kicks off her shoes as if they were grabbing onto her toes and won't let go.

"Hallo darling," she says breathlessly as she kisses me on both cheeks. "I tried to ring but your mobile phone has been off. I decided to attend the Tantra course with you." She straightens up and furrows her eyebrows, turning me 360 degrees as if I were a shop mannequin. "Good God, what has happened? You're so thin you've lost your bum!"

My mind is having a hard time catching up with her stream of chatter. Tantra course? Oh yes, at one time I did want to go to a Tantra course. And my back. The pain is gone, and I didn't even notice it.

"I need a drink," she says, flopping at the wooden kitchen table. "Charming little house, isn't it? At least that strumpet did something right. What do you have alcoholic around here?"

Strumpet? Is she referring to Val? I shake my head and clear my throat. The only communicating I have done in the past few weeks, apart from buying food at the local store, is screaming in the woods. I try to switch my mind into gear, but all I can come up with is grinding gears in space. I give Chloe a closer look. I haven't heard that offhand, devil-may-care tone of voice for over a year.

"I thought you *stopped* drinking," I say, glancing toward the door. "Where's Jean Luc?"

"Jean Luc's passé, I'm afraid," she says in an all-too-breezy way that tells me all.

I open the refrigerator to grab the bottle of white wine that I had found waiting for me when I arrived.

Chloe pulls a pack of cigarettes out of her bag and looks around for a lighter. "Matches? I seem to have forgot mine."

After days of early nights and self-reflection, I find myself struggling to regain my social graces. I pour the wine into a large glass and give it to Chloe, who immediately takes a large gulp as she follows me into the sitting room.

"How are things?" I ask as I stuff a few logs into the stove. "And if you say *Jolly Good* as if you don't have a care in the world, I won't buy it."

Chloe throws herself onto the sofa, pulls a piece of paper from the coffee table in front of her and flicks her cigarette ashes on it. "I need to be me again. The me I know is free to do what she wants, with whom she wants, when she wants. She smokes and drinks and has lots of men." She downs the wine in one go. "I can't wait to get back to London and begin my old life again."

"Uh-huh. That's why you've driven all this way to attend a course in Austria."

"Oh *that*," she says, taking another drag from her cigarette. She covers her mouth to stifle a cough. "Tantra courses are great for meeting men."

My eyes focus on her hand. It is shaking so much that her glass of wine looks like a stormy sea. "Has Jean Luc done something to upset you?"

She reacts as if she has been struck by lightning. "Of course not!" She tosses her hair defiantly and flicks a few ashes onto the floor. "He's just *too* French. The French are, frankly, too *foreign*. How can you take anyone seriously who doesn't have English as a mother tongue?" She drains her glass, wiggling it in front of her with an expectant air. Reluctantly I refill her glass.

"What about *I can love Jean Luc, but not like him in the moment?*"

"Not *like* him?" she barks. "I am *beyond* not liking him. I *loathe* the man. He is an egotistical, philandering womanizer who has no respect for anyone of the opposite sex."

I rub my eyes with my fingers. She has just described herself to a tee. Suddenly I feel very tired.

Chloe runs her fingers through her hair, pulls the sunglasses off and drops them on the coffee table. "Can you imagine, he was still with Val when we met at that Tantra course! Making love with me, making love to her, taking me to Paris, taking her on dirty weekends when I was working." She looks as if she is going to explode. "And to think I invited that woman into my home."

Val with Jean Luc? "You mean they were together when Max and I saw you?"

"No, he stopped seeing her romantically by then. When he said he *loved* me." She almost spits the word out.

"So then was then and now is now. Besides, commitment was never a big deal to you."

She glares at me as if she didn't have to be reminded of this.

I give a little cough. "Wouldn't forgiving him be a lot easier?"

She throws herself against the sofa, her arms fluttering theatrically above her head. "How can I trust a man like that? To think we talked about having a family."

I scratch my ear. I must not have heard correctly. The Chloe I know never wanted a family. I give her a blank stare.

Her voice sounds huffy. "What a joke. With a Frenchman. Was I mad?"

"No, no," I say distractedly. "You're in love."

She stops talking, her shoulders dropping under the weight of the utter hopelessness of her situation. Nervously she flicks her fingernails. "I can never forgive a man. It's a contract I made with myself when I was at boarding school."

"Even more so."

She glares at me. "It's over. *Fini.* Let's not even go there, shall we?"

When she uses the royal 'we' I know better than to push her. Besides, I need to get to bed, and soon. "So you are following a rule you set, uh, twenty five years ago?"

Chloe gives me a look as if I am an annoying fly that won't go away. "Can't we talk about the weather or some other mundane subject?"

Just then the door bangs open. We all jump up as Jean Luc, looking unusually unkempt, storms in. His eyes are bloodshot, his chin stubbly, his hair tussled, and he is *angry*. Jean Luc throws the keys to his car on the table and walks over to Chloe without a glance in my direction. Chloe's mouth opens, then closes, and I see her eyes immediately drop into a half closed I've-seen-it-all look. She flicks her hair seductively from side to side as if to feel it flowing along her back, then relaxes her body into the sofa like a puma watching its prey.

"*Merde!*" he says as he sees her. "You hang up on me, you do not answer your phone, do you think I could not find you? I had to drive here from Paris to find you."

"*Bonjour* Annabel," she says, her voice imitating Jean Luc's accent as she flutters a remarkably composed hand in my direction. "*Ow nice to see yew.*"

"I am perfectly capable of talking for myself," Jean Luc says heatedly. I can see he is using every ounce of energy to remain composed. He turns to me. "A kiss to you, Annabel, I know you are in trying circumstances, and I apologize for bringing our *difficulté* to your solitude, but I am too French to be civilized at a time like this. Excuse me."

I feel as if I have just landed in the middle of a firing range. I clear my throat. "What time does the Tantra course begin?"

Jean Luc thrusts his finger like a poker in Chloe's direction. If he could growl, he would. "That's why you came, isn't it? To pick up men. Then I'm going too."

"Why don't you show me around," she retorts. "You probably used this house as a little love nest with your little strumpet."

He turns full force on Chloe. "Shall we go to the bedroom? We have a conversation to continue, and I would prefer if we did it alone."

Chloe looks at him through half-lidded eyes. "Oh well, it's getting late anyway," she says, ho-humming her way out of the sofa and following me to the guest bedroom. I pull out fluffy towels and place them on the antique wooden bed. The sparks in the air are so fiery that

I feel as if I have been caught in an electrical storm. The room begins to spin as energy purrs and prickles up my torso, turning my legs into rubber. They buckle underneath me, and with a sigh, I sink to the floor and stare, discombobulated, in front of me.

Chloe jumps forward, but Jean Luc reaches me first, putting his arms around me to help me stand up. It's not easy — my legs are quivering like a newborn foal. He sighs once, takes a deep breath and exhales loudly, shaking the tension from his shoulders. Then he looks at me. Really looks at me: my loose, unkempt hair, the dark circles under my eyes, the pallor of my skin, the way my clothes hang as if they are one size too big, but I see it is my eyes that he stares the longest at. Instantly the sparks disappear, and I feel, rather than see, his eyes becoming deeper, more solid, as if he is taking the entire situation in with his glance. He puts a hand on my shoulder.

"*Mon Dieu.* You're in the middle of it, aren't you?"

The eyes are the windows of the soul. His unwavering gaze tells me all. A wave of relief washes over me. Jean Luc has lived through this. I will always know who has suffered through this. The depth of a person's gaze will tell me how deep within themselves they have gone.

"Am I going crazy?"

His hand feels warm and strong on my shoulder. "No, no," he says, as gently as if I were a small child. "It's the opposite. You're becoming sane."

Chloe hasn't made a sound. She is crouched by the bed, one part of her wanting to help me, the other wanting to crawl under the sheets and forget about the entire thing. "You're okay?"

"I'm fine," I say with an unsuccessful attempt to smile.

Jean Luc places a second hand on my shoulder. "I want you to light a candle, take a long bath with some lovely bath salts, wash your hair, and get a good night's sleep. Your only responsibility is to make yourself beautiful for your first Tantra course tomorrow."

As I turn and walk out the door, I hear it close with a determined click, and then a flurry of words. I turn and walk up the stairs, intent on following the doctor's orders. I can't think of a nicer thing to do.

5

Gründonnerstag
Maundy Thursday

"Darling, this is a Tantra course! You can't wear that!" Chloe says as I walk into the kitchen. She looks more rested than the night before, yet I still see lines of worry imprinted on her forehead. Dressed in a flowing sarong, a soft flowered silk shirt buckled at the waist; she looks more as if she is about to take a holiday in the Caribbean than attend a course in the Austrian countryside.

"I don't know what goddess clothing are," I mumble, looking down at my fleece and jeans. In this fragile state of mind, facing a crowd of strangers feels unbearable. I'm already cursing myself for agreeing to go.

Chloe responds by digging into the bag at her feet, pulling out a long slinky frock in shimmering orange and a beautiful pale pink scarf. "*These* are goddess clothes. You're a woman, remember? Here, put them on."

Jean Luc, looking a hundred times better than last night, walks toward me in jeans and a polo shirt, a red silk sash tied around his waist. He tries to help Chloe sit down, but she shrugs his arm off with an irritated shake. The tension running between the two still feels like a faulty electrical cord. I escape into the privacy of my bedroom to pull the silky dress over my head. A woman? There was never time for femininity in my profession. As a journalist, I wore sensible blazers and suits with straight lines and solid colors. My world consisted of deadlines and sandwiches at my desk, late nights and harsh camera lights that show every hard earned wrinkle.

Femininity is a new concept to me. I look down at the flowery mixture of soft colors and feel as if I have landed in a tropical fruit basket. The clothes feel so light and free, as if I were wearing nothing more than a summer breeze. Coming down the stairs, I self-consciously hitch the dress up with one hand, surprised by the soft feeling of silk swirling around my thighs. Downstairs, as Jean Luc beams like a proud uncle, Chloe applies blush to my cheeks, then dabs some jasmine oil that smells like a fresh spring day behind my ears. Then, spinning me around like a globe on its axis, they both nod and give me an approving hug.

The conference center is situated in a roomy *Schloß* in the middle of Mondsee town. The large, two-story beige stone building contains massive L-shaped wings that envelop numerous courtyards and fountains and even a small chapel. One wing houses a five star hotel, another a chic spa, a third outbuilding — probably the ancient stables — holds various conference rooms, the largest of which is where the Tantra course will be held. The weather is perfect — blue skies and crisp cool air — the setting is beautiful, all I have to do is get used to the *content* of the workshop, and I'll be fine.

In the beginning, I'm pretty good at convincing myself that I'm going to enjoy it. I imagine myself after the course, a liberated woman, smiling seductively at anyone I feel like. What I'm about to do can't be any more difficult than my excruciating work with Lisa. I feel at ease getting out of the car, semi-okay as we are walking toward the hotel, but by the time we reach the conference room, my bravado begins to slip. With each step I find my heart racing in my breast. My stomach does summersaults. Studying Tantra in a safe environment with Lisa is one thing, but doing it with a room full of people I don't know is something else. Questions whirl in my brain. Who attends a Tantra workshop? Will there be weirdoes? Will I be forced to do things that I don't want to do? My feet feel heavier and heavier, and finally they stop like a bump in the corridor outside the conference hall, with the ultimate question, the queen of questions that has been racing around my head all morning, on my lips.

I grab Chloe's arm. "You don't go *naked* in a Tantra course, do you?"

Chloe's mouth drops open, and if she had her cigarettes, it would have been a perfect time to pull one out and light up. I feel stupid, standing here, asking such a pathetic question in lieu of everything else in my life. Chloe's eyes flicker to Jean Luc, who steps into the void and puts an arm around me, easing me forward as if I were his next patient, his voice as smooth as ice cream.

"Of course not," he soothes. "Everyone keeps their clothes on."

I fiddle nervously with my hair. "So what type of people will be here?"

"All types. Some will be here because they are curious. Others because they are lonely. Some, like you, because they want to get to know themselves."

"But how will I know who I'm going to do the exercises with?" I'm whining, I know it. I hope I don't look as uptight as my voice sounds.

Chloe speaks to me as if I were a child. "Singles can choose a partner for the duration of the course, or they can alternate with each exercise. Couples can either stay together or not. It's up to you." She puts her hand on my arm, trying to ease me toward the door, but my feet refuse to budge. They are frozen to the ground. With fear.

Jean Luc gives a slight nod of his head to Chloe, indicating for her to go on. She gives my arm a light squeeze and flounces ahead, her tawny hair bouncing behind her. As I watch her, I feel almost jealous. Chloe never has any hang-ups when it comes to sex. Jean Luc's arm pulls me away from these thoughts.

"You remind me how I felt when I attended my first Tantra course."

"Were *you* nervous?" I raise my hand to my forehead. It is moist to the touch.

He nods his head. "It's *healthy* to be nervous."

I throw him a doubtful look.

He smiles. "It's true. If you aren't nervous, then your intention isn't to get to know yourself."

"Chloe isn't nervous."

He smiles. "Of course she is. She is just showing it differently than you are. Besides, forget everyone else. You want to explore a part of you that is beyond your current understanding of *who you are,* right?"

He watches me nod my head.

"So. It is perfectly natural to feel frightened."

I look at the ground, frowning. "But I have a problem with sexuality. You don't, neither does Chloe. Not anyone here."

He throws his head back and laughs. "Annabel, *cherie.* If we were so perfect, why do you think we want to attend the course in the first place?" He gives my shoulder a squeeze. "Stop thinking you are the only one who is damaged. Remember, *most people* have a problem in this area. You're just one step ahead of the others because you know it."

My shoulders relax a little. "But what about — I mean — I feel so stupid." I grab hold of his hand. "There won't be *group sex* will there?"

Jean Luc is about to laugh, but when he sees my eyes begging him to answer, he stops. Within seconds, he's no longer Jean Luc, friend and boyfriend of Chloe, but a Harley Street eye surgeon talking to a patient. He shakes his head with the authority of someone who knows.

"That is the *image* of Tantra, portrayed by people who do not understand it." His words are firm. "No, there will *not* be group sex. It is *not* going to be an orgy. Tantra is the study of energy, sexuality and spirituality. Because these subjects are taboo, misunderstood or denied by our society, it gives Tantra a mysterious, forbidden air. But you'll see. Qualified professionals run this workshop. It is a therapeutic practicum designed to help people embrace their inner fears, restore their well-being and promote healing, both psychologically as well as physically. Is that understood?"

A warm smile of encouragement spreads across his face. Then, seeing me hesitate, he wraps me like a long lost daughter into his arms. It feels so reassuring that a pin pricks my insides, and a big bubble releases in me, making me cry big gulping sobs of fear. I hate myself for crying, but I can't help it. With infinite patience that makes me want to hug him even more, Jean Luc waits for my tears to run their course, then digs in his pocket and hands me a tissue. Treating me as gently as a newborn baby, he edges me into the building.

"Relax, *ma chère!*" he murmurs as we walk. "Tantra is a tool to get to know yourself, and an excellent one at that. So go in with an open mind and heart. And remember, you don't have to do anything you don't want to do."

He tries to extricate himself, but I reach out to grab his hand as if I'm afraid to let it go. He puts his hand over mine and leads me, step by step, toward the room. At the threshold, he turns to me. "One more thing. It *can* be fun, too." With that, he gives my hand a squeeze, and leads me into the room.

The hall is open plan, with a wood beamed ceiling, tall windows, a polished wooden floor and a mountain of mats piled along the edges of the room. Inside, it feels as if I have entered another world. Everyone is dancing. The swirl of colors and energy and music is as palpable and aromatic as a ripe mango in sunshine. A deep rhythmic music makes everyone's bodies sway like palm trees in the breeze. At first glance, I'm relieved to see that the group looks fairly normal. There is a balanced mixture of women and men of all ages from thirty to seventy. Most women are wearing flowing skirts and blouses, sleeveless tops or t-shirts with simple sarongs; the men are wearing t-shirts, shorts or cotton trousers, some with brightly colored sashes tied nattily around their waists. I estimate there are around forty people in the room.

"Dance! Move your arms, feel how your body moves. Choose a partner, or if you prefer, close your eyes and dance alone," a woman calls out as I remove my shoes and place them on a pile of footwear in the corner of the room. "Go inward and connect with your body. Everyone respect each other, please, so if someone is alone, leave them be."

Instantly my fear cassette loops around my head in full volume. *Close my eyes? In a crowd like this? Is she mad? This room is lethally dangerous.* I shy away from anyone who looks too open and free and move toward those people who feel safer, those who look as cautious as me. With the air of a martyr, I dance quietly in the corner, keeping a wary eye on all potential predators *just in case.*

In this room of whirling limbs and loose bodies, watching people smile and laugh as their bodies sway to the music, I feel the walls of my prison squeezing me. They are as thick as stone, so impenetrable that they prevent me from expanding or letting others in. It reminds me of the story Herr Dietmayer told me of how an elephant is trained in India. When it is small, one leg is chained to a tree. Soon the elephant becomes accustomed that it can move so far without its leg being restrained by the chain. When the elephant grow up, all the owner needs to do is to hang a chain around its leg. Although the elephant could walk away, it doesn't, because it still thinks the other end of the chain is tied around a tree.

This is what happened when I grew up. I was molded into what was *expected* of me, rather than allowed to develop into *who I am*. There is no blame to this realization, only sadness. My parents did it to me, just as their parents did it to them. And that is what unconsciously I will do to my children, if I have any.

How I used to love to dance when I was a little girl! I remember being invited to spend the night with a girl friend when I was around ten years old. This invitation was very important to me, one of the many small initiations that leads a child into a teenager. The moon was shining so brightly that we couldn't contain ourselves any longer, so we slipped into the back yard to dance barefoot in the moonlight, singing to the night time fairies as we spun in circles, giggling and laughing — until my friend's mother pulled us screaming inside the house. I was sent home in disgrace. Memories of that night begin to surface, the feel of the soft grass, still wet with dew, the lightness in the air, the soft shine of the moonlight.

Slowly, like a flower budding in springtime, I begin to dance, moving like I remembered so many years ago, before I had begun to be molded, corrected, squeezed into a little box stamped Annabel Jones.

310

I take a deep breath and look at the class in front of me with the eyes of a young child. I have a choice. I have a sacred space in which I can begin again, and I have forty people to help me along the way. An Irish ditty comes to mind.

Work like you don't need the money
Love like you've never been hurt
Dance like nobody's watching
Sing like nobody's listening
Live like it's Heaven on Earth

Dance. Really dance. My breath begins to open as I feel my energy rise, and before I know it, my smile becomes broader, my body a little looser, and for the first time in a long while, I start to enjoy life again.

6

As the music dies away, the crowd stops, panting as they catch their breaths, then everyone grabs a pillow and sits on the floor in a large circle. There is one co-facilitator running the course — the second is expected this evening — but there are at least eight assistants helping people around the room. It gives me a feeling of being looked after, protected. The atmosphere is light and bubbly, as if the room were soaked in champagne. The parameters of Tantra seem like any workshop. The course will last six days; time enough for all of us to get to know each other well. The day will be split into three parts, with sessions in the morning, afternoon, and evening, and meals and free time in between. Dancing, I am told, helps us get in touch with our bodies, so every time we regroup, we will start by dancing. Each session will contain one or two exercises that are performed individually, in pairs, or in small groups. Each exercise will end with feedback from the entire assembly that helps integrate the experience. Lastly, I'm relieved that there are rules, and they are to be respected.

So far, so good. As the day wears on, my confidence mounts. Many of the exercises are similar to those I did with Lisa: practices to stimulate energy in our bodies, to find anger, to learn boundaries and to speak our truth. A hundred times I could kiss Lisa's feet in gratitude for the grueling work we did. Many times I find people in a panic when confronted with exercises that now seem like kindergarten to me. They show me how far I have come, and keep me humble when I see how much further I can go.

The day begins, for those like me who are single, with the ego crushing, unnerving panic of choosing a partner. Asking a man to do an exercise with me brings up all my insecurities of the dating scene: *Am I good enough? Oh yuck, not him! How do I say I don't want to? Am I doing this right?* In fact, the group dynamic reminds me of junior high school. There are the cheerleaders, the quarterbacks, the academics, the nice guys, the bullies, the shy and awkward types, and yes, even a few nerds. Negotiating a group of forty strangers with respect, self-restraint, and an open heart takes all the Tantric skills that I have learned with Lisa.

The exercises, both psychological and physical, are incredibly private. Not sexual — sex can be anything but personal — they are *intimate.* They are intended to break down the barriers of self-protection that we have built over the years, and nudge everyone to *get real.* To know what we like, what we don't like, and to express our demands and feelings with compassion and respect. We do simple rituals like gazing, where we sit in pairs, staring at each other's eyes for minutes on end. We learn how to give and receive massages — not sport massage, but how to inspire sensuality and listen to the body's wisdom. Not just the sexual areas but all bodily parts— foot, hand, finger, elbow, stomach — are considered sensual and are therefore honored. Our body is very democratic, only we have become very narrow-minded. We do psychosomatic exercises to re-enact how sexuality was approached in our families, we learn to shake up old patterns and to open to new ways of seeing ourselves. Each hour becomes a beautiful and sacred adventure.

But the main word I sense is *respect*. I have never felt so feminine, so sensual, and so honored. The day passes with such speed that I can't believe it when dinner arrives. If I hadn't been so nervous, I might have enjoyed it.

By the time evening rolls around, my skin feels soft after a massage with aromatherapy oils, my nose overwhelmed by fragrant smells, my bare feet enjoy the smooth feel of the polished wooden floor. My senses have come alive in the soft glow of candlelight, the beautiful words *sacred sexuality, devotion, heart salutation, wave of bliss* echo in my ears. Sitting on the floor, my back leaning against a pile of pillows, I gaze with new eyes at everything around me, then glance at my watch. Why I have been wearing Time like a chain around my wrist for so many years? With a shake of my head, I banish my watch to my carryall, where it stays for the duration of the course. I feel cocooned in a protective bubble where no one from the outside world can touch me.

After the course ends I remain in the room, chatting with newly found friends when a gust of cold air sweeps through the space. I look up to see the double doors of the conference room have swung open. It feels intrusive, as if our womblike interior as been invaded from the outside world. Two figures appear, their bodies backlit by the harsh lighting that seeps in from the hall. Compared to our flowing energy, they seem so rigid, so constrained in their street clothes. The door shuts behind them as they walk into the room. I observe the smaller figure's rolling gate, but I don't pay attention until I see Jean Luc stand up and walk over to shake hands with the taller of the figures.

It can't be. I rub my eyes in disbelief as a sharp needle hits me in the heart, bursting the balloon of freedom within me. The ease flows out of my body, leaving my stomach taut. The tall man is Eugen. I squint at the smaller man next to him. It might be the lights, but I could swear his eyes are twinkling in my direction.

"*Guten Abend!*" Herr Dietmayer waves at me with a smile that says he knows it all.

7

Chloe appears out of nowhere, looking as if she is about to explode.

"Jean Luc can room with Eugen. Let's go home, I need my space," she hisses before storming out of the room with a banshee screaming at her tail. I barely have enough time to put on my shoes before she is out the door.

"Slow down!" I call as I wrap myself in a shawl, pulling it around my shoulders.

Things don't happen like this in real life. Herr Dietmayer here? I remember him telling me that coincidences would become humdrum when I started following this path, but *still!* The rain drumming outside disperses my scattered thoughts as I wrap the scarf closer to my face. I inhale sharply, hating leaving the magical cocoon to return into a world of drab browns and greens. I dash toward the car.

"Did you know Eugen would be here?" I shout, trying to open the door.

"Are you kidding? I didn't even know *I'd* be here," Chloe says as we slide into the car and whoosh down the winding road, the wipers desperately flipping side to side. In ten minutes we are home, in fifteen minutes our wet clothes are piled on the floor and we are bundled in fleeces and corduroys and thick socks. It is only when we are in the kitchen that I chew over the turn of events. Eugen and Herr Dietmayer. They looked like they knew each other, but in Tantra you can never tell. While Chloe helps herself to a glass of wine, I make myself a sandwich, piling everything I can find in the refrigerator between two slices of brown bread and take an enormous bite. I haven't been this hungry in weeks.

Before I have the chance to eat half of my sandwich, Chloe pulls out a pack of cigarettes and lights one, blowing the smoke into the air with a pathetic look on her face. Gone is the ultra breezy confidence of this morning. Slumped over the table like a half filled potato sack, her once fluffy mane wet and bedraggled, she looks as miserable as a kitten that has been caught in the rain. And yet, there is something so tender in her eyes that it takes my heart away. She takes a last puff, stubs the cigarette in the ashtray and pours herself another glass.

I drop the sandwich on the table, hoping to be able to eat it later, and clear my throat as I shake the crumbs from my fingers. I might as well go for broke. The truth wrapped around her heart is squeezing it so tightly it can't beat without fluttering.

"This is the first time a man has hurt you, isn't it?" I ask quietly.

Instantly the wet kitten disappears, and I see the rigid, got-it-all-together cloak descend like drawbridge and lock into place with a hollow clang. She sits up, sorting and hiding all emotions with smooth efficiency. In a few seconds the old Chloe stares me in the face.

"Men can't hurt me," she shrugs. "I don't become emotionally involved."

Her expression is in such contrast with the chaos within her that I wonder why she can't feel it. "You look beautiful. I *like* to see you show your vulnerability."

Chloe's eyes get larger and larger, and suddenly tears start to brim. With enormous self-restraint, the tears remain where they are, but her face looks as if steam is percolating dangerously within. Her face becomes redder and redder, and then the restraint buckles under the strain and she explodes.

"Shit!" She throws her wine glass across the room. The glass hits the side of the kitchen wall and shatters, splashing wine and spraying shards over the floor and onto the walls.

"I *don't* cry over men," she spews. "I have a good job, I have money. I *use* men. That way, I never get hurt."

The sound of shattered glass lingers in the air. It makes me breathless and dizzy to feel her trying to keep everything under control. I look at the glass, wondering if I should get up to sweep the shards away. But if I lose momentum I might never have the courage to tell her what is in my heart. I wrap a blanket around her shoulders and move her onto the sofa.

"We all need each other, and hurting is just part of the deal." I begin to stack logs into the oven, then go to the kitchen to sweep up the shards of glass. Outside, the rain pelts on the roof so loudly that it sounds like the animals in the forest are performing a barn dance above our heads. By the time I return, the comforting smell of smoke drifts toward me. If Chloe were considering settling down with Jean Luc, I understand her pain. In my open state, I feel it as my own. In that moment a swell of water sloshes inside of me and rises up and pours out my eyes.

Chloe gives me an annoyed look. "Why are *you* blubbing?"

I wipe away a tear. "It — it hurts me to see you in pain."

With that, the hardness flows from Chloe's body. She sinks into the cushions, the tension sliding from her body and onto the floor as if it were a puddle in the rain. The atmosphere softens immeasurably. We give each other a long teary hug.

"What a mess we're in," she says, ruffling my hair. "How insensitive can I get? Are you OK with Eugen being here?"

The sound of his name acts like a pin that pricks me, causing my breath to whoosh out of my lungs.

Her eyes shine black in the soft light. "You still love him, don't you?"

I drop my head. "I blew it, and some part of me will always kick myself for it. You wouldn't believe what I've been through the past forty days." I toss about the idea of trying to describe it, but then give up. "It has left me with a love so big that it swells out of my heart and into my eyes to form this." I dry my tears away. "*Tears.* That's all they are. Whether it is because of sadness, anger or gratitude, tears are love in a liquid form. The more I cry, the more I love my tears because they open my heart."

Chloe's mouth drops open. "Earth to Annabel. Where did this come from? One day of Tantra and you turn into romantic mush. Where is the liberated woman in you?"

"Stop kidding yourself. That's emotional detachment, not liberation. You're just playing a man's game." I see her looking at me in surprise, but I don't care what she thinks, I am more focused on trying to find the words. "I think women have done a great job learning to become men. We've learned to hide behind our armor of masculine control, not trusting men, not trusting the world. Cut off from our natural strengths such as feelings and heart, dismissing our instincts and understanding of the natural rhythms in life, we have become numb. Numb to pain, numb to love. But we can't have one without the other." I reach out and take her hand in mine. Her fingers are so thin and cold that they seem as if they would break if I squeeze too hard. "We are women, and our power stems from the ability to feel and connect with our emotions. We've proven we can be equals in a man's world. Now it's time to go one step further, to have the courage to own our power. Not as men, but as women."

Chloe's eyes soften as she hears my words. "And how do you propose to —"

I rub her hands between mine. "Surrender and guide the relationship, rather than throwing it away. Forgive him and move on."

She pulls her hand away. "Just forgive him," she says. "You say that as if it were so easy."

"No, it's not easy at all. If anyone uses the word forgiveness lightly, then they haven't done it. I blamed myself for killing someone. I left a man who said he loves me. And I abandoned the man I love. I know how much pain I have caused. Forgiving myself has been the hardest thing I've done." I put my hand onto her heart, where her vulnerability lies. "*Why* are you angry? I know he was unfaithful, but go deeper than that." I try to encourage her with my eyes. "*Why* do you feel hurt?"

As the minutes pass, I watch a fury of emotional waves crash through her. At first her chest puffs up. She glares defiantly at her surroundings as if she were in a Greek restaurant and had just thrown her last plate at the wall. Her face twitches as thoughts come and go, some accusatory, others angry. Her mouth twists, she bites her lower lip, and then something happens. Her shoulders slump, allowing the anxiousness that she was holding on them to roll off like a long, gentle wave.

"I trusted him more than I have ever trusted a man in my life." For a moment we both contemplate the rain pattering on the roof. "Perhaps that's why I'm so hurt," she says in a quiet voice. "I trusted him, and he hurt me. How can I trust him again?"

Trust. I never could trust when I was young, but what about now? Can I trust? Not trust in an individual, but trust the process. Trust that whatever is happening is for the best. *Trust life.* The rhythmic drumming of the rain soothes me, making me appreciate the safety and warmth of our little chalet. My heart murmurs. I listen to its words. They express feelings I never would have owned a month ago.

"I don't know if I can trust Eugen. Not because he abandoned me. Because he abandoned his ex-wife."

Chloe raises her head. "I'm glad you said that. If he could do that to her, he could do that to you."

"Yeah," I mumble. "I knew that too. I think that's why I left him in the end."

The moment the words come out of my mouth, they surprise me. My truth often does. I listen to the rain tapping a Morse code on the roof.

"During the day," Chloe mumbles, "I tried to connect with Jean Luc, but we went through the exercises as if we were acting roles in a play."

I nod. "I know what you mean."

I look at my wrist, but I have left my watch in the conference room. The downpour continues. Water. I read that earth is masculine in energy, and water is feminine. Water is powerful — it wears down stone — but it is also forgiving and adaptable. When I drank gallons of it, it helped me get through the dark sticky feelings of my first emotional battle. Water running from my eyes cleanses them of the sadness within.

"Water," I say to myself.

Chloe gives me a confused look. "What are you talking about?"

"It purifies."

"Oh God, It's Maundy Thursday," Chloe mumbles. "That's when Jesus washed his disciples' feet."

I smile at her. "I forgot you were raised Catholic."

321

She pushes her hair from her face. "Don't remind me of my schooldays in that dreaded Catholic primer. Those nuns were something else."

I hold her hand and look at her, woman to woman. "I'm not talking about religion," I answer. "I'm talking about what is *under* religion. Everything can be considered symbolic, even the crucifixion." I smile as I see her shocked expression. My eyes fall on two plastic buckets resting under the table. "If we hurry, we can reach the hotel before the night porter goes to sleep." Then I get up from the table and put both buckets under my arm. I know exactly what we need to do.

8

The conference center is dark by the time we arrive. Each holding a plastic bucket under our arms, we sneak up the back stairs, a narrow, twisted and creaky affair built a few hundred years ago for servants to navigate without disturbing the guests. At the top, I hold my breath and listen, but there is no sound except for the dim patter of the rain on the roof.

"Water is forgiving," I whisper, then pause as a board under my foot creaks, causing Chloe to panic and lose her balance. Her arms pinwheel in the air. I reach out to steady her. "It can shock but it won't cause harm."

Chloe nods as we tiptoe into the bathroom at the end of the hall. Stepping lightly onto the tile floors, we make our way to the two basins in the corner and carefully place the plastic buckets under the taps. I test the temperature of the water with my finger. We don't want to scald anyone. In the silence, the water dribbling into the buckets sounds like a pneumatic drill.

"This could backfire," she hisses, placing her hand under the running water to prevent it from splashing so loudly.

"It could," I whisper, turning off the faucet. "Do you want to stop?'

She shrugs her shoulders. "What do we have to lose?"

We lug the heavy, sloshing pails down the corridor to the room the night porter indicated to us when we arrived. The unlocked door squeaks softly as I open it. The room is large, with two single beds resting against the wall at the far corner. Luckily, the curtains have not been drawn. A faint light from the parking lot filters in through the windows. On the right, Jean Luc is sleeping facing up, his mouth open, one arm splayed outward. On the other, Eugen, so tall that I can see his feet sticking out from under the duvet, sleeps on his side, one arm curled under his head like a pillow. We position ourselves by both beds and look each other in the eye. I can barely make out Chloe's face, but I sense she is grinning. With a joint nod, we slowly tip two gallons of warm water over each man's head.

Pandemonium. Eugen leaps up from the bed, wilding karate chopping the air. He only succeeds in thumping Jean Luc, who is on his feet, hitting his hand on his ear, where water sprouts in rhythm with each hit. Water is everywhere, on our feet, on the floor, on the walls, dripping from the beds, trickling down the bedside table, seeping like invading damp onto the rug lying between the beds.

"What the hell?" Eugen blusters, blinking in the dark, trying to shake some sense into a situation that doesn't make sense at all, as Jean Luc gropes like a blind man toward the lamp on the pine bedside table. As the lamp clicks, a pale golden glow illuminates two bewildered naked men in sodden cotton boxer shorts. They look like boys caught with their hands in the cookie jar. Jean Luc, repeatedly hitting his head to shake the water from his ear while snarling obscenities under his breath, looks so ridiculous that we fall on our knees, doubled over with laughter. For a moment Eugen looks deadpan, squinting through the water dripping down his face, and then, miracle of miracles, his mouth starts to twitch, then crinkle into a smile. With as much dignity as he can muster, he reaches down and pulls the sheet from the bed, wiping his face with it as if it were the finest Italian linen handkerchief.

"I take it that you two have something to say to us?" he says, wringing out the sheet before passing it to Jean Luc. "Unless this is a new Tantric greeting that I have not been introduced to."

Jean Luc twists a corner of the sheet into a thin point like a cotton swab. "It is certainly *not* a Tantric greeting," he fumes as he plugs it into his ear. His sense of humor failure only makes us laugh even more.

"I can't take anyone seriously with a sheet sticking out of his ear," Chloe says as she plunks the empty bucket on the floor. She looks in my direction, unsure what to do next.

The warmth spreading into Eugen's eyes feels like honey on my soul. It worked. The moment that the water splashed on Eugen's head, my anger slipped away with the droplets. I move my jaw, hoping the words won't get lodged in the back of my heart and I'll be left standing with an open mouth and nothing coming out.

"I want you to get how hurt I am," I whisper. I'm speaking for Chloe, but my eyes are on Eugen. "For leaving me when I needed you most. And for abandoning your wife, when she, too, needed you." My heart pounds in my chest. I look around, hoping no one can hear it. "Also I want you to know — really know — that I'm sorry for hurting you. That was never my intention."

Chloe shades her eyes as she stares at Jean Luc. "And that goes for me. Oh sod it, I love you, you philandering French bastard. That's why it hurts so much." She sighs, as if all the air has left her body. "There, we've said it," she says softly. "Now it's up to you boys."

Arm in arm, we slowly walk out of the room and down the hall.

9

Ostern

Easter

The water episode brings Tantra into a new phase. There was the course *before* the splash, then there is the course *after* the splash. Before, Jean Luc and Chloe were at loggerheads, I felt awkward attending the course, I was petrified of Eugen. After the water splash, the hard knot between Jean Luc and Chloe dissolves, I begin to enjoy myself, and, although I can't say Eugen and I become close, at least we don't avoid each other.

The days of Easter roll by, first *Karfreitag*, the crucifixion, then *Karsamstag*, Easter Saturday, and culminating in *Ostern* or Easter itself. These days are no longer the parable of Jesus that I read when I was young. There is no separation between this story and my own. I'm not alone in my wounded world. *Everyone* has been crucified in their own way, and everyone is working through personal issues. The clean-cut Englishman wants to heal a broken heart. The Belgian housewife has difficulties in her marriage. The German couple received the course as an engagement present and want to start their marriage on the right foot. Although we come from different cultures, backgrounds and points of view, we overcome our differences and begin to trust each other. This happens gradually, day by day, as we peel away our protective armor. In doing so, we become *family*. Lying on the floor late at night, pillows scrunched underneath us, we cry our sadness, scream our anger, whisper our fears and laugh like children, opening up our deepest fears and darkest secrets to each other. Like innocent teen-agers at a slumber party, we comfort each other, holding hands and sharing such intimate moments that we end up weeping— in sadness, in gratitude, in laughter. As we dig inside ourselves, we discover a great secret, one that has avoided many of us for years. Our hopes and dreams and fears are, at the end of the day, so similar it takes our breath away. On the surface we may be different, but deep down, we are the same.

It is at this moment, when we start to accept ourselves for *who we are*, rather than who we *ought* to be — we begin the long arduous road toward healing. The journey may be painful, but it feels divine. The magic that happens when we begin to trust each other — wholly, intimately, completely — with our hearts open is more than beautiful: it is *sacred*. That in turn becomes our strength, because it is this trust — in ourselves, in each other, in life itself — that we were looking for anyway. This is why working in a group is so rewarding. Although we find it through each other, we own it deep within ourselves.

And who is presiding over this transformation? No one else but the man who sells smiles, my newspaper vendor, Karl Dietmayer, a.k.a. Tantra workshop co-facilitator. There he is, my teacher, bald head gleaming in the soft morning light, wearing a plain white t-shirt and beige sarong with such dignity that he looks like a smiling monk. Standing behind the podium, looking as if he were in a deep theological question, he radiates contentment and a warm masculinity that has nothing to do with age or looks. I can't believe that he is over seventy years old. Even his limp has become attractive, because it is a unique aspect of *him*. Me, in a Tantra class, attended by Eugen, being taught by my *Trafikant!* Herr Dietmayer — I mean Karl — did tell me that magic would come into my life. How right he was.

For the past five days, Karl has led us on an expedition into the truth of ourselves. It is a step-by-step process, and this morning is no different. Today, he explains, is *Ostern*, or Easter. It is a time of resurrection, a time of rebirth. He places his palms together and looks us all in the eye. On this day, he explains gently, we need to choose a person with whom we want to share the most intimate part of ourselves. We are about to do the most challenging exercise of the workshop. It is called a pelvic healing.

Pelvic healings, Karl explains, are an extension of Wilhelm Reich's psychosomatic work. Karl's eyes skim to mine as he says this, and I remember our conversations about Reich while I bought my daily newspaper. As Reich proved that emotions — or energies-in-motion — are often locked in muscle tissues, they also can be lodged around the genitals. Intrigued, I watch as Karl unravels an anatomical diagram of the human body. As I examine it, his voice wafts in my ears.

"A fetus is gender neutral," he explains, running his finger along a drawing of the female genitals. "It contains both sexual characteristics. As the fetus grows, it *becomes* male or female. But both sexual parts remain within the body." He smiles broadly, as if anticipating our reaction. "You might not realize it, but a clitoris is what is left of a woman's *vajra*." He pauses to see how long it will be before we get the ah-haa. "And the prostate gland is a man's inverted *yoni*."

He shifts his weight before continuing. "Now you might wonder why I am telling you this. It is because these places — the *vajra* and prostrate in men and the *yoni* in women — are the most sensitive areas of the body."

A man in front of me raises his hand. "Is that why so many men suffer from prostrate cancer? Because we don't know how to express emotions?"

Karl shakes his head. "We can never be sure why anyone has cancer, and I'm not a doctor so I can't answer that with authority. What I can say is that there seems to be a correlation between the two. I see it, and so do others."

Jean Luc speaks up. "And some of us are even doctors."

Karl waits for the laughter to die down. "But this isn't new. Osteopathic doctors in France pointed out this correlation in the nineteenth century. It was they who coined the term pelvic, or sexual healing. They were trying to understand why genital areas become numb, and how they could reverse these affects. Studies proved that if certain areas around the genital area were pressed, it produced a painful burning sensation. If the light pressure continued, this sensation increased, gathering in intensity, until a release occurred, either by an emotional outburst or an energetic release, such as a bodily tremor. If this procedure was done carefully and consciously, it brought about outstanding results. Numbness was greatly reduced, and, with time, feelings and sensations began to return to the damaged area."

A man next to me raises his hand. "So why haven't I heard of this?"

Karl smiles. "Since when have you had an emotional check up of your reproductive organs?"

We all laugh.

He becomes serious. "Wilhelm Reich was thrown in jail because his work was far too advanced for its time. Now, take a pelvic healing. This takes Reich's work a step further. The concept that emotions are held in bodily tissues — especially in an area that we can't even *talk* about without shame — holds too many taboos. Give it about fifty years, and you may start to hear about it."

Karl's words fascinate me, until I start to consider the logistics. If pressure needs to be applied in order to release the emotion, someone has to do it. My mind does a back flip. He can't be suggesting —

Karl's words bring me back to the present moment. "This exercise is so profound that we have divided it into two days. Today, the men will receive a pelvic healing, tomorrow, the women." The assistants start to circulate amongst us, distributing plastic surgical gloves and bottles of almond oil.

"We're doing this in a *group?*" The question zings out of my mouth.

Karl looks me in the eye. "It is *best* done in group. You'll see. You'll be so absorbed that you won't even notice the others. But you will feel their presence, and this can help your partner open up more than he might normally do. A group makes you feel part of something larger than yourself, and that provides a lot of power."

I think about this for a moment as my mind paints a picture of men lying on their backs, legs open — I stop again. "We're going to be *naked?*"

He shakes his head. "No, because you will be doing the healing. Men, it's up to you. You might choose to wear a t-shirt or sarong, or have a pashmina or shawl to cover yourselves. You will be lying on your backs for a few hours, and probably will experience hot and cold flashes as energy releases, so give that due consideration."

His words act like a javelin thrown into the middle of the room, changing the atmosphere into hushed uneasiness. Karl's voice remains level and calm.

"Now. Once you have chosen a partner, find a space on the floor where you will feel both comfortable and safe. Men, you will be on your backs, leaning against pillows, as if you were about to give birth. Women, you are the midwives. You are responsible for creating a sacred space for your partners, and to be there for them at all times. The areas to concentrate on are the inner thighs, and, if your partner wishes, the *vajra* and eventually the prostrate. This is extremely subtle and delicate work, so it will need all of your concentration. The important thing is to keep connected to your partner — physically, emotionally and energetically — until the emotion has been released."

He opens his hands wide. "It is up to you to do what you want with this opportunity. The tendency might be there to have fun. Whatever you choose, I, plus the assistants, will be here in whatever capacity you need us." His voice becomes almost stern. "Right. We'll break for lunch. Eat lightly — no alcohol — and we'll meet back here at 1:00pm precisely."

I'm no longer listening. I can't think of lunch. My stomach feels like a tumble dryer on full spin. Slowly, I walk outside and sit on the small bench within the courtyard, bringing my knees to my chest as I look onto the hills in the distance. My chest feels so tight I can hardly breathe. I drop my forehead onto my knees and squeeze my eyes shut. I have just found my limits. This is one thing that I cannot do. Will not do. Period.

Chloe walks up to me. "I had *no idea* we were going to do this. Jean Luc told me this is pretty advanced for a week course." She puts her hand on my shoulder. "And this is your first time, too. Are you up to this?"

"I'm fine," I lie. "Don't worry about me. Go find Jean Luc, he's probably looking for you."

Chloe gives me a long look, but I glare defiantly at her, willing her to go away. I want everyone to go away. I put my chin on my knees and stare into the distance. Out of the corner of my eye I see Chloe giving her head a shake and huffing off. She's nervous too, but doesn't want to admit it. I watch her conferring with Jean Luc, then both of them turn back into the conference room.

A few minutes later, I feel a presence behind me, calm but firm. I turn around. It's Karl.

He smiles. "Do you mind if I sit down? My leg hurts after all this standing."

Anyone else, I would mind. But not Karl. Dear, sweet Karl. He eases himself on the bench and places one hand lightly on my back. "Is anything the matter?"

I'm so in control it's frightening. My voice is level, my eye contact firm, my manner strong. "Don't worry about me," I say, speaking in a got-it-all-together voice. "I'm just exercising my option to opt out, that's all."

He gives me a gentle nod. "Good. You don't have to do anything that you don't want to do." For a few minutes, he watches me. I stare at the horizon. At least that is fixed and unchanging, unlike everything that is happening in my life. If I'm lucky, I'll stare long enough that Karl will get the message and leave me alone. Instead, I feel his soft grandfatherly hand on mine.

"What is it, Annabelchen?"

The way he says my name — Annabelchen, little Annabel — does it. A great wall of darkness descends on me as my eyes swivel in his direction. I breathe out, and with it goes all my bravado.

"You're asking me to touch a man's sexual parts? How could you be — so — *disgusting!*" The vehemence in which I say that last word takes me by surprise.

His eyes hold mine. "I'm providing an opportunity for healing," he answers quietly. "Perhaps the methods are unorthodox, but if you have experienced Reichian work, you understand how this process works. The only difference is that we will focus on a specific area."

He removes his hand from my back and places it in his lap. Normally my glare can shut anyone up, but not Karl. He continues to talk, his voice quiet but firm. "I can imagine how you feel — I felt the same way when I was introduced to this many years ago. It was me who brought this knowledge to Austria, and who has encouraged other facilitators to share it." He pauses, hoping to see a change of heart within me, but I continue to stare him down. Something shifts in him, and his voice becomes softer. "This is the most profound healing method for sexual wounding that I know. You might not need it, but you won't know until you've done it." He pauses while watching me absorb his words. He smiles gently. "Either way, it's up to you."

There is so much compassion on his face that it is me who drops my head in shame. I can't fault his logic. But just the thought of doing something like this makes my stomach turn.

"I've reached my limit, Karl," I whisper. "I can't do it. I just can't. It's too much, asking me to work so intimately with someone I don't know."

He reaches out to rest a hand on my knee. With the other, he points toward the end of the courtyard. "And if it is someone you know?"

There, sitting on the ground, arms looped around his bent legs, is Eugen. He too is staring into the distance. Maybe it is the way he holds himself, but something sets him apart from the rest of the group.

"You're not the only one having difficulties with this exercise."

"But he studied Tantra with his ex-wife. He's an expert."

Karl pats my knee. "It doesn't matter where you've studied, with whom, or for how long. It only matters how far within yourself you can go. By the looks of it, this is a big one for Eugen." His eyes rest on mine. "Perhaps even more than for you."

Then I remember. Vandana's diary. *Eugen's sexual problems are a nightmare. A tantric healing might help him. I try to explain that at the turn of the century French osteopaths developed a procedure to heal the pain we hold in our genitals, but he won't listen. 'You're not going to stick your finger up my ass!' is all he can shout.*

My God, this is what she was writing about. She wasn't writing about sex, she was writing about healing. "You mean he's never done this?"

Karl shakes his head. "Never was able to. Opted out, every time."

I pause as I think about this. Eugen? The person whom I thought knew so much, was never was able to do this exercise?

Karl's voice lowers. "Let me tell you one of the greatest secrets about healing. It's a two-way process. By helping others, you help heal yourself."

I can't keep my eyes off Eugen. Karl trusts me to do this with him? But Eugen knows so much more about Tantra! No, I stop my thoughts so that I can get a good look at them. That's an old tape playing in my head. I'm much more than the person I thought I was. Perhaps I'm not giving myself credit for how far I've come.

"We're not together anymore," I say slowly.

"You don't have to be a couple to do this. This is about learning how to be friends. You might have fallen in love, you might have wanted to get married, but neither of you learned what it is to be *friends*."

He puts his hands on his knees and stands up with a long sigh. "Whatever you do, it's the right decision." He leans forward, gives my shoulder a gentle squeeze, and walks slowly away.

I look at the hills for a long, long time, reflecting on the enormity of the path I've walked in the past year. I put my chin on my knees. Love. That's what this all leads to. At the end of the day, it is all about love. Slowly I get up. My body feels heavy as I walk over to where Eugen is sitting. Dressed in jeans and t-shirt, his salt and pepper hair disheveled and uncombed, Eugen's head sags between his knees as he gazes blankly at the ground. He looks tired. It takes all my reserve not to put my arms around him and cradle him like a small child.

"This is difficult, isn't it?"

He meets my eyes in a way that would have been impossible five days ago. If he is surprised to see me, he hides it well. He pats the ground next to him. A minute ago, I wanted to burst into tears, but now, I feel calm and centered within myself.

"I'm sorry about reading Vandana's diary," I say as I sit next to him. I place my chin on my knees. "I was too quick to judge."

For a moment, neither of us speaks. We don't need to.

"I opted out," he answers. "I did it with you, too. Always did. Always will."

I'm not sure if he is talking about the pelvic healing, or leaving me, or both. I feel heat radiating from my chest, and know that I am connected to my heart. And that gives me courage to repeat the words it is saying to me. "I fell in love with you, I moved to Vienna to be with you, I wanted to marry you, and yet I never understood the first thing about loving you."

He looks at me a long, long time.

I would like to touch him, but don't want him to misinterpret my actions. "I want to become friends. I'm not sure I can do it, but I'm willing to try."

He tilts his head to one side. "And what do friends do?"

I give him a small, humble smile. "They understand each other, support each other. Love each other for who the person is, rather than who they are expected to be."

We stare at each other before I look away, too overwhelmed by the consequences of my next words. "They help each other heal old wounds."

Eugen reaches out to gently take my hand. "You'd do this with me?"

I bring his hand to my face and hold it there, enjoying the coolness against my cheek. "I wouldn't want to do it with anyone else."

The familiar crow's feet crinkle around Eugen's eyes as he smiles. "Are you *sure* you are the same person who came to Vienna a year ago?"

"Ahhh," I answer softly, wondering if he can hear the gratitude in my voice.

Maybe it is the warmth of his eyes, but this time, I know it will be all right. Everything always will be all right.

10

When we return to the conference hall, an almost churchlike atmosphere pervades the entire group; even the most rambunctious members are quiet as everyone prepares their spaces. I fetch a soft blanket from the pile in the corner of the room and lots of large, fluffy pillows, then meander outside to pluck a few wildflowers and return to place them on the floor next to us. It is as if no time has passed, that Max never existed, that Eugen's girlfriend never was. There is only the two of us, here and now, preparing for a ritual of ultimate importance.

Chloe and Jean Luc arrive, and we all collapse into a long, silent, four-way hug. As we separate, both men slap each other on the backs, gazing in each other's eyes like warriors going into battle. Karl places a plate with lubricant and surgical gloves on the ground next to us and moves on. Those people we talked to and bonded with — the German couple, the shy Englishman — place their pillows close to us. It makes us feel as if we are surrounded by supporting friends.

As Eugen settles on the pillows in front of me, he breathes deeply, closes his eyes and opens his legs. I edge myself between his legs, hands forward, as a midwife might do. With the eyes of a martyr, he gives me an almost imperceptible nod and, keeping my eyes glued to his face, we begin.

Soon he is bathed in sweat, his breath is short and sharp, his inner concentration so intense that I sometimes have to wait for minutes before he motions for me to continue to another area. His body reacts just as mine did during the Reichian session— and just as Karl said it would. If I press a spot where the muscles were taut, the entire area wants to pull away from my fingers. Sometimes minutes pass before, with a sense of surrender, his limbs shiver as waves of electric energy release from the spot, radiating outward, arms and legs twitching along the way.

Hours pass. Time becomes a fluid stream of pain and release, pain and release. My back is killing me, but I ignore it. By now, I understand the process and can physically feel the e-motions, energies in motion, caught in his muscle tissues, and can help them release. I also know how difficult it is to dive *there*, into the knots of fear that are held within. At one point, when Eugen is having a particularly difficult time with a spot that I am having a particularly challenging time working with, I notice his jaw clenched so tightly that all the muscles in his neck begin to bulge. His face is red and bathed in sweat. Why does that expression look familiar? I study his face, thinking back upon all the healing sessions that I have undergone in the past year. Sifting through my own shifts in consciousness and awareness, I remember a certain time when I, too, looked just like that. Jaw clenched. Lips in a grimace. Mouth closed. And — I *remember*. I lean forward, careful to keep my finger pressed in the same spot.

"Scream," I say softly. "You can, you know."

Thousands of cords that have held him tightly together start to snap like taut electrical wires. Eugen's eyes narrow with a fury I didn't know he possessed. His awareness goes within and I watch as he forgets the future and the past, forgets who I am and where we are, forgets about everything except this moment. Like a diver leaping from the highest cliffs, he plunges into the source of the pain — and explodes. Like a raging bull, he begins to scream, his body contorting as if all of his electrical wiring has gone haywire. As he roars with rage, the waves of pain emanating from his body make my heart jump out of my breast. I feel as if I am riding a bucking bronco. I've lost all sense of time; I have forgotten my aching back. It is all I can do to concentrate.

I feel Karl's hand on my sweaty shoulders. "Good girl," he says. "Just keep matching his energy with your own and you will be fine."

It is powerful, intense, and strangely exhilarating, like participating in a death and a birth at the same time. Here I am, in the place of a midwife — *sage-femme* in French, Wise Woman — helping Eugen birth more of himself. The moment crescendos, opening into one long powerful scream, his body twisting and convulsing against me, against the heavens, against life itself. We could be here forever, the both of us, dancing this strange dance of healing, but suddenly the intensity begins to fade, as if someone has pulled the plug from an electrical socket. Whatever emotions he was holding in that spot are now gone. He collapses into large, heart rendering sobs that continue for a long time. Then silence. He falls back on the pillow, his body trembling and twitching as if recuperating from an inner earthquake. Slowly the twitches become less and less. Everything else seems to unwind and relax around that spot, and I know that my job is done. I slowly run my fingers over all the places of Eugen's body where I had been working. It is a miracle. Before the muscles felt stiff and rigid as a piece of sinew, now they are soft and pliant. Covering him with a blanket, I tuck him in like a small child while stroking his forehead with the tips of my fingers. After a few minutes, I help him sip water. Then, and only then, do I lean back, rubbing my sore back, and wipe my sweaty forehead with a towel.

Eugen struggles to sit up. He wants to talk, but his voice is too far gone.

"Shush," I whisper, giving him more water. "Just recover your strength."

He takes a sip, his trembling hand sloshing the water on his chest.

"The diary," he whispers. He clears his throat once, but his voice is hoarse. "Vandana wrote it long before you came into my life."

When I try to make light of the subject, he shakes his head. "No, you must know. Come, lie next to me, I'm too exhausted to sit up."

It no longer seems strange to be in a large room filled with partially naked men and women. I pull the blanket over the both of us, then spoon my body against his, just like I used to.

"You know I sent Vandana to Steinhof because I thought she was going mad." His breath is warm against my neck. "She wasn't crazy. She was just going through her shadow. Like you have been doing. And me."

His words bring up memories that I thought were dormant. I no longer see the battlefield of sunken men and exhausted women, but view her face, gazing at me. "How do you know what was happening with Vandana," I whisper. "You were hardly in Vienna for all the time she was ill."

I can feel him rubbing his eyes with his finger. Round and round his finger goes, over his long eyelashes as if he were wiping away tears. I wait but nothing more is said. After a few minutes I move my body against his, hoping that will stir him into answering my question.

"I never left Vienna."

My body freezes as if all of my senses, my sight and touch and smell and taste, are all concentrated in what my ears have just heard.

"*What* did you say?"

His voice gains strength. "I was never away on business. I didn't abandon Vandana in her illness. I was with her right up until the moment she died."

My heart catches in my throat. Throwing off the blanket, I sit up and swivel around so that I can look into his face. It is drawn and haggard, but there is stillness in his eyes that I have never seen before, a serenity that comes from having nothing more to hide.

He coughs slightly. "Within days of discovering that she had cancer, she began to transform, radically transform. But it was too late; the disease was too advanced. I knew that if I didn't spend time with her, I would regret it for the rest of my life. She needed me; I loved you. I didn't know what to do."

"You could have told me the truth," I say quietly.

His gaze becomes less secure. "At the time, I rationalized to myself that I didn't want to hurt you. That you wouldn't understand. But now I know. I wasn't being noble. I was simply afraid that you would leave me."

He gazes at me with such pain that I have to look away. The candlelit room feels as quiet as a morning after a large storm. The stillness is punctuated by touches of soft music and the occasional whisper. I feel a catch inside me, as if the tight belt around my breast has opened another notch, allowing me to breathe deeper into my belly. I can hear the roar of blood in my ears and my heart flutters as if it were dancing on air.

Forgiveness. It seems like such a banal word. I remember looking it up in the dictionary while sitting in the farmhouse in Mondsee. *To stop resenting somebody's behavior or to excuse somebody from a wrongdoing.*

"All that time I thought you had abandoned me. Abandoned — *us.*" Until that moment, I had never thought of Vandana as an ally.

But now I get it. I shake my head silently. All women are sisters. No wonder I had punished myself for going after another woman's man.

He rests his hand softly against my cheek. My face feels so delicate under his hand, as if I were a fragile doll. Gently, he uses his thumb to wipe away a small tear that slips down my cheek. "I'm sorry for leaving you when you needed me. But I couldn't abandon her. Not when she was dying."

Forgiveness. It rustles inside of me, as light as a butterfly's wings. How easy to say I forgive you, but to do it is monumental work. Not forgiveness of Eugen, but forgiveness of myself. I begin to cry. I try to stop myself, but the memories of our tender moments of love overwhelm me.

A deep, powerful smell of rose permeates the room.

"Do you smell that?"

Eugen breathes in deeply, closing his eyes as he pulls me close to him. "Roses. Like by the fireplace. How long ago that all seems."

The very memory of that night breaks my heart.

Now it's Eugen's turn to cry. Tears begin to stream down his cheek, large, wet tears. "I was so afraid you would see her. I couldn't sleep, worrying that she would tell you everything."

"I did see her." I breathe in once; the smell of rose still embraces us, soft and fragrant. "A few weeks before she died."

Eugen brushes a hair from my face. "She didn't say anything to you?"

I remember her sallow skin, her thin body. But her eyes, as black and shiny as a beetle, had held my gaze. A cacophony of emotions erupts within my breast and I collapse onto Eugen's chest in deep, wracking sobs. Vandana knew the truth, but she had kept quiet. In her heart of hearts, she had wished us well.

May
Vienna
Tag der Arbeit

Vienna is transformed by the time I return. The sun is shining, the brightness making the buildings glow in pastel colors underneath a blue sky. As I drive around the broad avenue that circles the city center, the majesty of the architecture comes alive before my eyes. For the first time I can appreciate how beautiful Vienna is. Like a bespectacled woman removing her glasses and shaking loose her tightly bound hair, the city casts off her cloak of necrophilia and decides that life is to be enjoyed. Even the Viennese shed their habitual grumpiness along with their winter clothes. It's May Day, the festive holy day celebrating the first planting in spring. The ancient Celts celebrated this day as Beltane or the day of fire. Bel - the Celtic god of the sun. In Vienna, stores are closed; there are parades running the Ringstrasse. People on the streets smile, horse drawn carriages clip clop by crowds milling the cobblestone streets, cafes and restaurants sprout tables and chairs filled with people relaxing over coffee and cake while vigilant sparrows dart amongst the tables. Magnificent horse chestnut trees raise their pink and white candle blossoms to the sky, swaths of red tulips and yellow daffodils grace the parks with their smiling faces, birds twitter and flit with busy excitement amongst the green, leafy branches. Everywhere I look, joggers and cyclists and street magicians and tourists decorate the city with a zest for life and youthful enthusiasm. Every flash of color, every shout of laughter, every sound of tinkling china and fragrant flower blossom proclaims that the long dreary months of winter are over and the warm weather is here to stay.

It was May, exactly a year ago, that I moved to Vienna to live with Eugen. A year ago, I hated this city. A lifetime has passed since then, and now I am back where I started, and yet I am different. After checking into a small *Pension* in the center of town, I take a walk to decide what to do next. Strolling past the sweet smelling lilacs lining the Danube canal, I view Vienna with new eyes, gentler eyes, and know that I look upon myself the same way. The stone angels gaze down from their lofty perches, welcoming me back to the city of death with compassionate eyes. Once you can hold life's shadow, they whisper, you don't mind heaviness. And they are right. I never thought I would miss this grumpy city, but now that I plan to leave, I am surprised to find that my parting will be bittersweet.

Just like it was with Eugen — was it only this morning that we said goodbye? Ever since my retreat, time has lost all sense of meaning. During the forty days, time became as rich and thick as pudding or as quick and fluid as mercury. During my own session of pelvic healing, with Eugen at my side, time became a monumental vastness, surging up and down like waves in a rough sea. As my pain emerged, a grief I never knew I had, it felt like molten lava had been poured into my *yoni*. As time looped and rolled during those long, drawn out hours, my body raced hot and cold, my limbs trembled, my teeth shook, and in one moment, the agony was so intense that I screamed myself into a dead faint. Eugen said he had never seen such a battle. I can't remember because eventually time became all loose and fuzzy, but afterward I sensed a respect in his eyes that I had never seen before.

The session healed something within me, emotional distress I never knew I had, the pains of birth, the anguish of my sexual abuse, the inevitable suffering during my confusing years of puberty, the sadness of all the times I made love because I felt I should, rather than wanted to. Emotions that I now recognize we all have. Pain that makes our hips and lower back sore, that can make us go numb, that may be one of the causes of vaginal infections and cervical cancer in women and prostate cancer in men.

At the end of the course, we were instructed to do a pelvic healing with a partner whom we trusted for at least a half a dozen times during the next year, or until the pain had worked itself out of our muscle tissues. Eugen and I looked at each other when we heard this. This was healing something between us, giving us a bridge that we were cautiously learning to navigate toward a deep, trusting friendship. As the workshop finished and we started the transition into our daily lives, Eugen and I circled each other, talking about Austria and work and life in general, but never talking about the future.

When he accepted my offer of a lift to Vienna, I thought it would give us time. I was convinced that was all we needed. And so, on the last day, my heart buoyant with expectation, I watched Eugen leave the conference room, his hair washed and combed into place, teeth flashing in the sun and a smile as bright and open as I had ever seen. With a carefree shrug, he swung his bag on his shoulder like a sailor coming home to port.

It was Eugen who saw the car first. A beige Audi convertible, the top rolled down. Leaning against it, a tall thin figure dressed in slacks and a blue blazer. A younger, more beautiful me. Her face was pointed in the direction of the hotel. She hadn't seen us yet. Eugen coughed and rubbed his eyes. It felt as if he divided into two, duty and desire pulling in both directions. And I knew, just knew, that my reaction to this moment would affect me the rest of my life. I had a choice. I could make a scene that would mess things up royally between them — or I could bow out gracefully. I glanced in his direction, my feet frozen to the ground, my heart beating wildly, hoping he would say something, anything. But that happens in fairytales, and I live in the real world. It wasn't up to him. It was up to me. Instead, I lightly touched his arm, and as he turned I lifted my cheek for him to kiss, then walked away as quickly as a wave retreating from a sandy beach.

That is how we said goodbye. It took every ounce of energy not to run after him as he turned to go. I could feel my heart lunging desperately toward him, but I kept planting one foot in front of the other as I walked toward my car. Once inside, I saw through the windshield as his arms embraced her, those arms I knew so well, and I tried to hold myself back from wishing that I was within them. No one was forcing Eugen to hug her, I told myself. He was doing it of his own free will.

This seesaw inside of me, this contradiction of feeling, wanting to be with him but wanting the best for him, twisted inside me, until I heard an inner crack and a wave of love emerged from within me, so great that my heart physically could not hold all of it. I opened my mouth and sucked in air, into my lungs, into my heart, as I felt it breaking open. Time and time again I inhaled like a bellows, deeper, fuller, letting in joy as tears swelled in my eyes and poured down my cheeks. My heart was breaking, physically breaking, and I could feel myself getting larger, expanding to accommodate this love. It felt phenomenally painful but liberating to feel love not attached to an object, but for its own sake. I thought that love was like a fairytale where two people lived happily ever after, and I love happy endings. But I never imagined that the happy ending wouldn't have me in the star role. *My cup runneth over.* Love isn't possessive, it isn't demanding, it knows no limits. Love is wanting the best for Eugen. Whether he is with me, or not. That is why I let him go. This time I would respect the woman in his life. I would try never to inflict pain upon him, or anyone in my life, ever again.

2

I had hoped my time in Vienna would be a short stopover on my way back to London. My plans, however, are dashed by my bank statement. Sitting on my bed in the hotel room, I watch it drop from my hand and flutter to the ground. Nothing. A year's salary, plus guaranteed bonus and residuals, gone. I've done everything right, I let Eugen go, I saved Max's project, I didn't rat on Rudi, and all I have to show for it is an overdraft.

And then the buzzing begins again, and nothing really matters anymore. Ever since my retreat, strange things seem to be happening to my body. A golden rain pours into my head and shimmers toward my feet. It is pleasantly powerful, and when it occurs, which seems to happen more and more frequently, all I can do is lie down. I feel as if I were in the center of a fast flowing river, powerful and yet connected to everything around me. Fighting this energy is useless, like trying to swim upstream. I lie on the bed, unable to move but able to observe everything happening to me with crystal clarity; the emotions washing through like waves, my breath rising and falling, my mind furiously calculating how long I have before my money runs out. I close my eyes, focusing on these prickling sensations, and a thought, like a miniature electric bolt, enters my brain. Talk to Karl. I chew on that thought like cud. Yes, and Emma. They are the only friends I have left in Vienna. And with that decision made, I close my eyes and surrender to the sensations inside me.

3

The shrill ring of the telephone wakes me up. Dazed, I see that the sun has already set. People's voices echo against the walls of the narrow alley outside the window, telling me it must be dinnertime. A glance at the clock confirms this. Three hours have passed. It felt like no time at all. I pick up the phone and sit up, hugging my knees to my chest as I say hello. My words come out as a croak.

"What are you doing sleeping? I thought you were on the job hunt!"

Good old Chloe never lets up. "I'm trying," I say, trying to shake the fuzz from my head. "But a lot of strange stuff is happening to me right now."

"What's with Vienna?" I can hear her drumming her nails on her desk.

I stay quiet for a long time.

"It's that television project, isn't it? Something was fishy about that."

My mouth opens of its own accord, my jaw moving up and down easily as the words pour into the air. "Rudi blackmailed me because he wanted to go to bed with me. And when I said no, he didn't exactly take it gracefully. That's why I quit. He owes me money. A lot of money."

A pause. "How waterproof is your contract?"

My shoulders hunch forward in preparation for the explosion on the other end of the line. "I don't have anything in writing. Don't tell me how stupid I was, I already know it."

Chloe is surprisingly levelheaded. "Don't beat yourself up, you were coming out of an incredibly traumatizing situation." She exhales. "Men have used money and security as a leverage to entice women for ages. If Rudi didn't get what he wanted, he'll use the one weapon he has. Money."

"So what are you saying? That I should have gone to bed with him?"

"No, you just need to understand how things work. Look, a woman's energy is like a lamp, always radiating outward. Men are attracted to the heat. Like insects, they circle it endlessly. That's their job. They are men. So instead of punishing Rudi for coming onto you, take it as an honor. When you know your boundaries, you will be able to say no. That means that a lot of situations that would have made you angry will now make you smile."

I drop my chin onto my knees. Can things really be so simple as that? "But it never works that way. Either I succumb to their advances — that's what happened with Max — or I get angry and walk away."

She pauses. "Can't you talk to Eugen about this?"

Eugen's name brings a soft flickering in my heart. How I would love to call him now, to tell him what is happening, to ask for his help. I'd do anything to feel his arms around me. "I'd like to, but I can't. But I'm going to see Emma. Perhaps she can do something."

"You'll not get much help out of that little lamb. I know the type well. Hubby is the bad guy; wife is the ever-forgiving victim. Complain complain but at the end of the day, the relationship is as she wants it." There is a pause. "Darling, you don't need money, do you? I'm happy to lend you —"

"No!" I cry. "You've helped me more than enough. I need to fight this battle alone."

The pause tells me she doesn't have an answer either. "Just sort it out by June." Her voice quavers. "In fact, by the fifteenth of June." Her voice rambles on, and soon it finds its own rhythm. "And bring something for the daytime and, um, perhaps a hat, and a sexy evening thing for a little dancing."

Curiosity helps my annoyance to drift away. "A new book launch?"

Chloe switches to that ho hum voice I know so well. "Oh not much," she says lightly as if she were talking about this year's skirt lengths, "It'll be a little civil ceremony in Chelsea."

"Chloe," I say, then stop. "Chloe More-Hamilton." I pause again, feeling a wave of warmth wash over me. "*You* are getting married?"

"We have to. After three months you start to show."

I drop back against the pillows. "And you're pregnant to boot?"

"Lots of women have children late in life."

"No, no, it's not that," I say as another wave of happiness hits me. "That's wonderful! But you always told me you never wanted children."

She lowers her voice. "I never knew life could be this way. Do you know what Jean Luc said when he asked me to marry him? He quoted Robert Browning. *Grow old along with me, the best is yet to be.* And it's true."

"I read Browning in Mondsee. He also said *Love is the energy of life.*"

She giggles. "Now listen carefully. I know you think you're life is falling apart, but it isn't. Jean Luc explained what is happening to you.

351

He told me it's like giving birth, once you are in the process, you don't have any choice. I thought it's rather an amusing analogy, considering he's a man, but he said to ask any woman who has given birth if they would do it all over again."

"And they would say yes," I answer for her. "He's right. As awful as it is, I'd do it again. Even though I don't know where all this is going."

"And if you need me …"

"I'll call you."

"You *will* come through it. Stick in there." I can hear her smiling as she speaks. "You'll see. And it will be beyond your wildest dreams."

4

The sun is low in the sky by the time I reach Grinzing, the hilly vineyards that cradle the northwest corner of Vienna where the *Heurigen*, or local family wineries, serve food and the season's new wines. Wandering along the winding cobblestone road, it's easy to see this was once the main street of a village before Vienna absorbed it into its city limits. The squat buildings on either side of me look like country inns, their tidy facades painted in autumnal colors of gold and ochre. Everything feels slower paced, the air fresher, the scenery tranquil.

Inside the *Heurige*, the interior is cozy and relaxed; the interconnected rooms are lined with dark wooden plank floors stuffed with long wooden tables. The atmosphere is loud and boisterous, the thick cigarette smoke already forming a hazy cloud under the ceiling. Waitresses, looking like Heidi in their the low-cut linen *Dirndls* with puffy sleeves and long aprons, scurry between the tables, their arms piled with trays laden with grilled *Schweinsbraten* and *Knödel* dumplings and carafes of *Grünerveltleiner* wine. Not seeing Emma inside, I thread my way past the tables to the wooden door in the back and heave it open, relieved to take a deep breath of fresh air. The sun has already set; is getting dark. I walk into a garden lined with lilac bushes. Dozens of picnic tables are scattered on the grass, laughter and the clink of china lilts on the warm breeze. The lawn tilts upward and away from me, ending in a quilt patchwork of multi-colored vineyards that fans out in every direction.

At the back I spot Emma sitting by herself on one of the benches. More round and sausage-like than ever, she waves a puffy hand, her dog peering guardedly from under her seat. Although she is dressed impeccably in a long dark green *dirndl*, she doesn't look well. Her eyes seem swollen in her face, her creamy skin puffy, as if it were bread dough that had been left to rise a bit too long. Emma gives me a once over from behind her glasses as I ease myself on the bench across from her.

"You look too good for someone who has just separated."

I watch her light a cigarette and blow the smoke in the air. She *doesn't* look well. Nervously she fiddles the cigarette between her fingers. "Why didn't you tell me that you were having difficulties? I thought we were friends."

I look over her shoulder at the vineyards in the distance. "I couldn't."

But she doesn't seem to be listening to me. "You were my power couple." She looks up into the sky, letting her voice drift on the warm air. With the sigh of a martyr, she reaches over to pour some wine into my glass.

I quickly cover with my hand. "Just soda water, please."

She rolls her eyes and plunks the carafe down, leaving me to serve myself. "You should see the woman who replaced you. Innocuous. That series would have been so much better with you. That's why Rudi is so angry."

"*Rudi* is angry!" The carafe nearly slips from my hand.

She nods her head, then leans over the table with a conspiratorial air. "Don't tell him I told you. He can be full of revenge when he's been wronged."

"*He's* been wronged!" I feel the flush in my cheeks as I pour myself a glass. I gaze in Emma's direction, but she's no longer with me. Her entire body seems to elongate, her chin rising in the air, lengthening her neck as if she were a giraffe eating a leaf from the highest branch of a tree. She raises her hand, waving excitedly above the crowd.

"Well, look who's here?" She turns to me and claps her hands together like a little girl. "Isn't this perfect timing."

I turn and squint in the darkness. All I can see are clusters of people sitting on the benches. I hear laughter and the sounds of crickets. And then my heart stops. A tall figure weaves through the crowd. When I see who it is, I whip back to Emma, who smiles at me innocently. Feeling like a caged animal, I watch her kiss Max on the cheek. Grinning, he brings my hand to his lips in a clumsy gesture. His hand feels warm and clammy.

"Hiya Annabel," he says, sliding in next to her as if it were the most natural thing in the world. Leather loafers have replaced his combat boots, instead of a black leather jacket; he is wearing a dark blue blazer. He tips his head toward Emma and gives me a big grin as he sloshes wine into his glass and takes a long sip before smacking his lips. Gone is the Max who adored me, who would do anything for me, the Max who wanted me to stay. In his place is a person I don't know, someone who looks vaguely like Max, but his naivety is replaced by a loud, blustery yuppie. I find myself wishing to see his ponytail again.

My eyes dart to Emma's face, but she looks blithely beyond me, her eyes doting on Max. "Annabel has just been telling me what she has been doing," she gushes. "Do you know she was on a retreat? Isn't that brave?"

Max laughs and pours more wine into his empty glass. "Mondsee isn't exotic enough. Annabel needs to travel to India. To discover the meaning of life."

"She can wear a sari," Emma says, giggling.

"Chant OM," Max answers. They laugh again.

I feel like a gnat that has fallen into a soup, the more I struggle, the deeper I seem to sink. I look Max in the eye.

"Do you know I was never paid?"

For a second, my words cut through their laughter. As Max bends down to feed a tidbit to Emma's dog, I can sense a flicker of doubt behind his bravado. But when he feels Emma's gaze upon him, he sits straight again. "I made Rudi promise not to sue you. Isn't that enough?"

"You owe me money. And you know it."

"This comes from a woman who returned from a spiritual retreat," he snorts. "When it comes down to it, you need money just like everyone else." He turns to Emma. "What do you think? He's your husband."

Emma'a eyes open wide, as if she is trying to see something that is just beyond her reach. Her hand flutters towards her eyes, then it changes its mind and rests, useless, in the air between us. She pauses before she speaks.

"It was already brave of me to come see you. If Rudi knew, he'd have my guts for garters." Her eyelids flick, once, twice, then she shudders. "I hate when couples separate. It is so awkward." She studies her hands.

I rub my hand against the back of my neck, feeling how tight my muscles are. "Do you let your husband dictate *everything* in your life?"

Silence descends upon our table. I stare at the ochre stucco walls that frame the garden, and watch the lilacs sway in the evening breeze. But the scene no longer feels tranquil. It is suffocating me. As I watch Max gallantly refilling Emma's glass and draping her cardigan over her back, I remember how eagerly he had copied Rudi's manners. He's been busy since I last saw him.

Emma looks at her glass, and then takes a dainty sip. "When you quit, Rudi didn't speak to me for days. Said it was my fault." She pouts in my direction. "Do you know how difficult that was?"

For a split second, I almost pity her husband. "You *let* Rudi walk over you, and then you act the victim."

She inhales sharply, as if my words have hit her. She blinks innocently before clutching Max's arm. "Max darling, it's time for me to go. Get the bill, will you?"

For a moment Max studies the situation, then, as Emma busies herself with her dog, he slowly gets up from the bench and stamps away without another word. Once he is out of hearing range, I lower my voice.

"Why are you angry at *me*?"

"You should have known better!" she snaps. "Nearly ruining Max's career. Rudi and I have been extra careful to support him during these crisis months." She leans down and swipes her dog on the nose. "Bad dog, dribbling like that, I will have to spank you when we go home."

I open my eyes and really look at Emma. Her puffy skin, her nervous eyes, the thick padding of fat around her chest, armor inches thick that she has created to protect her sensitive heart. I feel my own heart, open and vulnerable. "You don't want me to leave Vienna," I say quietly. "You find it hard to live here, and need a friend." It's a statement more than a question.

"People like you come and go, but I have to stay," she says, looking beyond me to the hills. "I should have known better than to invest the time in our friendship."

I breathe out slowly. The chatter disappears into the background as I gaze into Emma's eyes. Gazing. It's something I learned in Tantra. To hold the eyes of someone while I open my heart. That's all. The first time I did this, it felt too intimate. After a few seconds, I gave an embarrassed laugh and looked away. But now I have nothing to hide. As I look into her eyes, I feel as if I have switched radio channels from the blaring, disjointed music of a rock station to the soft lilt of classical music. The moment stretches. I hold her gaze, my face as emotionless as a mirror, welcoming her to see *who I am*. Her eyes flicker away, but when I don't move, they swivel back to mine as if drawn by a magnet. Like magic, my anger dissipates as I feel what it is like to be in her shoes. To be Emma, to live in a life of compromise. All the time she says yes, her body adds another kilo of protection. I see her eyes widen. Tears well up — but then she looks away and snap — the connection is broken. A curtain descends between us, cutting her off from me, from the world, from herself. Flustered, she digs in her bag and pulls out a crumpled tissue to stop a tear slipping down her cheek.

"Can't you see?" she cries, dabbing her eyes. "Things are a trade off in my marriage, but at least I *have* one." She twists the tissue around her fingers. "Every time I see you, I start hoping things might get better with Rudi, but they won't. I feel pressure from you, and that pressure is bad for my marriage." Before I can answer she jumps up, yanking her dog's leash so hard that he winces. As I watch her flee the table, I know I will never see her again.

By the time Max returns, a waitress in tow, I am slumped at the table, staring into space. "Emma's gone."

Max orders another carafe of wine, then slides onto the bench across from me. "She's mentally imbalanced."

I give Max an incomprehensible look. "I thought you were friends."

"You should hear what Rudi says. She needs psychiatric help."

"You'd need it too if you were living with a man like that." I take a sip of water, listening to what the liquid has to say to me. Truth. Tell the truth. I nod my head and lean forward. "Be careful with Rudi. I couldn't tell Emma that. But I can tell you."

Max looks at me coldly. "Rudi and I are best friends."

My mouth opens up on its own accord, and before I can stop it, the truth rolls out as smoothly as a golf ball on a putting green. "Rudi came onto to me on the dance floor. Tried to kiss me. When I said no, he threatened to pull out of the deal. It would have ruined you. That's why I quit."

Max's eyebrows rise in disbelief. He brings his hand up to ruffle the top of his hair. "Rudi would never do something like that. He's an aristocrat."

I look him in the eye. "So is Eugen, and according to Rudi, he did it all the time."

"Don't play miss innocent on me," he snaps. "I saw the way you were looking at Eugen on the dance floor. You were sleeping with him, weren't you? Good old Max, taking you in, giving you a job, and that's what I get, you two-timing trollop. That's why you never wanted to make love to me."

Max's outburst feels like a blast of cold wind. My voice feels as brittle as a dry twig. "Where did that come from?"

He smiles triumphantly. "Rudi told me."

I roll my eyes to the sky. "Do you believe *everything* Don Juan says?"

He throws me an alcoholic leer and pours more wine into his glass. "You sound like my father. He needed psychological help, too."

I think of Max talking to the grave of his dead uncle and wonder how he defines madness. "Strange that all the women you and Rudi are with need psychological help."

He looks up, his eyes as large as when we did that strange fortune telling on New Year. As if what we are talking about has another meaning, a deeper meaning, that only he can see. "It's true. Both you and Emma *are* mentally unbalanced."

"So you won't pay me."

He gazes inside his glass, as if trying to read his fortune from within the liquid. "Prove it."

"*How* can I prove this to you?"

"That's not my problem. I'm a journalist. I need facts." He wipes his mouth with his hand, then places it, now sticky with wine, on my sleeve and gives it a squeeze. "I hope one day you'll be able to find yourself." He leans back and gives me the smug smile of a used car salesman. "And another thing. Let me tell you a lesson Onki taught me. Never trust anyone. Especially the person who is sharing your bed. Life is easier that way."

And with that, he downs his glass of wine and walks away.

5

Christi Himmelfahrt

Ascension

I pace up and down the stairs for a good five minutes before sitting on the bed and picking up the phone. Rudi answers on the first ring. If he is surprised to hear my voice, he doesn't show it. "To what do I owe this pleasure?"

I imagine him sitting in the stately grandeur of the State Opera House under the portraits of Verdi and Puccini and Richard Strauss, smiling into the air filled with centuries of musicality.

"My salary," I answer. "According to the contract —"

"I don't recall you *signing* a contract." His impeccable manners whisper how crude I am to even bring the subject up. An uneasy silence follows.

"I was living with the producer who signed it," I answer, "and if you recall, I quit rather suddenly. I don't think Emma, or the EU commission, would want to know why."

He hears the threat. I hear the clunk of the receiver on the desk and wait, realizing that he has probably gone to shut the door of his office. In a second, he wheezes down the line. "I would be happy to discuss this with you, Ms Jones. In person."

"When shall I come to your office?"

"No, no, no. I have a rather busy schedule, let's see, Friday would work. Can you make five?"

When I agree, his voice becomes efficient. "Good, Hotel Orient, Friday at 17:00."

I can't believe his brazenness. "That's not a place to do business."

"That's how *I* do business," he answers, his voice hard. Before I can say another word, Rudi politely signs off and the line goes dead.

6

I slam the phone in its cradle. Then, looking about my room, I know that I will bounce off the walls if I don't do something, now. Like a tornado, I burst out of the hotel and jump on a passing tram, but not being able to stand its slow pace, I hop off and walk the bridge spanning the Danube. By this time, it is dark. The hills of the Vienna Woods undulate against the nighttime sky, the last birdsong hangs in the air. The moon, bright as a penny in the sky, lights the buildings of the United Nations shimmering on the other side of the water. A deep yearning overwhelms me. I am homesick, homesick, homesick, but I don't know for where. I think of all the places I have lived, but none of them satisfies this longing. The feeling is so intense that it hurts. I feel like crying and screaming at the same time.

The Danube island is a large, manmade park crisscrossed with bike paths, its shoreline lined with trees. During the day, it is filled with walkers and picnickers, but now, at night, the island is as silent as the waters flowing by. I walk to the shore and collapse under a cottonwood tree. It feels safe here. I begin to cry with frustration. I'm tired. I'm tired of everything. I'm tired of waiting, tired of doing inner work, tired of my life falling apart. I can no longer go it alone. I need help.

Keeping my mind on these thoughts, I start to breathe deep breaths. I sense something, a small movement at the bottom of my spine. Unlike the previous Reichian session, I now am able to follow energy. It enters me from the ground and wants to travel up through me to reach the sky. Within minutes the familiar waves of energy begin to ripple up my spine, and this time, I'm working with it consciously, allowing it to grow and expand. I breathe, and breathe again, trying to remain actively passive as I open myself. Focused inward, I feel something shift, as if a trapdoor has opened within me and — bang! A writhing hot energy shoots up my torso, twisting like a snake. *Trust. Trust the process* I hear a little voice inside me say. My neck gives an extra sharp wiggle as the energy shoots through my head like a steaming percolator. Unable to do anything but go with this energy — resisting it isn't an option — my mouth drops open and a scream from the deepest part of my belly shoots up my spine and out my mouth. The scream is more than primordial; it is the sound of the universe, the source of life itself. And it is all within me.

It is the most wonderful, powerful moment. There is no past, no future, no pain, no fear, only the awe of experiencing the power of life itself. Finally, after what seems to be a lifetime but was probably no more than thirty seconds, I drop forward, panting as the energy drops down my spine. My body is wet with perspiration, and yet it hums and purrs like a motor. For the longest time I keep my eyes closed, trying to make sense of what happened. The buzzing and purring that I had felt earlier was nothing compared with this.

When I finally open my eyes, a different world greets me. At first I think that someone must have placed 3-D glasses on my nose. Everything looks so fresh and clear, as if it had been washed. In the vast ocean of time and space, little tadpoles of energy flicker in the nighttime sky. Glancing at the tree next to me, I see shimmering energy glimmer from its branches. Everything around me — the trees, the insects, even the hills and the water — is alive.

I move my neck and back. Although they have just been through a washing machine on full spin, they feel as lubricated as a well-oiled joint. And that is when I realize it. I *am* this energy. It is so powerful that I could light up the city of Vienna if I wanted to; it is so gentle that I am aware of the water lapping at my feet, the frogs croaking in the distance, the splash of a fish across the shore. Nothing can harm me, because I am inseparable from the universe. There is nothing to fear, because there is nothing outside of me.

I look down at my body. What did Karl say? Inner pollution means outer pollution. All my fears are the fears of the world. As I transform myself, I am transforming the world. I start to smile, and then laugh. All my life I have searched for the magical. And it has always evaded my grasp. Once I achieved a goal, I could never relax into it. And only when I stop, do I find it under my nose. *I am that.* It seems almost too simple to be true. I pull out my mobile phone and do a search for Karl's number. I have to speak to someone about this, and now.

7

Dressed in a long sleeve cotton shirt and a pair of beige cotton tie up trousers, Karl opens the door to his apartment and waves me inside with a gentle smile, then walks in his curious rolling gait behind me. As I step into the apartment, I feel a twinge of guilt that I called him at such a late hour. Austrians are not known for being night owls. But when I rang, he assured me that he was awake.

Karl's studio looks like any middle European living space, crammed with non-descript wooden furniture with doilies, a faded brown velvet armchair and sofa, a red rug with large paisley swirls and white crochet netting hanging on the window. Only the large bronze Buddha sitting in serene dignity in the corner of the room gives a hint of Karl's unusual perception of life. Although the apartment is only one room, it is well placed in the center of town and has a miniature balcony lined with white flowers and palms. On the table, a pot of steaming tea awaits us. The night is still warm. We settle on rickety garden chairs, pulling the cushions underneath us. My body is humming so strongly that the chair underneath me jiggles against the floor. Karl looks at the chair and smiles.

"Now do you believe what I meant when I said that everything is energy?"

I nod. "This is weird. Really weird. I feel connected to everything. As if I had a generator inside of me and didn't even know it."

He pours the tea into two cups and hands me one.

"The more you clear heavier energies like anger and sadness and fear, the more you can open yourself to love. Most people want love, but they don't want to feel the yucky stuff first. But it doesn't work that way." When I give him a confused look, he puts his cup of tea down. "Life is always in balance. Night is balanced by day, shadow by light, men by women. So the more shadow you hold, the more light you hold, too." He beams as if looking upon a star pupil. "I thought it could happen."

I give him a strange look. "You *knew* something would happen?"

He quickly shakes his hand in the warm night air. "No, but I could sense that you were at breaking point. Ready to drop your shackles. And when a person is ready, the teacher will appear. It happened to me in Cambodia. Mine happened to be a Buddhist monk who nursed me back to health after I lost my leg in a minefield. But they come in all different shapes and sizes." He grins. "Even newspaper vendors."

"So you're not really a *Trafikant*?"

He raises his eyebrows. "I sell smiles, remember? I *want* to work. It makes me happy. It is the easiest way that I can meet people. Then I can spot those who are ready to pop like champagne corks. Like you."

"What *was* that?"

"That," he says with a smile, "Was Kundalini. It's something, isn't it?"

"What's Kun-da-lin-i?" I say the word slowly to make sure I got it right.

"It's a Sanskrit word meaning coiled like a snake, because it is said to reside in the base of your spine." When he sees I don't understand, he tries another track. "It's the energy of the universe." He beams. "You have discovered one of the secrets of the universe tonight. Heaven's only a breath away. It's all inside of you."

I nod my head as I close my eyes, feeling the purring within my body. "I'm never alone. This is *in* me, not out there."

He drops his head onto his chest as if laughing at his own joke. "Oh my. Today is *Christi Himmelfahrt.*"

"*Himmel* — that's heaven. *Fahrt* — that's trip," I translate to myself.

"Ascension." He smiles. "It puts all those biblical stories in perspective, doesn't it? I think we need to celebrate with another cup of tea." He pours me another cup, but my hand is trembling so much I have to put the cup on its saucer and lean forward to sip it.

"Now don't forget the finger pointing toward the moon. Tapping your Kundalini is also just a tool."

I smile. "I know, I know, it's not the experience, but what it gives me that matters."

He stops pouring tea to look me in the eyes. "Did your body jerk a lot?"

"All over the place, especially my neck. Is that normal?"

"All those jerks were dams that were preventing the energy from coming through you. Those blockages are parts of yourself that are still closed down. Eventually you will be able to hold even more energy." When he sees my look, he adds, "What happens to a reservoir when a dam breaks?"

"The water surges through ..." My eyes light up. "Oh, I see. My dams are now disappearing, so I can hold more of my own energy. Is that what makes me feel dizzy during the day?"

He nods his head. "You're body is increasing its voltage, so expect all sorts of strange things to happen, and know that it is all part of the process. The energy you are experiencing is what Wilhelm Reich called Orgon."

"Wilhelm Reich knew about this?"

"Yes and no. Reich never incorporated spirituality into his practice. However at the end of his life, he started to realize that underneath body armor, everything is energy. Just like Albert Einstein. Physicists also know this. God, or the universe, is democratic. Every one of us has received the means to experience this energy. Most people do it through sex. That's why most religions try to put restrictions on sex."

I give him a confused look.

"An orgasm is a flicker of Kundalini. You no longer need religion, because you can now communicate directly with God. Not through belief — which is in the mind — but in experience, which is in the body. You just experienced what happens if the tap is turned on. Imagine what you would feel like if you could open to this when you wanted to."

"I can?"

He smiles. "It only gets better."

"Is that why people are so addicted to sex?"

"Right. They are looking for what it will give them, and now you know that you can't love another person more than you love yourself. You have just made love with yourself and with the universe tonight. But in relationship with another human, there is an additional factor. The heart."

I think of my experience in the retreat. "Everything is inside of us. Good and bad. Shadow and light. Black and white."

"Yin and Yang," he answers. "Just like people are left and right brained, we are left and right bodied. Our right sides are masculine energy, the way we express ourselves in the world. Our left side is feminine energy, how we receive the world. Until recently, you have been functioning using your masculine energy, and now you are opening to the strengths of feminine energy. In doing so, you are becoming whole."

For a moment we look onto the city. Vienna has pulled a black mantle of stars around herself, with only the steeple of St. Stephens Cathedral glowing in the darkness. Silence floats on the still air.

"So what made you angry?"

"How do you know I was angry?"

"There must have been a reason to go to the Danube Island."

I lean back in my chair and look at my mentor. He might as well know my story. So I tell him about Eugen, Vandana's death, moving in with Max, working with Rudi, and finally leaving my work and Max behind for my forty day retreat. "Now Rudi won't pay me. He wants me to meet him in some sleazy oriental hotel."

Karl looks up with a smile on his face. "The Hotel Orient! That's a wonderfully quirky Viennese institution. It's not sleazy, but it's also not a place to do business."

"I need that money," I say sadly. "My budget is getting low, and I can't work with all this funny buzzing energy. The Orient is a hotel?"

"Dedicated to all that is forbidden." He starts to chuckle.

"It doesn't sound very spiritual."

"It isn't. It's carnal. But be careful in thinking that spiritual things are better than anything else. All rivers lead to the ocean."

This makes me think.

He smiles. "So. Your Kundalini has just awoken. What has this experience brought you?'

I close my eyes. "I'm deep within my body. Maybe that's why I'm at peace. I feel powerful, too."

"Good. So let's put everything you learned in Tantra into practice. Do you feel powerful enough to go to the Hotel Orient to get your money back from someone who owes it to you?"

I open my eyes and start to laugh. "I don't feel afraid to meet Rudi!"

"I thought so. You never need to be afraid of men like Rudi again." He gets up and stretches. "We have to catch that man in a compromising position," he says, more to himself than to me. "Not easy, considering the hotel is extremely discreet." He pulls out his cell phone and looks at it, his forehead wrinkling as he smiles. "You know how to text people on your cell?"

I nod my head. I take him fully into my gaze, his short, stocky arms resting lightly against his beige t-shirt, his hands relaxed and slightly curved, the way his good leg seems so firmly planted on the floor. He reminds me of a puma, so full of muscles, and yet so flexible and light, as if he is ready to spring into action if he needs to. I glance at his leg, but it is so much a part of him that it, too, has become beautiful. He is beautiful, inside and out. Strange. I feel more comfortable with this elderly man than with most people I have ever known. Together we gaze over the city of Vienna. My eyes sweep over the steeples and onion domes stretching into the inky night, the higgledy-piggledy patchwork of roofs stretching as far as I can see.

Karl leans forward and puts a soft grandfatherly hand on my arm. "Eugen could help us."

I turn to look into his eyes. "Are you in touch with him?"

"We meet at a *Kaffeehaus* now and then."

"Are you friends?"

He smiles. "That's why I wanted to contact him."

I rub my eyes, trying to let my thoughts drift on the night air. "No."

Karl doesn't press the matter.

I drop my head. "I try not to think of him too much."

Karl tilts his head in my direction. "But *do you?*"

I turn my gaze toward the rooftops. My silence is the answer to his question.

8

Pfingsten

Whitsun

I watch as Lisa scribbles a few notes onto a piece of paper. She taps her pencil on the desk as she regards me.

"Has your energy changed! You look radiant. Fresh."

I tell her about separating from Max, my retreat and the Tantra course. "And then I had this sort of explosion. You know, the snake like stuff that runs up your spine?"

"Your Kundalini awoke?" She drops the pencil on the desk. "No wonder you look so good. Do you know people spend lifetimes trying to make that happen?"

I feel pleased without knowing why. "It sort of happened."

"Well, I don't need to teach you any more about energy," she says.

"And my body. It's changing shape. I used to have a big bum."

"Of course," she says in a matter of fact way. "Women hold unexpressed emotions in their hips, men hold them in their bellies. Now that your energy is moving, you're starting to lose the fat pads you had there."

"What!" I look at her as if she were Einstein.

I must look so ridiculous that she bursts into laughter. "Remember, emotions are only energies that flow through you."

"E-motions," I add. "Energies in motion."

"There are certain places where energy gets stuck. The energy we call anger is often held in the upper thighs and lower back. Fear in the solar plexus. Sadness around the heart. Men are often barreled-chested to protect their vulnerable hearts, and women often have big asses because they can't express anger. Not all the time, but this is the general pattern."

I think of Emma. All those compromise moments held in her thighs. "What a revolution for the health and fitness industry," I say. "If people only knew that all they had to do was some shadow work."

Lisa laughs. "That's what I thought. But there is a catch. Hardly anyone wants to do shadow work. They prefer to take a pill, or diet or pummel themselves in a sport club and think that they are being healthy. But self-inquiry? Never."

I stand up, twirling myself around in the mirror. "I see it. I can see the changes in me. Outside and inside."

"Good." She leans forward and puts her hands on the desk. "So let's bring what you've learned into your daily life. I got a call from Karl this morning. He told me about Vienna's Don Juan."

I nod my head. "The last time I saw this man, I reacted aggressively."

"And he responded aggressively."

"Exactly!"

"The world is your mirror. Remember. You are no longer a frightened rabbit, so he won't respond like a fox on the prowl." She puts the pencil down. "You can start by using a woman's greatest weapon."

I pause. "My heart?"

She smiles. "A woman's vulnerability and femininity are her *best* weapons, when used consciously. Now. The indiscriminate woman chaser's weakness is his heart. The moment you react positively to him and stay connected to your heart, he'll run a mile."

"Because that is the one thing he is afraid of. Love."

She nods her head. "You can't fake it. You have to connect to his heart while remaining centered within yourself."

What she says triggers a memory. "Wait. I did that when I met his wife. We were arguing. I don't know what happened, but I began to feel what it was like to be in her body." I wince at the memory. "The pain that she was carrying was something."

"And what happened?"

"She told me we couldn't be friends. It hurt, but at least she was honest."

"You see? You spontaneously gazed with her, and it helped her get real."

I nod my head. "Eyes really are the window of the soul." A wave of gratitude wells in my heart as I look at my teacher. "Thank you."

She gives me a rare smile. "It's nice to see a student do their work. Wasn't it an eye operation that began you on this path? You are starting to see inside yourself as clearly as you are seeing outside yourself. That means you can help others do so."

"But not everyone has done the work I have. Like Rudi. He won't notice."

"It doesn't matter what anyone has done. If you are connected with yourself, you'll help him do the same." She closes her notepad and smiles one last time. "So go get him, goddess."

9

Kalte Sophie

Cold Sophie Day

The summer weather breaks the morning I am supposed to meet Rudi at the Hotel Orient. The temperatures plummet and a bitterly cold wind forces me to rummage in my closet to find my winter coat again. When I go to buy my newspaper, Karl's temple shop is full of grumbling, shivering Viennese. On everyone's lips are Pankratius, Servatius and Bonifatius, the *Eisheiligen*, or the Icemen. Karl, bundled in a hat and scarf, explains that before the fifteenth of May, Cold Sophie Day, these three saints always manage to bring one last cold snap, just to remind everyone that winter is never far away. We all sigh. Typical Vienna. Never trust anything, even the approaching spring. Karl gives me a conspiratorial wink as I leave. My stomach turns upside down as I think about what we are about to do.

That evening I hurry toward the Hotel Orient, wrapping myself tighter in my silky shawl, wishing I had worn warmer clothing. Vienna is clothed in shades of gray, its buildings, streets and overcast, despondent skies waiting patiently for the sun to shine again. By the time I leave my hotel, a cold wind blows along the dark street, wrapping everything in a melancholy gloom. Shivering, I arrive at the hotel.

From the outside it looks like an unprepossessing fin-de-siècle hotel, its art nouveau façade faded and worn. The entrance is quiet and dark.

I pull my cell phone out and check that it is on vibratone, then place it in the pocket, just like Karl told me to do. Then, taking a deep breath, I push the brass handle and walk inside.

A woman appears. She is dressed from head to toe in black, her blond hair sleeked into a ponytail. She peers out from under a pair of horn-rimmed black glasses. "Can I help you?"

In front of me is a small and intimate reception room lined with dark wood paneling. "I'm here to meet Dr. Brandemberg."

She flashes me a discreet smile and waves me into a small room behind her. From the large oil painting of the reclining Venus to the small discreet nudes on the wall, it is an Edwardian salon dedicated to all that is forbidden. The room is just large enough for three small tables and a mahogany bar. The lighting is dim, soft music plays. Rudi, looking suntanned and handsome, stands up from a table in the corner and smiles. My stomach flutters as he raises my hand to his lips in the formal Austrian greeting.

"You look wonderful!" His eyes dance over my hair, my clothes, my skin. "Your hair," he concludes as he helps me sit down on the banquet next to him. "It's longer. I like it." As I cuddle myself into my shawl, I feel his eyes wander to the woman perched on the barstool behind us. They must be old colleagues. I find myself wondering how many women she has watched sitting at this table with Rudi.

He places his jacket around my shoulders. "I'm glad you look normal. When women go on those self discovery trips it can ruin them forever."

I flash a flippant smile. "You can call Tantra that."

Rudi's eyes nearly pop out of his head. "*Tantra*?" If he were a dog, he would be drooling. I now have *all* of his attention.

"And when I started to evolve sexually, Max found it challenging."

With a nod of his head to the woman in black, he orders a bottle of champagne. "Max would find that difficult." He fiddles with his tie. "He tries too hard to fit in, poor boy. It will be his undoing in the end."

I glance sharply at him, but he is too busy adjusting a cufflink to notice. *Max is a fool to trust this man.* I've learned my lesson. No one needs my protection. I look up as a bottle of champagne arrives on a silver tray.

Rudi gazes longingly at me before picking up the glasses. "You have a fascinating way of seeing the world. Tell me about Tantra."

"Let's talk business first." I take a glass from him. "I didn't like the way our last meeting went."

He grins. "Neither did I. Let's try again, shall we?"

We touch glasses. My voice softens, and so do my eyes. "I want you to play fair. Pay me what's in my contract. Plus three month's severance for abrupt dismissal."

He breathes in sharply, as if pleased to hear the air rattling down those nasal passages of his. I can see that he has already done his sums. "And what do I get for this?"

"A drink with me." I tilt my head and smile.

He shakes his head, his eyes glittering with seduction. "Not enough."

"What *do* you want?"

He leans back. "Show me Tantra, and I'll pay you everything you want."

I look at him. All of him — his impeccably chosen wardrobe, his perfect teeth, his suntanned skin — the desperate look in his eyes. *Foolish man.* I smile broadly. "Deal."

He looks like a cat that has caught the fattest of mice. "So," he says as he puts an arm around my shoulders. "Why does Tantra have such a bad image?"

I take a sip of champagne. "First let me tell you what Tantra is. It is energy, sexuality and spirituality. And that is where the misinterpretation begins."

His eyebrows bounce up and down, reminding me of two caterpillars fighting. "But it is *sexual*, isn't it?"

"Tantra is a path of meeting and embracing your fears." I am amused to see the woman in black peering from around the bar. I suppose our talk is more interesting than most of the conversations she overhears. I raise my voice so she can hear. "Let me start at the beginning. Tantra began in India around 5,000 years ago. It is the yoga of relationship. Yoga means *yoke* in Sanskrit, because it yokes you to God. So far so good?"

"Mmmm," Rudi says. He seems genuinely interested, so I continue.

"Yoga evolved into two schools of thought, the Right Handed School and the Left Handed School. The Right Handed School is popular in Buddhist countries, and is taught through celibacy."

"What a pity," Rudi comments. "Like having cake without the icing."

I give my shoulders a slight shrug. "Each to his own. In the Left Handed School, Tantricas were encouraged to do whatever they were most frightened of. For Indians, that meant eating meat if they were vegetarians, or having sexual relations outside of their cast. The Hindus called it *Living in freedom*. Tantricas recognized that only our fears limit us. Once we begin to delve into them, they lose control over us. We learn to discern. Choose. Act. Instead of re-act. Because whatever we fear in others, we fear in ourselves. Whatever we say about others, we are saying about ourselves. Once we understand that, we become free."

As I talk, I hear movement on the stairs. If I hadn't been looking, I would have missed the woman in black glancing at the doorway as a couple scoots by. With a diplomatic *Auf Wiedersehen* she nods her head as they vanish into a waiting taxi.

Isn't life funny? A year ago, I would have rather died than sit in the Hotel Orient, having a drink with a girlfriend's sleazy husband who is trying to get me into bed. I look around me at the tired, worn wallpaper, the little brass tables and the woman in black, gawking at me as if I were a mannequin in a display case. It feels naughty, dark, *verboten*. That's what sexuality feels like when it doesn't involve heart. That's why it doesn't interest me. But — I smile as I think this — it no longer frightens me, either.

We both look up as the main door opens and shuts. Like a snake, the woman silently slides off her stool to greet two guests. For a few minutes I hear bustle and hushed words, and then, as quickly as they appeared, the couple disappears up the stairs. A waitress glides toward the bar, places a bottle of champagne and two glasses on a tray and discreetly follows in their wake. Karl's right. It is a fascinating institution. I might as well enjoy myself; I'll never be here again.

"Are all the hotel rooms different?"

Rudi nods. "Completely. The only way to see a room is to rent it. Many guests are too famous to want tourists combing the halls." He slips his arm under the blazer resting on my shoulders and begins to play with my shoulder strap. Like it or not, I feel myself being enticed into the atmosphere.

Rudi refills my glass, placing it in front of me like an offering. "So tell me more."

380

"The most famous image of Tantra were women dancing wildly on gravestones in the middle of the night. People thought Tantricas crazy, but there was a method to their madness. The reason they were sent to cemeteries was to overcome the fear of death. Every fear, from death to sexuality to anger, is embraced by Tantricas as part of life. Tantra is an excellent tool for people who are goodie goodies, because it helps them accept their darker sides. Like me." I grin when I say this.

His caterpillar eyebrows rise so high up that it makes his forehead wrinkle. "You don't look like a goodie goodie."

I smile, as if taking in what he is saying but not feeling the need to respond. Like or not, my head fills with Eugen. How he would react if he knew that I was sitting in the Hotel Orient with Rudi? I bet he would probably find it amusing.

As amusing as seeing me standing in the Belvedere Museum, admiring the paintings by my painter nemesis, Gustav Klimt. I had to go one more time before leaving Vienna, to stare at the canvases that had so disturbed me a year ago. I remember standing in the large marble hallway of the Belvedere Palace, my mouth open. There they were, those society femme fatales, looking at me with their sultry eyes. That billowy fabric, those Byzantine designs, the long limbs of swirling flesh and dress. Goddesses. That's what Klimt painted. This was a man whose entire life was in homage of Woman. Under his creative eye, he portrayed females who owned their power, women who had incorporated Kali - at least while he was working with them anyway. It was said that Klimt had affairs with most women he painted, and it looked that way to me. Lust, passion, sexual abandon stares me in the face. No wonder the Nazis destroyed some of his canvases when they arrived in Vienna. If what Reich said was true - the Nazis were sexually repressed - they would have had a fit when they saw what Klimt was painting. His pictures are from the same era of The Hotel Orient. An era that was exploring sexuality, but still not incorporating the heart.

"And what about me?"

I sigh and bring my attention back to the work at hand. I look at Rudi and smile gently. "Often Tantra attracts people like you, but for the wrong reasons. In India, if a person has sexual relations outside of his caste because it titillated him, then he shouldn't be doing Tantra, but going into what *he* fears. Perhaps for someone like you, a monogamous relationship is a challenge."

Rudi's eyes dart from side to side as if the room has become too small for him. "Spice is the variety of life."

We are both quiet.

"What I best like about Tantra is that the female is considered sacred."

"I never knew you could put the words sex and sacred together," Rudi says slowly. He looks pensive. "I wish Emma could hear that."

"Does Emma mind that you come here?"

He starts to rub the back of his neck. "You didn't tell her, did you?"

"Why would I tell Emma?" I ask. "She'll know anyway."

He squirms. "She doesn't care. She doesn't like sex anyway."

I wonder what he would think if he knew that his wife rented sex videos in hotel rooms. My smile becomes softer. "You love Emma, don't you?"

He fiddles with a napkin wrapped around the champagne bottle. "Let's go to our room, shall we?"

And that's how I know it. He *does* love his wife. The thought brings a smile of comfort to my face as I get up from my chair. I gather my shawl and stand up, but the room tilts before my eyes. I grab hold of the table, trying to steady myself, but the floor keeps slipping from

382

under my feet. The champagne! I knew better than to drink alcohol. I shake my head, trying to clear the increasing fuzziness as I follow Rudi through the maze of corridors. We stop before a small discreet door at the end of the corridor.

"This is the only room I ever use. The Oriental."

Feeling a trickle of nervous perspiration dripping down the small of my back, I slip my hand into my pocket to touch my cell phone. I should have texted Karl sooner. Squinting in the pale light of the hallway, I make out the number of the room as Rudi fumbles with the key and opens the door.

When we walk in, I gasp. The interior is a stunning temple of eroticism. The small foyer, an intimate sitting area under a tent of billowing fabric, is on our left. The bedroom, decorated with the paisley fabrics, is to our right. On one side of the room stands a wooden Bombay chest and two leather chairs, on the other, under more voluminous folds of fabric, a large, low bed. At the end of the bed, a massive gilded mirror hangs at a downward angle so that the couple on the bed can watch themselves in action. Everything is red, the color of raw sexuality.

There is a discreet knock and a waitress — complete with white apron and lace cap — appears with a bottle of champagne, caviar and grapes, which she leaves on the table. As soon as the door closes, Rudi comes up behind me and slips his arms under mine. Now that I am no longer afraid, I can feel how powerful sexuality is. Even though I don't find Rudi attractive, the eroticism in the room is so thick it takes all of my energy not to fall into it. I can already feel the small snaking energy at the bottom of my spine.

I frown, trying to clear my brain. Turning to Rudi, I hand him his blazer, then, without saying a word, I slip into the bathroom. As soon as I lock the door, I close my eyes and lean against the door, breathing heavily. *I knew better than to have had that glass of champagne!* Slowly I take off my shoes and pull my stockings off, concentrating on the cold marble under my feet. Once I can feel my feet, I take out my cell phone and quickly type

we're in room 5 the oriental

I punch the SMS button, imagining the message popping up on Karl's cell phone. I hope he isn't far away. Then I brush my hair, adjust my make up and splash some water on my face. Realizing if I stay any longer I might lose my nerve, I take a deep breath and open the door.

Rudi is lying on the bed, his hands behind his head, eyes closed. His jacket is on one of the chairs. When he hears the door, his eyes open languidly. *Where are you Karl,* I think as I sit on the bed next to him.

"How long do we have?" I ask as lightly as I can.

"All night," he answers with a dreamy smile. "Normally you rent a room for three hours, but I have it for the night. I don't like to rush things." He runs a finger lightly down my cheek as he speaks.

My heart pounds in my breast. I can feel my body tugging at me, wanting me to close my eyes and abandon myself to the moment. It would be so easy, I am single, I am no longer friends with Emma. *Why not?* I hear Chloe's voice. *You want to be free, so be free!* But I know that voice, it isn't Chloe, it's my mind, testing me. *Go into the feeling,* I tell myself. That's the way out. Steeling myself, I allow the seat belt on my mind to snap, letting my imagination go wild. Fantasies spark everywhere like fireworks on a starry night. There we are, making love on the bed, twisting and writhing, our arms and legs intertwined. On my back I gaze beyond Rudi's naked shoulder toward the mirror.

My eyes widen. It's Vandana. Her eyes tell me what I need to know. Poof! My fantasy pops like a soap bubble, and with it, the spiraling energy of sexual desire flows down my spine, into its cave and closes the door, leaving me with a focused head and a clear heart. Maybe Chloe could have done it, but I can't. It has nothing to do with prudish feelings, nothing to do with Tantra. It's not *who I am.* I take a deep breath and will my body to relax. Slowly, my thoughts begin to wane, and as they do, I hold out my hand.

"Come," I whisper softly. "Let me show you what Tantra is all about."

Rudi allows me to bring him into a sitting position, then, like a rag doll, he rests while I remove his tie and open the top button of his shirt. I shake my hair and feel it falling over my shoulders, then adjust my skirt so that I can sit cross-legged in front of him. We face each other, so close that our knees are touching.

"This is Tantra," I whisper. I place my hands as if in prayer in front of my heart, indicating for him to do the same. Intrigued, he presses his hands together and smiles self-consciously as I bend forward, nodding for him to imitate me. As he leans toward me, our eyes remain focused on each other until our foreheads touch. We are so close that I can smell his skin and feel the warmth of his breath on mine. Our eyes meet, only inches apart.

"I honor the divine in me, through you," I whisper.

The room disappears, our bodies disappear, the only thing that matters are our eyes. In a period of ten seconds, the atmosphere changes radically. Everything seems bathed in a warm glow of soft shades of rose and green. Time feels like liquid warmth. After a few seconds, we pull back, our eyes still locked. But when he wants to look away, I shake my head, inviting him to look even deeper.

At first his eyes move from side to side, as if my gaze is too intimate for him to bear. As I continue to gaze into his eyes, I start to feel behind them, into his soul. I'm surprised to see so much depth, so much tenderness. In an instant, I am in his shoes, and I know what it is like for him to be alive. Under his aggression is a painful shyness. Heartbreak, pain flickers deep within him. When he was young, he had far too many restrictions, too much responsibility, not enough love. Never enough love. He leans forward as if trying to listen to what my eyes are telling him, whispering something he used to know before he resigned himself to become his father's son. Before he forgot who he was.

He gulps a few times, and I know that if I can feel him, he, too, can feel me. His jaw starts to twitch. There is something he is trying to hold back, a welling of emotion that he is trying to keep down. "May I?"

He swallows and nods stiffly as I rest my hand gently on his neck. It feels as stiff as a pipe of steel. As I lightly move my fingers over his throat muscles, I massage the skin with feathery touches, my fingers willing the muscles to loosen. Rudi gulps again, then coughs. Tears start to brim in his eyes. And in that split second, a realization hits me. *Oh my God, he is going to explode!*

Like a volcano, the feelings burst through his throat like high-pressure water valve. His jaw drops, and with it, the armor holding his persona into place cracks as a wave of sadness erupts from his soul. *What have I done?* My mind leaps to attention and begins to furiously list multiples of possibilities of what I need to do. *Call the reception — no, Karl!* But another part of me knows exactly what to do. I throw everything I have read or experienced away, put my mind in my back pocket and continue to gaze at him. No smile, no judgment, only let him drink from my eyes. Like a drowning man, his sobbing increases.

My mind calms down and everything slips away, the reason I came here, the money he owes me, the scene in the Opera Ball, my anger at his wife. The only thing that matters is for me to continue to be a mirror for this man who, for the first time in his life, is seeing himself. I feel it all, the emptiness and loveless within. That is what was behind the years of gallivanting. He has been looking for love, running from his heart. The moment stretches into infinity. He is still sobbing by the time I hear a soft click of the door opening. Briefly Rudi's eyes flick behind me as I speak, but with the thirst of a dying man, he returns to drink from my eyes.

"Don't bother with the camera," I say quietly, never taking my eyes off Rudi. "Just close the door and come sit with us."

10

Of all the things Karl was expecting, it was not to see me sitting, fully dressed and cross legged on the bed of one of Vienna's most erotic hotel rooms, with Rudi bawling his eyes out. I feel the bed bounce softly and out of the corner of my eye, I see Karl crawling behind Rudi, sitting behind him with his legs on either side so that Rudi can lean against his breast. Like an exhausted warrior, Rudi collapses against Karl's chest. He doesn't blink, nor does he question what is happening, all he can do is drink from my eyes and feel the waves of sadness erupting within his breast. Time feels pliable, soft, and tender; it could go on forever, but finally I can feel the eruptions getting smaller and smaller, until with little hiccups, Rudi starts to come to. Silently, he brings his hands to his face and rubs his eyes. Then, he looks down at the strong, thick arms that are holding him, turns around to gaze into an unknown face, and returns to give me a confused look. He is deeply moved and very fragile.

"That — that was the most extraordinary experience I have ever had." Rudi's voice sounds hoarse. "It was as if I could see my entire life flashing before my eyes. Images of when I was small; when my mother died." His voice drops to a whisper. "When I was three." Then it is as if he is seeing me for the first time. "Why did I want to seduce you?"

I laugh when he says this.

"I mean, no offence, but —" He clears his throat, then reaches in his pocket and pulls out a handkerchief and blows his nose. "What *was* that?"

Karl helps him up. "Yourself, young man," he says softly. "When Annabel gazes at you, she acts as a tuning fork. If you engage with her — which you obviously did — your body adjusts to her frequency. She's deeper in her body, so she helped you come deeper into yours." He pats Rudi on the back. "Good work. That's probably fifty years of emotions held within your breast, so don't be surprised if you feel light headed. You might even find you won't be frequenting here so much, because whatever you were looking for, you've found in yourself."

Rudi starts at Karl's words. He wipes an arm across his forehead as Karl helps him off the bed. My legs are cramped and sore, so I bend down to stretch before standing up. To my surprise, when I turn to say goodbye, Rudi envelops me in a bear hug, squeezing me so tight I can hardly breathe. He whispers a thank you in my ear before turning to take Karl's arm. I know I don't have to ask whether he'll pay me. He won't think twice about it.

Feeling woozy, I return to sit on the bed. Karl presses my hand. "Good girl. Promise you won't get angry with me." He gives me a mysterious smile. "You'll see. Now, time to take this courageous warrior home."

"To Emma," Rudi says quietly, looking at Karl as if he were a long lost brother. "My wife. I want to go home to my wife."

"Your wife," Karl repeats, putting an arm around Rudi's shoulders. He picks up Rudi's jacket from the chair as they move into the foyer. Slowly, their arms around each other like two soldiers returning from battle, they leave, closing the door behind them with a soft click.

11

I look around the bedroom as if in a daze. What did Karl mean, don't get angry? I shake my head. Trying to gather my thoughts as well as my clothes, I start as I hear a knock on the door.

"I'll get it." The voice comes from the foyer.

I pull myself up from the bed and peer around the corner just as Eugen gets up from a chair, stretching his long legs before walking toward the door. He looks as fresh as a spring day, barefoot and dressed in a simple polo shirt and jeans. His shoes are resting by the entrance of the door, where he must have taken them off when he came in. When he opens the door, a waitress appears with a large bottle of sparkling water with lemon, explaining that the two gentlemen who just left ordered it as a gift to us. Eugen takes the tray and closes the door, then places it on the small round table in the foyer before sweeping his gaze appreciatively around the room.

"Isn't this something?"

I lean against the wall. "What are you doing here?"

He gives me an innocent smile before opening the bottle of water with a short, sharp twist. "Karl needed me."

"Karl doesn't need anyone." My voice sounds sharper than I intend.

Eugen's eyebrows rise as he hears my words. "I didn't mean in *that* way. I meant in a practical sort of way. He couldn't rent a room on his own. This is a *Stunden* Hotel, a hotel you rent by the hour, a love hotel. Couples can rent rooms. Men and women. Or men with men. Or women with women. Or even a group." He places a slice of lemon in a glass, then pours the water into it. "But a *single* person *can't* rent a room. It's not allowed." He smiles to himself as he watches me mulling over this. "So, when Karl gave me a call, I dropped everything." He puts an arm around me and helps me sit on the bed, then gives the glass to me. "Besides. *Someone* had to stand on watch while he picked the lock. We were in the Roman room when you texted us." He looks around. "I like this room better. I feel as if I am in the Arabian Nights."

As I take a long, thirsty drink, he helps himself to some water and sits next to me. "Impressive work. You might consider changing professions."

"As a what?"

"A shaman, a witch, a healer, that sort of thing. You really can move energy."

Images of ancient spinsters in floppy black hats and warts on their noses dance before my eyes. Don't shamans wear snakes around their necks and rattle rainsticks at bad spirits? I give him a deadpan look. "I don't know what I did; I only knew that it was the right thing to do."

Eugen gives me a gentle smile. "You don't have to *look* the image of a witch or shaman or healer to *be* one. People like you don't have official roles in our society, because this role isn't sanctioned by our society. So they have to be other professions, like newspaper vendors." He grins when he sees my eyes light up with understanding. "Journalists. Writers. Teachers. Personally my favorite word for women like you is *Goddess*."

"I'm just taking my power as a woman," I say slowly, hearing the truth in my words. I hadn't realized this until it came out my mouth. My body feels heavy as it always does when I say a deep truth. Instantly my shoulders relax as I surrender into something that is greater than me. Holding me. Not Eugen. Earth. *Mother* Earth. Resting in her arms. Resting in the mother. I feel assured. Comfortable.

"That's why I came here," Eugen adds, tucking a strand of hair behind my ear. "To thank you for allowing me to break up the way I needed to."

"Break up?" I say softly. My heart stutters in my chest when I hear these words. I feel as if I have gone to the depths of myself and have now started the long voyage home.

"How long have we been —" I glance where my watch used to be.

"Two hours."

"No wonder I'm tired." Wrapping the shawl around my shoulders, I stand up, my body feeling like lead.

Eugen takes my hand. "Don't go." His eyes engage me, inviting me to look at him. "Ever."

We gaze at each other silently. Warmth envelops my feet, as if I could feel each thread in the carpet under my toes. A vertical pull downward from the center of my body. I keep relaxing. Allowing myself to expand beyond my body. Not a bad heaviness, a centeredness. Support. Being held. Resting in myself. In this space, no one can touch me. In this space of comfort, I am connected with myself, and Eugen. I can love him without losing myself. From this space, my heart never needs to close. I can give and receive love. I feel safe. Safe to open my heart. How strong I feel when I'm safe. From this space, I look around the room with new eyes.

"Goddesses. Don't they like to celebrate?"

I watch the speckles of gold dancing in Eugen's eyes as he looks around us. He laughs, genuinely amused. "I didn't think you *liked* these types of places."

As I sweep my gaze around the room, I feel a surge of emotion at this confirmation of just how much I have changed. "I think you'll find there are a lot of things that I didn't like that might not be true anymore."

He raises his eyebrows in mock surprise. Then, pulling himself upright, he bows deeply, clicking his heels in the old fashioned Austrian formal greeting. As he raises my hand, he stops just before his lips touch my skin — the ultimate sign of respect. "*Jawohl* my queen."

There he goes, making me laugh again. I smell the warmth of his breath, admiring his long eyelashes resting on his cheek before he raises his eyes to look me squarely in the face. I return his gaze, my eyes unwavering. Looking in the mirror behind me, I see that my eyes are smiling. He kisses me. And this time, I kiss him back.

Acknowledgements

It took me eight years, five countries, four re-writes and two continents to complete this book. I wouldn't have been able to finish without the support, encouragement and patience of friends and teachers along the way. In Vienna, where I returned to re-write my book for the umpteenth time, I would like to say thank you to Lisa, Heinrich and Maria Berg, Baldip Khan, Dietfried and Christina Mayer, Martina and Gisi Podreka, Camilla Redfern and especially Stefanie Winkelbauer who patiently read through all previous versions. Thanks to Susan Haynes and Margaret Bentham in the UK, and in France an enormous thank you to Ileana Altmann, Philippe Dennery, Herve Lalin and Abbey Peruzzi for encouraging me toward publication of *both* books. During the last stretch in the USA, I couldn't have done it without Mindy Felcman, Maria Florez, Danielle Leinroth, Bob Loverd, John and Laura Woodhams and the woman who helped me organize my thoughts, Christel Ibsen. Finally I would like to express my profound gratitude to all those who taught me so much: Elisabeth Asenbaum, Mildred Carabanero, Veni Labi, Surabhi and Michaela Trpin in Austria; and in the USA, John Davis, Shina Richardson and especially Lorraine Weiss for helping me become who I am. The next one will be easier I promise.

Bibliography

Health & Healing

BRENNAN, Barbara. *Hands of Light: A Guide to Healing Through the Human Energy Field.* New York: Bantam New Age Book, 1987.

JUDITH, Anodea, *Eastern Body Western Mind.* Berkeley CA: Celestial Arts, 1996

MYSS, Caroline, *Anatomy of the Spirit: The Seven Stages of Power and Healing.* New York: Random House, 1996.

NORTHRUP, Christiane, *Women's Bodies, Women's Wisdom.* New York: Bantam Books, 1998.

Psychology and Somatic Bodywork

COPE, Stephan, *Yoga and the Quest for the True Self.* New York: Bantam Books, 1999.

FRANKL, Viktor, *Man's Search for Meaning.* New York: Simon & Schuster, 1984.

FROMM, Erich, *The Art of Loving.* London: Harper Collins, 1995.

JUNG, C. G., *Memories, Dreams, Reflections.* London: Random House, 1989.

MILLMAN, Dan, *Way of the Peaceful Warrior*. Tiburon, H.J Kramer Inc, 1980.

REICH, Wilhelm, *Character Analysis*. New York: Farrar, Straus and Giroux, 1945.

REICH, Wilhelm, *The Mass Psychology of Fascism*. New York: Farrar, Straus and Giroux, 1969.

REICH, Wilhelm, *The Murder of Christ*. New York: Farrar, Straus and Giroux, 1953.

EISLER, Riane, *The Chalice & the Blade*. San Francisco: Harper Collins, 1987.

Spirituality and Consciousness

CAMERON, Julia, *The Artist's Way*. London: Pan Books, 1995.

DE MELLO, Anthony, *Awareness*. New York: Doubleday, 1992.

HUXLEY, Aldous, *Island*. London: Flamingo Books, 1994.

MCKENNA, Jed, *Spiritual Enlightenment*, Wisefool Press, 2002.

SATPREM, *Sri Aurobindo or the Adventure of Consciousness*. Institute for Evolutionary Research, 1984.

TOLLE, Eckhart, *The Power of Now*. USA, New World Library, 1999.

WALSH, Neale Donald, *Conversations with God Book I/II/III*. New York: G. P. Putnam's Sons, 1996/97/98

WILBER, Ken, *The Marriage of Sense and Soul*. New York: Broadway Books, 1998.

ZUKOV, Gary, *The Seat of the Soul*, New York: Simon & Schuster, 1989.

ZUKOV, Gary, *The Dancing Wu Li Masters: An overview of new physics*. London: Rider, 1991.

Relationships & Sacred Sexuality

ANAND, Margo, *The Art of Sexual Ecstasy.* New York: Tarcher/Putman Books, 1989.

BYRON, Katie, *Loving What Is.* London: Rider Books, 2002.

SCHNARCH, David, *Passionate Marriage.* New York: An Owl Book, 1997.

DEIDA, David, *Dear Lover.* Austin Texas: Plexus, 2000.

FROST, Gavin and Yvonne, *Tantric Yoga.* Maine: Samuel Weiser, 1989.

GARRISON, Omar, Tantra: *The Yoga of Sex.* Harmony Books, 1964.

HENDRICKS, Gay and Kathleen, *Conscious Loving.* Bantam Books, 1990.

WELWOOD, John, *Journey of the Heart: The Path of Conscious Love.* NY: Harper Perennial, 1990.

The da Vinci Code Journey

This article was written as the cover feature for the Naples Daily News. Andrena continues to run workshops and journeys to sacred sites in Provence and other locations across the globe. For more information see her website www.andrenawoodhams.com.

I'll let you in on a secret: I pay attention to coincidences. I consider them part of life's inexplicable magic. I listen to them like I do a good stock tip, knowing that when they occur, there is bound to be a dividend or two hanging around somewhere. If I hadn't acted on these instincts, the da Vinci Code Journey never would have happened.

Months before I left my home in Austria for my annual visit to the US, I had been feeling like a walking Who's Who of *The Da Vinci Code*. Everywhere I looked, I knew friends connected to the bestseller. My adopted godfather was the Grand Master Emeritus of the Knights Templar in London; my best friends in Scotland were descendents of the aristocratic family who built Rossyln Chapel, even my drycleaner miraculously had become Deputy Marshall of Westminster Abbey in London. It was Paul's appearance at Westminster that clinched it. While in London on my way to Naples, Florida, I had decided to make a quick visit to that venerable institution to see Sir Isaac Newton's tomb, one of the major locations featured in the book. I was pondering the idea of a small, select Da Vinci Code Tour, and was looking for something special. As I roamed through the Abbey with my guide-phone pressed to my ear, I wandered too close to the exit door and set off the Abbey's alarm system, which began to wail ferociously. As I stood, red-faced and guilty, trying to pretend that the screeching whine was *not* emanating from the plastic object in my hand, a small dapper man in a long red mantle swooshed toward me. With a benevolent smile, he gently took the phone from my clutches and quickly pressed a few buttons. The piercing whine cut abruptly, and everyone breathed a collective sigh of relief. And that is when the magic happened. The man looked into my eyes and blinked.

"I know you."

Tying to shake the buzz from my ears, I shot an uncomprehending glance at him.

He grinned. "It's Paul. You know, Paul, the drycleaner."

Yes; it was indeed my Irish drycleaner from my London days — over fifteen years ago. The absurdity of it all began to sink into my consciousness as I gazed at Paul standing before me, transformed and stately in his long red mantle.

"Retirement bored me," he explained in his lilting Irish brogue.

I lowered my voice as my eyes wandered along the stone frieze of one of the most beautiful religious monuments in the world. For a thousand years, this was the historical seat of the protestant Anglican Church. "If I remember aren't you, um, *Catholic*?"

Paul's eyes twinkled. "Ahh yes so I am, so I am," he answered softly, pausing appropriately before adding, "And they say God doesn't have a sense of humor."

In that discombobulated way that happens when two people meet in extraordinary circumstances, we chatted randomly about our lives: I explained that I was living in France, writing about — I spoke carefully as I'm never sure how this will be taken — subjects covered in *The Da Vinci Code*. When Paul didn't flinch, I mentioned my tour.

To my relief, he beamed. "Ooh, that'll be lovely. What shall we do, close the Abbey and have a verger — those men in black coats — take you for a private tour and a candlelight dinner? I know exactly the verger. Benjamin makes history positively sing."

My eyes nearly popped out of my head. "Westminster Abbey *does* that?"

He chuckled mischievously. "Oh no, no. Not yet, anyway. But leave it to me."

That's when I knew my idea for the Da Vinci Code Tour would work. Shortly afterward, I met Pat Classen, a tour operator in Naples Florida, who jumped at the idea of a small, select journey based on the bestseller. Pat and I honed the journey to four locations — London, Scotland, Paris and Provence — and added a sprinkle of superb restaurants, a dash of adventure riding the wild white horses of the Camargue, and a pinch of spirituality with a pilgrimage to the cave of Mary Magdalene. But the key was my knowledge of the subject and the opportunity to be invited as a guest in the homes and clubs of my friends connected to the book. The result was an intimate and, at $18,500 per person, selective Da Vinci Code tour, a Town & Country Travel Club Exclusive and once-in-a-lifetime journey for six people. And it all began by coincidence.

When *The Da Vinci Code* first appeared in 2001, I found it to be a thriller that contained a lot of information that I already knew. It is what I call a bridge book— something that takes ideas or notions that are currently outside the current understanding of society, and puts them into a form that makes them accessible to the larger public. Whether you loved it or hated it, *The Da Vinci Code* was a work of fiction that forced people to examine what they believe. Why did this book make such a splash? First of all, the plot: *The Da Vinci Code* purported that Mary Magdalene was not a prostitute, but Jesus' companion, and, sacrilege of all sacrileges, that she was the mother of his child. The author, Dan Brown, inserted the Provencal legend that Mary Magdalene fled to France, and added a twist from the controversial bestseller *Holy Blood Holy Grail* that Mary's daughter began the Merovingian line of French royalty. Finally, he wove in the legend of the Holy Grail, the mysteries of the Knights Templar and the dark secrets of the Priory of Sion.

And so, the journey began by examining the plot of the book. Hinduism uses a spiritual practice called *niti–niti,* which translates as 'not that, not that' and then examines what is left over to discover what is true. In that spirit, I began our two-week tour in London, the home of the Enlightenment, and where Paul's magic came into play.

The May weather was perfect, the late sun just setting as our little group of six swept past the crowds of tourists pressing against the iron railings of Westminster Abbey and were waved inside the cavernous interior. Everything was bathed in a velvety late evening light, beams of soft pale rays glimmered through the carved windows, highlighting the worn, honey-colored arches and the multitudes of memorials carved in stone. The Canon of Westminster greeted us warmly as we were shown to the carved wooden benches called quire stalls to attend Evensong. There we passed a serene hour listening to the beautiful boys voices floating upward as we relaxed into the comfort of ritual. Whatever the Church's past history, it was important to see it as it is today, performing a daily worship of song and prayer. Then the congregation left, the massive wooden doors closed with a low thud, and we were left alone with a thousand years of history. As Benjamin the verger whisked us into every corner of this magnificent pile of stone, jetlag disappeared as we fell into the timeless wonder of history coming alive.

Finally we stood in front of the monument of Sir Isaac Newton, reclining on a sarcophagus with his elbow resting on stone copies of his greatest tomes, many of their scientific principals still valid today. All around him, the walls were jammed with statues of architects and artists, writers and poets, politicians, explorers — and scientists. Who said religion and science were diametrically opposed? Benjamin the verger nodded his head. Pointing behind Newton to a pyramid with a celestial globe with the zodiac signs, he noted that astronomy and astrology were one and the same a few hundred years ago. Even Newton's unorthodox interest in alchemy, the mystical art of turning metal to gold, wasn't so strange, I added. Lead into gold applied to personal transformation and growth. When religion moved from *esoteric* to *exoteric*, it became available to a broad public people, rather than a select minority. It changed from a practice of examining the inner self to that of obeying a set of pre-ordained rules. Esoteric translates as *inner* — only recently has it taken on what some considered New Age connotations.

With these new ideas swirling in our heads, it was time for a glass of champagne before sauntering up a long flight of stone steps into the small oak paneled dining room where Paul, and our candlelight dinner, were waiting. Afterward, as a special surprise, a friend whom I had invited to join us reached down and pulled out a set of bagpipes for an impromptu serenade. The music acted as a catalyst to bond our group together. As Pat shed a few emotional tears, Paul glanced along the polished long fifteenth century oak table and smiled knowingly.

"Well well well," a guest said as we hopped into the waiting cab to take us to our hotel. "One of the most memorable nights of my life. How will you top this?"

Yet events didn't top each other, but unfolded in layers, so that slowly a picture began to take place. Three days in London flew by in a very British blend of crumpets and tea, drinks and dinners, with the occasional visit to a historical monument to tie everything together. Like Sherlock Holmes with his magnifying glass, we followed in the footsteps of coincidence, seeking to discover with each delightful step how much of the plot of *the Da Vinci Code* was true.

Or not. The major underpinning of *The Da Vinci Code* is the mysterious Priory of Sion, a centuries-old secret society whose Grand Masters were some of Europe's most influential artists, scientists and creative minds, such as Leonardo da Vinci, Isaac Newton, Victor Hugo and Jean Cocteau. Over dinner with American journalist Vicki Barker and William Cran — one of Britain's most respected filmmakers — at their wisteria covered Georgian home along the banks of the Thames, we watched Bill's documentary on the subject, which hammered that theory. The Priory of Sion was a forgery. The Dossier Secrets, the supporting documentation of this allegedly ancient society, were less than twenty years old. Once we knew that da Vinci wasn't a Grand Master of a secret society, we later moved on to the effeminate figure he painted next to Jesus in *The Last Supper*. Hugh Buchanan, one of Scotland's best-known watercolorists and his wife Ann, an art historian, nailed that one. As many people in Leonardo da Vinci's times were illiterate, it was common practice to paint religious figures in a way that they could be easily recognized. It is well known in art circles, she explained, that St John the Baptist was portrayed as an effeminate figure without a beard.

On to the Knights Templar, the monastic military order that reputedly held a treasure that, according to *The Da Vinci Code*, proved that Jesus and Mary Magdalene were married. Dinner with Grand Master Emeritus of the Knights Templar General Sir Roy Redgrave and Simon LeFevre, Grand Prior of England, Scotland and Wales, was a night to be remembered. Into the foyer of the sumptuous Cavalry &

Guards Club we sashayed, our heels clattering on the black and white marble floors, and puffed discreetly up the red-carpeted staircase lined with massive oil portraits of Britain's greatest generals, before scooting into the library where Sir Roy and his wife Lady Valerie were waiting. As the two of them expertly worked the room, making each guest feel special, I sat back to watch my friends in action. Roy wasn't well-loved because he was a British General, or a Knight, or Head of the British Armed Forces in Hong Kong and Berlin, or Grand Master Emeritus of the Knights Templar, but because both he and his wife were delightful people with wicked senses of humor, as the guests soon found out over dinner. While Valerie guided us through the etiquette of drinking port, Simon gave an after dinner talk on the Knights Templar. Formed in Jerusalem in the twelfth century to guard the pilgrim routes in the Holy Land, the Knights Templar were a chivalric order to bring peace to an otherwise mayhem of Christian vs. Islamic 'this land is mine, no, it's mine' free-for-all-slaughter. We learned that the Templars invented the modern concept of banking, allowing people to deposit money in one of their buildings and withdrawing it in another country; that they invented the checkbook; and that probably that they had become too powerful, hence their downfall. But the story of the Knights Templar treasure was, as far as Simon knew, stuff of myths and legends. The modern day Knights Templar was a recent Christian charity formed on the ancient principals of this society.

By the time we arrived in Scotland, we had *niti-niti*-ed ourselves out. Pulling at all the strings of *The Da Vinci Code's* plot, we discovered, one by one, that most weren't historically valid. Then again, Dan Brown always did say he was writing fiction.

But wait. The second part of the *niti-niti* process was to examine what was left over. What about those strange grimacing faces that lined the inside of the Temple Church in London, or the statues of Mary

Magdalene dressed as an Egyptian or as a Black Madonna, or the very odd stone carvings called Sheela na Gigs — hags that looked, well, as if they were about to be examined by an OB/GYN? Those figures were all on Christian churches. Perhaps the plot of *The da Vinci Code* might not stand up to scrutiny, but there was still something there.

The mysteries culminated when we reached Rosslyn Chapel, a few miles south of Edinburgh. From the outside, Rosslyn looks like a small nondescript stone chapel on a windswept Scottish hillside. Only when we walked inside did its power hit us. Every inch is covered with carvings: celestial stars and moons, medieval instruments, vines and lines and biblical characters, unicorns, dragons, kings and knights and queens and a host of intricate illuminations bombasted us from the ceilings, the walls, even the floors. It was easy to see why this extraordinary building acquired the name 'cathedral of codes'. Built by Sir William St Clair in the fifteenth century, it obviously had a lot more going on than just 'stonemason's quirks' which was how these symbols were dismissed until recently. Baron St Clair Bonde, direct descendent of Sir William St Clair and in whose seventeenth century Robert Adams manor we were staying as guests, confirmed that although legend stated the Knights Templar treasure was here, it was hardly likely. But who said treasure was tangible, he added with a cryptic smile in my direction.

On cue, I pointed to a bulky line running eye-height along the inside of the chapel. Upon closer scrutiny, it was a thick, leafy vine. Every twenty feet, the vine was interrupted with round, full cheeked Bacchus faces, men of different ages with foliage for hair, beards of leaves and twigs, and branches sprouting from open mouths. The legendary Green Man, I explained. Like King Arthur or Robin Hood, myth and lore were ways to keep the old ways of thinking alive. The Green Man, the power of nature. *Mother* Nature. Now we call her

Mary Magdalene, but before that she was called Artemis, Isis, Ishtar, the divine mother, or simply, the sacred feminine.

For thousands of years, Asian cultures have understood that the world is governed by polar opposites called *yin* and *yang*. But in the west, the past thousand years were ruled by warrior-like perception of the world, called the patriarchal age. During this time, the feminine way of thinking went into hiding in myths and legends such as the Green Man or Mary Magdalene. Whether you believe in astrology or not, we have entered a new astrological age, the Age of Aquarius, the era of communication, which is feminine in nature. Hundreds of books on the feminine have sprung up in the past fifty years, but it was Dan Brown's novel that brought these ideas to the popular market.

Nations also have tendencies toward masculine or feminine, differences that became apparent when we traveled from the United Kingdom to France. London was decorated with statues of fierce lions and generals honoring warriors and bloody battles. In Paris statues were of sea nymphs and voluptuous women, writers, poets and musicians. No surprise Dan Brown began his novel here. With vigor we began to relish the story behind the story of *The da Vinci Code*, absorbing the senses and rhythms of life while we admired the Mona Lisa, craned our necks to examine the St Sulpice church, and savored what the French call culinary science in the ornate private dining room of Le Grand Vefour, Paris's grand eighteenth century restaurant.

Then with a gentle sigh we left *The da Vinci Code* behind to descend to our last stop, a rented fairytale chateau that was to be our home for the rest of the journey. Provence, home to painters and poets, endless lavender fields, and the cult of Mary Magdalene. Like her predecessors such as Artemis, the patroness of nearby Marseille, the feminine is worshipped in rituals and traditions, many which involve the enjoyment of the senses — food, perfumes, soaps, oils and paintings. Every night, our chef Michelle, a native of Provence who was well versed in local customs, created a symphony of mouth-watering delicacies using local, homegrown produce. Try to live with the rhythms of nature, she explained, and your body will thank you in kind. Gradually the pace of the journey began to slow down. We talked less, slept soundly, laughed more, foraging through markets for fresh bread and wonderful soaps and scarves that were soft to the touch. We were flowing with life, rather than against it. And it felt wonderful.

And the legend of Mary Magdalene? We did ride the white horses of the Camargue to visit the forsaken wilderness where she supposedly arrived in 45AD. But it was where it was said that she spent her last thirty years that we found her. Along a path lined with wild thyme and sweet smelling rosemary, we wandered high above the Ste Baume hills just north of Marseille, finally reaching a small stone courtyard carved into the nearly vertical rock face. We peered behind two heavy wooden doors to cautiously examine the yawning cave sparsely decorated with a few wooden benches, a simple stone alter and dozens of flickering red candles. On the steps outside the cave Father Henri Dominique, one of the five Dominican priests who lived in the chapel next door, greeted us as he did all those who make a pilgrimage to *her*.

"What a coincidence," he exclaimed, his white robe swaying in the wind. "Yesterday I was interviewed about *The Da Vinci Code*, and I said no one had found us."

"So is the legend of Mary Magdalene true?" one of the guests asked, his voice echoing in the open space. The silence was so loud that it was almost palpable.

"We can never historically prove she *was* here," he answered. And with a shy smile, he beckoned to us. "But I feel her presence now."

The breeze whispered a serenity rarely experienced in daily life. And we knew he was speaking the truth.

Printed in the United States
138082LV00001B/4/P